P9-DOB-067

THE BARTER

THE BARTER

Siobhan Adcock

DUTTON
est. 1852

DUTTON
— est. 1852 —

Published by the Penguin Group
Penguin Group (USA) LLC
375 Hudson Street
New York, New York 10014

USA | Canada | UK | Ireland | Australia | New Zealand | India | South Africa | China
penguin.com
A Penguin Random House Company

LIBRARY OF CONGRESS CATALOGING-IN-PUBLICATION DATA
has been applied for.

ISBN 978-0-525-95422-4

Printed in the United States of America
10 9 8 7 6 5 4 3 2 1

Set in Fairfield LT Std
Designed by Alissa Rose Theodor

For Connie, Andrew, and Averil

THE BARTER

CHAPTER ONE

She's been waiting for something to happen, and now it has.

Bridget is sitting in the glider in Julie's room. It's past four in the morning and her thoughts are wandering, trailing through familiar places, picking up slight objects and then putting them down again. Julie is sick with a summer cold and cutting two teeth, waking every three hours to cry so piteously that even Bridget, a steadfast cry-it-outer, can't leave her baby girl to wail in the dark. So here she is, sitting with a warm, buttery bundle of mostly sleeping girl in her lap.

And, as has become more or less customary for her, Bridget is thinking about death, plucking at it in her mind like fingers plucking at the curled edge of a bandage. Later, when she is at her most terrified, she'll wonder whether she brought the ghost into her house somehow just by thinking about death so habitually, so unwisely. *When I should have been thinking about educational toys, I was thinking about death. When I should have been thinking about weaning or baby swim classes, I was thinking about death. And that's why she's here. That's how she found me.*

Bridget wouldn't call herself morbid by nature. If anyone were to ask, Bridget would say she is fixated on death for two perfectly good reasons: One, because she is a new mother, and motherhood—as everyone tried to tell her, and as has turned out to be completely true—means imagining the worst that can happen, every day, all day long. And two, because she's married to an interactive game developer. All the ways a body can change shape, change definition, die, and avoid or cheat death—these are the things, Bridget thinks, half asleep and rocking gently, that preoccupy mothers and technologists alike.

Now that Bridget is home full time and thinking more about Mark's job than she feels safe thinking about her own (the job she left behind, that is, her job as an attorney at a midsize firm up in Austin), she finds herself with more time to think about this stuff.

Gently, she touches baby Julie's hair, the feathery spot right at the sleeping girl's temple. The fact is, *everything* that other women tried to tell Bridget about motherhood has turned out to be true, and yet it still surprises her to realize that no one was lying. It *is* different when it's yours; you *do* like other people's babies more after you have one of your own; the weight does take nine months to come off, if it ever does; and then the worst, the most ludicrous and pat saying about motherhood there is: You don't know what love is until you have a kid. All of it, all just as unilluminating and condescending as it was before Bridget gave birth, and all of it true. The weird, dreamy fixation on death, though. No one told her about that. But everybody must feel that, too; everybody must think about it.

No. Probably that's just me.

Probably that's my problem.

But if everybody isn't thinking about it (because *she's* thinking about it, here in the glider with her daughter snoozing in her lap), how else to explain all the movies and shows and books about it? Every time she looks at the news or the TV, she sees something that reinforces how vulnerable children are, to neglectful parents, to glib and hilarious sitcom parents, to breakfast cereal advertisers. And to worse, of course, far, far worse. *Aren't we all,* she thinks, drowsing and gliding with her ten-month-old daughter in her lap, *deviled and tormented by thoughts of our little dear ones coming to harm, and isn't it true, after a while, that those feelings of torment come to be sensations we long for—manufacture, even—in order to prove that we're capable of feeling tormented, in the same way that conservatives and liberals long to hear each other say something infuriating?* A seductive self-justification, sure—the former attorney in Bridget can recall constructing stronger arguments to prop up flimsier claims.

And not just death in general, but death in particular, death as a particular inevitability for all the people she loves. Case in point: Lately it hits Bridget with increasing frequency that her own mother, Kathleen, currently alive and well and living three towns away with her second husband, might die—*will* die, is *bound* to die eventually—and the howling loneliness she feels at the thought is (she muses, half asleep) probably not unlike how Julie feels upon waking up in her crib, with her imperfect sense of time and object permanence. For Julie, the universe begins anew after every nap, with terror and curiosity and the aching search for the familiar: Mother. Mother.

So (pushing with one foot so that the glider's rocking motion lengthens), what if her mother were to die. What kind of world could Bridget inhabit if it turned out to be possible for Kathleen to leave it. Or, okay, what if Mark were to die. What would she and Julie have to do, how would they have to live then—when she, Bridget, has just taken this strange huge step of exchanging her old life for this new one and is, for the first time in a decade or so, without any means of supporting herself, or any other creature for that matter, without help from someone else? Or, what would Mark do, for that matter, if Bridget were to die—who would care for Julie?

From there, Bridget's next irresistible thought is the really unthinkable one: *What if Julie were to die.* How would Bridget live in a world where Julie was not. Bright, plump, fearless Julie, with her throaty, truck driver's chortle and her endearingly spazzy baby ways.

She can't know it until later, but it is at this moment, just as she is finishing this peculiar logical circle in her mind, the one that has led her so naturally to thoughts of her own daughter's death, that she first senses the ghost nearby. There is a scent in the air, a smell that someone half-asleep could mistake, at first, for the smell of summertime, for mown lawns and flourishing shrub beds, and it moves into the room like a secret and brushes across her face like a veil, sweet and sorrowful.

In the days to come this scent will become synonymous with panic, and hiding, and heart-stopping fear, but in this moment it is almost comforting, familiar. In the yard alongside their house, there's a strip of ground that's always a little bit muddy and damp, even in the heat of summertime, thanks to a creek that used to run through the neighborhood and now resurfaces between the houses only during the wetter spring and winter months, the merest temporary glimmer, like a bracelet emerging from a velvet pouch. Bridget likes to see the little creek surfacing and receding, likes the way its muddy scent floating through the window screens means the start of the green season, although both she and Mark have wondered whether it might be undermining their foundation. Their neighborhood is all new construction, quickly planned—the houses here aren't bulletproof. She knows from her neighbors that some of them have poor insulation, bad drainage. She thinks tiredly, *We should get that side of the house looked at for cracks, I guess. I'll have to talk to Mark about it.*

When Bridget hears the noise out in the hallway—a thump, something heavy and soft meeting the wall—she assumes it's Mark, even though he never gets up with the baby, or hardly ever. Mark works, she doesn't; ergo, she gets up with the baby. The logic seems straightforward enough, even when the execution of that logic leaves her stumbling and glassy-eyed and foulmouthed, and when Mark complains constantly that *he's* tired, which Bridget is always too tired to challenge. Still, she sometimes loves being with her little girl when the world is dark and it's just the two of them. The turtle night-light in Julie's room glows warm orange, as if the world is shining through a piece of amber. To pick up a reaching, sweet-smelling baby girl in the orange turtle light, to tuck her head under your chin, to shuffle sleepily to the glider chair and settle in for some long, edgeless minutes while the trees shush outside in the heat and the air-conditioning blows a soft, cool breeze—it is lovely to be clung to by a curled-up baby in the middle of the night. Bridget still nurses Julie sometimes, when Julie's half-asleep anyway and won't be made impatient by the scantiness of Bridget's milk, which was never plentiful to begin with and which began to dry up when Julie started solids. Bridget is nursing Julie when she looks up and sees, for the first time, what has just moved through the doorway into her daughter's room.

At first her mind supplies a nonsensical explanation, and she thinks she's seeing a piece of furniture—a white couch—that has somehow reared up, massive and shambling and improbable, and is trying to bump into the room. But immediately, by the horribleness of its continuing movements, that first comical impression is erased. Because it is clearly human, and yet not. Even before Bridget sees what it is, what it is doing, her breath stops.

It moves as if struggling for every inch; each step has to be swung for, lunged into. Every movement costs it something.

Then Bridget sees a hand.

It hits the doorframe with a slight, soft thud that makes Julie twitch in Bridget's lap. The baby's weight feels like all that is keeping Bridget attached to the bottom of the world, all that's keeping her from following her insanely accelerated heart in a flight backward out the bedroom window and into the black-and-green night. It takes several long moments for Bridget to realize she is not breathing, and she swallows a gasp of air.

But the air itself has changed, and she suddenly feels as if she can't get enough oxygen into her lungs. The smell of earth, of soil and moisture and things growing out of the dark, has gathered close around her even as the quality of the air in the room seems to have thinned, as if all the nourishment has been sucked out of it. *This is what it's like inside a coffin,* Bridget hears herself thinking over the terrified hammering of her heart. *This is what the air tastes like inside a coffin when you wake up and find you've been buried alive.* Bridget lunges forward in the glider and gasps for breath again, the lungs in her chest feeling flattened and strained.

The ghost, pulling herself painfully through the doorway, pauses and shifts at the sound, with a sharp, quick snap in Bridget's direction, and unwillingly Bridget finds herself looking directly into her. Her eyes are like glittering wells, like stone-rimmed quarries, deep and cold. Bridget feels her own hand clap over her mouth, feels her other arm scoop around Julie's back, creating a barrier between the ghost and the girl on her side on her nursing pillow, still mostly asleep.

The ghost is a dead woman. Her hair, like her eyes, is black, and she seems to be wearing white, or to be made of something white, but it is nearly impossible to tell anything else about her because the edges of her body, her head, her limbs, seem constantly to be shifting, growing enormous and grotesque and then shrinking, angling away, diminishing to an equally grotesque size, out of proportion to what her body seems to want to be. It is like watching a maddened Picasso try to struggle out of its frame. Impossible to tell whether the ghost really has two eyes or just the combined force of two eyes, impossible to see whether she is slender or full figured or weak or strong. She seems to be dissolving and resolving through a field of static.

Now she moves toward Bridget, bringing with her that smell of damp earth. Watching her move is horrible, each step a reminder that the body can die. But watching her eyes is worse.

Bridget doesn't think of herself as a brave person—it doesn't occur to her to confront the ghost or to fight, for example, although later she will wonder what might have happened if she had. Her first instinct is only to lean forward to cover Julie's small sleeping body. "Don't," Bridget pants. Her lungs are white fire. "Please don't, please don't."

The ghost stops in the middle of the room and with difficulty lifts her arm, or the haze of impressions that seems to be her arm. Is the ghost pointing at her? Gesturing for her to rise? Beckoning for her to come? Begging? Bridget's eyes are now blurred by hot tears. *No no no no no.*

The baby sleeps on, peaceful and unaware. Bridget can't bear to look away but can't bear to keep looking, either. Finally she buries her face in her baby's side, eyes burning, chest aching, breathing Julie's smell of sun-warmed skin and pee and laundry detergent. *Now she'll strike.* Bridget realizes her mistake too late: She should never have looked away from the ghost, even for a second, even to blink, because now, when she looks up, the ghost's face will be there, inches away, glaring and staticky and furious, before it becomes a huge black mouth and swallows them both whole.

Panicking, Bridget weeps into the crook of her daughter's small arm. The baby sighs. *Oh God, please save us. Save her.*

When Bridget looks up again—it could have been moments later, or it could have been hours—the ghost is no longer standing in the middle of the room. The smell of wet mud is gone. Bridget kisses Julie all over: her fat thighs, her cheeks, her sweet starfish hands. Julie latches on again and nurses for a few moments, then falls back asleep. Mark finds them both there in the morning light.

The house has a strange smell the next day. A tang.

Ignoring the smell, Bridget and Julie go ahead with their normal Bridget-and-Julie routine. Playtime, morning nap, out in the car for errands, back for lunch, afternoon nap during which Bridget dozes off herself on the couch, then some distracted housework, then some more playtime while Bridget returns a couple of emails on her phone, then yet more playtime (bored by now, so heartfailingly bored, and counting the hours until Julie will be asleep) and dinner and bathtime and bedtime and waiting for Mark to come home, which he won't do until much later, after Bridget herself has fallen asleep. It's as if nothing has happened at all. Bridget hasn't exactly forgotten the ghost so much as decided it is unlikely she will see her again—the ghost was some product of a dream, not even a dream itself. And so, the night after seeing the ghost for the first time, Bridget puts Julie to bed as usual and goes to sleep waiting for Mark as usual, albeit later than she'd expected to, given her uncomfortable, long hours in Julie's glider, folded in half around her baby with tears of relief and terror drying on her face.

Julie awakes crying at three A.M., and Bridget opens her eyes and sees the ghost standing close at the side of the bed, filling the room with her watery indistinctness, her coldness, her smell like a fresh-turned grave.

The ghost is waiting for her, black eyes neutral and expressionless.

With her heart stuttering and her eyes already tear-filled with horror, Bridget scrabbles for Mark's hand under the covers.

He murmurs, "Not you."

The ghost turns and effortfully begins slicing her way out of the room.

"Marshland," Mark says, still in a dream he doesn't know is a dream. *He smells her, too.*

Bridget lies stiff with fear until she realizes the ghost must be going to Julie's room. Then she throws back the covers and flies out into the dark hallway, heedless and terrified. "Mark!" she cries. "Julie!"

The ghost is entering Julie's room as Bridget hits the upstairs banister and rebounds, hip singing with pain. She's never moved so fast, and yet suddenly she doesn't seem able to catch the ghost in her slow, struggling deliberateness. Her breath is short again, and she can't seem to get enough air into her lungs—it's like being on top of a mountain, where everything is cruel and thin.

Mark is awake now, calling worriedly from bed. "Bridget? What happened? Is she all right?"

Get up and help us, damn it! But Bridget can't speak: Horror and airlessness have stopped her voice. The ghost is standing next to Julie's crib, turning to face Bridget as she halts in the doorway to the baby's room.

The ghost lifts her arm, as if pointing in Bridget's direction. For the first time, but not the last, Bridget understands that it is a command.

To do what?

Bridget can't keep herself from snatching her sleeping baby up and away, out of reach. Her movements are the jerky, panicked whirs of a clock reversing its wheels. And then Bridget has Julie in her arms and finds herself standing two feet from the ghost, the closest she's come, close enough to feel the radiant coolness coming from the dead woman's form, almost like a soft wind that her ceaseless shape-shifting seems to create, the kind of wind that would stir light curtains at a window in the half hour before a rainstorm.

At this range, surrounded as she is by a shifting cloud of static, she is even more clearly dead—dead and moving, dead and yet alive, dead and yet standing before her, an abomination.

"Who are you? What are you doing here? Go away!" Bridget whispers fiercely. But her lips feel numb, she's shuddering to breathe, and she staggers with Julie's weight and falls against the wall near the crib's headboard. "Go away and get out of my baby's room!" Julie is fully awake by now, jostled out of sleep and crying—wailing, really. Her face is a mouth; her eyes stream tears. Bridget clutches her daughter. "Go away!"

The baby cranes her neck around, still screaming, looking in all directions until she locates the source of her troubles. The ghost. Bridget's heart falls. *She can see it.*

Julie points a chunky fist at the ghost—shakes it at her, in the way that she does when something angers or excites her.

The ghost watches Julie. In her mother's arms, Julie begins to still herself and grow serious, staring at the dead woman.

Mark shuffles belatedly, sleepily into the room.

"What's going on? What's wrong? Is she okay?" Without fully opening his eyes Mark takes their little girl from Bridget and cuddles her, and as always, Julie responds by grabbing him around the neck while simultaneously craning to keep her mother in view. *I can have this, but you have to stay mine, too.* "What's the matter, little Jujubee? Mmmm. Little bee. Bzz bzz."

Julie leans into her father and extends a balled-up fist toward her mother, who closes her own hand around it. Bridget feels knock-kneed, dumbfounded—her jaw, she's sure, must be hanging open in stuporous shock. The ghost is real. Her daughter can see it. Her husband can't.

The ghost is still there, right next to Bridget at the side of Julie's crib. But the dead woman isn't looking at them anymore. Her gaze seems to be fixed out the window. Bridget can hardly bear to look at it, can hardly bear the thought that it is still here, still real—*Jesus, no, she can't be real, but she's still here, she's still here, look at the way Julie's* looking *at her.* She swallows, hard.

"Do you mind if she sleeps with us tonight?" Bridget asks hoarsely.

Mark sniffs and gives Julie's cheek a game smooch. "I thought that was a bad idea, you always said. Crib death. All that. Is she sick or something?"

"Maybe. I don't know. I just want her close by so I can watch her." Bridget puts a hand on Mark's lower back and gives him a gentle push, trying to herd them all out of the room, back into their bedroom, where she can shut the door against the ghost and keep them all safe.

"Should I be worried? Are you worried? Don't let me roll over on her."

"I think she'd squawk before she'd let you do that," Bridget says, guiding Mark and Julie out, away, but keeping her eye on the ghost, flickering in stillness near the baby's window. As soon as Bridget's small family is out in the hallway, she can breathe again, and she begins to really push, shoving Mark along as swiftly as he'll let her.

"Hey. Whoa. Hey. I'm still half asleep here, Bridge. Take it easy."

She shuts the door behind them and quietly locks it while Mark settles Julie in the middle of their mattress in the near dark. Bridget turns on the closet bulb and closes the closet door partway, creating a warm triangle of light across the floor that will almost reach the three of them, snug and safe in the bed.

Julie whispers some nonsense words. She is happy, if confused. Bridget crawls into bed next to her and opens her pajama top to let Julie nurse. Mark rolls onto his side to face them and sleepily pats Julie's hair, then Bridget's shoulder. *Nothing can reach us here. Nothing can harm us as long as we're together.*

"Good night, dear ladies," Mark murmurs. Julie nuzzles in. Bridget closes her burning eyes in relief, exhausted, every part of her body humming with satisfaction and tiredness. They'd gotten away. The three of them, all close, all safe, here in the dark.

Julie and Mark are asleep, and Bridget is almost asleep herself, breathing the heat and scent of the little blanket-shrouded valley between parents where baby Julie sleeps—detergent, skin, a faint whiff of pee (she should have changed Julie first, she supposes)—when the bedroom door opens and the smell of dirt enters the room.

In the days that follow, the ghost invades. But slowly.

Bridget learns to avoid places where the scent of wet earth is strong. The second morning, climbing the stairs to put Julie down for a nap, smelling grass and mud more distinctly with each step, feeling a bit short of breath but attributing it to the climb (and to her own denial that this could be happening, that this could really still be happening, to them, in their neat little house), Bridget almost walks right into the ghost standing in the upstairs hallway at the top of the steps near the door to Julie's room, still and alert.

She's looking for something.

It's the first thing that comes into Bridget's mind—and once she has the idea, she can't help but think and rethink it, over and over, because for now it's a question she can't begin to imagine how to answer: *What is she after? What is she after?* Julie makes a small, low sound in her throat, and Bridget kisses her head, in her favorite spot, right at the little girl's feathery temple. *It can't be her. If the ghost wanted the baby, she would have just taken her, or tried to. She's after something else. Got to be. Got to be. What does she want?* The ghost turns toward them, and Bridget backs away down the stairs, keeping the ghost in sight—promising herself she would not make the mistake, ever again, of shutting her eyes. Better to see the unimaginable than try to imagine what it could be doing while you're refusing to look. The ghost doesn't pursue them, and Bridget brings Julie downstairs to sleep on the couch, which the little girl does almost right away, with her mother leaning over her in protective terror, her breath coming fast and shallow.

It's not lost on Bridget that Julie seems less afraid of the ghost than she is herself. The ghost is, for all Julie knows, just another grown-up in the house. Just another strange person watching over her. For all Julie knows, they could come in all sizes and shapes, every variety of solidity and transparency. *Sure. Why not?* If the ghost is just another watchful presence in Julie's life, that would explain why it seems to spend so much time flickering back and forth between the hallway, her mother's bed, and Julie's bedroom, a field of static restlessly shifting channels on itself in an endless loop between the window, the bed, and the stairs, the window, the bed, and the stairs. *She probably seems more real to Julie than her own father does. She's certainly around the house more.*

She's looking for something up there. But what?

Bridget can sense the dead woman nearby at all times, even in the broad light of afternoon, but the ghost never seems to want to come downstairs—at least not when Bridget has been around to notice—which makes her easier to avoid. Like a lot of other things in Bridget's life at home with a baby, maneuvering around a ghost in the house soon becomes a sort of challenging-but-doable routine. The ghost stays upstairs all day, doing God knows what, and Bridget contrives ways for herself and Julie to stay away from her. Sometimes, when she and Julie are in the living room, Bridget senses the ghost looking down over the banister at them, flickering and watching, but when she looks up, nothing is there.

It is only during the dark hours that the ghost seems to come looking for them. Night after night, Bridget surfaces from a miserable half-sleep to feel her breath coming shorter and shorter, the scent of damp earth approaching, even before the door to her bedroom opens and the flickering presence in the hallway makes herself known.

Sometimes it's possible for Bridget to believe that she isn't frightened. When she's out of the house with Julie, mostly—at the neighborhood pool, or aimlessly wandering the aisles of the grocery store, or driving the long way home. During the hours that Bridget is not in the house, which naturally have begun to spread and lengthen with the ghost's arrival, she can almost decide it's funny, almost hear the jokes she would tell if anyone, anyone at all, were prepared to believe her. *The thing I don't get is why she doesn't do some fucking laundry if she's just going to be hanging around the house all day.*

She's looking for something. But what?

In her deepening exhaustion, Bridget can only guess that the ghost, in the fashion of most ghosts she's read stories about, wants something specific—an offering of some sort—and what, exactly, she should do about it finally comes to her days later, on a sparkling Wednesday morning that she spends, like every Wednesday, at the coffee shop with the redoubtable Gennie, Gennie of the beautiful thick hair and the well-behaved, artistic toddler. The ghost wants something from Bridget's house—something from Julie's room, perhaps?—and Bridget will have to give it to her. An offering. A sacrifice.

They are at a Starbucks, of course. In their mid-Texas suburb there is no other kind of coffeehouse. The four of them, Bridget and Julie and Gennie and Gennie's nineteen-month-old son, Miles, arrive after the morning rush and before the afternoon loiterers and poem writers, just post morning nap, and immediately squat in the plushest, most remote corner and proceed to cover it with rice puffs and little bits of half-eaten tofu cubes and cooked apple. A guy at the other end of the room is trying to read the paper and keeps sighing loudly and glancing at them as he turns the pages. They all ignore him.

"I can't believe Julie's cruising already! She's going to be an early walker," Gennie is saying. "Yes, *you*!" This last is addressed to Julie, who has been wriggling ardently in Bridget's lap, trying to reach for Gennie, just get *at* her, with no thought of what she'll do once the object of her searing baby desires is achieved. Bridget knows she should try to listen to Gennie but can't seem to stop herself from staring into space, thought after thought drifting out into blackness like a series of hapless astronauts stepping out of the capsule. She is dead tired. It's been days.

What can she offer the ghost. What should it be. Some little thing from Julie's room, some token of appeasement? Bridget finds herself cataloging Julie's less-favored toys in her mind as Gennie talks. Floppy Bunny—too crusty. Laughy Giraffey—too crusty. Plus, Julie still sucks on his legs when her gums hurt. That horrible monkey thing Mark's mom gave her—inappropriate? Would the ghost somehow guess it didn't matter, that she'd been given something valueless? But how could anything from the world of the living—particularly from the world of a plump-wristed, rosy ten-month-old girl, with bright eyes and a beating heart and a pulse just discovering what it could do—be of no value to the dead?

It is a sign of something that I'm even considering this. It is a sign that some corner has been turned, Bridget thinks, as if being stern with herself somehow excuses it. *But this can't go on. This is worse than sleep training. I'm being chased out of my own house by a ghost, like Ms. Pac-Man.* So she will offer the ghost . . . something. A talisman. Or maybe it's more like a payment. *I'll pay up.* Julie is so little and easily pleased, she'll never miss whatever it is Bridget takes away to give to the ghost—who will . . . what? Pick it up in her hands? Flow through it like a sunray? Or shove it hungrily into her mouth?

But Bridget is trying not to go into that dark place—she's trying to be reasonable and practical about it, which seems possible at least while she's here, in the coffee shop with Gennie.

Gennie takes one of Julie's hands and swings her arm gently in space. "I thought maybe we could come up with a budget cap for the craft projects so nobody gets too crazy—you know some of the mommies will make this into a bigger deal than it needs to be. Yes, *hello*, sweet pea," Gennie says to Julie, who, judging by her grasping and reaching and grunts of effort, seems to want to change mothers. Gennie's son, Miles, meanwhile, is playing quietly on the floor with some kind of nontoxic wooden puzzle. "I do hate to sound judgey about other moms. I do."

If only I could talk to Mark. If only. But even if Mark could see the ghost, which he can't, he's never around, and at any rate the two of them aren't exactly in the practice of solving problems together. Not now. Maybe they were once, but not anymore.

The very first person Bridget realized she couldn't talk to about the ghost was, of course, Mark. The ghost is invisible to him, even though she stands over his bed every night. Even though she's there waiting when he comes home close to midnight and crawls into bed with his wife, and she's there in the hallway when he rises early to beat the traffic in. Throughout the dark hours, Bridget is a sentry for Mark and Julie both, overtired nerves sensing and scenting, seeking the ghost, imagining where she might be. She's never far. And every night, while Bridget lies in bed, fluctuating between stiff terror (*she's here, she's right here with us*) and helpless half-wakefulness (*the hallway, the top of the stairs*), punctuated by periodic visits to Julie's room to stand guard over the baby while the ghost flickers near Julie's window, Mark is asleep.

More frightening than the ghost is the suspicion, which Bridget briefly entertained, that she might be utterly bonkers, a complete lunatic. But as far as Bridget can tell, she is not insane, inasmuch as she knows the ghost is real. Mark may not see the ghost, but he *smells* it—she's seen his face change when he enters a place the ghost has recently occupied, as if he's smelling something off and is too polite to mention it. Since Bridget's been at home, Mark has become cagey about anything that might be construed as a critique of Bridget's housekeeping. He made one harmless comment too many when Julie was small and still up half the night, and Bridget laid into him with real ferocity, whisper-screeching that he could do them all a favor and sweep the kitchen himself if he was so sick of catching crumbs on his fucking socks, which, by the way, *I wash for you so what exactly is your problem exactly?* It's not a sexist thing in him, not really—he's just never been as tidy or fastidious as Bridget, and even before she quit her job to stay home, Bridget was doing most of the housework. Almost all. Mark helps with laundry and handles the trash and does ineffectual puttering things, like pruning the houseplants. Which is actually fine, really fine—she'd rather do it herself and know it's been done right than have to nag Mark to be sure he wipes the little rim behind the toilet seat. It's only when Bridget is exhausted that she minds.

And she's exhausted all the time now.

Gennie says, "Sometimes I wish that we could all just hang out *without* talking about the kids, because inevitably we start *comparing* the kids, I don't know how it happens but it always, always does. And then I think, well, Jesus, what the hell would we all talk about if it *weren't* for the kids, you know? So that's part of why I really want to make this work. I just want to give us something we can share and do together, as a group, without it becoming a competition."

At this point Bridget realizes that Gennie has actually been talking to her about something on and off for a few minutes. A summer project Gennie's come up with for all the neighborhood families with little kids. And she ought to at least pretend that she's listening to her, her good friend Gennie. (*But oh God, this,* this *is a matter of life and death: There is a dead person in my house who stands over my bed at night, and sometimes over Julie's, and I might be crazy or I might just be tired—of course I'm tired—but oh God, Gennie, I couldn't tell you, I couldn't ever tell you in a million years what I'm really thinking right now, and it's not just because you're what I'm not, not really, not in my heart, not even though that's also what I am.*)

It's the art camp. Gennie has been talking about the art camp she's been trying to organize for the summer, an idea she may have read about in a magazine or just come up with on her own, so creative and kind- and sweet-hearted is she: Gennie and Bridget and the other mothers they know with young children will each take turns hosting an art camp morning once a week all summer long. Week one at Gennie's: Make your own superhero capes, design your own sidekicks! Week two at Pilar's: Finger painting outside on the deck and sidewalk chalk! It sounds fun. It's a nice idea. *Please, oh God, let this be the end of it, let us escape the ghost and have art camp. Floppy Bunny will be fine. In her mouth.*

To prevent herself from thinking of the ghost—from clutching at thoughts of the ghost the way one clutches a handlebar, and for the same reasons: the instinctive physical reaction to fear, the sensation of falling—Bridget bends down to Julie and lands a series of kisses, *swock* after *swock*, all over the dear little musk-smelling head of the child in her lap. As Bridget does so, she is aware that Gennie is watching her do it, and that the look on Gennie's face is tender and appreciative but also, and here's the slightly menacing thing, proud. Bridget has seen this expression before, on Gennie's face and on the faces of other mothers they know, and to her, that familiar expression says, *We got you. We so got you.*

Bridget's phone buzzes in her skirt pocket, and she plucks it out from under Julie's plumply diapered butt and peers at its screen, entertaining half a second's hope that it's Mark. But in fact it's Martha, an old friend from law school who is also a mom and also an attorney (although Bridget supposes she can no longer call herself that, strictly speaking).

quick q? about estates. ur my only hope. call me!

She is too tired. She puts the phone on the wobbly little table in front of them. Gennie has taken the opportunity to check her phone, too. Like all the mothers they know, they live and die by their phones. "I know that women used to do this without smartphones," Bridget says by way of apology, "but I can't imagine how."

"What, you mean motherhood?" Gennie smiles absently. She's still reading something on her screen. "Yeah, it does seem impossible. I take a picture of Miles every day, probably."

"I'm not even talking about the camera. Although that's obviously good, too. It's more like the news and the weather and the clock and the messaging other humans with vocabularies. How did women get through the *day*, I'm asking."

Gennie gives Bridget a half-wink over the top of her phone—she's tapping out a message. "They talked to other women, probably. Instead. Like I should be talking to you. Instead. Of doing this." She finishes, looks up. "But you know, compared to our washing machines, smartphones are like the *least* important advancement in technology for women like us."

Bridget smiles, but her tired brain is circling the words "women like us," like something caught in a drain. *But I'm not like you, I'm not, I'm not. I like you, but in my heart I'm not.*

Gennie goes on wryly, "Living without a phone might be boring, but if I had to wash my own dishes, I might as well go live in a box in a hole in the ground."

"A hole in the ground?" Bridget shivers and stands up suddenly, pretending she needs to stretch her legs. She is adept at pretending she has been listening when she hasn't been, a skill she developed in her former life as an attorney, and which she's certain will be useful once Julie starts to talk in earnest. "Sorry, I'm sorry. Let's talk art camp. I'm listening."

"It'd be easier if we could do it in a neutral place and not at people's houses, I know," Gennie goes on, agreeing with an argument Bridget hasn't even made. "But the playground's too hot and the pool's too crowded and the clubhouse is too much. I looked into it, believe me. But we'll just make that a ground rule: If a kid has a meltdown at someone else's house, no one can hold it *against* anyone. You know?"

Bridget smirks and puts Julie on the ground so that she can cruise alarmingly between small, easily toppled tables and find bits of napkin to put in her mouth. "You're thinking of Sandra."

Sandra is one of those mothers who finds a way to blame other mothers whenever her son misbehaves. *At my house he never does that! Oh, but I guess I don't leave stuff like that out for him to find.* In the group of neighborhood mothers that Bridget and Gennie run with, Sandra is known as a bit of a pill, which, perversely, is just what makes her so indispensable—to Bridget, at least. As Bridget put it to Mark one night, crowing, a little drunk after all, "No one joins a mothers' group—no one *hears the words* 'mothers' group'—without thinking, shit, that sounds awful—unless there's a chance *that they all might kill each other*!"

When Bridget first quit her job, she'd had not a single stay-at-home friend, and she knows that as new friends go, she is truly lucky to have found Gennie, and not only because of Gennie's many lovely qualities. Gennie is the tacit leader of their small group of neighborhood mothers, and her friendship has paved Bridget's way right into the center of their social set, a position she's not sure she would have tried to achieve on her own steam. Because, actually, it had been more a sort of prurient anticipation of lurid mommy spectacles that drew Bridget into the mothers' group at first: She'd imagined lunacies erupting over snacks and playdates, and she'd imagined herself retaining the slightly superior attitude required to be entertained by them.

But the truth is she understands, even truly likes, these women of her new world. They are all kind of lonely, and they live near each other, and they want their kids to have other kids to play with, and really everybody is mostly pretty nice, in the way that people are. They've gotten to know each other, the mothers, at Friday evening neighborhood cookouts in the central green in their subdivision (Gennie organizes, texts everybody with details, makes sure people know what to bring), cookouts to which everybody comes early, with coolers full of snacks and drinks, and from which everybody leaves drunk, with their kids asleep and sticky in their strollers. Sandra's the only one who says things like "I saw a kid with her nanny at the pool today and I just felt sorry for the little thing" and "I just think working mothers are kind of selfish, you know? Like, what could be so important about their jobs that they'd miss out on being with their own children?"

Bridget's law-school friend Martha tried to warn her against becoming too entrenched in what she calls the "mommy scene" when Bridget "opted out," as Martha insists on calling it. "Before you know it," Martha said, not quite winking, "you'll have twenty things to do every day and you'll be trying to figure out how you got so overcommitted when the whole point was to have all this time to focus obsessively on your baby. Basically, don't hang out with any grown women who refer to other grown women as mommies. But even then you might not be safe."

The last time Bridget saw Martha, about a month ago, they'd arranged to meet up for drinks at a Mexican place while Mark put Julie to bed, not very successfully, and Martha's husband, Graham, put their two kids to bed, in equally calamitous fashion. If their husbands were a little more competent they'd have dinner more often, they agreed, and then ordered another round of margaritas. It was then that Bridget told Martha about the summer cookout-and-drinking scene that Gennie had organized in their neighborhood, and Martha was drunk enough to sigh, "God, that sounds nice. Can I come sometime?" Which of course she could, and Bridget arranged it by texting Gennie that very moment. Then Martha changed the subject to something happening at work—she was at a larger firm than the one Bridget had left—and let slip some comment about how glad she was to have something to really *do*, you know? Something to keep her in the *world* when the kids felt overwhelming. And Bridget was drunk enough to say, "Gennie says she doesn't understand women who get their identities from their jobs."

Martha snorted. "She's five years younger than you. She opted out before she ever *had* a real job."

"You're right." Bridget nodded.

"The first time you quote *me* to Gennie, I'd really like to know. I'd like for you to give me a call when that happens," Martha declared.

Mark, somewhat to Bridget's surprise, can't stand Gennie. "She's too cute" is all he'll say. To her face he's as polite as an auditioning tenor, but whenever Bridget brings her up—which is, she'll admit, weirdly often—he tends to grimace and shrug and be generally dismissive. While Bridget tries not to take Mark's tepid judgment of her friend as anything more than a lack of interest, she can't help but feel betrayed, a little, in the sense that Gennie is exactly the kind of person Bridget is supposed to want to be now. Gennie is a choice, essentially, that she, Bridget, made in order to benefit all three of them, and Mark should at least try to be consistent in what exactly he's after in a wife. If it's not Gennie's best qualities—her humor, her charm, her thinness, her creativity and patience on rainy days—then Bridget will have to admit something she's not prepared to admit, beyond the obvious fact that Gennie is a person and not a symbol, a convenient one that Bridget herself has constructed. She'll never be as good at this as Gennie, even though she is what Gennie is now, even if in her heart she suspects she's not.

Gennie checks her phone again for the time. "We have to go soon. You're coming to the mommy yoga class, right?"

"Yep. My only exercise."

"You get plenty of exercise just chasing her around," Gennie says cheerfully.

"Do I?" Bridget watches Julie plump herself down on the floor, in frowning study of a found, probably unclean plastic cup lid that will within moments make its way into her mouth. She honestly cannot think of a single occasion when she's chased Julie around. Bridget thinks this is something that mothers of boys do and assume that all mothers do also, because otherwise they'd try to trade their sons in for girls.

"Well, you're doing something right. You look great."

Bridget manages not to roll her eyes, but as she removes the cup lid from Julie's chubby fist, prompting a bellow from the girl, she is forced to acknowledge that this is precisely the sort of blithe, perhaps willful generosity that Bridget associates with Gennie, because Gennie is the one who looks great. She's actually slimmer now than she was before she had Miles—Bridget has seen her wedding pictures, over at the house. Gennie has milkmaid skin, chestnut hair, and a twinkly air, and wears only delicate, handmade jewelry. Just looking at her makes Bridget happy. And, of course, jealous. But mostly happy.

"Gennie, you are a force for good," Bridget says, again without quite thinking what she's saying, but this time she means it.

Gennie's cheeks flush prettily, and she smiles with real pleasure. "So I guess that means I should go punch that huffy guy with the newspaper right in the neck."

Oh, it takes them many, many long minutes to gather all of their things, all of their snack cups and sippy cups and half-finished lattes. And the act of stuffing the rest of the apple crumb pastry that Bridget has forced herself to eat only half of into a paper sack and thence into the trash causes her a real pang (three dollars, plus think how delicious it would have tasted after yoga, warmed in the car by the sun), to add to the pangs already in process: The pang of guilt for poor Floppy Bunny, destined for some ghostly subsummation that Bridget can't think about right now, not when an hour's worth of normalness with Gennie and the kids have pushed the ghost to the back of her mind. An ongoing, aching pang of love, constantly tolling like a huge distant bell, for her darling baby. And with it, a similar, nonstop pang of low-level remorse or something like it for her old life and her old job, which wasn't God's work but was hers, in a way that she liked. Pangs for Mark, even, of the sexual, envious, and doubting varieties. Part of the reason she's been going to yoga classes with Gennie is to try to recapture some of her own former spryness and energy, her *vim,* as they might have called it in the nineteen fifties, because some stubborn part of her persists in believing that Mark might actually notice.

But in fact there is a text from Mark on her phone, as Bridget discovers once she has gotten Julie into her car seat and settled herself behind the wheel to follow Gennie's car to the yoga studio. (Could they have carpooled? Would it have saved a polar bear if they had carpooled? Index under "pangs: first-world problems, caused by.")

b home late tonite. sorry. love.

It's not his fault.

It's not anybody's fault. But it would almost be easier if she believed he was having an affair—with, say, some frisky young developer at his mobile gaming company, a pixieish, overpaid recent college graduate bending over for him in the heat of the server room late at night.

It's not another woman, though; it's just work. She knows because she was the same way before she quit her job to stay home with Julie. Bridget and Mark have been married for two and a half years now, and before Julie was born, they had still had appliances from Bridget's bridal shower they'd never used. Vacation time they'd never taken accrued like cholesterol in their calendars; unread magazines piled up in slick stacks under the coffee table, so high sometimes that it seemed the table's legs must be about to lift off the floor.

They still haven't taken a vacation, actually. That's the joke. How could they now, on one income? *Ha ha ha. A week full of ha's.* It's not his fault. And she's not so cruel as to throw that irony in Mark's face.

Other than the ghost, the only thing that makes Bridget feel terror, real terror, is the thought of how dependent they are on the guys—young, slick, prone to handing out business cards—who own Mark's company, PlusSign. (*It's called "PlusSign" because it's a digital gaming company,* Mark once explained to her, in an email from the office his first week on the job. *If they made dog collars or shoehorns, they'd be called "Plus Sign."*) The little boat of Bridget and Mark and Julie is now entirely afloat on the sea of PlusSign; for better or worse, they have entrusted their small family's fortunes and future to two young men in their late twenties who made an enormously popular mobile game in which you run from house to house in an increasingly complex warren of animated subdivisions, sneaking into people's homes and robbing them, the old-fashioned way, while they sleep. Stuffing their belongings into a sack—which, in a metaphor that Bridget supposes is the analog of Mary Poppins's carpetbag, expands infinitely to accommodate your loot—while you caper and cavort and race the sunrise and other robbers. In this game, you get extra points if you stop to clean out your victim's refrigerator.

Bridget rereads the text from Mark on her phone, then turns her eyes to the rearview mirror to gaze at Julie, snug in her rear-facing car seat and looking expectantly into the mirror Bridget has affixed to the car's back window, so that both of them—just inches away from each other but cocooned in their separate seats and facing in different directions—can look at reflections of each other, just like they're doing now, whenever the fancy strikes them. Bridget raises her phone to the rearview mirror and takes a picture of Julie, smiling into two mirrors at her mother. She sends it to Mark. She doesn't expect a reply, although a reply would be nice. She looks at the picture of her daughter, her daughter with her clear hazel eyes and her beautiful lashes and the curls of dark hair just now growing long enough to fringe her shell-pink ears.

"Baby girl," Bridget announces, "we are not going to yoga."

Because the strange fact is, sometimes she wants to see the ghost as much as the ghost seems to want to see her.

CHAPTER TWO

Rebecca Mueller, pretty and much admired, married at an age that was not exactly young. She didn't marry for money, although she probably could have. But what made her accept John Hirschfelder, with his handsome wood-frame house and his large acreage west of town shot through with feathery cypress trees and sunburned grass, was not exactly love, either.

She married two months after her twentieth birthday, in the second year of the century. She left her father's immaculate brick house in town—the unused piano, the gas lamps, the heavy, severe parlor furniture, the lock of her mother's hair—and moved to the new house that John Hirschfelder had inherited along with sixty acres of good land when his parents died. In the months leading up to the wedding it was said, and Rebecca herself often felt, that if her mother were still alive she might not have married a farmer.

Why did she marry him then. Well. Rebecca and John had always known each other. They'd gone to school together in the stout brick schoolhouse in town. But she'd gone to school with other boys, too, whom she'd always known, who had annoyed her when she was younger, and who had grown into men who stopped by the house to try to impress their suitability on old Dr. Mueller and his daughter. At the time that Rebecca Mueller married him, she couldn't articulate why she'd chosen John over the others. He had a handsome face, and a good sense of humor, and long, browned hands. She liked him. She'd always liked him. She wasn't especially easy to please—oh, yes, some might say she was impossible—and she liked him.

In fact John was generally well-liked among the few hundred Texans—mostly second-generation and immigrant Germans—who peopled their town, a thriving ten-road outpost in the lower-central latitude of the state. Even before he somehow managed to convince Rebecca Mueller to marry—and to marry him, of all people—the town loved to tell and retell how young Hirschfelder had lost both parents to influenza within days of each other. The town loved even better the story of how he, their only child, barely well enough to walk himself, had made sure his parents were buried properly. He was a favorite in town. He was a favorite of Dr. Mueller's, and Rebecca's, too.

Rebecca knew that her old friend had seen a terrible year. The deaths of his mother and father had made him grave and intent. John's father had purchased a new acreage the spring before his death, and John was now responsible for the improvement of that land, besides the acres that were already producing. He had two outbuildings to construct, and half of the upstairs rooms in the new house still weren't finished. The farm's prospects excited and terrified him at once, and John was smart enough, even at his age, to admit that. But not to just anyone.

He admitted it to her, one soft evening early in the spring following the hard months in which he'd buried his mother and father. He came by the Doctor's house to take Rebecca for a drive—or, rather, to steer them both out to where the town's perimeter met the roads that led out toward the farms and then relinquish the reins to her so that she could drive, as she loved to do. Riding down these country lanes in his parents' buggy was something they had done together since before they were teenagers. Better to do it in the evenings, when the earth seemed to give up in a long, slow gasp the heat it had collected all day.

Now that they were older, of course, this kind of behavior actually meant something—it wasn't the companionableness of childhood, or even the stormy friendship of their adolescence, but two grown people, a man and a woman, climbing into a buggy together to ride out into the country. In other, less wild and independent places, they would already be considered a scandal. They were no longer children.

All this Rebecca knew. That night in the buggy, she wore a sage-colored dress and a fierce look. She could see the road opening out in front of her, and she almost felt that she could see straight through the man next to her on the unembellished, flat seat. The boy she'd grown up with had been completely transformed, wrung out by what the winter had done; for the first time in his life he had been made to understand what it meant to be a man. The change in him was so absolute, she saw, that he expected everything else in the world to have undergone a similar shift of gravity. Including her.

Maybe there was something scandalous about them after all, she thought. They made each other nervous.

"I'm feeling tired and different these days, Beck," John said to her that night, when he'd finished telling her about his plans for the farm, and about how certain smells or tunes, certain slants of light, affected him in ways he couldn't always predict or account for—"peculiar moments," he called them.

"Are you?" Rebecca's eyes, a gray that her many would-be beaux swore reminded them of everything from storm clouds to silverware, turned back to the road out ahead of the horse's ears. She was afraid. Or, even if she wasn't afraid, she sensed in herself all the physical symptoms of being afraid—the shortness of breath, the lightness of head, the quickened clumsiness of perception, which all, perhaps, amounted to the same thing, regardless. "You don't seem much changed."

"I don't?" John had to laugh. It wasn't a happy sound.

"All right, you do." Rebecca sighed. "I don't know why I said that." But she did know why she'd said it—she was determined not to let John Hirschfelder say anything she would have to agree with. She felt she had to stop him from asking her anything, any question at all, that she might say yes to. "I just mean to say that *I* think of you the same way as ever," she said relentlessly.

John cleared his throat, but she was too uncomfortable at the thought of causing him pain to look at him. Instead Rebecca blinked down at her gloved hands, holding leather reins, which were, really, among the strangest things on earth, when you thought about them for a minute—that these rough straps had been made by some human hand for this purpose exactly: to connect her to an animal, to let her express her wishes to an animal without their being able to communicate in any other real way.

"I'm sorry," she said. "I'm being untruthful. You're different. Everybody knows it. I know it, too," she added quietly. But John had already decided to speak.

"Well, the honest fact is I think I'm frightened, Beck." John was now the one whose gaze had turned out toward some distant point across the fields. His admission had been sudden, and it aroused an unfamiliar sensation in them both. *Is this what it's like. Is this what it would be like, us two.* In an instant she saw the two of them at the kitchen table at his house, in the morning, at breakfast. She saw herself passing him something, some little thing. She saw him reach for it, his brown hands. "I don't know how I'm going to manage."

"Manage what?"

"Everything. There's too much . . . land. I sometimes think I'm killing myself at it," he said, and he meant it as a joke, but of course one didn't say such a thing as a joke, particularly if it were true.

She was alarmed but tried not to show it. "Oh. I—I know so little about farming," Rebecca said, lamely. "You know—we've always lived in town, my father and me. Everything I know about farms I know from listening to—to you," she rushed on. "You seem to know everything, you always make it sound so easy. You practically ran the place even before . . . your parents' passing—I'm sorry. I don't mean to bring it up that way. But I believe you can do it. If anyone can do it, you can."

The funny thing was, of course, she meant it. For all his fears he was considered the most capable of the young men in their community, and he probably knew it, and if he didn't, well, there, she'd told him. Dark-eyed John Hirschfelder and his easy, competent, surprising—Goddamn it. This was his way; this was how he got to her when she didn't mean to let him think she could be got to.

She'd be a terrible farmwife, and she knew it even then, even that night in the buggy, on the road between the fields.

She would be the first to admit it: She didn't know how to do anything. Her father, the town doctor, had raised her himself, with the help of his poor spinster cousin Fräulein Adeline, whom Rebecca had always half respectfully, half irreverently called Frau and who oversaw all the cooking and washing and housekeeping and made sure the Doctor had coffee at three o'clock. Frau kept house pretty well, but she hadn't made it her especial priority to teach Rebecca how to do it. Oh, Rebecca could sew, at least she could do that. The thought of marriage made her miserable, even shy—she, who cared so little about what people thought. She supposed she'd have to do it eventually, get married. She supposed she could do worse than to marry someone who loved her well enough to overlook the fact that he'd have to survive on cornmeal cake and boiled potatoes.

Oh, for God's sake.

"You don't have to tell me anything," Rebecca blurted.

"I know. I know, Beck. I want to, though. You know I do," John said tiredly. Her heart ached with pity for him then. The air was purple, and the fields stretched out to either side of them like long hounds under a tent of sky, and her childhood friend sat next to her on a wagon bench, weary and worried and still grieving for his mother, and longing for *her*, for Rebecca Mueller of all people, without much hope. How could she be so cruel, she wondered, not to love him back. How could she be so foolish, when half the women in town would dearly love to take her place, take his hand, here in the dust and clatter where no one but the two of them existed or cared. *You stupid girl. You know what you have to do.*

So she held the reins with one hand and with the other reached over and clasped John Hirschfelder's hand with her gloved fingers and squeezed hard, harder than was strictly romantic. Too hard. Dark-eyed John Hirschfelder, with his beautiful face and his strong back and his good heart. The poor man.

W*hy do women marry, anyway. To make a house? To have babies?* It was a question she couldn't answer yet herself. Unless it was to build a life with the one person who seemed to understand you even a little bit. She wasn't sure she loved John, but she knew she admired him. And he wasn't afraid of her, old Dr. Mueller's daughter with the odd temperament, the pride and the vagueness and the sharp gray eyes, and—as she was forced to admit—the confounding ignorance about how to do most of the things women were supposed to know how to do.

They were to be married in the Lutheran church in town, and in the short weeks before the wedding that spring Rebecca took steps to avail herself of some little understanding of what might be expected of her as a farmwife. She consulted Frau, who managed in the amount of time they had left under the same roof to teach her how to tend the stove and bake a loaf of bread, which at least gave Rebecca some confidence that she and John wouldn't starve. Also she got a few lessons in cooking and laundering, which went as poorly as she thought they would—not because the principles themselves were especially difficult but because laundering was as backbreakingly boring as Rebecca had always suspected it to be, and because the kitchen in the Doctor's house was infamously smelly and hot and unventilated. Rebecca began to grasp with some disappointment that she probably could run a farmhouse, after all. Not well enough to please her own pride but well enough that she might not kill her husband or his hired men through her own negligence or ignorance.

Frau taught her as much as she could about managing a kitchen garden, which was considerable. Frau had accepted the humiliations that life had forced on her as a foreign spinster—and an ugly one at that—who spoke little English and lived on the charity of a distant widower cousin, and she compensated for the long hours of boredom and halfhearted work and scripture reading by becoming a remarkable gardener. (Or it might have had nothing to do with Frau's ugliness and unmarriedness. It might have just been in her all along to grow a lovely, abundant garden, given the opportunity and the leisure.)

Still, it was difficult for Frau, an instinctive expert in pruning and soil moisture, to take a long-enough step back from her own intense interest in her growing things to be able to explain to a newcomer just what she was doing or how she did it. The hours were beautiful, anyway. They spent quite a few of those May afternoons in the kitchen garden, Frau talking mostly in German, Rebecca half-comprehending and meditative, pinching bright-green leaves and breathing in the scent of the sweet earth and its good promises.

"I wish I were as good at something as you are at this," Rebecca said one afternoon a few days before she was to be married to John Hirschfelder. The bees were drowsing around in the grass, and Rebecca was trailing Frau through the vegetable beds.

Frau turned on her the warm, indulgent expression she'd worn half her life. Frau was the Doctor's favorite aunt's only daughter; her true name was Adeline. She said, charmingly, in English, "Oh, your mother wasn't good at anything, either."

"Except making men fall in love with her," Rebecca answered, eyes shaded.

"*Ja,* except for that." Frau laughed and then coughed. Frau had known her mother, who had died shortly after Rebecca's birth. Rebecca understood that her mother had been instrumental in convincing the Doctor to take Adeline in, and that the two of them, despite their inability to communicate in the same language, had been merry conspirators against the Doctor's dourness and pipe smoking. Rebecca's mother had been of Italian descent, beautiful, strong willed, and all the other things that one said about long-dead, romantic mothers. Frau loved nothing more than making Rebecca unhappy with stories about her. "Well, they say you're good enough at that, too," Frau allowed.

Rebecca snorted, patted Frau's shoulder, and went up to the house to try to find a cool, dark place to sit and think. Of these there were many: The Doctor, her father, had one prevailing philosophy when it came to equipping a house, and that was to furnish every available corner with a place to sit and read a newspaper. Rebecca pulled herself through the kitchen door and made her way, blinking like a fish at the transition from the bright afternoon to the dim murk of the house, to a chair she favored in the dining room, where just that morning she'd laid a thick old copy of *Practical Housekeeping,* which had probably been given to her mother when she had married. It read like a good joke. A practical joke. One that Rebecca was going to be relying on to keep her and her good-natured husband alive. Not for the first time, Rebecca reminded herself that she wasn't a prairie forty-eighter who had to learn to survive a harsh winter in the Dakota Territory. She had only to learn to live in a farmhouse without an icebox, for heaven's sake.

In the warm dimness of the room Rebecca gathered the book into her lap and sat down, feeling the weight of it on her thighs. She reached into her bodice and pulled out her reading glasses, which the Doctor had insisted upon, to save her eyes.

And suddenly there he was, looming overhead.

"Your John is coming here for dinner?" the Doctor demanded. Rebecca looked up at him. Typically her father's sudden appearances and disappearances had an invigorating effect on her, although she suspected they were calculated to surprise. *Swoop, here I am in my chair under the lamp, frowning at a newspaper. Zop, I am gone to my office to see patients and I may not return for dinner. Whish, here I am standing over you in the doorway between the parlor and the dining room as you sit down to read and be alone—nothing escapes me, and especially not my freedom to do as I wish; I am an old man.* The Doctor's summer suit was pressed and fresh; he held his watch in his hand. *Live forever,* Rebecca thought suddenly, and almost managed a smile up at his unamused face.

"Papa, how should I know? He has a lot to do on the farm now. He'll come to dinner if he can."

At this rejoinder the Doctor looked at her approvingly, which nevertheless reminded her that she ought to have smoothed her hair and washed her face before she sat down. "I like it better when he comes here. You and Frau bore me."

Rebecca snorted again and balanced her glasses on her nose. "I might be more diverting if *I* knew how to break a field or build a chicken coop?

"You might!" the Doctor almost bellowed in his glee at the thought. "*Ja,* you might!"

For all his intelligence the Doctor had raised her unthinkingly.

She'd gone to the village school, and at night in the parlor she'd read the newspaper with him, or novels, but if her father had ever considered sending her to college, he'd never mentioned anything about it, and she wasn't the type who would beg for such a thing. Her mother's family was all dead or in New Orleans or back in Italy. In a more adventurous version of her own life, Rebecca imagined, she might have traveled abroad to know her mother's family better, but she didn't believe herself to be a particularly adventurous person.

She was modern enough—she'd been up to Austin, of course, and to San Antonio and Galveston, like many of the other girls her age. Trips to the cities reinforced for girls like her just how country they were, but still, the modern way of thinking found them all, even out here in the hill country. Some girls Rebecca knew wondered "what they'd do with their lives," what it was that would make them happy the way they believed they deserved to be. One thing—every man, woman, and child gets one thing: It is the thing you must seek out and sacrifice for, the thing that will make you happy. Perhaps for one girl it's mothering babies; for one girl it's an ambition for the stage; for another girl it's marrying well; for another girl it's an education and a large life in a strange city. But one thing only, one key. To desire more than one thing, to pursue more than one thing in the name of your life's happiness, was unseemly and greedy.

Rebecca still didn't know what her one thing would be, and that above all was what caused these smothering moments of panic. She supposed she'd always believed she'd have more time to think about it; she hadn't anticipated life rushing at her like this and demanding that she step into its cold, busy current before she'd even had a chance to take off her shoes.

"I am endeavoring, you see, to be of use to you and Mr.

Hirschfelder, too," she said mildly, lifting the corner of her book and letting it drop again. Her father made an unflattering sound and moved toward the kitchen door, on his way to smoke on the back porch. As usual, her father had no remark to make on the subject of her moving out of the house. "Boring or not, you'll miss me, *mein Herr,*" she warned his retreating back.

When John next came to visit—it was that evening after all—Rebecca told him what her father had said that afternoon, just to make him laugh, which she loved to do. "I have to wonder what the good Doctor's reaction was when you asked him permission to marry me," she teased.

They had gone to the backyard for some fresh air after dinner and found the night loud with insects, and heat lightning scattering the breezes, and the small-leaved bushes clustered around the house trembling.

John walked close enough to her that his sleeve brushed hers. "He said, '*Gott im Himmel,* you?' "

Rebecca halted midstep. When she saw that he wasn't making a joke, she cackled with laughter. John smiled on—he was used to this sort of outburst from her, she thought. Still, she sensed she wasn't behaving quite correctly toward her fiancé, and wiping her eyes, she said, "I'm sorry, John. I think we owe you an apology. He's just a rude old thing."

"Oh, I didn't mind. I don't know but that I had the same thought myself at the time."

"Don't say that," Rebecca said warmly, and she smiled up at him and then her breath caught. His brightness was back. She never knew what to do with it. "He just loves to make a man's knees knock if he can," she hurried on. John, meanwhile, had slipped an arm carefully around her waist. Her heart struggled. She was painfully aware that the fabric at the small of her back where her shirtwaist and her belt met was damp: The day had been hot, and the air in the dining room stifling. *Don't touch me there,* she wanted to plead as a favor—she didn't want either of them to be embarrassed. *Oh, not there, I'm not at my best at the small of my back.* Her neck was damp, too, the curls at her nape sticking and clinging; her palms were clammy with nervousness. There was no part of her, it seemed, that *was* at its best. She felt light-headed. John's hand was gentle. It didn't feel as if he were guiding her or pressing—that is, he didn't make it feel that way. His arm was about her waist because he longed to touch her, and that was all.

"Is this all right?" John said in a low voice. Rebecca nodded, her throat dry.

In four days they would be married.

She knew, naturally, what that would mean. She wasn't stupid. It wasn't just gardening and cooking that she'd have to learn. Marriage was an entire vocabulary she didn't know yet. A married woman was a wise thing, an experienced thing, a careful thing. A married woman has crossed an invisible bridge.

So she forced herself to turn in toward John Hirschfelder, there in the humid, flashing night on the grass, her whole body tense like an arrow just shot. Something coursed through the tree branches overhead, and she realized it was only the wind, not a ghost, not her soul, not a tribe of witches. Her lips parted, and she took in the disturbance of the breeze with a little click in her throat. She closed her eyes and then forced herself to reopen them.

Rebecca was known as a tall woman, with a slim figure, but John stood several inches taller than she. John was well formed and well built, but like her he was thin, still thinner than most men in town. *I'll feed you,* she found herself thinking in that moment, looking up at his brightness, breathing the gentle heat of his breath. *I'll nourish you, it can't be so hard.* His face had never been so close to hers, and she found that she liked it; she liked to see his broad cheek and his dark lashes, she liked to see his strong mouth, with lips that curved up on one side and down on the other, and she liked the straight dark hair that fell over his forehead. "You're looking at me strangely," he said to her.

"Am I?" she whispered. Her lips were tingling as if someone were tickling the roof of her mouth.

"Like you're an animal who wants to eat me." John grinned. He was joking, of course. His sense of humor, famous, irrepressible, even when she wished he'd be serious. "I recognize that look. I shot a mountain lion once for giving me that look, on a hunting trip with my father." But he did not move away from her; he stayed close, where she could study his face, his *brightness*—the term she'd begun to attach to a phenomenon she'd noticed early in their engagement and kept noticing, even when it made her unhappy. When she looked at John sometimes, in the mornings or evenings, it was like looking at a gem underwater. Parts of his face would seem to glint at her, like a mermaid's hair glimmers to a drowning sailor, and she saw now where it originated: around the eyes, yes, but also at the corners of his mouth, sometimes—yes, just there. And his arm, still around her waist, and she, still so close to him, but she could step closer, couldn't she? Yes, to be sure.

John's smile had faded, but the brightness was still present. They were still for a moment, and then Rebecca seemed to feel as if she'd been holding her arm aloft, and then simply let it fall, softly, so that her hand rested on his chest—with that same sense of muscular relief she experienced when she realized she'd been sitting hunched over a book or a piece of handwork and simply stretched her neck and pulled back her shoulder blades.

When he spoke, his voice was hoarse. "Are you all right, sweetheart?"

"You had better kiss me, John," she said raggedly. "My heart—"

"Mine, too," he said. He smiled at her, with what they both knew to be false bravery. He brought his lips to meet hers. To her surprise—and his, she thought—a small sound escaped his throat as their lips touched, and her body tensed in response to his. It broke her heart.

At the altar in the Lutheran church. Everyone at the ceremony looking at the two of them, seeming to know something they didn't know, seeming to nod at her wisely, smile at her encouragingly. Rebecca had never known before what terror was, and now, when she most needed her heart to beat true, she felt almost faint with heat and the rush of blood. She felt glittering and thin like a soap bubble. *What am I so afraid of,* she kept asking herself. *What could it possibly be.* When the priest invited them to kiss after announcing that his incantations had worked their invisible, unsurprising results, Rebecca turned to John so quickly, seeking his strong mouth, that the congregation laughed, approving. She had wanted that mouth, more of it, ever since his kiss in her yard (even though that night she'd broken away and excused herself with a hot, blushing inarticulateness, and raced upstairs to throw herself into her room in the dark and stare out the window and listen to her heart, her heart, her heart).

John looked more handsome than she'd ever seen him, in a dark-gray suit, his eyes sparkling, and she knew herself she was pretty today, wearing an ivory embroidered dress with lace at the sleeve tips and collar. She kept John close to her throughout the wedding reception that afternoon, leaning on his arm when she could and leaning to keep him within sight when he had to move away. He brought her cold tea, fried chicken, sweet light peach cake that Frau and some other women had made for the party. The Doctor's house was fairly turned upside down. The old man was nowhere to be seen.

At five o'clock Rebecca and John were to leave for the farmhouse. Frau showed the young men, John's friends, where Rebecca's trunks were—her clothing and books and small possessions, and the wedding gifts that had been sent to the Doctor's house. John told Rebecca that there was a pile of presents waiting for them at the farmhouse, too, dropped off by their country neighbors, including "enough pickle and pie to keep us until next summer, probably," a bit of good news that Rebecca tried to absorb with equanimity. *Now begins my life in the kitchen,* she thought. *Now begins my life in the vegetable patch; now begins my life in the coop, in the barn, in the cold cellar. Now begins my life as a woman who has married a farmer instead of staying where she belonged, in a chair by the stove in the dark, with an old, grumpy man reading a newspaper under a light across the room, and a furtive, friendly spinster waiting for me to take her place.*

At four forty-five Rebecca began to hunt for her father in earnest. He couldn't possibly mean to send her off to the farm without wishing her well or indulging in a few archly delivered parting words. She couldn't find him. Upstairs, downstairs. Oh, their good house. She was looking for her father but she was finding evidence that a trap had sprung around her: It was going to happen, after all. She was going to move from this good, comfortable house, with its kitchen and garden and yard from which came delicious and good-smelling things, on a leafy street in town, near stores where she could buy cakes of soap and bricks of butter, near the post office where mail and magazines came, near the seamstress, the laundress, the school, the sidewalks where she could meet and talk to neighbors. . . . From here she would step back in time. She would go to a place where she could no longer be careless about bread, or buttons, or jelly jars.

She had been thinking about her future, knowing she was about to step back in time to meet it. She had come to some conclusions, but not enough of them for her own peace of mind. Unlike the world in which, say, Rebecca's German grandmother had been raised—the Doctor's mother, who had in fact been married to a forty-eighter—the world that Rebecca had inhabited here in a small town in the beginning of the new age was one in which a woman received both less and more training than her mother had had. She knew that until now, she had needed to be neither talented nor clever nor useful. Indeed she had needed to be very little to anyone, even to herself. And now, she thought, she would step backward into a place where a woman, her comfort, and everything she cared about could be destroyed in one bad season if she weren't all three. *Am I talented and clever and useful? Dear God, please let me be. Don't let me fail myself—it's the only test I'll ever get to take.*

Her mother, Florencia, by all accounts talented and clever, had not been especially useful, at least not in the traditional way. Rebecca had grown up listening to chapters in the saga of Florencia's ineffectiveness at keeping house; it was one of Frau's more hilarious subjects. Most of Frau's stories about Florencia concerned some disaster brought on by an unwise choice or impulse, for reasons that perhaps seemed plain given the strange choice Florencia had made in marrying the Doctor to begin with, and given the fact that she died so young, so far from her family, and after only a few years of marriage.

As Frau told them, the stories of Florencia's adventures in housekeeping were never intended to help Rebecca absorb any of the useful knowledge that her mother might have lacked. The stories tended more toward fairy tales than *Practical Housekeeping,* and usually traced the same plot: Florencia has decided to do something she's never done before—make a cake for a church social, get out a bloodstain in one of the Doctor's shirts, sew a dress for a party—only to fail resoundingly, with consequences ranging from sorry to ridiculous to dangerous. In one story, Florencia almost burns the house down; in another, she almost kills one of the Doctor's patients after ambitiously restocking the medicine vials in his traveling bag. The young woman's pride prevents her from asking for Frau's help, which would have been gladly and lovingly given (no doubt for the younger Rebecca's benefit, when Frau told these stories, she tended to paint a portrait of Florencia as a bright but inexperienced child rather than a grown married woman). Just as Frau discovers Florencia's predicament and is on the point of teaching Florencia the right way to do whatever it is she's attempting—and at this point in the story, Frau always leaves the kitchen to go down cellar for more apples for the cake, or goes upstairs to find her needlework kit and put it to use—the good world intervenes on Florencia's behalf. A magic stone smashes the bloodstain out of the shirtfront; a cat knocks a tin of milk into the batter; a bird singing to her from the backyard reminds her to check something twice. "The good world loved that girl as much as she loved the world, and it never once forgot her," Frau liked to conclude.

Rebecca finally found her father out in the yard, near the small shed where they normally kept the buggy and the Doctor's one horse, the mare whose name Rebecca liked to change every month or so since she had always figured horses to be too indifferent to care—on her wedding day the horse's name happened to be Lucy.

Even though she had gone to search for the Doctor, the effect of actually finding him was still as if he'd come around a corner to surprise her rather than the other way around. She had been tired and dispirited, but the sight of his trim, compact self, whiskered and competent and yet endearingly helpless, invigorated her as it always had. Nothing could be so wrong in a world in which her father still lived. The Doctor was sitting on a low bench near the horse shed, squinting into the dusty stillness where Lucy stood, bored, staring in the way that some horses do.

"Papa," Rebecca said, then cleared the dust from her throat. "We are going."

"Yes, Mrs. Hirschfelder." Dr. Mueller stood as briskly as if she hadn't just found him in an attitude of inert melancholy and faced his daughter. "Come here and give me a kiss, dear girl. And you had better rename my horse one last time, too."

Rebecca moved toward her father and embraced him tenderly. It wasn't his fault. However she felt now, however unprepared and unstudied and untethered, it wasn't the Doctor's fault. She could only blame herself for never having bothered, never having tried. And now she would see what she was made of.

"Primrose," she whispered, and gave his cheek a peck. "Or, no. Patience."

"Patience, *ja*. Like 'patients.'" Her father smiled at her. His eyes were wet. "*Sehr gut.*"

"*Ja*." She smiled.

"You are not a German girl," Dr. Mueller reminded her. "You are an American girl. Go be an American wife."

He led her on his arm around the house to the farm wagon in the street in front of the porch, where John Hirschfelder waited to take her away, and where the wedding guests had gathered to see them off. When her father had led her down the aisle that forenoon, Rebecca had hardly been aware of him. She had been thinking of how good her dress smelled, the fresh, clean linen smell of the new fabric, and how hot it was in the church; she had been thinking about the cool, stiff stems of the rosebud nosegay she held; she had been thinking about John's arms, the yard, the nighttime. She had allowed her father to relinquish her at the altar without so much as a second glance back at the old man, and she had stepped toward the spot where she would stand and be married like a high-strung pony steps into a market stall, all the same bright anxiety and prancing dismay and all the same fundamental lack of understanding of how she had come to this place.

Now, as she neared John's wagon, she turned and embraced her father again the way she felt she ought to have in the church. She was sorry for him, sorrier by far than she was for herself. What had he raised her for, after all. To keep her dead mother as close to him as he could, for as long as he could, until at last he had to open his fingers and watch her walk toward another.

CHAPTER THREE

As Bridget and Julie drive home from the coffee shop, avoiding mommy yoga with Gennie while driving heedlessly into something more terrible by far, Bridget distracts herself by telling Julie a story. Other than imagining the worst that can happen every day all day long, she's learned that the other main job requirement of motherhood is being able to summon a story on command whenever the occasion demands it. *On your way home to confront a ghost? Not sure you can think straight? Worried that your baby girl can smell the fear rising from your skin like smoke? Time to play Scheherazade. Extemporize.* This, too, seems like a skill from her working life that she's redeploying in a new way. In fact, when Bridget is short a plot line for a Julie story, she will often borrow one from an old case (heavily tarted up with fantastical objects and locations, since as an estates attorney her cases had not tended toward the entertainment of a baby, or anyone else) or from games Mark has worked on at PlusSign. For an attorney, she has a pretty good imagination, and she's got something of a knack for magical powers, escape hatches, and talismans, more than a few of which even made their way into some of PlusSign's early successes, back when she and Mark used to talk to each other about work. Or anything much.

Bridget is pulling into her driveway when her phone begins ringing, and so she parks and answers it, thinking it's probably Martha buzzing her about the estate case she gives absolutely zero fucks about.

"Bridget! Where are you? Class is starting. I thought you were right behind me." Gennie's tone is fretful. "Are you okay?"

"I'm sorry, Gennie." She is extemporizing again, talking fast. "I was partway there and then Julie had this enormous poop—it's all over her car seat. I had to take her home. I just pulled up, actually." Bridget has to wonder sometimes where her advanced powers of invention, which some would call *lying,* actually come from. Her father, probably.

"Oh God. Good luck with that. Your car seat probably has the removable cushion, right?"

"Right into the washing machine. Serenity now, goddamn it," Bridget says, and Gennie laughs, because everything Bridget says is funny to Gennie, even if it's not—just another of Gennie's gratifying personality traits.

"See you Friday? You're still bringing your friend Martha to the cookout this week, right? I can't wait to meet her."

"Yep. Have good limberness and inward focus. Tell Miles to really work for that shoulder stand." As she signs off, Gennie is still giggling, which leaves Bridget feeling a bit wistful for Martha after all—she's harder to amuse. Bridget wouldn't mind having to work a little harder for the laugh track.

Sitting in her car in her driveway, the engine ticking and cooling, Bridget feels the familiar conflict arise, feels her breathing accelerate. *Go in. See her. Don't go in. Don't see her.*

"What do you say, Miss Jujubee? Should we go inside?"

Julie looks expectantly at her mother in the twin mirrors and lets loose her pterodactyl screech.

Meanwhile, Bridget is still holding her phone. Before she can second-guess herself again, she taps the button for Mark's work number, hoping to catch him between meetings. *Be there, love. Be there, love. Be there, love.*

Julie squawks. "Ssssssh, baby," Bridget says, and that is when Mark picks up.

"Bridge. What's up. Everything okay?" His voice is not altogether warm. He does not sound altogether happy to hear from her. Once, he told her (and was promptly forced to acknowledge that it had been a mistake to do so) that sometimes at work he forgets that she and Julie exist, and that it doesn't even have to be a particularly busy day for this forgetting to happen, although most of his days are busy. Sometimes he'll just be putting out fires over email and drinking his coffee from his travel mug and thinking about whatever project he's going to do next, and it'll be an hour or so before he'll even remember who he is, much less that he has a family, a rosy little baby girl and a fine, strong, lawyerly wife. He'd meant to sound amazed at himself, Bridget thinks. He'd meant for it to sound like he couldn't believe the way his mind worked. But it had just sounded cruel, at the time, and she wept, and then a few days later she told her mother.

"Yeah. Thank God you're there." Bridget closes her eyes and puts her head on the steering wheel. Julie screams again, once, without much conviction.

"What's going on?"

"Nothing," Bridget lies, light-headed, heart pounding.

She'd wept at the thought of Mark forgetting them partly because she needed so much to be remembered, to leave a part of herself in the world outside of her car, her errands, her playdates, her daughter, her daughter's naps, even if that part was just the figment that Mark carried around with him through his day. But she'd also wept, she thinks, because she remembers that feeling herself, that absorption into the hours. She remembers feeling that way, of course she does. She can't say it's the best feeling or the healthiest—how good for anyone can it be, after all, to tether blank-brainedly to a corporation that runs on her time, her talents, her precious life's minutes and hours. Losing oneself in one's work is a pathology, not a badge of honor. But so is losing oneself, period, and there are plenty of ways to do that. Plenty.

She remembers being absorbed in something important but small. Work never felt like an enlargement of herself, exactly. But she misses how the hours would pass, quickly, and she misses being able to lose them. *And now there are two women lurking around the house, looking for something. Maybe I should just tell her to get out because* I'm *supposed to be the ghost around here.*

Mark says, "Where are you guys? You sound echoey."

"I'm in the car. In the driveway." *Now, why didn't I think to lie about that, I wonder.*

"In the driveway? It's like ninety degrees out. You guys should get inside. Do you want me to call you back?"

"I want you to call me back. Yes. Please. Do that little thing."

"I will. I promise. I will. Twenty minutes."

"Twenty minutes."

"Are you all right? Bridget?"

"Oh . . . Oh, I'm fine." Bridget rubs her eyes. This isn't going the way she thought it would. She realizes what she wants is a little bit of bickering or bantering, something to remind her what it feels like to be a normal married couple whose house isn't haunted. She must sound awful. She must sound frightened out of her mind. Or maybe Mark is just overcompensating to prove he's a sensitive guy. Men do that oftener than they like to admit. "I'll talk to you later. Sorry to bug you at work. Are you having a good day?"

"Mired. I'm mired. I feel like a stubbed-out cigarette."

"That's quite a metaphor."

"I don't think it's really what I'm trying to say, which I guess is what makes it a metaphor." She understands what he means. They think alike, the two of them. And now he sounds tired, too.

"Don't think about it too much. It's just games. No one will be hurt if you don't give two thousand percent."

"I know. I'm not saving lives. I know," Mark says irritably. Now Bridget feels badly: She has said the wrong thing. Of course. No one likes to hear that his contribution to the world doesn't really matter and that he might as well just stay home and fold socks and wait for something cool to be invented without his help.

"Sorry. You are saving lives. What about all those poor people who would otherwise die of boredom? What about the poor children, all across the country, with nothing else to do but look out the car window or talk to their parents? You're saving their *lives.* We've *got to think of the children.*"

"Someone, please, think of the children," Mark agrees, deadpan. "They're our only hope for the future."

"Do it for the children. Save the children!"

"Somebody save my baby!" Bridget cries.

"I left my baby in that burning building! Save it!" Mark rejoins, a little dorky, just the way she likes him. Then says, "How is my baby, anyway?"

"She's good. I think she's starting to get hot. I should go inside." Bridget feels better. It is comforting to know that someone else out there is as unspecific and strange-feeling as you are, and that is why, she thinks with satisfaction, human beings get married to each other.

"Okay. Do you still need me to call you back in twenty minutes?"

"I don't *need* you to call," Bridget says, with a lightness she does not quite feel, not quite. "Would I *like* for you to call? Maybe. Yes. Probably." *And if I don't pick up, it's because the ghost got us; send help. Send Bill Murray.*

"I have a meeting but I'll call you after that. If you probably maybe would like me to."

"A *meeting*. How intensely professional. I didn't think PlusSign even had conference rooms." Here she goes again—she can't seem to help herself. Cheer him up, tear him down. Praise his effort, belittle his work. Where, where, where does it come from, this compulsion to make him hate what he's doing? She used to make him feel proud of what he did. And now, now that they're all dependent on him, now that all three of them need him more than he's probably ever been needed in his life, she makes these remarks, where do they come from, like the tiny moths in the closet that you never see but that you know must be living there because they've contrived to ruin your favorite sweater.

"Where else are they going to keep the Ping-Pong table?" Mark sighs. It is of course a relief that he hasn't allowed himself to be baited, but in another way it's a measure of her diminished influence. Which she shouldn't be measuring at all, much less in units of passive-aggressive snark. *Where, where, where does it come from.* "I have to go. You got my text? I'll be home late tonight."

"That's okay," she promises, even though it isn't, exactly. She has to make up for herself. "You got the picture I sent?"

"Yes. My little muncher. Give her a kiss from her daddy. I miss Jujubee today," Mark says longingly, and she doesn't doubt it. She would, too.

"I'll kiss her enough for you and for everybody else in the world besides. What time will you be home, do you think?"

Mark sighs again, musically this time. "Ohhh, God, I don't know. I sort of don't want to think about it, you know?"

This again.

"Okay. Love you."

"Love you, too, Bridge."

And here she is, in her car again, with her baby, running out of ways to avoid going into her own house.

As usual, the instant she's off the phone with her husband she wants to call him right back and do it all over. Whatever else she and Mark may lack as a pair, they've always enjoyed a little telephone banter—indeed, phone conversations, as Bridget has pointed out to Mark on more than one occasion, probably make up well more than three-quarters of their marriage.

Mark is a hard worker—he's always excelled. Mark also happens to be a good-looking geek, so his was not the typical story of the nerdy, scrawny guy with the small coterie of similarly nerdy guy friends, one skinnier, one fat, one acne scarred. He and Bridget met online, like about forty percent of the couples they know, when they were in their late twenties, but they also went to the same college at the same time about ten years ago, where their paths never crossed.

Mark didn't leave the computer lab much in college, except to smoke up with his friends and listen to jam bands. Bridget, too, was a grindstoner, so determined to get into a good law school and get internships and then an associate position at a good firm that she hardly looked up for about four years, and then for about another seven years after that.

They bought a house together—this house—right before they were married, at about the same time that work began to pick them both up and propel them windward. Bridget has always loved their house, but never more than when they first bought it. She loved how smoothly all the new fixtures operated. Sometimes she walked from room to room and just squeezed things, the overstuffed arm of a chair or a smart, shiny banister. This was before they really knew any of the other young married couples in the neighborhood—although she and Mark both saw their next-door neighbors sometimes, in their cars, in their driveways.

And then, once they were finally married, they fell into lonesome habits almost right away. She would bring home casework and nod off at her desk at home, waiting for him to be released from his office, where product delivery dates kept his entire team on a maddening schedule and a debilitating diet. She drank what seemed to be oceans of tea, but she never managed to stay up long enough to see Mark come in. She slept next to him every night, both hands closed into loose balls. He slept heavily; he slept through her alarm every morning. She reset it an hour later for him. She left before he rose. That was her whole week.

Saturdays she usually spent in the office, especially after she started getting assigned to larger cases. At the time, they'd been married less than a year, and she'd been swept into a kind of helpless acceleration of briefings and research and memos that had made her, she knew, short-tempered and prickly. Then Mark had been assigned to direct two important projects at his software company, and suddenly Sunday to Friday would pass without their having seen each other—awake—more than two or three times. At her corporate Christmas party they'd snuck up to the roof of her office building and stopped just short of rangy, difficult sex in view of downtown, warming their hands inside each other's clothes, grinning incredulously at each other like strangers pleased to find they had so much in common. Because they were still excited about what they were doing, who they were—the two of them so delighted by their own success that it seemed natural to have sex every time they saw each other, and more natural still for Bridget to go off the pill, and ultimately (here is where Bridget acknowledges there had been some magical thinking going on) to be pregnant and still working until nine or ten at night seemed like the final symbol of their badassery, their martial marital bonhomie. *We are so damn good at this we hardly need to even see each other to make it work.*

With Julie's birth, though, that kind of spontaneous goodwill vanished. Once her mother went back home and Bridget found herself alone with a newborn and doing everything on her own, she was surprised (surprised! as if she couldn't have expected it!) at how tired and resentful she felt. She'd begun, unconsciously at first, to establish a refined sexual algebra of permission, refusal, and frequency. She wasn't sure yet whom she was trying to punish, or what she was trying to prove. Sitting in her stuffy car in her driveway, she's sure that's another reason why Mark finds it easy to forget her.

But if she feels like she's been disappearing—from her husband's mind, from the world outside her neighborhood—well, it's her own fault, and she can admit it. *Sure. Yes. It was me.* Because she'd been the one to suggest that she quit her job after the twelve weeks of her maternity leave elapsed. The understanding between Mark and herself seemed to be that in exchange for her increasing competence at home with Julie, Mark was prepared to take on sole financial responsibility for the three of them.

Bridget remembers the night they talked about it. They'd been lying in bed in the dark after a long and difficult day, the baby asleep but about to wake up in an hour, he frustrated and she near tears, both of them whispering fiercely at each other as if they weren't alone in their own house, as if some other grown-up might overhear and shout from the living room that they should stop talking and go to sleep.

"I need sleep," she whispered helplessly.

"I don't see how this is going to work if one of us doesn't slow down. We're already running on fumes and you're not even back to work yet."

"I feel like I should stay home."

"You should, if you want to." He paused. "We should run the numbers."

And they had, and even though the numbers hadn't even come close to working, she'd felt so wildly incompetent and powerless as a new mother, and so wildly in love with her little girl, that she voluntarily relinquished everything other than trying to be better at motherhood—even and including all the other things she used to be good at, like the law, or being well and truly married, or having friends outside the neighborhood. So now here they are, ten months after Julie's birth, and for Mark, other than the sex, it is almost as if nothing has changed—he still works long hours; she still cleans the rim behind the toilet seat. Whereas for Bridget, every day feels like time is spinning itself out, a spool of thread knocked across the floor. Mark knows nothing about the way the hours inflate, substanceless but not quite weightless, like plastic bags filling with cotton balls. Bridget loves her baby girl with a clear intensity that reminds her why she's alive, but even for her, love isn't enough for all these strange, expanding, swelling hours and days. *I'm the ghost around here, lady. This particular job is filled.*

She's been feeling herself dissolving, losing substance, as if she were disintegrating inside the cotton balls herself; joking grimly to herself that she'd been rendered a mommy mummy, a formerly powerful personage crumbling to spicy pieces inside of the carefully applied shroud that was intended to hold her together—there it was again, she was thinking about death—and now this, this ghost.

What is she after? What does she want?

Haven't I already given up everything I was supposed to?

Bridget finally opens the door to the driver's side, letting in a swath of concrete-baked summer air, and Julie begins to scream in earnest.

"Okay, my darling. Okay. Hang in there." Bridget hurriedly snatches her tote bag from the passenger seat and decides to leave the yoga mat where it is, wedged against the door. Impossible to carry it and also get the baby out of the car seat. These small unpremeditated driveway compromises are why the inside of her car looks nothing like the inside of her house—ten months of deciding to come back for it later have added up in the predictable way, and it makes Bridget uncomfortable to look at the inside of her car from the outside, the way a person parking next to her might. *She put a car seat—a* baby—*in the middle of all that mess? Who could do such a thing?*

Julie's face is an unhappy mouth now. Wailing, she locks onto her mother through the rear window, and her mother opens the door and swings down toward her with a gentle series of sounds and assurances. "Okay, okay, okay, okay . . . Jujubee, Jujubee, Jujujujujubeeeeee . . ."

It doesn't really help. Julie is still unhappy when Bridget heaves them through the front door, holding the baby under the armpits and dangling two bags from her shoulder and almost losing the keys. Still bleating, outraged, Julie nevertheless holds herself stiff and still against Bridget's side. The baby always seems to sense when she runs the risk of actually being dropped.

The door swings closed behind them although Bridget doesn't feel herself kicking it shut—she knows she must have done it, one of those movements so routine it becomes unconscious, the way you'll lock your front door on the way out, thinking about something else, and then spend the entire drive to work wondering whether you locked the front door. She must have kicked the door closed. It doesn't close on its own.

Bridget and Julie both smell it immediately, the earth, the wet, cold dirt, the banks of a creek on a spring day, the newly broken sod. They're on the threshold, both of them pausing before the next breath, looking into the bright living room, the staircase, and the hallway to the cool kitchen. Julie wails. Despite the fact that she's never seen the ghost downstairs, Bridget is suddenly seized by the conviction that if she were to turn her head just a hair to the right, there the dead woman would be, her impossible face inches away, staring blackly, waiting for her sacrifice.

Bridget drops her bags on the floor in the entryway and gathers Julie close. Julie is whispering Julie words now, breathing through her mouth, looking around with gleaming eyes. Bridget's own heart is hammering. *She's here. She's always here.*

As impossible as it seems to move, to take even one step, Bridget realizes she must. She cannot stand with her baby in her arms just inside her doorway all afternoon. She must move.

Julie whimpers. *She's hungry,* Bridget thinks, and then shudders.

"Nothing to do but what must be done," Bridget murmurs, then decides to sing it. "Nothing to do but what must be done, Jujubee, Jujubee, Jujubee. . . . Nothing to do but what must be done, oh deedee, oh deedee, oh deedee . . ." The song, breathless though it is, helps get her stiff limbs moving. *Move. Don't breathe too deeply. Don't look around you. Just go, just go.* "Oh deedee, oh deedee, oh deedee . . ."

Bridget is in the kitchen now, where she sets Julie down on the floor to crawl around on the slick surface the little girl loves, while she opens the refrigerator in search of something to feed her. The smell of mud is stronger in here. Bridget looks determinedly into the bright, harmless interior of the fridge and tries to keep singing. "Nothing to do but feed you lunch, Jujubee, Jujubee, Jujubee. . . . Nothing to do but give you much, oh deedee . . ." She clears her throat, and as she does, she thinks she sees something white slide past her field of vision, something moving past the breakfast table on the other side of the kitchen counter.

Why am I so convinced it's down here with us?

Without turning—unable, for the moment, to force herself to do it—she says, "Julie?" Her voice is shaking.

Julie doesn't answer immediately, and Bridget whips around so quickly that the bottles in the fridge door shelves clink.

Her darling baby, sitting in the middle of the floor with a measuring cup in her hands, looks up at her. "Ha," she says in her small voice.

Nothing. She didn't really see anything. There was nothing there after all.

"Ha," Bridget echoes, smiling at her daughter. The smile is unforced. Even in the presence of death, Bridget can't help smiling at this creature, all chubby legs and velvety skin.

"Ha," Julie responds, warming to her theme. "Ha. Ha."

"You don't say."

Then they both hear it. Something slides across the floor over their heads and lands with a thud in the upstairs hallway.

Julie's face reflects the change in Bridget's expression in the instant before Bridget is aware that her own mouth has stretched wide, her own eyes have become glassy with fear. Julie begins to cry, and Bridget corrects herself and snatches the girl up off the floor. "Oh, don't cry, Jujubee. Don't cry, sweet pea." Julie stops midsob. Like all babies, Julie mostly just wants to be held, and she settles into the curve of her mother's left arm comfortably and begins to look on the counter for her lunch.

With one arm, Bridget pulls out plastic containers of finger food from the fridge and puts them on the counter. As she does so, she is conscious of sliding footsteps in the hallway upstairs, moving toward the landing.

"Jujubee, Jujubee . . ."

It is difficult, but Bridget has done it before: opening plastic containers with the scrabbling fingers of one hand, tipping the contents out onto the tray of Julie's high chair, which Bridget always leaves on the kitchen counter once she's washed it after breakfast.

"Dah. Dah," says Julie, unremarkably.

"Dah," Bridget answers, impersonating conversation for the girl, the theory being that someday, when she learns to talk, she'll understand the give-and-take, the rules of talking to others. Bridget is also performing in this moment the real way conversation works, which is to say that even as the words are being spoken at least one of the parties to the conversation will invariably be thinking about, concentrating on, listening for, something else entirely.

The footsteps are now creaking slowly somewhere near the top of the stairs.

Bridget lifts her chin and swallows. *We're fine, oh deedee.* She takes the baby and the high chair tray to the breakfast table, buckles Julie into her high chair, snaps the tray on. Scoots back into the kitchen for a cup of juice diluted with water for Julie's lunch.

As she's pouring the juice, there's a sliding, heavy sound midway down the stairs. A dead step.

It's coming down.

Bridget begins her song again. "Jujubee, Jujubee, oh deedee, oh deedee."

"Dah!" Julie shouts, but as Bridget returns from the kitchen she sees that Julie's face is quite serious. She's staring down at the scattered chunks of cold steamed vegetable on her tray, deciding where to start.

It's coming down. For whatever it's looking for.

The shuffling, sliding sound on the stairs is growing closer now. Bridget can almost believe that the ghost is trying to hurry.

Nothing to do but what must be done.

Bridget puts the juice cup onto Julie's tray and leans down so that they are eye to eye.

She whispers, "Listen to me, my baby girl. I'm going to go take care of something real quick. You just sit here and eat your lunch. And be quiet. Please, please, please be quiet. Don't let her know you're in here. Okay?"

She knows this is an impossible thing to ask of a ten-month-old who likes nothing more than to greet each morning with a triumphant yawp. But her heart is pumping so hard and so fast she can hardly think above the blood rushing through her veins. She feels electric, singing with tension, afraid to touch Julie lest she somehow transmit a current through her fingers.

In this moment of heart-wringing panic, Bridget forces herself to remember the fact that the ghost has never touched Julie, despite having had many opportunities. For whatever reason, the ghost has never tried to snatch her away. In fact, Bridget discovered the ghost standing directly over Julie in the baby's room just yesterday morning, while Julie sat playing with her blocks and occasionally looking up at the ghost, and Mark, who was ostensibly watching the baby while Bridget took a shower, sat in the glider, reading email on his phone, oblivious.

She wants something. Something more. From Julie's room? Or from me?

Fine. I can negotiate.

An idea comes to her: what she's prepared to offer up in exchange for peace from the ghost. It's something dear to her, indescribably dear, and it's right here, downstairs. She thinks—she wants to believe, anyway—that a ghost will understand its worth. A ghost might understand better than anyone would.

"Okay. I'll be right back. Please, please be quiet, Jujubee. Don't let her know you're here. Okay? I'll be right back." Bridget is backing away, whispering, casting her face into a huge, theatrical smile. Julie watches her, chin lowered, and grins conspiratorially. This is all a good joke.

The ghost is dragging her way into the downstairs hallway now. Bridget can hear her. More to the point, she can smell the ghost, the wave of scent she seems to push in front of her, for all the world like a mound of soil being cupped and pushed by a pale human hand.

Bridget slides out of her sandals. She has reached the archway that leads into the family room. Their house is an open circle downstairs: Proceeding counterclockwise from the entryway, a hallway leads back to the long kitchen that occupies half of the first floor, with entryways to both the family room and the dining room, which also opens to the living room, which in turn is visible from the entryway. When the ghost reaches the bottom of the stairs, it will be flickering in its staticky way at the point in the house where the entryway and the living room meet.

She might just have time—if she can run. If she can run silently and outflank her.

Bridget turns and noiselessly flies into the family room on bare feet. It's here, on the shelf over the television, that she finds what she is seeking and clutches it so tightly she feels her own fingers creak. It's not from Julie's room after all, but she knows its value to herself; therefore she thinks she knows its worth as an offering. Meanwhile there is no sound from the hallway, no signal from the dead woman. Bridget tiptoes as quickly as she dares through the dining room and peers into the living room.

The ghost is not here, but Bridget is momentarily overcome by the smell. It is like a grave. A grave has settled over her rugs, over the hood of the antiqued brass lamp (like a friendly alien head bending on its stalk) by the reading chair in the bay window; a grave has fallen on the shelves of books, the deep sofa where Mark likes to sprawl to read his email, the canvas bins of toys under the west window, the strewn-about remainders of her baby daughter's morning explorations of the world: coasters tossed from the oval table onto the rug, books pulled from lower shelves, a plastic egg crate that Bridget has saved for her to play with, filled with colorful interlocking shapes that have been sorted according to an emerging sense of logic, pure logic with no obvious motive—an adult would have arranged the shapes and colors to create a palette or, even worse, a playful facsimile of randomness, but a ten-month-old is, Bridget knows, guided by instincts at once less measured and much more acute. No other combination of colored shapes slotted into the shallow cups of a clear plastic egg crate could have been more Julie—looking at it now, holding her sacrifice in her left hand, Bridget can for a moment imagine that she's looking at her daughter's DNA.

Nothing to do but what must be done.

Bridget tiptoes into the living room and leaves her offering on the floor, in the center of the broad, patterned rug that anchors the room, next to the egg crate and its shapes—the altar where she hopes the ghost will find her payment.

Bridget backs out of the room swiftly on her toes, and once she's back in the kitchen, she opens the back door communicating out onto the shady patio. The heat of June in Texas, the insect song and leaf rustle of afternoon, steals instantly into the house and warms Bridget's air-conditioned, fear-chilled skin. The scent of baking grass and warm brick erases all traces of the ghost. Bridget turns back to her girl, half expecting to see the ghost framed in the kitchen doorway.

But there is only Julie, with her back to her mother, busily playing at her tray. Bridget watches her plump wrists, the curls at the back of her neck.

It is the work of a few clumsy, desperate moments to seize up her daughter's entire high chair—with her too-startled-to-squawk daughter still in it—by the seat and bump it shin-bruisingly outside onto the patio, next to the outdoor table, under the striped umbrella. Bridget then slams the kitchen door and rests her back against it, pressing her palms against the hot metal alloy, relief striking through her like a clock chiming the hours. *She's trapped,* Bridget tells herself.

Julie stares at her with a bewilderment that's almost like hurt.

"It's okay. Finish up your lunch, Jujubee. Then we'll play under the tree." Bridget moves without hesitation to the outdoor storage chest and rummages inside, pulling out the picnic blanket, a ball. It's hot enough that they won't be able to stay out here long unless Bridget can keep the baby cool somehow. She has left her sandals in the kitchen, but she crosses the hot surface to the corner of the house in her bare feet and picks her way to the small cluster of shrubberies that conceal the outdoor spigot. She twists the knob and turns on the sprinkler so that it sprays a gentle arc for Julie to toddle through and scream about. Here in the side yard where Bridget stands on tiptoe, the ground is a little bit spongy because of that underground creek. Her toes are muddy. The grass feels cool and wonderful. She pauses to catch her breath.

She's actually not sure what she thinks she's doing—did she really just drag Julie's entire high chair outside? When have they ever played under the backyard tree on a picnic blanket in the middle of the summer? When have they ever, for that matter, spent much time on the patio in the summer, except in the evenings when Bridget sometimes serves their supper out here, or when she and Mark come outside after cookout nights, once Julie is in bed, to swat mosquitoes and drink white wine and gossip quietly about their neighbors?

The grass will be prickly; the shade will be unconvincing; the heat will overpower. Why is she cast out here in the heat with her child? Why did she give her house over to a ghost?

My offering needs time to do its work.

Bridget squints across the glare of the afternoon toward her daughter in her high chair in the shade. Julie has thrown her juice cup over and is kicking her feet, sure signs that the postlunchtime squall is about to begin. The grass here at the side of the house is soft and feathery, more signs of the little creek that used to run through her side yard. Bridget lets her gaze sweep the street in front of the house. It is empty. It is always empty. Texas schoolchildren play inside during summer vacations. There will never be a gang of kids riding bikes in the street or playing catch in the cul-de-sac in the afternoon.

Mad dogs and Englishmen.

But I can't go back in there.

Bridget tells herself that she will bring Julie to the shade of the tree with the blanket and the ball, and they'll play for just long enough for her to catch her breath, and then she'll take Julie through the sprinklers for a laugh, and then they'll go back inside and change. By then everything will be fine. Her heart rate will have slowed down enough to get her through the long, quiet afternoon and Julie's nap, which is always the worst and best part of the day (before the ghost, Bridget relished having those hours to nap and clean and zone out—now, however, the afternoons are spent convincing herself not to be afraid).

She focuses on her daughter, who is beginning to cry. She has to get back to Julie and pick her up and clean her off.

She begins her wincing steps across the hot artificial planking toward Julie's patch of shade near the back door, passing, as she must, the glass sliding doors that also communicate onto the patio from the family room.

The sun's glare against the glass obscures her for a moment, reflects Bridget back to herself; nevertheless, Bridget cannot help but see her.

I won't turn and look. I won't turn and look at her.

The ghost, just inside the sliding glass door, her terrible face inches from the glass. Staring furiously at Bridget from inside and holding the framed photograph Bridget has left for her, the one treasure of hers whose value she imagined a dead woman might understand. It is the only photograph Bridget has of herself (in the photo she is a baby, not quite a year old) with her older sister, who died when Bridget was two, and their mother, Kathleen, the guiding star of Bridget's life. The ghost has picked this photograph up somehow and is holding it in her flickering claw. Holding it like something she would crush.

CHAPTER FOUR

With her penchant for telling tales (not all of them happy), Frau had, naturally, told Rebecca the story of her own birth and her mother's death many times, and it was this story that Rebecca found herself thinking of the night of her marriage to John Hirschfelder, in the middle of the night, sitting alone at the kitchen table, after everything had happened.

This was how Frau usually told it:

Florencia's labor had come on suddenly while the Doctor was on a call a day's drive away, and the birth soon became nightmarish (Frau invariably used the word "*furchtbar*"). Florencia had endured a troublesome pregnancy, and no one had expected the baby so soon. Both mother and child were in mortal danger when the midwife called for her sister. The midwife's sister lived alone and was rarely seen out in town, but when the midwife called for her, she never failed to come. She arrived at midnight.

Rebecca's mother was roused from semiconsciousness. The midwife stood by in a corner, while her sister, Ilsa, crouched over Florencia and touched her forehead, not ungently.

Frau, telling the story, would intone in the mysterious Ilsa's stern voice, "Do you want to see your child live?"

Florencia's weak reply: "Of course."

"Then listen carefully to me. What would you be willing to barter for your wish?"

"Oh—everything, anything! My own life!" (Frau always gave Florencia a higher-pitched voice than any grown woman ever possessed—it was an effect Frau applied in all her Florencia stories to make Rebecca's mother sound young, charming, steerable.)

To this Ilsa said, "That won't be necessary. But perhaps an hour?"

Here Frau, in guileless imitation, typically strained her head forward with difficulty, as a struggling woman would attempt to lift her head from a pillow. "Only an hour? For all her life?"

"An hour."

"What mother wouldn't sacrifice an hour of her life for her daughter? Of course I will do it!" Florencia was stirred to indignation. The midwife rushed forward to calm her, but Florencia swatted her away—this imperious gesture, too, Frau loved to reenact.

"An hour may seem very precious to you," the midwife's sister judged, "once you realize you will never have it."

"I would give the most important hour of my life for her!" Florencia declared.

"I must be clear. I don't mean an hour of your life only. I mean an hour of your life, and also an hour of hers." Standing at the bedside, Ilsa then put her hand on Florencia's belly.

According to Frau, in this moment, Florencia showed some pride, and no little courage: "'I accept,' the girl said. Never would she try to bargain or ask for mercy. These were the terms, you see."

Ilsa said, "I will need a tear." Florencia tried to comply, but she could not simply cry on demand ("no *Mimöschen,* she," Frau observed), so Ilsa blew into her eye until it watered, then caught the drops in a tiny glass jar. "Now I must have a kiss." So Ilsa bent low over Florencia, and the little mother kissed the soft corner of her mouth. Ilsa went out into the night, toward the woods.

The midwife waited with Florencia, whose pains were unbearable ("*unerträglich,*" Frau always said, fixing Rebecca with a gleaming eye). Shortly before dawn, however, Rebecca came through safely.

With the sunrise, the inscrutable Ilsa returned from the forest. "The girls are fine, fine!" the midwife exclaimed happily. Florencia lay with Rebecca in the bed, exhausted and feeble. Ilsa went to Florencia and touched her forehead again.

"You may sleep well with your daughter today and tonight. But the hour you bartered is the hour you would have seen your second daybreak with her. I did what I could." Ilsa went away.

According to Frau, Florencia had not expected to live. "She would have almost a full day with her little miss—what was a sunrise? She lay with you in her arms and thought no more about the midwife's crazy old sister."

But as the sun set, Florencia did begin to think—and she began to harass the midwife. What if the crazy woman had really accomplished this exchange? Had she been cursed? Almost a day—one hour short of a day. Surely Ilsa could have spared them the last hour of one day—was it so much? Florencia's temper rose. She ordered the midwife to fetch her sister again.

Ilsa came and stood over the bed.

"Why can't we have a day?" Florencia demanded weakly.

"You gave up your hour—that was the hour needed to make a day. But your daughter will live. You gave that to her."

"But you didn't tell me which hour!" Florencia cried. "You tricked me!"

"There is no trick. You pledged an hour. One hour from both of you, in exchange for her whole life. If it consoles you, the barter you made has given *her* a chance at everything." Ilsa nodded to the little pale girl with the head full of thick black hair, nestled against Florencia's side.

At this Florencia seemed to resign herself to her fate, to the extent that she ever resigned herself to anything.

"She slept curled around you, and before daybreak, she died."

As they rode down the country lane toward John's farmhouse on their wedding night, Rebecca and John talked in a lively way about the wedding and the party. They'd always enjoyed a bit of gossip together, even when they were school chums. This much about married life, at least, felt comfortingly the same to Rebecca. Their talk didn't slow until the wagon reached the gate in the early evening, and John said, "Would you like to see the place, sweetheart?"

She accompanied him on a tour of the land that had become his entire universe, and was now hers, too. John drove the horse as slowly as the animal would allow at the end of a long day with hay waiting in the barnyard. He was quiet as the wagon skirted the north end of the property, bordered by a copse of oak trees that swayed and whistled in a low wind. But Rebecca sensed him watching her in the gathering darkness, and her hand found his again on the wagon's board and clasped it as they surveyed what seemed to be the blessed end of the earth. In the dusk, the green merging with the violet and black, the long rows of young oats bent back into wind-traveled channels, the soft, pliable shadow of the fields. It was as if the farm itself were showing off for her. Texas was vain; it had a vast, dark heart.

"Do you know where you are, John?" Rebecca demanded quietly, somewhat short of breath.

"Let me show you the house," John said, and his voice was warm with joy.

It wasn't until the next morning, after things had gone so terribly wrong, that Rebecca saw for herself the simple, well-planned prettiness of the house where she would live. It had the straightness of a house where every nail and board had been put in place by a family who knew only how to do things the right way. The dining room cupboards were built into the wall on either side of a broad window facing west. The kitchen faced east and was cool in the evenings and warm in the mornings, with a trim new stove and a pantry clean and fresh. The wall above the stairs had been papered in a climbing vine pattern with a background of pale-green stripes, and the wood floors and banisters had been well planed and polished. Another little stove stood in the sitting room, this one potbellied and just for warmth, looking judicious and expensive in the bright candid light of the first morning of her married life, the first morning she'd awakened and known herself to be a cruel woman, a horror to herself.

But that night, that first night, she saw as much as the lamp would allow, which was plenty to assure her that the place was comfortable, as sweet and tidy as a newlywed girl could ask for. John pointed out the riches in the pantry and the cold storage room below the kitchen, where they also found cool, sweet milk in jugs, evidence that the cows had been tended that day by the hired boys. Since the wedding lunch had been long and rich, and since it was now dark and hot and they didn't want to bother with starting the stove to cook, he and Rebecca sat down to a slice each of a neighbor's pie and a shared mug of milk at their kitchen table, which John had made himself last winter, before he'd gotten sick.

Once she had finished exclaiming her delight in the place, she found that both her approval and his evident pleasure in it had exhausted her. The talk between them faded again. Rebecca couldn't help herself; she yawned mightily.

"Would you like to get ready for bed, sweetheart? The bedroom is upstairs. I'll bring up your valise." He avoided her eyes. He didn't say "our bedroom," not yet. Rebecca wondered at him suddenly. What was to keep him from just taking her hand and leading her up there, she wondered. Kissing her again. Where had that feeling of brightness gone, that one she'd been thinking of and leaning toward all the afternoon? Where, when she needed it to remind her how she should feel and act?

"Do you get tired easier now, John? Earlier than you used to, I mean?" she asked hopefully.

"Because I was sick?" John shrugged, squinted away toward the window, where the night was blueing outside and the shishing sound of trees came from past the kitchen garden. Even in the dimness she saw him deciding to lie. "I've got some good help. The Heinrichs—Paul and Martin. We've been working out here all spring, and I've never felt better in my life." He turned to her then, seeming to unleash the whole force of himself on her in a moment, his determination, hope, desire, fear, that brightness—it was too much for Rebecca, who almost leaped out of her kitchen chair in her instinct to escape. Yet at the same time panic kept her rooted to her seat just as if she'd grown out of it.

"And I've never been happier in my life than I am tonight, Beck," he said to her, either tactfully ignoring or not seeing the reaction his loving, unhurried words were having on his wife. The panic sent stupid thoughts skittering like a handful of spilled dry beans across Rebecca's consciousness. *I won't be swallowed! Close your mouth!* "You know—you must know—I've always loved you."

"Oh God," Rebecca moaned. She put her hands over her face.

She felt, rather than heard, John's hesitation. Then he stood and moved toward her, putting his hand on her hair.

"Don't be afraid, Beck."

Misery and embarrassment kept her still.

"I'm sorry, John," she said through her fingers.

"It's all right," he said gently, although she knew from his tone that he couldn't have understood her.

"I'm not . . . strange." She kept her fingers over her eyes, breathing into her palms. She stammered—how unlike her, she thought, who is speaking, who is saying these things. "I'm not a monster." *I'm not special. I'm not anything. I'm not a nurse or an actress or a saint or a teacher. I would still like the right to decide what makes me happy.* "I think I'm afraid of what we just did, today—getting married, I mean. I'm afraid of being unhappy. But I believe in you, I believe in you."

John touched her hair again. "If you do, then everything will be all right." His voice was troubled—instantly, she had to work not to hate him a little bit. Oh, he was a good person, one of the best. And she . . . What could be wrong with her, to say these things without thinking of what they meant or whether she even meant to say them? She was wild and stupid and afraid, an animal, not a reasonable adult. She felt a deep disgust in herself and an equally bottomless pity for her husband. How could she rescue them in this terrible, idiotic hour?

"I do," she promised. She reached for bravery. "I do love you. Let me—let me show you." She stood and took his hand, which closed tightly around hers.

The kitchen was black now and very quiet. John gently pulled her into his arms, and she could hear the raggedness of his breath in the instant before their mouths touched again, for only the third time since they'd known each other. Her lips opened under his; she felt everything that was herself opening, a slow, reaching movement like that of water that has been spilled over hard-packed earth, seeking its widest circumference before penetrating into the ground. There was that sound again, that broken sound from the battered cavern of his chest, where his sadly strained heart lived. Her John's heart. She must be careful with it. She flattened her hands against his chest. She would be brave. She moved her hands down to his belt. His body stiffened. Knowing how she affected him gave her power, and she longed to use it. The plane of her hand dropped down over the meridian of his belt buckle; she was no longer thinking now; there was no need for thought. Or was it rather that she was thinking harder, calculating faster, than she ever had in her life?

John broke away first. His breath was so uneven that Rebecca wondered briefly whether this was something he was strong enough for. *Maybe I should stop. I don't want to stop. I don't want to begin.* In the darkness his expression just registered—either startled or angry or hungry. It didn't matter. His mouth was on hers again, and he had pulled her against him.

And now a peculiar thing began to happen: As her actions grew bolder, her mind wandered further and further away. Why this should happen, she didn't know, couldn't say. As she sensed that John had lifted her onto the kitchen table, as she felt herself bringing her legs around his waist, and as she felt herself—her own fingers—pulling the hem of her cotton traveling skirt up so that the fabric gathered around her thighs, she had already stepped across the room and begun to develop—well, *theories,* it was the only right word. Theory one: She did this because she wanted to, but perhaps she wanted to because she knew she had to. Theory two: She was the best actress ever to have stepped foot in the state of Texas, because that was the best explanation she could offer for how well she made their bodies fit together, how she matched her gasping breath to his. Theory three: It was possible that someday she would be in love with her husband and desire him in the way he deserved to be wanted, but that day wasn't today. It wasn't today.

She saw herself arch her spine in a curve like a sickle above the surface of the kitchen table; she sensed his mouth on her throat, on her bare breasts; she heard them both try for air that seemed to hang above them, charged and trembling, like an afternoon disturbed by the ringing of bells.

When it was over, or seemed to be over, John picked her up from the table and she leaned into him gratefully. It seemed to her that she had seen the entire event but had felt very little of it. He carried her to the foot of the stairs, where she slipped out of his arms to climb the steps in the dark herself, holding his hand as he climbed behind her, feeling disheveled and glorious and eerie, like a ghost, and then when they reached the bedroom, John took her in his arms again and undressed her reverently and began the process anew. The process. Within minutes, her bare back sweating into the mattress, she began to feel tired, bored, anxious. *More is required of you! Give yourself up!* the Rebecca watching from across the room demanded unreasonably.

The Rebecca in the bed, though—oh, she was beginning to see the mistake she'd made. This, this tenderness and sweetness, was what she had to expect and endure, and not the bright, hard newness of the kitchen table. You could crave brightness when it shone at you from almost any man. You could endure sweetness only from a man you loved.

She began to feel angry.

John lingered over her body this time, kissing her throat, her shoulders, the curve where her brow met the bridge of her nose. Rebecca was hot, uncomfortable. John wasn't an especially hairy man, but in the damp heat the hair on his chest was curling and clinging to her, which was maddening and awful; his chest and shoulders were slick with sweat and his forehead, too. For her own part, she was drenched—the bedclothes beneath her felt as if they'd been rained on. And she was sticky and sore between her legs, of course—everything down there felt bruised and burned, but most horribly, she could feel the stickiness in her own pubic hair, and one particular sore spot where a hair (or more accurately, if she could bear to think accurately in such a moment, a small *clump* of hair) kept pressing, sticking, itching, borne repeatedly into a tender, miniscule spot by the pressure of his weight on her. If she dared reach down and just sweep the hair to one side with her finger, the relief would be exquisite, excruciating. If she dared push him away from her, just end it—this, this was worse than unenjoyable; it was painful; it was infuriating. Downstairs, on the kitchen table, she had suspected that they were doing something differently from how it was normally done, and that had contributed both to her enjoyment of it and to her curious abandonment of her body in the place where it set her free. It had been almost a hopeful act.

But this, oh, this—that spot—*it has to end! Why won't he just end it?*

Having so recently spent himself, and having loved her so long, however, John could no more bring himself to end it than he could thrust his own hand into a glowing stove. So Rebecca was forced to wait, to feel everything she wanted least to feel—smothered, hot, sticky, frictional, unloving, unrelenting. At length she shut her eyes tightly and turned her head to one side on her pillow, which John seemed to mistake for a sign of her own passion, and which prompted him to arch his hips into hers hideously, harmlessly, ludicrously—*now, now it's over, oh God, this can't be me.*

John lowered his face into the pillow to the left of her head. The hair at the nape of his neck was moist against her cheek. His body was relaxed, and heavier and hotter than anything she'd ever imagined.

She wished she felt like laughing. It should have been funny. His expression—the sounds . . . But she wasn't that mean.

Not mean, but she *was* enraged. Not at John, exactly. She didn't blame him, exactly. It wasn't his fault. That wouldn't stop her from punishing him, of course. Making John miserable was, after all, the best and most efficient way of making herself miserable. For she was angriest at herself, at her stupid, animal, trusting idiot self, who had hoped that a mistake she made knowingly would turn out all right, and in so hoping had dealt them both an inhuman blow. *It starts and ends here, tonight. This farce. I hate myself. I hate myself. I hate myself.*

John rolled over, off of her, leaving her body—in itself an unpleasant sensation, leaving as it did a hot puddle between her legs on the sheet. *I am expected to sleep in this because I am expected to be in love with him,* Rebecca thought furiously. *This is no one's fault but my own.* She sat up and impatiently threw off the bedsheet, swinging her legs over the opposite edge of the bed and looking down at her naked body. She was a beauty, was she not? Perfect, if a little thin. She had long legs, full breasts, a narrow waist, thick hair. Her eyes were famous in four counties. She saw blood and moisture on her thighs, nothing she hadn't expected. In the blue darkness, her white body showed itself to her—*remember, this is yours, and almost all that you have.* Two of John's chest hairs clung damply to the swell of her right breast. She lifted a hand and emotionlessly picked them off, flicked them to the floor.

"Water," she said coldly. It was a command.

She heard John propping himself up on his side in the bed behind her. "It's in the pitcher on the washstand, sweetheart. Can I get you . . . anything? Are you hurt?"

"I'm fine." She stood, her spine as straight as a queen's, and crossed the room in the hot blue night to the washstand, where she found the pitcher of water, warmed by the day, sitting in an old-fashioned porcelain basin atop a carefully folded white cloth (she guessed old sheeting, hemmed and repurposed by John's resourceful dead mother), which she swiftly moistened and applied to herself, neck and face first, then her arms and hands, even as the fire and tackiness between her legs screamed out to be soothed and cleansed away. She parted her legs without vanity and cleaned herself, aware that John could see, if he dared watch. When she finished, she carelessly threw the soiled cloth into the basin.

She turned to the bed then. Her young husband lay naked on his side, watching her with some anxiety, the bedsheet precarious over his hips.

"I'm sorry if I hurt you, Beck. It'll get better. It will."

What would you know about it, she thought but did not say.

What she did say was, "You didn't hurt me. Where is my valise?"

John pushed himself up, squinting to see her clearly. "Come back to bed for a moment, Rebecca."

"No. I would like my nightgown, please." She forced herself to stand straight and clenched her fists at her sides.

"Of course," he said simply. "Your bag is still downstairs, by the door. I'll bring it." John rose from the bed. His nakedness was not as shocking as she had thought it would be. She was able to watch him without embarrassment or shyness as he moved through the room, the way another woman might examine a hat or a dog or a plate she thought she might buy. *Here is my husband, handsome and prosperous, as God made him, in his bedroom, in the house he helped make himself.* John stepped into his trousers and, bare chested, opened the bedroom door—it hadn't registered on her, earlier, that he had shut it behind him, as if they were in danger of being overheard by anyone, as if there was anyone else in the house—and then she heard his tread descending the stairs.

She stood naked in her bedroom, relishing the sensation of air moving across her skin, grateful for every moment she didn't have to spend sweating in the bed. That bed. She eyed it now critically. The mattress was far too soft—she already knew she'd sleep poorly in it. The bedding was too heavy for the weather. John seemed to favor a superabundance of pillows. Something in the sheeting had smelled—not quite stale but vegetable-like. She knew, because he'd mentioned it in passing, that he had a hired girl from one of the big Czech families, and she suspected that he didn't know how much laundry soap to insist upon. She wasn't sure herself, come to that.

She allowed herself to think about the bed's history. When John's parents were alive, they had probably slept in this room, because it was the largest one upstairs and one of only two that she happened to know had been finished, with sanded floors and closet doors and furnishings the Hirschfelders had ordered from Austin last summer. But this wasn't their bed. Before he proposed marriage to Rebecca, but not very much earlier, John had probably moved his own bed into this room and put his parents' bed into the smaller neighboring room where he used to sleep. She knew this because it would have been the right thing to do and the right way to do it. She knew it because she knew John's unfailing instinct to do the correct and honorable thing. God damn him.

John reappeared in the bedroom doorway after an absence that seemed to both of them a mite too long. He could not, even in the darkness, conceal his pleasure at the sight of her.

"You're more beautiful than I could have imagined, Beck. You really are." His voice was low.

Rebecca cleared her throat and stepped toward him in a businesslike fashion, belied ridiculously, she knew, by the fact that she was naked. She reached out for the handbag in his grasp.

"No, let me." On a low dresser between the washstand and the door, he set down the bag, opened it, moved his hands inside as if petting a cat. He pulled out a white cotton gown, new and fine, made especially for her trousseau, that she'd folded tidily on top. He turned and brought it to her, and as he moved closer, the nightgown in his hands, she realized he intended to touch her again. And indeed, before she could process the surprise of this realization—wasn't her haughty stiffness effective? would she have to practice and perfect it?—here he came, and John's warm hand had swept behind her, smoothing down the small of her back, following the curve of her waist, cupping her hip.

This she could not allow. The nightgown was between them, a membrane. She snatched at it.

John stepped back, releasing her. She found herself glaring at him, feeling real hatred for the first time in her life.

"I won't ever do that again," she declared venomously. "Don't ask me. Don't touch me. Don't approach me. Don't beg me."

John stood still before her, obviously unsure how to respond. She threw the nightgown over her head and thrust her arms through the sleeves. The fabric settled around her calves. She raised her face defiantly, her hair tucked beneath the gown's collar. When John still said nothing, when she felt her blood cool, when she felt herself to be a bit ridiculous—did she really mean for their marriage to be chaste, forever?—she let loose a breath and reached up to pull her hair out over her shoulders. She realized that she did, in fact, mean for their marriage to be chaste, forever. That she would really prefer it that way. That she should never have married him and that she had broken his heart saying what she had just said, so she might as well go ahead and make it worse, make him hate her, make him regret her choice as much as she did, since neither of them could have much left to lose anyway, and because it was late, it was so late, and she'd never been so tired.

"I mean it, John," she said.

"You mean you don't love me."

"I do not," Rebecca said stoutly, then amended, for honesty's sake, "Not—not in that way."

John was silent, and the sound of it was awful, cricket filled— She felt her knees weaken. How much more of this could she—could *he*—endure? "How could you have married me?"

"I didn't know," she replied. "I know now."

John made a small movement then, as if she'd hit him or thrown something at him. He turned jerkily toward the bed. "You know now," he echoed hollowly. "And I suppose you don't want children."

She knew that he couldn't bear to look at her. Her heart thudded heavily in her chest—it really felt as if her heart, the organ, were literally shrinking or falling, in some way losing its place in her center. She didn't know what she was going to say until it escaped her lips, and then the horror of it struck them both so forcibly that the disaster of their marriage was complete and irrevocable.

"It doesn't have to be like this. I'll be your sister, John. It will be like nothing ever happened. I could love you that way. I know I could."

Incredibly, he almost seemed to laugh. His expression was agony itself to her, but his eyes were bright, his lips parted, his teeth shining in the blue night. He glanced out the window past their bed; then, in a series of motions so swift and graceful that they were finished before she understood what he was doing, he went to the bedside, picked up his shirt, and was out the bedroom door, swinging himself into his sleeves and then gone.

She waited up for him in the kitchen.

It took her many long, anguished minutes to find a lamp and then matches. She wanted badly to make coffee, but when she tried to start a fire in the stove, she couldn't get it to do more than smoke, which forced the humiliating realization that she'd need to wait for daylight to figure out how to work the dampers—it was a different and more modern stove than the one Frau cooked on at her father's house. Then again, she thought bitterly, John might as well get accustomed to the kind of house she was prepared to offer him: a comfortless one, no warm stove or hot coffee or willing wife.

She sat at the kitchen table with the lamp giving out a low light. She listened to the wind outside. She stroked the wood of the table itself with fingers that felt unresponsive and stiff. As she waited, she thought of her mother. She imagined that her mother, if she had lived, could have told her, long ago, that this was how she would turn out. Her mother could have spared her and John this mistake. She would have arranged it with the Doctor; they could have sent her someplace else to live, far out of John's way, a city maybe, where there might have been other cruel and unpleasant people like herself; she could have lived in a boarding house, taught piano lessons, lived cheaply, died alone, without hurting anybody or expecting anything in particular from herself. Such an existence would have seemed like a blessed, heroic one in comparison with what she had done and what she had to face now.

One of the stories Frau had told her about Florencia concerned her stubborn refusal to acknowledge her family in any way once she had married. They had cut her off, and she'd responded in kind. Florencia and the Doctor had eloped. They'd met in New Orleans, in the lobby of a hotel, because her hat had blown off her head as the hotel doors opened in a storm, romantically enough. At that time, Dr. Mueller, who was thirteen years her senior, had spent the previous five years practicing medicine in Fredericksburg and was in New Orleans to equip himself for practice in one of the newer German-belt settlements growing along the railway that ran through New Braunfels and Austin. His description of the land, and of the pretty country ways of the old-fashioned communities that clustered there, had persuaded idealistic Florencia to marry the odd, funny gentleman. Or so Frau reported. They boarded the train to the frontier together, as many ambitious couples were still doing in those days—as, in fact, one of Florencia's older sisters had done just the year before with a rich banker fellow who had investments in Denver. Florencia's old German medical man was a horse of a different color, however. "She wrote to her family from the train as they traveled to Texas—twenty letters, she always said. Twenty letters she wrote." Frau would usually give Rebecca a sidelong look here, indicating that she had reason to doubt the number. But then she would continue loyally, "And never did a letter come back. Once your mother understood that her family had no use for her, she had no use for them. Her back was forever turned. Whenever your father would suggest she visit or write, she said no. Even when she knew she would become a mother—no. No letter to her mother." Frau typically shook her head here, ignoring Rebecca's mute misery, and concluded: "And when you were born, she died with this regret. But she was proud." The lesson, like the lessons in most of Frau's stories, was unambiguous.

You stupid girl. You know what you have to do.

When he comes back, I'll tell him I made a mistake. I'll apologize, and I'll speak to him sweetly. I'll lean into him and put my arms around him, and even if it feels as obscene and insane as seducing my own older brother, I'll bring him back to bed with me and pretend I was just a hysterical bride, losing her temper in a moment of panic. Nothing's been said that he wouldn't be glad to pretend had been unsaid. Nothing's been done that he wouldn't be glad to see undone.

Even as she counseled herself, she knew he wouldn't be fooled. He was no idiot, the man she'd married.

Still she would try. She should try.

He was a good person.

She wondered if she would ever feel like a good person. *What must that be like.*

Rebecca put her head on her forearms and breathed down onto the table's surface. Her lips brushed the soft, oiled wood. She yielded to the temptation to kiss it and then realized she was very sleepy or very strange, or both.

When she next looked up, the quality of the darkness had changed around her, like she'd been under a blanket and a corner had been lifted, and John was in the kitchen, stirring the stove with his back to her. He had found the pot that she'd brought out and then done nothing with, and the fragrance of coffee filled the room. It was not yet daybreak. She had the sense that John had been gone for a long time, that he'd been wandering out in the fields in the darkness—his clothes carried the scent of earth and summer night, and the pungent greenness of growing plants.

Without in any other way acknowledging that she was now awake, John turned and put a tin mug of coffee down on the kitchen table in front of her.

"Thanks," she tried to say, but her throat was dry and it came out a squeak. Which she reflected wasn't a bad effect, after all—it made her sound timid, more timid than she felt.

"You're welcome," John said.

She cleared her throat and took a welcome sip of coffee, into which he'd dumped a hearty spoonful of sugar so that it was strong and dark and sweet, just as she'd preferred it when she drank with her father and Frau in the afternoons. The Doctor's house already seemed as if it had never existed. With her throat warmed and moistened once more she said, experimentally, "I love you."

"Stop." John turned where he stood. His eyes were terrible, dry and cold. But of course. He wouldn't have been weeping out his love for her in the fields. Not him. "Just stop it right now."

"I do. I love you as much as I—as I seem to be able to. I love you like my own brother. I would never want to make you as unhappy as I've made you. It's killing me to think that I'm doing this to you."

"If you keep . . . talking . . . ," John said through clenched teeth, "I'm going to do something I will regret. Just be quiet. Please. Just don't say anything else. For a minute. Please."

Rebecca pressed her lips together hard. *You see, I can be obedient.*

He shook his head, watching her. After a moment he said, "It never even occurred to you that you might drive me away, did it?"

She didn't dare to lie. "No," she replied.

"You can have the bedroom. I'll take the east gable room. I have an old bed in there." John rubbed his eyes. "The hired girl comes in the mornings and will help you—she does most things, but you should give her directions. Otherwise you can do whatever you want with your days, just don't come out to the fields. We should be all right for a while, if only we don't see each other too much. But you know and I know that this can't last. This can't be what it's like forever."

This last seemed to be a direct appeal to her intelligence. But she didn't want to say the first thing she thought, which sounded meager and sniveling even to herself: *Why don't we try it and see?*

"Whatever your ideas of marriage are, Beck, you have to know I don't want you for a sister."

She knew she'd insulted him, but not until now had she understood just how deeply offended he was.

"Wouldn't it be better that way? Wouldn't it be better after all to know that we were still friends than to feel as if you were forcing me?"

John's lips parted. He stared at her.

"Beck, what could I have done to you that was so terrible that you'd . . . I don't . . ."

It was a terrible thing, but now that she had hurt him as much as she would ever hurt anyone, she wanted badly to touch him again. She wanted—she wanted mad things; she almost followed an instinct to throw herself against him, thrust her hands into his trousers, back him up against the burning stove and take him in her mouth.

Instead she rose unsteadily and said, "You didn't do anything." She met his gaze frankly. She made her voice clear. "I made a mistake. I'm sorry. Come here."

She raised her arm and extended her hand to him over the table.

CHAPTER FIVE

Bridget makes her way downstairs in her pajamas, holding Julie, who swings one leg cheerfully, swatting her mother with her chubby foot.

As she descends, Bridget's eyes are fixed on the photograph in its frame, lying on the floor at the bottom of the staircase: the picture of her mother, her sister, and herself. She half expects it to look different—some kind of horror-movie special effect, all the eyes blacked out or all the faces dripping blood. But when she picks it up and examines it, it's clear that it's the same as it ever was. The three bright, girlish faces shining out of the frame are merry, knowing, as if the photographer, Bridget's father, has just told a family joke, which perhaps he had. The photo, which Bridget was given in high school and which has been with her ever since—the first thing she packed when she went off to college, the first thing she unpacked when she moved into this house—is unchanged. Nothing has happened to it. No harm has come; no malice has been acted upon. She's not sure why she doesn't feel more relieved.

"Let's go get breakfast started, Jujubee."

It is in turning that she sees it. The ghost is standing near the living room window with a look of contempt and fury in her eyes. But here, now, in the morning brightness, the ghost is less recognizably a woman; she seems to be enveloped by that crackling whiteness, seething. Staring out at Bridget from a dark place.

There's a dead thing—a deadening thing—in my house.

It feels suddenly as if the ghost's hatred has swept down into Bridget's throat and blocked her windpipe.

The ghost has full rein of the house now. Yesterday, after making its way downstairs and collecting its offering, it roamed through the lower story of the house all afternoon and night in its slow and staggering way. Looking for something else, Bridget supposed. Looking for its payment. She and Julie, meanwhile, slipped upstairs and hid in the little girl's bedroom—for once, the only place in the house the ghost showed no interest in. Bridget pushed the little bookcase in front of the door, and they read stories; they napped curled up together on the glider; they woke and played with Julie's toys. After dark, Bridget gave her daughter a bath and put her to bed, then crept into her own bedroom next door to hide until Mark came home. The ghost did not disturb them.

Now Bridget picks up Julie and moves into the kitchen with her, clutching the photograph, and sits very, very carefully on the cool, comforting kitchen tiles with her daughter. Blindly she reaches out to pull a few measuring cups from a drawer for Julie to play with, and then Bridget puts her own forehead on the floor, just so, just so, until she can catch her breath and be sure she won't cry. *Why is it here, what have I done, what have I not done.* The stench of the wet ground.

She is alone with Julie in the house; Mark left for work at sunup. He'd been at the office until late the night before, and she could dimly recall his explaining something to her while he undressed for bed, talking fast and loud like someone who's been on urgent phone calls for hours, and seeming to be only half aware that she herself was already in their bed, trying to sleep or, more accurately, waiting in a glazed, exhausted stupor for the ghost to make her nightly appearance at their bedside. Mark had said something about a product delivery deadline moved up by a new marketing opportunity. It had sounded convincing. Or had it?

She didn't know whether to believe her husband; she's long since stopped being able to judge whether his workplace war stories are plausible or not—the digital gaming business is a strange place. All she knows is that she and Julie are alone in the house with the ghost, and they can't be. They can't be.

She stands, grabs a handful of their earthly goods from the kitchen counter—car keys, wallet, juice cup—and takes Julie and herself out of the house via the back door, walking in her sandals and pajamas around to the driveway. She puts the baby in the car seat and starts driving.

And here they are, Bridget and Julie in the car, on the run. Driving the roads that used to be—and Bridget can remember this from her own girlhood—surrounded by sleepy country on both sides; the former farm-to-market roads around Austin all have transformed into tucked-in plazas and subdivision entry points. This road was still half wild when she was a girl, golden hills sloping away in all directions and flattening into green lines. Now it is different.

It's Julie's morning naptime, and the little girl has begun to nod off, although even from the driver's seat, Bridget can see Julie fighting it. The eyes drift closed. But then the eyebrows go up high: *No! No sleep!* The eyelids raise, the little head bops to one side, then the other, and the eyes widen, try to focus out the window. *Whoa, stop sign. Whoa, tree. Car. House. Sleep.* The eyes drift closed. But then, oh, the eyebrows go up high: *No! No sleep!* And again the head moves, the eyes widen. *Whoa. Parking lot. Sign. House. Sleep.*

Bridget estimates that they left the house around seven thirty in the morning. At some point she'd picked up breakfast from a drive-through and pulled over to eat it at a picnic table near a forlorn-looking playground on the banks of a small, scummy pond, the centerpiece of an unimpressive little park, in which the two of them were alone with the sound of traffic on the nearby road. After breakfast, Julie cruised around the table and crawled a bit in the grass, until Bridget discovered the grass was riddled with goose poop. So she picked up her baby and put her through her paces at the playground, and when Julie began to look tired, Bridget unearthed a snack from the bottomless reserves of left-behind-but-still-useful packages of gently processed edibles in the backseat of the car, and then let Julie play a little with the water coming out of the drinking fountain in the playground, and then loaded her back into the car seat, both of them still in their pajamas past ten in the morning, and started driving again.

Nothing to do but what must be done.

Julie is asleep.

I will stay with my mother for a few days.

Oh God, what a fucking fabulous idea—she is going to put it into practice this very instant. The relief attending this thought is almost as gratifying as the coffee and the shower she also desperately wants. She can't leave Mark a message because she left her phone at the house, but it doesn't matter—he's so busy at work he'll probably be glad that they're out of his hair. She won't go home to pack. She'll get on I-35 in twenty minutes and be at her mother's office by the time Julie awakens, hungry for lunch.

Something stops her, though.

No, even if your house is haunted, you can't show up unannounced to your impeccable, beloved Texan mother's workplace, wearing your pajamas at noon, without so much as your diaper bag, bearing a hungry baby with an unchanged diaper who is also in pajamas and has been in a car seat for most of the day. The shame of it would give almost any woman pause, even a formerly hardworking, IRA-contributing career woman who really—let's be honest—*is,* now, what her stay-at-home mom friends are, even though in her heart she's not.

What would those mothers think of her if they could see her now? Even Gennie, friendly and tolerant Gennie, would find it hard not to judge. *You gave your daughter breakfast from a drive-through window. You haven't changed her diaper since this morning. You are not wearing underwear—like, any underwear of any kind—and you are out in public in your pajamas, and so is your kid, and by the way, you just gave her a snack from a container of oat puffs you found in the backseat of your mobile landfill of a car. That's it, then. You've taken the final step out of line, and there is no community of decent women on earth that will consent to have you.* And besides, she needs to fill up the gas tank.

No, the drive to her mother's cannot be undertaken, not just yet. What can be done, and it gives Bridget some comfort to think it: She can drive to the Starbucks over in the next town that has the take-out window, and she can get a coffee and a something, some kind of fatty, awful something, and then she can suck it up, yes, she can, and she can go to a gas station *that's nowhere near her house* and be one of those sloppy, horrible people who gets out of her car and pumps gas braless, underpantsless, wearing slept-in, crusty yoga pants and falling out of a tank top.

This much she can do. Because she is bold. She is brave. She is in a neighboring town that is not as nice as hers. And she is a mother who does what she needs to do, when she needs to do it, no matter who's watching. Right.

But first she has to get some money out from a bank with a drive-through ATM, so she drives around looking for one of those, and it doesn't matter if it's her bank—she's decided she'll eat the cheating-on-you fee this once. The first machine she finds, however, won't accept her card. Or something. The second bank she drives to, which is right across the street but requires about a hundred right turns to reach because of all the meticulously landscaped median strips in the mini-mall maze she's wandered into, also won't let her withdraw cash. *"Transaction cannot be completed." What the hell is this.*

She finds a branch of her own bank after another ten minutes of driving. No drive-through teller; it's showtime. Bridget parks as close to the vestibule as possible, draws up her chin, puts on a pair of sunglasses she finds on the floor below the passenger seat, and rolls down the windows of the car for Julie. She will walk as stiffly as possible so as not to let her breasts swing beneath her tank top or let her thin yoga pants ride into the crack of her ass. But she will be quick, too, so that nobody can see that she's left her sleeping child to broil or be kidnapped in an unattended, open car in the sun.

Nothing to do but what must be done.

She waits until no one is in line, then scoots. Go, go, go. Watching her car through the plate glass front of the building. Insert card and then pull out, but not too quickly—*shit. Okay, do it again. What would I like to do? I'd like to find some kind of a drive-through where I can buy a fucking bra and a package of diapers, that's what I'd like to do.* She cannot stop to wonder why she feels so exposed, so horribly outflanked. Julie is alone out there in the car, and it's starting to get hot.

After the second failed attempt, it dawns on Bridget to check their account balance.

There's nothing. No money in their shared checking account. Bridget tries to think how this could possibly be. She'd taken money out last Friday, before the weekend, and there'd been several hundred dollars left.

Bridget hears someone clearing his throat behind her and steps aside for the man who's been waiting to use the bank machine. In the frosty air-conditioning of the vestibule her nipples have become noticeable, and of course the guy looks at them as he passes her, of course he does. She swipes her sunglasses back down onto her nose furiously.

You're not going to cry, are you? Seriously?

No, she is not going to cry. She's going to try to think this through. Bridget marches back out into the harsh sunshine and starts up her car, rolling up the windows and blasting the air-conditioning—in the few minutes she's been inside, the car has already become uncomfortable. She and Mark pay all their bills from a separate checking account they designated for that purpose. Well, Mark pays all their bills, yes, but she makes sure the electronic transfers happen on time. When Bridget stopped working, they did some financial housekeeping and agreed that it was better to have one untouchable account for bills and necessities and then one special, sort of *discre-*

tionary account, which was to be separate—that way no payments would ever bounce, and they could see exactly how much they had to spend at any moment. Yes. A good idea. It should have worked. Except that money from the *discretionary* fund got used for necessities all the time, and then sometimes money from the bills-only account would need to be moved over to the spend-me-like-I'm-on-fire account, to keep them liquid between Mark's paydays. Had they decided to consolidate everything after all? They must have. *Think, Bridget.* She could almost manufacture a grayscale memory of that conversation: *Let's just move everything into one place since the shifting back and forth is getting annoying. Okay, I'll do it. Will you remember? I will, I promise. I'll remember. I'll do it the next time I have a minute and I'm online.* Except which of them had promised? Which of them had come to the conclusion about what to do? Why hadn't anybody clarified that they should move everything into the fucking account for which they actually had fucking *debit cards,* for Christ's sweet fucking sake?

And now she does cry a little bit, but out of fury and frustration and not humiliation. Although, yes, there's some humiliation in it, too.

The funny thing was her mother had tried to tell her this would happen, or something like it.

Hadn't she? Yes. Bridget can remember *this* conversation, at least, quite clearly. In fact, at this moment, the memory of it could be said to uncurl in her mind, like some deranged, poisoned daisy in a burned-out lot, with all the same loathsome cheerfulness. Bridget, in her car, wipes tears from the corners of her eyes, but her chin has become a walnut, and she can't suppress a sob that has nothing and everything to do with the bank and the money and the idiot mistake that has been made. (*Oh, for God's sake, don't be so self-indulgent, you childish cow. There's a dead woman in your house. This isn't even your biggest problem.*)

She and her mother are at lunch at a pleasant-enough cafe—a mini-chain, one that specializes in sandwiches and soups and undrinkable coffee—near Bridget's old office. Julie is ten weeks old, asleep in her stroller. The decision has recently been made—by Bridget or Mark or perhaps by both of them—that Bridget will not be returning to work, and Bridget has just gone in to her old office for a morning, to formally tender her letter of resignation at her law firm and to gather up the stuff from her desk.

Bridget's mother, Kathleen, drives down to babysit while Bridget has the valedictory conversations with her now-former coworkers, her now-former boss. HR will be in touch. The wheels are in motion. She's about to be spun free from the machinery. Her mother is buying her a quick lunch and then heading back to her own office for the afternoon. It has taken Bridget the better part of three hours to extricate herself from a job she held for eight years, and trained herself to hold for another three years before that. But Bridget gathers that Julie has been her usual amiable infant self and made Kathleen's morning an easy one.

Opposite her mother at the table, Bridget swiftly answers a text from Martha. *Yup. Easy cheesy. Everyone super nice about it.* Then looks up to find her mother watching her with tears in her eyes.

"Are you all right, Mom?"

Kathleen nods and begins to dig into her bag, an elegant short-handled tote that looks as expensive as it is, for a tissue. Kathleen keeps her tissues in a little case in her bag. Her bag is mostly filled with thoughtfully selected little cases of this type: She has a glasses case that opens on a nifty top hinge like the door of a DeLorean; a silver lipstick case she bought on a trip to Paris a half decade ago; a small makeup bag, because there is not a woman in Texas who doesn't carry a makeup bag and sometimes two in her purse; an e-reader encased in a supple peacock-blue leather sheath; a cell phone protected in another leather sheath, this one a very pretty pale green. Things don't just knock around together inside the bag of Kathleen Goodspeed, née Hanratty. *She* does not have stray crumbly gum wrappers or floury-smelling wrinkled tissues in her bag, and never shall she. Bridget watches her mother with admiration and bemusement as she removes from her bag the quilted lilac-and-pale-green-patterned case that holds, just so, a plastic packet of tissues.

"Pretty," Bridget says, indicating the case.

"Yes, I liked it," Kathleen says simply, her throat sounding full, and she blows her nose with no little efficiency, then says, "I'm sorry, Bridget. I'm happy for you."

"You're that happy for me? You're so happy you're crying?" Bridget says, with a twinkle that feels forced. Because it is forced.

Glancing down again at her phone, she decides to ignore the latest blip of Martha's electronically wielded sarcasm. *Did somebody already claim your stapler? And/or your paralegal?*

Her mother says, a trifle lamely, "I don't mean to seem upset. There." She compresses the used tissue in her hand. Kathleen is a tallish Texas beauty of a certain age, which is to say it is all still there: The hair is buoyant and thick and expertly kept; the figure is slender in the right places and pillowy in the rest; the skin is clear and wears its bronzer well. She remarried a few years ago. The guy is a bit younger than she and runs his own business. Something financial. Or maybe it's real estate. But Kathleen kept her first married name, Bridget's father's name. She became Kathleen Goodspeed one day thirty-six years ago and will remain that woman for the rest of her life.

Kathleen is the sort who doesn't like to make a fuss over tears, and she has clearly decided to pretend that her brief, therapeutic cry has refreshed her: "I'm just thinking about you when you were a baby girl. And how I felt like I would do anything, give anything to protect you. You must be so excited to spend this time with Julie. You'll see. Every day you'll wake up and wonder how much more you could possibly bear to love a person."

Bridget looks at her sleeping, tiny daughter, a little bean in a blanket with caterpillars on it. "I know. I think—" She turns back to her mother and widens her eyes. "I think! Oh God, Mom. What did I just do? Is that mine?" She gestures wildly toward the baby and laughs, and her mother smiles, too.

Kathleen has always been Bridget's hero, but a particular kind of hero, the kind that also requires some protection of her own. Kathleen has had to enclose herself in a kind of armored carapace in order to be of use, more Batman than Wonder Woman. As the country song or the women's movie script or the psalm goes, she has battled through hardships, mostly alone. All the money she's ever had in her life—and by now, she has had a lot—she's earned for herself. Perhaps it is enough for now to say that Kathleen Goodspeed knows whereof she speaks when she says, not very distinctly, over a wilted salad in a lame lunch joint near Bridget's newly old office, "I just worry about you and Mark finding that it's not easy on one income."

"A man is not a plan," Bridget says, and rolls her eyes, and twinkles again to show that she's not really angry, although she is, of course she is. What kind of a thing is this to say to her, on this day? Are they really going to have this argument?

Kathleen rises to the challenge. "That saying should really be 'A man is not a *job*.'"

"Raising a family is not a job?"

"Oh, it's work. But work is not a job. A *job* is a job. You know when you have one because you get paid for it."

Bridget's annoyance reminds her of the one bad thing you can say about Kathleen as a grandmother: She never babysits. Hardly ever. Because she can't. She's still working. She took a week off to help Bridget at home when Julie was born, but she doesn't babysit. She doesn't even offer, not even to let Bridget and Mark go out for dinner on a Friday night, as Bridget would dearly love to do.

"You chose your career, I chose my kid," Bridget says brightly, but this feels like a line that's being read to her from a cue card somewhere behind camera. Other lines of this type that she has delivered today, while saying good-bye to her former coworkers: *I just want to be there when she has her firsts, you know?* And, *They're only little once, and these years are so important.* And via text to Martha, *Uh, excuse me, counselor, don't you have to go file or email something while I'm breast-feeding my baby?*

"How do you mean, sweetheart?"

"I just mean, you chose your career," Bridget says tiredly, not even sure now what she meant to say in the first place.

Her mother looks at her, quizzically at first, but then hurt. "No, I didn't."

Bridget is forced to backtrack merrily—horrible, horrible. Of course this is the most wounding thing she could have said to her mother, possibly the worst thing she has ever said to her, ever. And where did it come from? The same place where she stores all of her special little excellent digs for Mark, no doubt. "Oh, I know you didn't really have a choice, Dad wasn't around, how else were you going to keep a roof over our heads, the whole thing. I just mean, you made sure that you were working instead of . . . I don't know. I don't know what you might have done differently." Bridget sighs and rubs her eyes, wishing for a cosmic eraser. "I mean, Mark and I just did the math, and it made more sense this way, for me to stay home. Compared to day care."

Kathleen actually laughs, but there's no joy in it. "You'd better get out that calculator again, sweetie. You think you didn't make more as an attorney than someone who works at a day care place?"

"No, I know. I just mean compared to what we'd be taking home. Minus the day care."

"I don't see it that way. What about your retirement savings? What about the money you're not saving while you're not working? What about the years of advancement in your career that you're never going to get back?" Kathleen leans forward, then seems to make herself sit back again. "I'm sorry. You know I don't want to sound like I'm sitting in judgment on you. You and Mark should do what you think is right for your family."

"We *are,* Mom. We are." But because she is still annoyed, Bridget adds to herself, *And thanks so, so, so much for your permission. Mom.*

"Look at this baby girl," Kathleen says warmly, gazing at Julie in her cotton blanket in her stroller. She's sleeping hard, like she never wants to wake up. Bridget takes a deep drink of coffee from her paper cup and looks at her sandwich. She's never been so tired. She's never been so hungry. She's never been so angry at her mother.

Who leans into the sacred tent of air above her sleeping granddaughter, smiling with delight, and murmurs to Bridget without even looking at her, very much as if she is remembering something, "You know, someday you are going to want your own money, sweetheart, and not because of you. Because of her."

Bridget finds herself at the curving green entrance to her own neighborhood before she quite realizes that she is driving in the direction of home. She's almost out of gas entirely, but some kind of mother-autopilot function in her brain has kicked into gear, navigating her to safe harbors while she woolgathers. Rather than taking the right turn toward her house, however, she turns left, toward Gennie's. Gennie and Miles are likely to be at home because it's just past Miles's naptime. After ten months of friendship with Gennie, Bridget knows Miles's naptimes almost as well as she knows Julie's.

As she pulls onto Gennie's street, she is constructing the story. *Took Julie outside with me to pick up the paper from the driveway and locked myself out! Took Julie with me on a quick dash to the grocery store and forgot my house key!* But of course, she has her house key—it's on the same key ring as her car key. Who keeps her house key separate from her car key? No one. She'll have to tell the truth. *I am afraid of a ghost in my house. Please take me in and give me a cup of coffee and a pair of underwear.*

Julie is still asleep, so Bridget detaches the car seat from its base and carries it toward Gennie's front door.

Looking back on it, she's not sure why she didn't notice anything different when she approached Gennie's house. Surely something might have tipped her off? But she is oblivious to the clues—the cars parked at the curb, the two strollers folded up on Gennie's porch—and walks right into her lowest, stupidest moment like a dog roaming into one of those invisible electrified yard barriers that are advertised in airplane seat-back catalogs along with all the other solutions to first-world problems, like automated cat feeders and bulb-changing poles for light fixtures embedded in vaulted foyer ceilings.

Gennie opens the door, and the first thing Bridget notices is that her friend doesn't seem the least bit surprised to see her. But then Bridget's appearance registers and Gennie's beautiful hazel eyes widen slightly. Because she's Gennie, though, she seems at once to know what to do.

She stage-whispers, so as not to wake the baby, "Bridge! Come on in, the others are all here already, we're having coffee and wrapping up—but come with me to my room first, we can put Julie in there—" Bridget is already following Gennie through the door into the foyer, coming into full view of the mothers, all of them, casually pretty in striped boatneck tees and denim miniskirts, draped tanks and slim poplin cargo capris, sleeveless blouses and linen skirts, arrayed across Gennie's living room looking as well turned out as young Southern mothers usually do and, taken as a group, absolutely and stomach-clenchingly terrifying, at least to Bridget, in this moment, as she sees herself imprinting on their collective consciousness the certainty that something is wrong. "—and that way she won't wake up until she's ready to call for mama—hey, guys, sshh, Julie's sleeping, be right back."

Gennie puts her hand gently at the small of Bridget's back, both guiding her away down the hall and seeming actually to shield her from view. Gennie's house is, as usual, not just immaculate but comforting and lovely—there are flowers, something was baked this morning, the coffee is special. Bridget knows from experience that the other mothers' homes are this way, too, and that they do it all themselves, proudly—never, ever in a million years would they hire another woman to help them; they are as far beyond help as they are beyond reproach. *Southern women make the effort.* It's one of the commandments Bridget herself grew up with. Kathleen, as a single mother raising Bridget on a bank clerk's salary, cleaned house every weekend, and kept her nails done.

Meanwhile the children are all playing on Gennie's spotless rugs and haven't so much as looked her way. It's a consolation that at least the kids aren't wondering why she looks like such shit. *It's like one of those nightmares,* Bridget thinks, *where you're naked in the grocery store, or where the toilet you're using turns out to be in the middle of the public library.*

Gennie goes on, "I'm so glad you could make it after all. I thought you might not be coming or something, but then I thought, Julie's probably napping at some off-hour and she can't get away. Here. Let's—let me draw the blind real fast so it's not so bright. Just put her on the floor? Between the bed and the door? And that way you'll hear her for sure when she wakes up."

"Thanks, Gennie," Bridget manages. *I am not going to cry. Kindness is not what makes you cry. Cruelty deserves tears, but not empathy, not tenderness of spirit. Keep your shit together.*

But then. "You look tired, hon," Gennie says feelingly, and that does it. Waterworks. Heart-deep misery. Slim, tanned arms around her shoulders. "What is it, Bridge? Is—is it Mark?" Gennie asks, hesitant. "Are things okay with you guys?"

Bridget snuffles a little bit, and instead of answering, she requests a tissue. It's perverse, not correcting her friend's assumptions immediately. It is unfair to Mark. But what can she say, really? "I've just had a tough morning."

Gennie is silent and fetches her a box of tissues from the master bathroom. She watches Bridget wiping her face and blowing her nose. Bridget is afraid to look at her. She knows that her nipples have hardened again in the frosty air-conditioning of the house, clearly visible beneath her tank top, again. She has a feeling that she's also displaying a shadowy delta of her pubic hair through her thin, stained pants. Her feet are dirty. Worse, her child is dirty. Julie is all crust and crumb, and she smells as if she might actually be sleeping in a pooped-up diaper—allowing this to happen is probably the true cardinal sin of motherhood. Bridget thinks, *I look like a woman who has fled her home. I* am *a woman who has fled her home.*

Finally, Bridget's conscience demands a say in this whole embarrassing tableau. "Mark's fine—we're fine, I mean. He had nothing to do with it. I'm just . . . freaking out."

Gennie is quiet a moment longer, then says, "You don't have to tell me if you don't want to, Bridge."

"I would tell you if there was anything to tell, I swear."

"Don't feel like you have to. It's okay. I just want to make sure you're safe and taken care of. As your friend—" Gennie pauses delicately. "When was the last time you saw him?"

Bridget isn't quite sure she's hearing correctly—didn't she just clarify that things are fine with Mark? "Last night. He's working a lot. This really doesn't have anything to do with Mark." Suddenly she is exasperated. "'This,' what is 'this'? I don't even know what I'm trying to explain. So I show up to the art camp meeting late and looking a little bedraggled. Sorry."

"You look fine," Gennie assures her. "Do you want a cup of coffee or something?"

"Oh God, yes. And Gennie, could I—could I just freshen up a bit in your bathroom?"

"Oh, of course, of course!" Gennie is so truly delighted by her request that she takes Bridget by the shoulders again and squeezes. "Use anything you need in there! I have this fabulous tinted moisturizer stuff. It's, like, super sheer—"

"And Gen, I'm so sorry to ask, I know this is weird, but . . . could I—" Bridget swallows. *No, I cannot ask for underpants.* "Do you have, like, a long sweater I could just wrap around me? Or something like that?"

Gennie stares at her, and then Bridget sees something incredible happen: Her friend's eyes well up with tears. "Oh, honey. Of course. Of course. I—I'll be right back, I have just the thing."

As Gennie disappears into her walk-in closet, Bridget has time to experience a whole new bottoming-out level of shame. *She thinks he's locked you out. She thinks he beats you or terrorizes you or something. Say something. Say something right now. Just make something up, before she suggests calling a domestic crisis hotline.*

"Gennie, I know I must seem like I'm acting strange—or not strange but . . . Look. Everything's totally fine, with me. And Mark, especially with him. He's great, he's just working a lot. And I—I forgot my house key and my wallet . . ." Bridget follows Gennie toward her closet, talking to her friend's back while looking at the floor. It occurs to her that she has never sounded less convincing, even to herself, and she wonders whether some terrible part of her isn't enjoying this a little bit. Playacting, or at least not being straight. And being treated, tended to. Why does this feel so nice? Gennie turns around with a long, belted cardigan, all-season cashmere, pale heather gray, impossibly luxurious, perfect. Bridget takes it from Gennie and appreciates the loveliness of the object, and also the gesture. It's probably one of the most expensive sweaters Gennie owns.

"I never wear this, and it's too bad. I got it for Christmas from Charlie's mom in Massachusetts, and on someone short like me, I just get swallowed up in a cut like this, it's so long. But on you!" Gennie says brightly, and Bridget ties the belt. "That's just right for you. You have such shoulders. Everything hangs well on you."

"Thank you, honey," Bridget says. "I mean it. You just saved my life, or it feels like it anyway."

Gennie responds by throwing her arms around her, and Bridget is a bit embarrassed. "Whenever you need to talk, I'm here," Gennie says, and because she is finally safe, for the moment, leaning her head against Gennie's sweet-smelling hair, Bridget rolls her eyes.

Karen, Pilar, Sandra, Asha, Jen, and Gennie have conducted the art camp planning meeting without Bridget and are now lingering in the general warmth and welcome of Gennie's home while watching their children, Madison, Honor, Aidan, Jashun, and Ruby, tearing apart poor Miles's playbox. To his credit, Miles is trying to be cool about it, but it's easy to tell that he's not entirely happy about seeing his toys, his precious things, carted and spun and thrown about the room. *Who are these people?* he seems to be wondering. *Who gave them my stuff? My stuff is important!* Bridget sips her coffee, hot and strong and sweet, and watches Miles with sympathy while trying to get up to speed: She has missed the entire meeting, and this means she has to go along with what whatever's been decided, okay, but it would still be helpful if someone would just tell her what, exactly, that was.

"So, Wednesday mornings?"

"I thought we said that, yeah."

"But aren't we starting on Tuesday next week?"

"Gennie's got the schedule. You wrote it all down, right?"

"Thank *God* for you."

"So nice of you to get down all the details and have us all over, G."

"You're welcome, J." This is how Gennie and Jen address each other, G and J, and it sort of makes Bridget a little bit jealous at the same time that it makes her want to flick both of them, very, very hard, on the kneecap, with a wooden spoon handle or maybe a pencil.

"So, Tuesday of next week but Wednesdays thereafter," Bridget clarifies. Not for nothing has Bridget done a few depositions in her day.

"Thereafter, yes." Sandra says this, and it's not exactly nice to hear the word echoed. *I* was *an attorney, you know, and it's not uppity to use a word your kids will learn in third grade.*

"Okay. And Sandra, you're first?"

"Yep, first at my house. On Tuesday."

"And what time."

"What time did we say? Eleven?" It occurs to Bridget that by skipping the meeting because she appears to be hungover—or still drunk—she might finally have demonstrated her outsiderness irrevocably to this group of women, and that this distracted vagueness in response to her questions might be masking a real unwillingness to answer. Maybe she's not invited to the party anymore.

Then Karen turns to her and asks, "But will that time work for you, Bridget? Is Julie napping at eleven now?"

"She'll be fine. And when is it my turn? Or, I guess, how do we know whose turn is next?" Suddenly Bridget's mind leaps to the impossible: all of these children, these darling babies that she really, truly loves a little bit, playing in her living room under the watching black eyes of the ghost, her whiteness shifting and twitching in the corners of the room, her eyes following them. *The babies. Oh God, what can I do? She hates me, hates me, hates me.*

"We did a lineup, right? A totally casual calendar. A TCC." Asha yawns. She's co-sleeping with Jashun and is always exhausted. "I'm totally trademarking that, BTW."

"You actually talk in text message," Gennie teases.

"I know! Or wait, I should say 'LOL'!"

Bridget waits for the two of them to stop laughing at this and then says, with a little more intensity than quite matches the mood of the room at the moment, "Okay, but, so when is it my turn?"

She sees Sandra shoot her a look. "Do you need Gennie to give you a firm date on the TCC, Bridget?"

"You know what, I might need to ask for one, too. As nice as it sounds to play it by ear every week, I'm so busy it'd just be nice to know when I need to plan," Pilar puts in.

"Is this too much work? Are we being too ambitious?" Asha asks. "Maybe we should just—"

"No! *No,* y'all!" Gennie bursts. She is pleading and laughing. "Come on, we can handle this, can't we? A weekly semiorganized playdate? I mean, for God's sake, haven't we each of us been responsible for harder things than a little once-a-week summer camp? You know? I mean!"

"You really want to do this," Jen observes, smiling. "Okay, G. Whatever makes you happy, I'll do."

She has this effect on people, Gennie. Bridget can't help but see it, but she is trembling at the thought of having guests, having the babies, actually in her house. Her house, where the dead woman is.

Her lips feel as if they've been clamped shut. Bridget is aware that she is breathing funny, heavily, and then she hears Julie crying in Gennie's room and leaps to her feet, bolting down the hallway, leaving a brief, puzzled silence in her wake.

She doesn't care. She's with her girl again. Seeing Julie awake and reaching up for her from beneath the buckles of her car seat, her little face squinched in its adorable distress as she cries, Bridget's heart does a familiar stutter. Ever since Julie was a newborn, Bridget has been trying to explain to Mark the peculiar, physical effect the sound of Julie's cry produces. "It feels a little bit like an electric pulse," she told him once. "Like a power wave that pushes through you and disables your neurological system for a second, then reboots it."

"Sounds like a neutron bomb," Mark observed at the time, half kidding and half frightened.

Bridget's fingers are as quick as Rachmaninoff's, and her upper-body strength is, by now, formidable. She lifts Julie into her arms and squeezes her, kisses her plump, soft cheek, takes in the unmistakable barnyard odor, and heads for Miles's room and his changing table. "Hello, Jujubee. Did you sleep well? Did you have a good nap?" Julie's hair is a fluffy halo, whorling out from a point at the back of her head that has been pressed into her car seat for hours. "My sweet Jujubee. Mmm, mmm, mmm." And so on. Oh, it is sweet to hold and comfort a sleepy baby. She indulges in several more kisses as she gently lays

Julie down on Miles's changing pad. Julie is cheerful now, alert and quiet and still as she usually is after her wake-up squall. She says, "Mmmma," and pretends to kiss her mother.

"Thank you, Jujubee." Bridget smiles at her little girl. "I love you, too."

"Are y'all okay?" Gennie whispers from the door.

"We're fine. Do you mind if I borrow a diaper?"

"As long as you don't give it back." This is their group's standard response to this question, which is asked by at least one person every time they get together.

"I think I'd better go, Gennie. I'll give back your sweater—"

"No, no, keep it. Keep it till Friday, I'll see you then. Or keep it till whenever, I don't need it." Gennie eases in, glances back over her shoulder at Miles and the others in the living room, and closes the door behind her. "Bridget. I'm sorry if I said anything off . . . about Mark."

Bridget pulls Julie's pajamas up and then pulls Julie into her arms. "You didn't," she lies. She kisses Julie's head and puts her on the floor, where she toddles toward the bedroom door, wanting to join the children she hears in the other room.

When Bridget looks back up at Gennie, she is pale and clearly struggling with something. It comes out in a whisper, after a tiny pause that is somehow as adorable as a mouse squeak, despite the disgusting horribleness of her question: "Is he cheating on you, Bridge?"

"What?" She stares. "Why would you ask me that? Of course not!"

Her friend is miserable. "I'm sorry. I'm sorry. Please—*please* just forget I said anything."

But hadn't she just been thinking this herself, albeit in a sort of jokey way, just yesterday? Even thinking it for the express purpose of dismissing the possibility—doesn't that mean it's crossed her own mind, too?

Suddenly she would like very much to sit down.

The bank stuff? Could it actually be because—could he really have taken everything? Constructed some kind of story about work, and then lit out of town with or checked into some hotel with or gotten on a plane with—who? Who would it be?

No, this is not happening. This is not possible.

"I just saw him last night. I just spoke with him yesterday afternoon. He—he was—" *Not overly happy to talk to me. Either of those times. And I haven't really been paying attention. No. Lately my attention has been, oh, let's call it divided.*

"It's okay. I'm sure it's okay," Gennie says.

Julie begins to pound her little hand on the door. She unleashes a wail. Gennie picks her up, but Julie isn't having it; she strains toward the door and lets loose again.

"God," Bridget says. "My God." She isn't sure what she's feeling, but she knows she can't be feeling it here. She has to go home. She has to go home because (*why? because suddenly you want to see her? this is all her fault and you hate her*) otherwise she'll say something to Gennie that she'll regret.

"Are you okay? Don't go yet, Bridge. Please. Stay and hang out and let's talk about this." Gennie stands between Bridget and the door, but now both Bridget and Julie are trying to escape.

"There's nothing to talk about," Bridget says firmly.

She slides her hands under Julie's armpits and lifts her away from Gennie, who lets her go. Julie gives a kick and catches Gennie in the shoulder, which Gennie ignores. She's saying, "Okay. But call me. Call me when you get back into your house. That's all I want."

"God, Gennie, mind your own *business,*" Bridget snaps, flinging the bedroom door open, and now of course everyone in the living room has heard her. There's another one of those funny silences. Bridget turns back to Gennie, ignoring Julie's shouts of impatience and distress, and kisses her friend on the cheek—soft and pear-like, just like Julie's. "I'm sorry," she whispers, contrite. "Don't listen to me. I don't make sense." *This is her fault. This is her fault.*

"It's okay. Really. It is." Gennie clears her throat. "Let me get Julie's car seat for you. You just go. Everybody, Bridget's going."

Bridget hurls her car around hedged street corners at speeds that make the tires squeak and make her little girl go silent in the backseat. *I hate her I hate her I hate her.* She wheels into the driveway and flings open the car doors and grabs Julie from her car seat. Julie laughs at the speed of her ascent.

"We're going to go kick that thing's sorry fucking ass out of our house, Juju. What do you think? What do you think about that?" Bridget says brightly. "And then we're going to call your dada and have him explain a few fucking things. Awesome! Fun! Let's do it! Let's go!" In Bridget's arms, Julie is bounced and is thereby delighted. Right now there is no room left in Bridget's heart for fear; her heart is full; it is bursting with a righteous sureness. *I should have done this days ago. Gotten angry. Demanded my rights. Claimed my house. Protected my girl.*

The front door swings open hard and fast enough that it boings against the little spring mounted in the baseboard to prevent the doorknob from going through the drywall, then swings back into Bridget's face—she catches it with one palm. She puts her little girl down on the floor in the living room on the rug, among her toys. "You play there for a minute. Don't go off anywhere. Mama's got to take care of something. I'll be right back." *I am ninety percent sure.*

Bridget's chin is high, her eyes wide, her shoulders back. She strides into the kitchen. She is smelling for the ghost, sniffing for her like a cat.

"Where are you?" she says in a low voice. Then, louder, "Where are you? Come out. Come out here right now." Through the kitchen into the rear part of the house. "I'm coming to find you." Julie says something encouraging from the living room, something like "Bidissus!" And Bridget actually laughs, although her eyes are filling inexplicably with tears again. "I don't know what you thought, but I'm stronger than you are! *I'm coming to get you!*"

Nothing. Nothing is here.

She spins back toward the front of the house. Upstairs. The dead woman is upstairs, probably in her baby's room. "You can't live here anymore," Bridget declares—mutters, really. She is feeling less bold by inches as she climbs the stairs. The smell is here; the damp grave has settled on everything over their heads. By the time she reaches the top landing and glances back down into the living room at her daughter, she is aware of her heart again. *My heart, my heart, my heart.* Julie is absorbed in a shape sorter, her plump starfish hands working inexpertly, her little head bowed in concentration, her breathing collected and heavy.

Bridget wipes tears from her cheeks and advances down the dim upstairs hallway.

The doors all open to the left from the landing, except for the bathroom at the end of the hall. The first door is Julie's room, and it is ajar. The wet earth, the bank of a creek, the bare yard after a rain. Bridget's arm is shaking, but she pushes the door open, and the sunlight in the room floods across the floor, warm across her feet.

She is there, by the window.

The sun flickers through her as if she were made of leaves.

"Get out," Bridget tells her. The ghost's attention snaps toward the sound of Bridget's voice, and then its hideous indistinctness shifts in her direction. Its black eyes rest upon her now. She is more transparent than Bridget remembers, more diffuse and staticky. Has she changed, or is it just the daylight? It doesn't matter. Bridget sobs, "Get out! *Get out! You can't live here!*"

And now it is moving toward her. Has it become stronger? It seems to move more quickly than it used to—still as if pulling its own deadness behind its intention, but with the awful segmented coordination of a spider.

"No!" Bridget points at it, shaking but insistent. "No, *you*! *You can't!*"

Can't she? What can't she do? Just because the ghost hasn't touched her yet doesn't necessarily mean she can't, or doesn't want to.

"Get out of here!"

The ghost's hands rise, her arms, her body still just channels of static that limit her realness and yet seem to make her limitless. With the sunlight behind her, the ghost is a series of shifting and flickering layers: a woman's face, a screen of smoke, a woman's shoulders, a wall of static, a woman's body, a white membrane. As the ghost shifts within herself, her form releases cool waves of air, like a wind off the surface of a pond, brushing Bridget's bangs back gently.

The ghost raises her hands, begging.

Bridget is crying hard now. "I won't help you! I hate you!"

The ghost's stare is fixed and bottomless. She makes sure Bridget is looking into her eyes; she waits. Then with effort the ghost shakes her head, once, a slow no. *No, you don't.*

The ghost's hands are raised toward Bridget, out and up, not to grasp but to plead. *Give me something.*

"You can't have them," Bridget gasps. "They're mine."

Anger flashes through the ghost's body like a shaft of light skimming across a river. Her eyes grow—the black holes in her face actually grow larger, deeper.

Bridget screams—she can't help herself.

Downstairs, Julie shouts in alarm.

The ghost moves toward her again, one more revolting dead step. Her hands reach. Bridget sees that the closer the ghost comes, the clearer she is realized, as if she is fighting her way through a curtain or up from the bottom of a microscope's lens. She is wearing some kind of dress, long white sleeves that are dirty with the earth of a grave. Her face is beautiful, sharply drawn—but her eyes, huge and black and angry, are terrifying. She has long dark hair and a high, fine collar. Her mouth—but Bridget cannot look at her mouth. Because it is opening. And there is nothing but hunger in there.

Bridget screams again and backs out into the hallway, hitting the railing at the landing.

The ghost pulls itself toward her, reaching for the door.

They both hear Julie crying.

Bridget lunges for the knob and slams the door shut, penning the ghost inside Julie's room. She pauses, ear close enough to the door that her hair brushes the wood, and tries to hold her breath long enough to hear whatever may be happening inside—but almost instantly, propelled by the ferocious pounding of her heart, air rushes out hard from her nose and mouth. *Pahhhh.* And still nothing. There's nothing.

Something metal slides, shifts. She looks down and sees the doorknob beginning to turn.

"No," she whispers. She grabs the knob with both hands and tries to hold it still.

A soft thudding against the door.

No. No.

The knob twists. Her hands are soaked in sweat; the knob slips between her palms. "*No!*"

As terrified as she is, she is helplessly aware of the sounds of Julie's cries and her toddling movements as Julie approaches the foot of the stairs. Looking over her shoulder as she clings to the doorknob and tries to still it, Bridget sees that Julie has cruised to the staircase and is, in her wobbly fashion, trying to climb the stairs toward her mother, her little hands on the third step, her plump feet on the step below, her face turned up toward Bridget's, crying for real, tears on her round cheeks. "Julie, stay there! Don't move!" The little girl shakes her head. *No no no.* "Julie, don't you move! Stay where you are!"

Bridget feels the tension on the other side of the doorknob slacken and release. *Is she letting go?*

She looks around wildly for something to shove in front of the door—it opens inward from the hallway, but something big to block it? A chair? There's nothing in the hallway. The bathroom hamper? What about the linen cabinet? It's just cheap particleboard, but it's full of stuff. Could she move it quickly enough?

Julie is on the fourth stair.

"Julie, goddamn it, *stop exactly where you are*!" Bridget screams (*why, why, why, didn't we put a fucking gate up there the second she started cruising?*). The little girl, crying, reaches up for her mother, who sees her losing her balance as she rears back and lifts her arms over her head. "Julie, please, please!"

Another horrible thump against the door, a dead body pushing itself up against a barrier, as if borne by a current of water.

Julie falls. She lands back one step, on her thigh, one pudgy forearm hitting the stair above her bottom. She doesn't hit her head, but the loss of altitude does startle her, and she begins to scream in earnest while starting up the steps again toward her mother, eyes practically squeezed shut with the intensity of her misery.

"Julie, stop! Stop right there!" She has no choice. Bridget relinquishes her knuckle-cracking grip on the doorknob and flies down the steps, scooping up her baby girl near the bottom before she works her way any further toward danger. Julie buries her head in Bridget's shoulder, grabbing a fistful of the hair at the back of Bridget's neck, as she is wont to do, and working her little fingers through the strands as she weeps, inconsolable.

Bridget, for her part, stands at the bottom of the stairs, holding her daughter tightly against her chest, watching the landing with a fear greater than any she's felt yet. Her heart pounds and stammers. Her knees shake. She finds she has to sit down, just sit on the floor for a moment, and sinks into a cross-legged position with Julie's legs and arms still wrapped around her.

Nothing happens. Bridget watches, listens, rocks her little girl. The ghost does not descend. Perhaps she's exactly where she wants to be.

CHAPTER SIX

Rebecca Hirschfelder's little boy, Matthew, was born at the end of the summer growing season, a blessing in a number of ways, not the least being that Frau came to stay with the Hirschfelders during that busiest of times. In the way of most of the Germans who farmed here, John Hirschfelder planted every cash crop his land could sustain and reckoned on no fewer than eight months of growing weather. The corn harvest, the threshing and binding of the oats, and the winter wheat planting all collided in early autumn—but thanks to Frau, during their short, sunlit evening suppers and noon dinners, John and the hired men were now eating better than they had in more than a year.

Dr. Mueller, who had attended the boy's birth with the help of a midwife from town, had left Frau and the hired girl, Dusana, rigid instructions about how and when their help would be required since, given the new mother's physical state, the baby's changing and bathing must fall primarily to them. Two weeks after the newborn's arrival, Rebecca was still bleeding and much reduced, weaker by far than she'd been when she first moved to the farmhouse the previous summer, and confined to bed when she was ready, more than ready, to be out of it. She stayed put only out of deference to her father. She hadn't liked the sorrowful way he looked at her, nestled with her boy among the bedclothes, the two of them each about as helpless as the other.

The bed itself, which Rebecca had always hated, was no help. She sank too far into the mattress and pillows, and the infant was too small, her arms too tired, her breasts too sore. One afternoon in September, finding herself, as usual, unable to find a comfortable position to nurse the boy, Rebecca sat up against the headboard and propped the infant in the crook of her arm, with a pile of sagging pillows in her lap to support his tiny body. The boy wasn't heavy, but holding him this way meant she couldn't lie back herself, as she would dearly have liked to do. The fall afternoon glowed outside the bedroom window, throwing outrageous light across the room, across the bed, and across the two of them swaddled and immobilized. Rebecca and her boy.

His small mouth—that wasn't the source of the pain, the midwife had told her. It was the milk coming down, not him, that caused the sensation of burning shears raking across the tip of her breast. She just had to wait for it to be over—count to ten and it would end, and she could breathe again.

One, two, three.

She wondered if John would come to visit them this afternoon—or wait until she was asleep again.

Four, five, six.

The side of his darling face. The plump, pretty cheek.

Seven. Eight.

Let me out. Let me out of this bed, this room.

Nine. Ten.

Almost always at its worst before it improved.

There.

Rebecca allowed her eyes to close, but the glow of the room was still visible as a rosy pressure on her eyelids. And the sweet, warm boy in his clean white wrappings, half-asleep and half-nursing, was there, always there, new and utterly unknown, and yet someone she felt she'd known and understood her entire life.

The bedroom door opened and in came Dusana. Rebecca recognized the girl's self-conscious tread without needing to open her eyes. Dusana emitted her usual snort upon finding Rebecca sitting up, holding the boy—Dusana generally snorted with derision whenever she was unsure what to do, and Rebecca had become familiar with the sound. She supposed that part of her breast must be showing. Dusana was only fifteen.

"He's all right. He doesn't need to be changed yet. He's been sleeping and just woke up," Rebecca murmured, again without opening her eyes. "In about twenty minutes, however, I expect we'll need your help."

"I be here, Mrs. Hirschfelder."

"Thank you."

"I let you sleep now. You should sleep. Try to sleep while he eat."

"I wish I could."

"My sister could lie down while her little girl eat. Could you try?"

"I'll try again soon. I promise. I know you're right, that would be more comfortable." Dusana was forever recommending the sensible course, the best way, and Rebecca, for reasons she herself didn't quite understand, was always resisting until she couldn't anymore. Ever since she'd moved into John's farmhouse and assumed her part in directing their hired folks, this was the way it had stood between her and Dusana.

"Cozy. Very cozy they always look." Dusana's waxed boots scuffed closer to the bed. "Sweet baby boy," she said warmly.

"You're a good girl and a good help to me, Dusana." It wasn't so hard to admit. There was no need to be so prideful, was there?

"You rest, Mrs. Hirschfelder. Everything is taken care."

Everything had taken care. Rebecca herself had taken care, more than she warranted. She realized she was very tired indeed.

"What is Frau doing? Where is she?"

"Frau?" Dusana asked, puzzled.

"I'm sorry. Miss Nussbaum. My aunt Adeline. Is she still in the kitchen?"

"*Jo,*" Dusana said stoutly. "She here, in the kitchen. She making pies for the men."

Rebecca smiled in a thin way. *I will not open my eyes.*

"She making enough to feed eight times the men."

"That's the way she is." Between feeding the men, preserving the last of the summer produce, and laying waste to Rebecca's sewing basket, Frau had informed Rebecca that she was already prepared to do the winter planting of the farmhouse's kitchen garden. All that remained was the digging, which could wait until the weather had cooled a bit. Rebecca wondered sometimes just how long Frau expected her to stay here, bed-bound in her hot little aerie.

Dusana sniffed to signal her disapproval of Frau's generosity toward the hired men, and this, too, was a sound Rebecca knew well. Rebecca shifted her arm under the baby's head, and he squeaked his own disapproval and then latched back onto Rebecca with a hungry *hawmph.*

"You rest. I come back."

Nursing the boy always had the effect of making her feel hungry and tired—not a drowsy, sleepy kind of tired but the kind of fatigue that comes in a wave after a day's long work. Rebecca was acquainted with the sensation. She'd never worked so hard in her life as she had in the past year. She'd never known what work was at all, she would admit, until she came to live on the farm and lost her husband's goodwill at the same time.

Not that he hadn't helped her, even in his coldness. She'd given him no other choice: He had to help her. Without reproach or comment he'd done a good deal of work that would otherwise have been hers, if only she weren't so incompetent and lost. Somehow, despite everything else he had to do, her husband managed to see that the cows were milked and the chickens fed each morning and night. Because he rose so early—earlier than she or Dusana could ever manage, although they kept long hours themselves—he got the stove warm every morning for her before daylight, and at some point each week, she could hardly imagine when, he freshened the tinderbox and organized the woodpile. She supposed that her husband's mother must have taught him to do these things when he was a little boy tasked with helping her around the house.

John disappeared to town some days and came back with soap, coffee, coal, thread, before Rebecca even realized they would soon run low. When one of her washboards broke, he replaced it with a better one. He, not she, had directed Dusana in planting last winter's vegetables, although Rebecca had failed to supplement with much pickle or preserve, and by February they had all discovered just how much salt pork and potato they could eat.

The one thing Rebecca could do well, almost from the beginning, was bake bread of all kinds, although her piecrusts were still starchy and burned. Although she tried to adhere to the principled schedules suggested by that old friend *Practical Housekeeping*, it was March before she and Dusana could contrive to get all the washing done on Monday in time to iron on Tuesday; indeed, one bleakly chill January week, the washing wasn't ironed and finished until Saturday afternoon. That had been a low moment.

It wasn't the work that Rebecca hated. What she hated was being bad at it.

Her failures were often less ones of execution than of an inability to see around corners: losing some meat in the cold cellar for lack of proper salting, losing potatoes in March because they'd never been looked into and were spoiled by moisture, running out of hot water at inconvenient points in the washing, never reaching the bottom of the sewing workbasket and wearing out socks and stockings as a result. Every day demanded that she be more strategic, more organized, more energetic. Every day she and John grew thinner and thinner.

For all that, truth be told, the work was enjoyable in its peculiar way. She had come to think of the farm as a sequence of basic math problems, just little math problems, like tangles of string, tucked into the corners of every room and divoted into the earth itself on every inch of every acre, and she liked it when she could solve a problem. She liked knowing that without her efforts, joined with John's and the Heinrich boys' and even little Dusana's, the farm would cease to run properly. They all had their parts to play in turning the wheel.

And from the very first night she'd loved the place itself. The smart little white farmhouse, poised on the merest rise with a view down a sloping orchard to the barnyards and the fields beyond, possessed in all its well-organized particulars a sweet correctness, the very spirit of John's wise, doomed little mother, who had had a hand in every detail of the house where she knew she'd live out the rest of her life, if God allowed it. It was John's mother's dream house, and even with the little wiry math problems tucked around the place, everything about it pleased Rebecca: the bright square rooms, the wide windows admitting the fresh air that wound its way through the house, the cool porches—even the built-in shelves, which seemed to be spaced at exactly the right height. Rebecca wasn't so ungrateful as to overlook the abundant evidence of the woman who had come before her, with the expertise and the desire to improve not just her own life but also those lives she touched, even these years after her death. It overstated nothing to say that Rebecca was simply trying not to spoil her mother-in-law's hard work, and it was this thought that often chucked her under the chin. The farmhouse was the engine that turned the fields, after all, and ever since her first glimpse of them, Rebecca had loved, without needing to know why, the immense, waving green-blue yellow of the acres they owned.

She'd always been the sort who relished a challenge, and transforming herself from a nearsighted, indolent bluestocking into a rough-thumbed, fireside-sewing, washtub-stirring farmhouse wife was nothing if not a challenge. There was something reminiscent of her dreamy page-turning days, too, in the march to the horizon that was farm housekeeping.

She still couldn't make a cake.

She was getting better.

She would conquer it. She knew she would.

If they would just let her get out of this damned bed.

She'd grown in the past year, even as she'd lost some of her fleshiness. She really thought sometimes, when she looked at her own arms, newly curved with musculature, that she had never seen them looking so well. As long as she didn't look at her hands. Well, those were ruined, even though she tried to remember to wear gloves whenever it was practical. Laundry was what did it. One couldn't wear gloves and do the wash.

Her legs, though still skinny, were wiry-strong like a colt's. She sometimes thought she could run the entire length of the farm's south pasture, just for fun. Someday she might even do it.

And her breasts had returned, as full and white as they once had been, only now with milk. She was a funny-looking scarecrow of a mother, all right. What a sight she must be. A sturdy, straightened stick, with bizarre relics of womanliness clinging to it like charms from a totem—her swinging black hair, her gray eyes beneath their delicate fringe of lashes, her aching breasts. Rebecca took in a deep breath and gently repositioned the boy. The pain began afresh, on the other side. She counted.

The hours drifted away, and when they came back, someone else was in the room with her, a wide, warm body blocking the low golden glare through the west window. At the same moment Rebecca became aware that Matthew's little body was no longer nuzzled into her side. She stretched out luxuriously in the bed, muscles aching and thanking her at once.

"Your mother is comfortable now, *Liebchen*." Frau's voice moved slowly back and forth before the window. Rebecca would not open her eyes, no, she would not. Not when the bed was all hers at last, and she could roll fully onto her side and stretch her legs out in front of her, making herself an L against the sheets, which were blessedly cooler and fresher on the other side of the bed. "We won't disturb her, no. We'll let her stretch herself and rest herself, won't we. Sweet sleeping elf. We love our mama. We want her to be well. Don't we."

Dusana's heavy boots skidded in and stopped short at the doorway. Rebecca pressed her face into the pillow.

"You hold him? Oh, let me see the little face. Oh, he's sleeping. Look at the . . ."

"The eyelashes. Yes. Long like a calf's."

Dusana snorted.

"You'll change the waters, please. There's a good girl."

Dusana obeyed Frau immediately, her thick-soled tread moving toward the washstand on the other side of the bed. Frau and Dusana were well matched. You could almost say the two of them were allies, although Rebecca hesitated to think of them that way since the only force they had to unite against was her.

But Aunt Adeline always seemed to strike the right tone, including the girl but not to the point of intimacy. Dusana, Frau seemed to have grasped instantly, was looking for employers, not a family. Family she had plenty of. What the girl wanted was instruction, importance, tasks that meant something. Not that she didn't appreciate a little friendliness, of course. And yet too much friendliness, too much praise, made her uneasy, in Rebecca's experience. Aunt Adeline had always managed the servants in Dr. Mueller's household—there had been men and women to help with the laundry, the animals, the cleaning.

"They both fall asleep?" Dusana asked Adeline. "I told her, nurse on her side so she can rest."

"She's resting now, I think," Adeline murmured, gently yet pointedly. Good old Frau. Dusana's next words were softer.

"He coming to visit them soon. I saw, he washing up at the pump."

"Mmm," Adeline said noncommittally.

Rebecca, meanwhile, felt a thread drawing through her body that pulled a warm tautness from her knees to her heart. It was an anticipation and an anxiety together: She was more resolved than ever to play possum, and yet eager for the women to leave the room so that she could—what? Prepare. Pinch her cheeks for color, brush out her hair, exchange her milk-crusted nightgown for a fresher, sweeter-smelling one. It was the old brightness returning—it had been returning, slowly and strangely, all the fall into winter into spring into summer, as she'd been forced to witness all that John did to care for her—without (it must be said, and here was the true mystery of it) in fact caring for her. Not even the little boy had brought John back to her—not even Matthew, perfect and shell white and long lashed, could do that. Matthew was too small and dependent and sweet to know any needs greater than his own: Mother, hunger, sleep. Mother, hunger, sleep.

The understanding of her little boy, which had apparently been born in her at the moment of his own birth, produced a sudden longing. Rebecca inwardly urged Adeline to bring her little one back to her. *See how my arm is extended? See the hollow right here where he would be comfortable? Bring him back to me. Bring him back to me.*

"Better if she wake up," Dusana said, experimentally.

"Perhaps not," Adeline replied, with perfect neutrality.

And here he came. She sensed the sweep of air before him up the stairs before she heard him arrive at the landing.

"Good afternoon," John said, and his voice made what felt like a thundercloud in her, low and electric.

She heard Frau transfer the little one into John's arms. Matthew didn't awaken, but he did make a small sound, almost a purr, met by an answering purr from Frau, raspy and pleased. She tutted and kissed. Rebecca heard John exhale with satisfaction. Another sensation with which she was familiar.

But she knew too well also its opposite: the frustration and pain of nursing him, and the weak fury of exhaustion that could not rest. It wasn't fair to resent John, or men generally, for never experiencing those things, but resent she did.

Keep your eyes shut. It's the smartest thing you can do.

The room was then quiet. She pictured them, close enough that she could have, should have touched them: her husband, John, his long legs in field-stained trousers, his shoulders straight and stubborn, his dark eyes shining down at his boy, and his good strong hands, one under the boy's rump, one under his tiny head. She heard a soft kiss, John's dry lips parting.

"He's a good boy," Dusana offered. "He not give us a minute of trouble."

John didn't reply for some minutes, during which Rebecca allowed herself to wonder if he spared a glance in the direction of his wife, his corpse wife, lying motionless, bloodless, and thin in what ought to have been, but for her own strangeness and rigidity, their bed.

"She's all right. She's resting," Rebecca heard Frau say. So he had looked at her. "We'll leave you."

"No. Please don't leave on my account," John said. "I have to get back." But still he lingered, still he held Matthew in his arms. Rebecca strained to hear what he was doing, telltale whispers of fabric and skin that would tell her where John's body was. Without moving she felt herself yearning toward them, her husband and her little boy, feeling very much as if she had died and was surging upward from the bottom of her grave toward everything she'd lost. *Oh, don't be sentimental, you stupid girl. Open your eyes.*

No, keep them closed. It's best.

So in the end, she waited until her husband laid Matthew back down on the bed next to her, without touching any part of her, deliberately or no. She heard Dusana follow John down the stairs to the yard, to continue hanging out the washing. And finally she heard Matthew begin to stir.

And she opened her eyes. Frau stood at the end of the bed, watching her. Without expression, like the dead woman that she was, Rebecca stared back.

In the year since they had been married, John refused to fight with her, and he proved devastatingly effective at defusing clashes before they began. After all, the Heinrich boys and Dusana ate dinner with them every day except Sunday, and often supper, too, and the five of them, John and the Heinrichs in the field and she and Dusana in the house, were too much together and too much occupied with the work of the farm for the problem between herself and John to be allowed to come down from their bedrooms upstairs—for that was where it undoubtedly lived.

Rebecca couldn't have foreseen it, but the problem of their inelegant sleeping arrangements, a problem she herself had created the very first night of their marriage, had initiated an ongoing sense of disaster in the farmhouse, like a train derailment that kept skidding and shrieking along, for miles and miles on end. John rarely spoke to her unless it was to communicate something about the farm—they both worked so hard that he was scarcely around to talk to anyway. Their old bond had been lost, and it was a bitter thing to think about their old bantering ways and how they'd once enjoyed each other's company.

And yet. When she thought back through the first year of her married life, her mind filtered quickly to those nights when the barrier between the two upstairs bedrooms became suddenly and inexplicably permeable, followed by long weeks when there might as well have been a stone wall and a moat between them. Often she'd gone to him, surprised at herself, as hungry and apprehensive as an animal emerging from close winter quarters into a biting spring. But there had been nights when need, or resentment, or the loneliness they shared drove him to her. When she went to him, it was because she was awake. Or bored. Or yearning. Or uncomfortable. Or carrying too much remorse and heartsoreness to stay away. It was never far from her mind that this was all her fault—*this, this, what is this?*—the ruins they lived in like survivors of a collapsed civilization, clustered around the fallen walls, bewildered, with their pitiful little fires at night. She'd done this to herself; she'd been willing but unloving, persuaded but uncommitted.

Not infrequently, though, she found herself exasperated with John. Didn't it seem ridiculous to hold a grudge this way? Didn't it seem childish? Why did he have to take her so seriously? Why couldn't he yield, just a little bit? She was trying; she was trying so *hard*. Her irritation and self-pity would take sinister root, then develop and bloom, sometimes over the course of weeks, into petulance and then anger and, finally and catastrophically, into contemptuousness, which she in her own moments of childishness would not bother to conceal.

She was able to observe that these slow-moving tides of rage provoked John's curiosity, his concern, and at last his sympathy—he was not a man who could live with an obviously unhappy person without at some point asking what was wrong, any more than he was a man who could fail to let a hapless animal out of a trap that had been set for a larger predator—and just when she saw him begin to bend, she would say something cutting, and he would retreat into his own anger and confusion. And then they'd exchange roles—her anger would disappear in an instant, swallowed up by remorse, and she'd be the one to watch him grow increasingly distant, cold, enraged, until a fissure finally erupted and his anger was released.

Never did he say a cruel word to her, though. No, John's way was to unleash a torrent of work. He would stay up all night to rebuild a chicken coop or repair a mower or sharpen every tool in the shed. He was painfully thin yet surprisingly strong. He never seemed to sleep. She thought sometimes that his disappointed anger was like an oven in him, keeping every vessel of his mind on a scalding boil, and indeed anything that remained too long within the furnace of his attention was likely to emerge scorched and burned out from within. Rebecca and Dusana and the hired men had learned that it was better, far better, not to tell John when something was wrong, or broken, or could be improved—better to let him discover the problem on his own; better not to ask even in the most casual way whether, say, his folks had ever considered planting the fruit trees in the field south of the house rather than to the west beyond the kitchen garden. Even such foolish, conversational notions could spark a flinty resolve in him to make improvements that required Herculean effort for negligible reward, and you might wake up to discover that John had dug up and replanted a row of young trees, or managed to come into possession of a half dozen peach saplings in order to start a new orchard in an experimental location down below the cow pen.

This kind of restlessness was what got farmers into trouble, and everyone who knew Rebecca and John's farm could sense what they were headed for. So they stayed away. It was true, as Dusana had often resentfully pointed out, that they had few friends to help during the harvest season, despite John still being as generally well liked as ever, and Rebecca still being as beautiful and admired and untouchable as she ever was when she lived in town as the Doctor's peculiar daughter. They had become lonely people; they had few visitors, and Rebecca rarely went calling on their neighbors. It was as if they were cursed, or as if their house was haunted. Rebecca and John never discussed it, but both of them knew where the root of their loneliness lay.

Rebecca had last seen her husband in her bed on an early June night that was moonless and dark. Her belly had a pleasing, firm roundness to it then, and her breasts were already full, although not to the point that they ached—not yet. Her color was high, her eyes a bright and lively gray, her hair even thicker and wilder than usual. She'd been experiencing a strange attraction to herself—something like vanity, she supposed; she would watch herself in the mirror and see an unfamiliar woman who was gorgeous, unrestrained, and uncanny. There was something powerful in her. She was impossible to ignore, no matter how dry the wheat fields got or how sick the new calf was. John, as busy as he was during that time, could not resist her. Didn't want to. Watched her and watched her, like a burned man wanting to drink from her hand. There was a delirious week when he came to her almost every night.

By then, their nights together had long since arrived at a pattern—

what amounted to a conjugal constitution—tacitly agreed to by both husband and wife in what seemed to be an effort on both sides to minimize further humiliation. It was purely practical—any advances being made by either of them were already quite freighted enough without adding the risk of rejection. So: Whoever came to the door did not need to knock, but etiquette required that a lengthy, respectful pause be observed between turning the knob and pushing the door open to enter the room. Whoever entered the room then took the necessary steps to close the distance between them—from the door to the dresser, from the door to the bed, or sometimes no distance at all. But whoever had been sought, whoever had been the object of that nighttime breaching of daytime barriers—it was the sought-after one's responsibility to touch first, to reach for the seeker's hand or waist or mouth. John always rose before dawn and left her, regardless of whose bed they were in. Although sometimes, to spare herself the agony of creeping back to her own bedroom in the morning light, Rebecca would slink away as soon as her husband had fallen asleep.

It was unusual for them to talk even on these nights. They both were still too stubborn, too hurt, too young to put into words what might have saved them. Their silence made them both feel deserted, and cheap. It made them both vow that the next time wouldn't be by their instigation—the next time, they would wait for the other to break down and arrive at their door, if it took months, if it took years. Nothing—no need, however human—could be worth this. *This, this, what is this?*

On that last June night it had been trembling and sweat, a ferocious consumption: His kisses, her kisses, were all teeth and tongue and little tenderness. They loved each other like they were half trying to murder each other. And then they lay on their backs, trying to catch their breath, until the sensation of lying on her back made Rebecca dizzy and she had to roll onto her side, the white of her hip the only half-moon in the room, everything else darkness and shearing crickets and heat.

She dared to say to him, in a low voice, "That felt good."

John cut his eyes in her direction, surprised. She lay on her side, her hair loosened from the coronet braids she wore in these hot summer months, her breasts tumbled together against her arm. His lips parted, and she thought for a moment that he was going to strain toward her and take the tip of one of her breasts in his mouth again, but then he said, "I'm glad you're feeling well. I hear it's not easy for some women."

Rebecca misunderstood him, of course. She sometimes forgot altogether that she was pregnant; she had been so overtaken by this strange and desirable force. A fire shook her, and her fists clenched. "What a stupid thing to say."

John sat up. His armor had already descended. He was too accustomed to this kind of thing. He didn't even rise to meet her anger; he merely retreated. "I meant your health, Rebecca. I meant the baby. I meant how easy it seems to be for you. I was glad." He was already standing, already dressing, and already close to the door. And Rebecca's remorse, that familiar thing, had already flown in through the window, shattered by her angry outburst, and alighted on her shoulder like the better angel that it was, whispering dismay and contrition.

"I'm sorry," she said, making her voice clear, although her throat had closed up. And her body was still aching, still angling out for his, even though she'd already done things that night she'd never thought a sister would do to a brother.

"Don't be," John said, and paused at the door. "I'll leave you alone. I think sometimes—" But he didn't finish the thought. He disappeared into the black heat of the upstairs hallway and had not returned to her bedroom since.

All throughout the long, harshly lit period of Rebecca's recovery, Frau stayed on, feeding the hired men and bossing Dusana around, soothing Matthew and sometimes taking him away from Rebecca so that she could rest and he could see a bit of the world. Some nights Frau would come to sit with Rebecca to keep her company in the intolerable evenings before sleep came, sensing without asking how it was between Rebecca and her husband, who slept in another room and who came to visit only when her eyes were closed.

On these warm black nights—so similar to the nights of Rebecca's childhood, when Frau would sit at her bedside and rehearse all she remembered of the Brothers Grimm, which was considerable and terrifying—Aunt Adeline liked to tell Rebecca the old funny stories about her mother's failed housekeeping efforts, and strange stories about her father, too, the Doctor, which seemed to reveal the old man in unpredictable ways. Rebecca would lie in the deep, swallowing bed, near sleep, listening, and at some point in the telling, Frau's stories would become part of the waking dreaming that was her life now, the bed that wouldn't release her, the sleep that would never quite come but never quite leave her, either. Frau's stories tended to blur the border between life and dream. Rebecca supposed it was a deliberate effect—that these half-dreamed family stories were intended to be a grown woman's lullaby. She found herself wanting to believe in things she hadn't believed in since she was a child. She wanted to believe these stories exactly as they were told.

"Your mother's first child, which I think you know, was a little boy before you, and he came early and died.

"*Abergläubisch,* Florencia. Or perhaps not superstitious—she had rituals. Perhaps that is the better way to say. She was Catholic, you know. You could have been Catholic, too, if you hadn't been raised here.

"When the little boy died, she wanted to plant a tree in the yard, to remember him. It took her some time to do it, though, and by the time she finally did, she knew that you were coming. So she planted two trees, one oak and one ash. Your father, he did not like this. He didn't argue with her, but he didn't like it. He knew she felt poorly that it had taken her so long to do. He felt that arguing with her would call attention to it. I understand him. I also wondered why she had waited, if it was so important to her. But never would I argue with her, either.

"Your father had a story about the ash tree. He said that one day in March, he saw a hobbling *Frau* with deep eyes and a velvet satchel passing through the gate in front of the house. She slipped in the yard, quiet as a spoon, and she rested against Florencia's little ash sapling. Your father said she looked to catch her breath. While she stood there, this *Frau,* she pressed the tiny ash leaves to her lips, to her heart, and to her forehead. From her satchel she drew a piece of bread and ate it, sprinkling crumbs over the ground where the little tree's roots were starting. And then toward the oak tree she turned, but your father came out of the house at that moment and demanded her business there. He told me the *Frau* looked surprised, and snatched her velvet bag and vanished.

"'You shouldn't have scared her off,' I said to him. 'Where did she run to?'

"And your father, he would say, 'She did not run. She vanished.'"

Rebecca thought of her mother often during these strange, trapped days. Mostly she found herself amazed: *I will survive this—I have survived this—but you did not.* She had borne something her mother had not been able to, even though Florencia, in Rebecca's imaginings (and even in Frau's retellings), was a stronger force of life, larger and more important in every way than she felt herself to be. Especially now. She felt so weak, like she was a fading impression stamped without enough force on the surface of the world.

Thinking of how her mother had died tended to make Rebecca pull her little boy in closer, close enough to feel his baby breath on her lips, and wonder what would become of him, what could possibly become of him, if anything happened to her. If she didn't get well after all, for instance. Because if the story of her birth were true (which of course it wasn't, it couldn't be—it was just another of Frau's stories and it only seemed true now because she'd been in bed so long and was losing her sense of what was a dream and what wasn't), Rebecca was missing an hour of her life. She'd bartered it without knowing it, in order to have an infant hour with her mother before her death. It was an hour gladly given, an hour she'd never thought, even as a lonely, angry child, of wanting back—if anything, she always imagined she would have given *more* hours, days even, if it would have meant prolonging her mother's life or her happiness. Rebecca didn't consider herself unusual or heroic in this regard—what child wouldn't give as much for her mother? As a child, the only thing that troubled her about the barter her mother had made for her was not knowing which one it was—which hour she had lost. Back when she believed the story, as a girl, she had imagined a few possibilities (it was the hour she would have met her great love, or the hour she would have had some extraordinary bit of luck) but resigned herself to the understanding that she might never know. The hour she'd lost might, in the end, simply pass without her even knowing it. And if that were the case, then how wonderful, how simple, to exchange something so small for something so valuable.

Now, though, the story Frau had told her made a different kind of sense, and hurt her in a different way. Holding her boy, watching him sleep. *Would you barter an hour of your life to save me, if you could? I would for you. Isn't this the secret contract between us? Everyone knows I'd die for you. But does anyone—anyone but we two—know what you'd give up for me? If I would dare to ask you?*

Rebecca dreamed of her mother often now, too. Usually in the dreams, Florencia was standing over her bed, looking down at her and Matthew, holding a child she didn't recognize—her first, Rebecca supposed, the one who had died and turned into an oak tree. Within the dream, Rebecca would be consumed by a terrible sense that something had just happened to John—that he was in danger and needed her help while she was lying here in bed. And there would be her mother standing at her bedside, holding a stillborn child, eyes black and hot with anger, and gesturing angrily for her to get up, get up.

CHAPTER SEVEN

After some length of time she can only measure in units of Julie's slowly diminishing sobs, Bridget stands, still holding her girl, and makes her way to the kitchen. She opens the refrigerator and gets Julie some sliced fruit to eat, and she puts the girl gently into the high chair and snaps on the tray. Julie smiles up at her mother hugely. All is forgiven, forgotten. *You don't know how lucky you are, my love.*

One ear still trained on detecting sounds from upstairs, Bridget calls her husband at work. He's not at his desk. Or not picking up.

She knows she must, must take a step backward into the realm of the real, the rational. The morning has spun out of control like a quarter over a tabletop, and only she has the power to rein in her own rampaging thoughts. Mark—her hardworking, affectionate husband and Julie's besotted, if distracted, father—has *not* blown town with their every penny and left them without any means of supporting themselves. He'd sooner leap out a window than bring Julie to harm. Bridget must be fair. She must be reasonable. She must remember that he works like a desk-bound mule. For them. Everything he does is for them. Partly because she's left him no other choice.

She leaves a message.

"Mark. Call me as soon as you get this. I need to talk to you."

Julie says, "Doooooooo."

"That's right. Need to talk to doooo."

"Mama."

"I also need to talk to my mama, yes." Bridget takes a breath. "It is time, I believe, to call in some reinforcements. Thank you. My baby angel."

She is moving back into the kitchen to get Julie's cup when she sees the photo again, on the floor near the cupboard under the sink, where she'd left it this morning just prior to their flight from the house. The photo of Bridget and her mother and her sister, taken by Bridget's father when the girls were very small.

She stoops to pick it up and puts it thoughtfully on the counter.

Bridget's older sister died in a car accident at age three. The little girl had been named Carrie-Ann, after that old song—*Hey, Carrie Anne, what's your game now, can anybody play?* Kathleen had raised Bridget alone because the accident and everything after had caused Bridget's father to surrender and retreat. He had been the one driving the car that day, although the accident wasn't his fault. Bridget hasn't seen her father in many years. After spending most of her childhood shuttling between towns out in the Panhandle, he moved to the desert in New Mexico and more or less disappeared there.

It's been a long time since Bridget has thought of her father with anything more than a sort of unembittered curiosity—*where did he get to, anyway*—which, Bridget reflects, is certainly a credit to Kathleen. If Mark were ever to really leave her and Julie, she doubts she would have the emotional wherewithal to somehow prevent her own daughter from resenting her father for his flaws, however human they might be. After Julie was born, Bridget sent a birth announcement to her father's last known address and got a wonderfully weird card from him, with a gift certificate for a baby store in a denomination that seemed fearsomely large for an unemployed desert drifter.

Time to call in reinforcements. Kathleen had made it, somehow, through that terrible time, which had gone a long way toward convincing Bridget (and Kathleen herself, for that matter) of her invincibility. As Kathleen often says, "If you've gone this far, you might as well go on": She not only survived the loss of her baby and her husband, not only raised a little girl on her own, but also, in the meantime, built herself a career as a personal finance advisor at the bank where she started as a teller—a career that, while not glamorous, subsidized some travel and a tasteful, selective shopping habit. Kathleen has outfitted Julie's nursery with beautiful things. Hers is the kind of true-grit, steel-magnolia story one hears told about a particular kind of Southern woman. She intends to work until she dies. Indeed she almost always phrases the things that she feels most strongly about in terms of them killing her: *I just love Julie to death. I would sooner die than sell my house. I'm dying for a cigarette, but I worked so damn hard to quit I'd rather kill myself than smoke again. This man is going to be the death of me, but I love him, I do. You and Julie are my life, Bridget. You and Julie are my heart, just walking around outside my chest—that must be why I feel like I've died and gone to heaven whenever I'm with that little thing.*

Bridget brings Julie a cup of milk, then sits at the kitchen table and watches Julie eat her snack while waiting for the telephone to ring at her mother's office. There is still no noise from upstairs, and Julie herself is quiet and cheerfully focused, faced with a tray of bright delicacies. She's a good eater, thank God. She's a good little ladybug in general. Bridget watches her, her long lashes and round soft cheeks, her sweet mouth and dark curls, and she begins to feel calmed.

Her mother's voice in her cell phone says, "Bridget? Hi! How's my baby?"

"She's good, she's eating a little something. We've had quite a morning."

"Tell me about it. I've been in meetings all day, and I'm dying for a coffee. I think, actually, while I have you on the phone, that I'll walk out and get a cup while I'm talking to you. Hey, so, have y'all decided whether you're going to Mark's family for Thanksgiving?"

Bridget has called her mother for a reason, but her mother has her own reasons to chatter. This is not exactly unusual. "Um, no, we haven't discussed it yet. But it's their turn—Christmas with you, Thanksgiving with them. This year. Look, Mom, can I ask you something?"

"Sure, honey. Oh, Christ, will you look at that—" There is the sound of a fumbling tussle. "I just missed the elevator. The guy in it looked *right at me* and didn't press the hold button. Or the door-open button. He basically did nothing. And here I am juggling this phone and my bag and my sweater and not moving fast enough to catch him. What a jerk."

"I hate that," Bridget says, distracted at what might have been a sliding, heavy step overhead. "Mom, I have to ask you something. Can you— Are you in a place where you can hear me?"

"Oh, yeah, hon. Just in the lobby here. You go on."

For a moment Bridget is unsure what she means to ask, exactly. *Are you ever mad at me for that thing I said? Do you think Mark might be cheating on me? Can telling yourself a story about something too many times make it real, whether you want it to be or not? Do you think about Carrie-Ann dying? Or me, or Julie?*

What she says is "Do you believe in ghosts?"

Kathleen Goodspeed laughs heartily. "What a question. I most certainly do."

Bridget is momentarily floored. "What? Really?"

"Oh, it's the Irish in me, I guess. Your grandfather used to tell me stories that'd scare me so bad I'd be dreaming of sleep. I'm in the elevator, honey, I might lose you. Hang on."

"Don't go—Mom—" Bridget says urgently. It was definitely a step that she heard. The door to Julie's room has opened upstairs. "Mom. Mom."

The line is bright and empty. Bridget stares at her phone. *He has not left me. She is not real. Nothing has happened that can't be undone.*

She is thinking this thought over and over—*nothing has happened that can't be undone*—when Kathleen calls her back. The background noise on her mother's end is louder now; she's outside, evidently on her way to the Starbucks across the parking lot from her office. Bridget remembers when she used to make early-afternoon coffee runs herself, to the coffee-and-sandwich chain across the parking lot from her office, the one where her mother waited for her the day Bridget left the firm. Bridget and her paralegal, Juana, a smart cookie from down around Corpus Christi, would make a dash together around two thirty, do a little catching up, half business, half personal, and on the way back Juana would excuse herself to go smoke a cigarette in the shade by the mercilessly pruned landscaping in front of the building, and Bridget would head back in and ride the elevator up by herself. Bridget remembers those times being weirdly satisfying, the humming of work in her brain, the scorched, earthy scent of a cup of strong coffee, the sunshine slanting through the building lobby on her heels, how good it felt to stand up and stretch her legs, how good it felt to know exactly what she was going to do when she sat back down at her desk. *There's something to all that, I guess,* Bridget thinks now. *There's something stupidly satisfying in a day's work, whatever it happens to be*—that and the rituals of working life, the coffees, the meetings, the conference calls, the harmless conversations over the sinks in the women's room, the smell of the supply closet like the first day of school trapped in resin forever.

Kathleen is not yet aware that they are connected, that the warm, warbling throb that in the cellular age has come to stand in for the sound of a telephone ringing has stopped. Bridget can hear the firm click of her mother's shoes on the pavement—they would be pumps, probably a closed-toe d'Orsay, a style that Kathleen favors because her ankles and feet, at sixty-two, are still slim and strong.

"Mom?"

"Oh, you scared me!" Kathleen laughs again. She has a laugh like a late Judy Garland, loud and chomping but nevertheless endearing. "Guess I was thinking about ghosts since you asked. And then there you are talking to me, from beyoooond the phooooone . . ." Kathleen is clearly in a good mood. Bridget allows herself a small smile. "So what's up, buttercup? Is there a ghost in your pretty little house?"

"Yes," Bridget says baldly. It doesn't make her feel better to say it; there's no release. Rather, she feels as if she's taking a step forward into a swirl of mummy wrappings that will bind her up tight.

"Oh, come on now," Kathleen says. "Your house is five years old, tops. You were the first owners!"

"Do you really think that matters? Don't you think ghosts can just show up wherever they feel like it?"

"Well, no, as a matter of fact I don't," Kathleen says, indignant but still amused. "I think there are, you know, special rules. But you're serious, I guess? You really think your house is haunted? Yes, I'd like a medium skim latte, please," she adds, and Bridget is forced to feel ridiculous again.

Do I press it or let it go? What help am I looking for here, anyway? The screaming of milk being steamed in the background on her mother's end of the line is making this whole exchange seem ludicrous. And then Bridget hears the footfalls upstairs. The sounds are not on the stairs, not yet anyway (*maybe I frightened her a little bit after all*), but the ghost is on the move up there. Looking out the windows with her blackly blazing stare. Dragging her deadness down the hallway. Looking for something—some piece of Julie, or Bridget, or Mark to fixate on, to stand over and hate.

"Bridget? You there? Is everything okay? Where's Julie right now, what's she doing?"

"She's finishing up her snack and she's starting to look bored. I should go. We need to clean up and get dressed," Bridget says decisively. There are clean clothes in her dryer; she'll fashion some kind of laundry-day look for the two of them out of whatever she can find.

"Get dressed? Why, it's almost one o'clock, Bridget," her mother says, genuinely startled, and Bridget is glad after all that she didn't get on the highway this morning.

"I know, I know. I told you it's been a rough day."

"What's going on? Are you all right? Are you safe?"

"We're fine. I'm sorry if I scared you. I'm going to get Julie out of her high chair and get us cleaned up."

"Okay, but—Bridget, let me call you when I'm back at my desk. I can barely hear you in here."

"Fine."

The shuffling sounds continue upstairs as Bridget, gritting her teeth, cleans up her little girl and puts her on the kitchen floor to toddle about while she washes up in the sink. Then it's off into the utility room near the kitchen, Julie yelping with delight at the sight of the dryer. Bridget puts clothes into the washing machine and starts it up so that at least there's a comforting, harmless sound in the house to compete with the dead woman's stealthy footsteps—this is a trick she has used many times since the ghost arrived. The other day she ran the dishwasher a full cycle for five plates, three cups, and a couple of spoons. *Oh, the polar bears.* The familiar pang of remorse striking like a clock chiming the hour.

Bridget finds tiny, fresh-smelling leggings for Julie and clean shirts for both of them. Underwear and a support camisole for her, and a cotton skirt. She dresses them both right there in the utility room and tosses their pajamas into the hamper. She hasn't shaved her legs, and in her short skirt she's conscious of the stubble, but the simple fact of wearing a pair of underwear feels so surprisingly wonderful that she almost doesn't care whether her calves are a little bristly. Almost. She's a Southern woman herself, like her mother and her friends. *But when did I become so tightly wound up that going commando for a half day makes me feel like I'm living in the* Lord of the Flies?

Her cell phone is ringing in the kitchen. Bridget picks up Julie, who wails at being removed from the scene of so much large, exciting machinery, and carries her into the living room, where most of her toys are. Then she jogs back to the kitchen and snatches at the phone just before its final ring.

"Hi, Mom," she says immediately, coming around the corner again back into the living room. "Sorry again if I worried you."

"It's Mark."

"Oh." Bridget is caught up short, both by her surprise at the sound of his voice, and by the fact that the ghost is visible at the top of the stairs and the black eyes are looking down at her steadily. *She's been standing there watching Julie. Waiting for her to come back into view from the landing.*

"What is your mom worried about?" Mark asks suspiciously, and suddenly all of Bridget's annoyance is back, triggered by anxiety and fear, but also ready and waiting to leap from its shelf like a canned snake. Bridget shuts her eyes tight to block out the ghost and hears terrible things begin to tumble out of her own mouth.

"Well, I haven't really told her anything to worry about, but if I felt like it, I could. I could tell her my husband moved all of our money into an account I can't access, so I'm totally and completely broke unless he *elects* to get some cash out for me on the way home." She hears Mark groan at this—*too little, too late, buddy*—and then continues mercilessly. "I could tell her I'm not sure I'll even *see* said husband anytime soon because he's home so late these days I could almost believe he's having an *affair,* if he ever smelled like perfume or booze instead of, I don't know, conference-room takeout and whiteboard markers."

"Funny," Mark says.

"Oh, am I? I've sure felt fucking funny all day long. I guess that explains it."

"I'm sorry about the money. I knew as I was doing it that I should have checked with you first. I *knew* I was doing something wrong."

"Well, it's all your money, I guess," Bridget says bitterly. "I suppose you can do what you want with it."

Mark coughs. "That's a hell of a thing to say, Bridge. I said I was sorry. Don't be shitty."

"*You* don't be shitty," Bridget counters nonsensically.

"You're picking a fight with me." He sounds tired.

"No, I'm not. I'm *having* a fight with you. Over a thing that you did that really affects me, really sincerely makes my day harder."

"My day isn't exactly easy, you know. I'm not just sitting here playing *Angry Birds,* Bridget. I did the bank thing quickly in between meetings the other day, and I fucked it up. Whatever. Give me an inch, here. Give me a little room for error."

"I don't have *any* room for error. Not even a little bit. All day long. If I don't watch Julie every minute these days, she might get hurt"—*or snatched up by a ghost.* "She's all over the place now that she's cruising. If I don't keep the house clean, I get little *comments* from you. If I don't stay on top of the laundry, you whine about not having anything to wear to work. If I don't make all the dinners and do all the grocery shopping and all the meal planning and all of that everything, no one else is going to do it and we waste money we don't have on takeout and restaurants, where, fucking, if we go, *I'm* the only one who ever seems to notice when Julie's putting a goddamn *pea* up her nose." She is aware, as she fumes, of how she sounds. She sounds like a pissy housewife. Like a cartoon of a woman, with a rolling pin and an apron. "Where's *my* inch?"

Mark is quiet. It's all too easy to picture him sitting on the desk in one of those open-plan work pods they have at PlusSign, instead of real offices where grown men can have respectable, dignified arguments with their wives, holding his forehead in the triangle between his thumb and first finger and looking down into his lap, where a silver laptop sits, six windows open, all of them pulsing.

He finally says, "She stuck a pea up her nose?"

Bridget laughs, relieved and ashamed. As she laughs, her eyes open—she's been squinching them shut, as if to help her focus on her sense of maltreatment and injustice. The ghost is now halfway down the stairs and is looking right at her. Into her. *Jesus, Jesus, where is Julie, where is Julie?*

"Bridget? Was that Julie?"

She must have made some kind of sound into the phone—a yelp? A screech? She can't wonder about it now. Bridget crashes around the banister into the living room, where Julie is leaning over her toy bin, trying to reach the bottom. She snatches the little girl into her lap (Julie squawks) and holds her, clutching the phone to her ear and watching for the ghost to finish her descent.

Moving down the stairs. Coming for them.

A low moan of terror escapes her. Julie squirms.

"Bridget? What's the matter? Is Julie okay?"

"Mark—" Bridget's throat is bone dry. She coughs. "I can't talk. I can't talk now. Please hurry home. Please don't stay late tonight, if you can. Please."

"Okay. I'm sorry. I really am. I'll—I'll try to get home in time to put Julie to bed. I promise." She realizes that he thinks she's choking up about—oh, who knows, the fight, the money, the things she might have cared about once but can't even make room for in her mind now with that shuffling noise coming down the steps—*that sound that dead body in my house she wants her payment.*

If her first offering—the one single object in the house that held the most value and meaning for her—was not acceptable, then what would it take? What was it after?

Fine. We'll try something of Julie's. But it's going to be something she doesn't care about—something she can afford to give. And that's all you get. I'm her mother, goddamn it, and that's all you get of her.

"Okay. Do that little thing," Bridget somehow croaks. She swallows hard. She decides to close her eyes. She is aware that in her lap, Julie has gone very silent, very still. "Mark? Are you still there?" It's better with her eyes closed, within the comforting darkness, as she sits in her sun-bright living room in the middle of the day with her baby in her arms, thinking of ways to negotiate the impossible.

"Yes. Bridge. I'm really sorry."

"I know. Just—I love you. I'm sorry I yelled at you. It's all stupid stuff. It doesn't matter."

"I love you, too, Bridge. Are you okay? You sound funny."

"Do I?" Without opening her eyes, Bridget clears her throat. The baby in her lap doesn't move. *Snake charmer, pied piper, it's like a spell.* "Mark. Is there something you can think of—something of Julie's—that you think we might not need anymore? Or right now? Like a . . . toy or something? A doll?"

"Um." Mark pauses delicately, clearly wanting to make the effort to answer the question despite its nonsensical flavor.

"I'm thinking of giving some of her stuff away. There's a charity looking for donations," Bridget lies. It's easy, as it always is. She is listening hard. The shuffling on the stairs has ceased abruptly. *She's listening to me. Oh God, what if this is it, what if this makes her stop and go away.* She can hear Julie's breathing, soft and slow.

"Um. Sure. There's a bunch of soft baby books she probably doesn't care about anymore—or *Pat the Bunny;* she's always looking at me like, 'Dad, this is for *babies,* what is *up* with this,' when we read that. Or the monkey thing from my mom. Or how about those dangly things that were on her activity mat."

Bridget allows that Mark has surprised her. He's right. Those are all exactly the things Julie has outgrown. He does pay attention. Of course he does. He's not an idiot, this man she married.

"That sounds good. Thanks," Bridget says quietly. Her eyelids relax over her eyes; they are no longer smashed tight. Then she adds, because he has reminded her of it, "But I love the line 'Bunny is eating his good supper.'"

"I've always thought that book was a little weird. Judy feels her daddy's face? Paul puts his finger through his mommy's ring? Aren't these kids young to be wife-swapping? Get that filth out of my house." Bridget snorts. "But you might want to do one last reading with Julie to see if she likes it again. She's always changing her mind."

The smell is gone. Julie shifts in her lap, squirms, tries to make a break for her toys on the rug in front of them.

Bridget opens her eyes.

"Thanks. You're surprisingly observant."

Mark sounds wounded. "Well, it's not like I never play with her. And I'm really sorry I stranded you and Julie without any money. I'll stop at the bank. And I'll be home before seven. I'll try. I really will."

"Okay." Bridget stretches out on the rug next to her daughter, who looks at her archly, delighted. "Uh-oh. I think I have to play mommy pile."

"Okay. I'll see you later." Mark pauses. "We should talk."

"Mmm-hmm."

Bridget puts the phone to one side and rolls onto her back. She closes her eyes again and says "Eh," and pokes her tongue out of the corner of her mouth. This is their game, and not until today has it ever seemed to Bridget funny or strange that she would play dead with their little girl. It just felt good: To make a game out of lying on the floor with your eyes closed? Genius. And of course Julie loves it. She puts her hand on Bridget's stomach and giggles.

Bridget peeks at Julie with one eye, then says "Eh," and flops back into dead pose again.

Julie lets loose one of her trucker chortles. *Heh heh heh.* She climbs up on Bridget's belly. Bridget says "Oof," then "Eh." Julie chortles again and rolls down so that her face is close to Bridget's, her little mouth breathing sweetly near Bridget's nose. *Heh heh heh. Ooof. Eh.* Eventually, Julie touches Bridget's face with her small fingers, Bridget's cue to come back to life, opening her eyes and squeaking, *Mommy pile, Mommy pile, Mommy pile.* Tickling. Whereupon Julie just about falls out, and Bridget hugs her daughter's small warm body tight against her chest, still tickling, until Julie says "pie" and rolls off.

Then they do it again.

And again.

Bridget hears her cell phone ringing somewhere and lets it go to voice mail.

It is dark. Julie is in bed. Bridget has taken a shower and watched some television and eaten a little bit of dinner—she's not hungry, which is unusual for her—and gone into Julie's room to pull *Pat the Bunny* from Julie's low white bookshelf. Her ears are ringing, and she is very, very carefully avoiding anything like real thought. If she thinks about how Mark broke his promise to come home on time, she might start looking for something of his to break, or shred, or stand over and hate like a ghost.

She places *Pat the Bunny* on the floor in the middle of the archway leading to the unlit living room, where she can smell but not see the ghost in the darkness. She will be standing in her corner, the ghost, gazing out the window onto the empty suburban street, perhaps listening for crickets over the faint whoosh and whir of the air-conditioning.

Without waiting to see whether her latest gift will be well received, Bridget am-scrays upstairs and climbs into bed, where she intends to wait with a stack of magazines at her elbow for her husband to come home. At which point she is unsure what she will do: tear into him, or treat him to stormy, tearful, girlish silence, or give him up to the ghost as a hostage. *If she'll even take him. She's already got Bunny.*

The best thing about *Pat the Bunny,* of course, and certainly its grubbiest, most well-handled feature in the copy that Bridget has just abandoned on its informal altar downstairs, is the book-within-a-book, "Judy's Book," which the audience is invited to read over little Judy's shoulder, and which the preverbal infants for whom the book is written tend to recognize as a miniature version of something familiar—always a delight for the miniature-human demographic. Judy's Book contains Bridget's favorite line: "Bunny is eating his good supper," which in the early, exhausted months of Julie's life often reduced Bridget to inane, helpless giggles. She admitted to Martha once that, probably due to sleeplessness, it took her several readings of *Pat the Bunny* to understand that the Bunny of the title, and the hero of Judy's Book, is actually Judy's stuffed animal Bunny, which explains why his physical attitudes while sleeping or listening to a clock or eating his good supper look nothing like a real bunny's—Bunny's arms and legs are always stiffened into a forward-facing position, as if he wants to touch Judy with all four paws at once. Martha's response was: "That's funny. I was so goddamn tired when I read that book for my kids I kept thinking, 'Who the fuck is Pat?'"

"Well, the other thing I couldn't figure out is who *wrote* Judy's Book, you know? She's reading the book, but it's about her stuffed animal Bunny? Wasn't 1940 or whatever too early for postmodern metafiction?" Martha didn't laugh—whereas if she had been talking to Gennie, that would've been a layup.

"It *is* meta," Martha claimed, quite serious and yet quite not, the way she always is. "The book you see Judy reading isn't the same book we're reading. Judy's Book is the one she's imagining reading—she's the narrator. In fact *Judy* is writing the book as she quote-unquote reads it. The act of telling stories about Bunny is what creates Judy's Book."

"The rituals she has with Bunny are the book."

"That's right. And we're also cowriters of the book; we observe her play with Bunny, and as she narrates what she's doing, we're her audience. We're the *pages*."

"You are totally losing me."

"It's totally obvious. See, this is what happens to your brain when you quit your job and the biggest thing you have to think about is whether your kids are eating too much sugar. Like, of *course* they're eating too much sugar, *any* sugar is too much for those little fiends. Listen," Martha went on in her courtroom tones, "the real problem in Judy's Book is this: In a book that's all about exploring the world, and, and basically *grabbing* things, there's a little girl who's written a book for herself—who's *trapped* in this book inside of a book—and what is her book about? There are like five fucking pages, and each of them is about being a little mommy to a bunny: feed the bunny, pet the bunny, watch the bunny grow, put the bunny to bed, watch the clock."

"'Hear the tick-tick, Bunny?'" Bridget quoted. She was neither agreeing nor disagreeing at this point, just signaling that she understood. She didn't entirely like the idea of Judy trapped in her own story—she thought it went a bit too far to say that little Judy was trapped. She didn't say so at the time. But ever since Mark mentioned giving it away—this book, this particular book out of the many he could have named—she's been revisiting what Martha said about it. Would a ghost trapped in a house be appeased by a story with a trapped little girl, or not?

"Exactly. And like I said, we're the pages—just by listening to it, we are *helping* Judy write this story about herself that traps her in place. In a book about tactile discovery and taking risks and play, Judy is stuck in a circular story about taking care of a bunny. And the fucking bunny is just going to grow up and put her in a fucking nursing home anyway."

This is the kind of half-serious abuse Bridget enjoys taking from Martha and no one else. Sitting up in her bed, unread magazines on Mark's pillow, her teeth brushed and her hair still damp, she briefly considers calling Martha. Getting her read on the situation.

No, this much she knows better than to do. She can imagine all too easily what Martha would say if Bridget were to tell her that she hasn't seen her husband awake to talk to in probably more than a week, that her house is haunted, that she doesn't have enough money of her own to fill up her gas tank so that she can drive to her mother's . . . and even if she could drive to her mother's, she's afraid of the message that might send to Mark. Have they really drifted so far apart, the two of them, that she believes *he* wouldn't notice or care if *she* left? Hadn't she seriously considered, just this morning, lighting out for Kathleen's house for a week without so much as telling him that they were going? Isn't she, after all, the one who's guilty of thinking about leaving?

Martha would say, *This is what the word "breakdown" sounds like, Bridge.*

Why would she leave? She has everything she could ask for here. Pretty little house. Healthy, funny, lovely child. Nice friends, a social life of sorts. Family nearby, or all the family she has, anyway. A handsome young husband willing to make money for her so she can stay home and raise their daughter.

But there are other things, other things she wants. It sounds terrible—*Who could ask for anything more?* as the song goes. But yes. She wants more. She wants—uninteresting things, nothing special. That's the worst part, maybe—she's not even thinking about saving the world or living up to some smothered artistic potential or fulfilling some long-held dream. She's not gifted, she's not going to do anything miraculous with her happiness, but she still wants it.

You're allowed to want things. You don't have to be special, and you don't have to be a monster to want more in your life than your baby and your house and your marriage. Even if those things are stupid, even if they aren't helping anyone or changing the world.

Well, naturally I am. Bridget feels impatient with herself again. These pangs, they are pointless, they lead nowhere, they are the luxury of the woman who leads the kind of privileged life she knows herself to have. And therefore these pangs are beneath her. She knows better than to self-indulge in regret when she's been given a lifestyle that many people would be grateful for—grateful! She should be grateful. She is.

She's had happy times at home with Julie, though, yes, she has. Nothing could have prepared her for the shocking joy that sometimes floods her when she is holding Julie, or giving her a bath, or watching her eat, or doing any one of the simple, silly things they do with their days together. It's the kind of happiness, bone-deep and fleeting, that makes Bridget wish for strange technologies: a chip in her brain, for example, that could record Julie's expressions or the sound of her squeaky voice for mental playback later, when both of them are older and less loving. Or a time machine, but a time machine that only works in increments of one minute so that you could relive a bit of goofy, wonderful goodness with your baby over and over until you've wrung every drop of joy there is to express from it, drunk it all up, and declared yourself ready to move on to the next minute, whatever it might bring. Or some kind of virtual consciousness currency that lets you barter moments of lazy thinking or inattention for heightened consciousness when it really counts: Imagine some bank where you could trade in minutes of wasted waking life, those hours spent pulling out of the driveway or changing diapers or walking up flights of stairs, and those minutes could be exchanged—not one-for-one, but at some rate that made you want to earn your own life—for superconsciousness that you could flick on, like a switch in your mind, when you sensed that you'd come upon a moment of daily joy, in this good old, sweet old world, and you wanted to *really* live in it, absorb its preciousness. Regular consciousness is not good enough for the kind of dumbfounding joy that parenting introduces, at its best moments. And, okay, regular consciousness is perhaps *too much* for the kind of repetitive, hourless routine that parenting also introduces, at its most mundane: the endless washings of small plastic containers, the tired-out play, the hours spent with a preverbal person when nothing, nothing is coming into your brain or out of it that is worth assigning value to. So, yes: Imagine a bartering mechanism whereby the good stuff can be made even better, and the boring stuff, the flatline stuff, the un-alive moments of being alive can be turned in, trimmed, released. Made into harmless dead matter, lint floating under the dresser.

Frustration and sleepiness overcome her simultaneously, and she eyes her phone, lying beside her on the covers, for distraction.

The message from this afternoon. She discovers it the way you might find a forgotten scrap of cash in your raincoat pocket. Better yet, she sees that the message is from Kathleen. Bridget prepares herself to relish the sound of her mother's voice—to make it the last thing she hears before sleep, how delicious, how lovely a gift. The magazines are swept off the bed, the light is dimmed, and Bridget snuggles into her pillows in the darkness. This is how a blessed child goes to bed every night. Mother.

"Bridget, honey. Just calling you back. I'm sorry we didn't connect earlier. Listen. Don't worry if your house has a ghost in it. And don't worry if you think you're crazy. I want to tell you a story.

"You and I went through some hard times when you were a little girl—I mean a really little girl, right after your dad left.

"And you know"—this sounds almost sung, after the briefest of pauses during which Kathleen seems to have taken a sip of her coffee—"I've always had my faith. It goes without saying that I wish I'd done a better job raising you to believe in something. I don't mean to tell you what to do, you're a grown woman. But I'll tell you, it's been a great comfort to me in dark times.

"Anyway. This was one of those times. I never knew what to make of it, exactly. But I think it might have been one of those times when God was reaching out to me and even if I didn't understand what it meant, something was really there.

"You were a little thing. You were . . . I think maybe two. Almost two." Bridget understands, without Kathleen needing to say so, that whatever she's talking about must have happened in the year after Carrie-Ann died, her mother's zero year. She hears her mother take another sip of coffee and then begin to talk faster, as if the caffeine has given her a jolt, or the remembrance has.

"I was in the kitchen, reading my Bible. I did that a lot at night in those days after putting you to bed. The apartment we lived in was always so loud. It was a tiny place, I don't know if you remember it. I was glad when we were out of there, it always had a bad—vibe, I guess." Kathleen laughs unhappily. Bridget's heart aches at the sound. "So I was reading my verses and feeling, you know, pretty low. I was working two jobs at that time, there was a neighbor lady who would watch you overnight, and I used to just sit at that kitchen table in the hour before my night shift and read my verses and just dream of sleep—oh, you can't imagine how tired I was. Can you believe it, I worked from ten to three every night, then I came home and slept for four hours and got you up and off to day care and then worked from eight till four, then I picked you up and played with you in the afternoon and gave you dinner and a bath and put you to bed, and then I sometimes took a little nap—although, jeesh, when I did that it was like I was even more tired, so I didn't always. This was one of those nights when I didn't sleep, but I wanted to so badly. I sometimes thought, thinking about it later, that I must have been asleep and dreamed the whole thing. But then, when I'm true with myself, I know it was real. It wasn't a dream.

"Anyway, what happened was, I turned the page of the Bible and suddenly there was this verse that just seemed to sing up at me. 'As a mother comforts her child, so will I comfort you.' I don't remember what chapter it was, but I remember it was like those words were blazing up at me, telling me to read them over and over.

"I sat back in my chair then and sort of, I don't know, lifted my hand to my face, to rub my eyes, and I felt, I swear I felt someone standing behind me. In my kitchen, in my home. With my baby girl sleeping in the next room. I was so scared. I knew there was someone there—I could feel, well, it was like I could feel something breathing over me. And then—and I know this sounds crazy, a little bit—but I felt something touch me. Just real light, you know. But something put a hand on my forehead and just pressed real gentle, like when you were sick and I would put a cool washcloth on your forehead and you'd be soothed that way.

"You would think I would have screamed or jumped or something, but you know, I decided to just let it happen. Just let it in. Maybe I was so tired I couldn't have fought anyone off anyway." Kathleen laughs. "I would've just given up. But it felt so good, and not frightening at all, that I just let it, whatever it was, just hold my head like that, and I felt so light, almost like I didn't have to think or work or feel anymore. I was so grateful. Just for a minute, to be at peace that way.

"I don't know how long I sat that way. But when it was gone I felt better. I went to work and if you can believe it, the very next morning at the bank was when I got my first promotion. That's the craziest part about it, almost! I'll never forget it. But it meant more money, so I could cut back on my nighttime job, and sleep more, and we finally moved out of that unlucky old apartment later that year. I finally began to feel like we were going to move on, to better things. After that night."

Bridget's tears, streaming down her cheeks, are making the slick glass face of the phone slippery. She reaches for a tissue from the box on the nightstand and misses a little bit of what her mother says next.

"—back to work, honey. You know, every minute of work I put in, even in those dark days, was sweeter because I knew I was trying to make a good life for you. So even though I felt like I was doing nothing but hours and hours, just putting in hours and hours, I had your sweet little face in my mind the whole time. Just thinking, that's my girl, I'll do whatever it takes for her. And it felt like when I was missing the strength to keep that whole machine going, for you, something came to visit me to tell me to keep it up. That I was doing the right thing, and it was going to be all right.

"So that's why I'll always say I believe in ghosts. I'll talk to you later, honey. Try not to worry. I love you."

In her sleep, in the darkness before awakening, she senses the air coming alive even before she hears the door to the bedroom open, the movement of air in the room, bringing with it the tang of death and earth, the two inescapables, the matched pair. She hears the footsteps, quick now and approaching.

She is afraid to open her eyes.

"Please, please don't," she whispers.

The footsteps stop short, but she feels the presence at her bedside. There is someone there.

"If she were here, she could see you, I think," Bridget murmurs.

There is a shuffling sound, a strong exhalation. Bridget emerges from sleep into the realization that it's Mark, not the ghost. But the scent—she opens her eyes.

He's there, looking off toward the window and not at her, moving toward the closet while unbuttoning his shirt. He's left the bedroom door slightly ajar. And the ghost is there, too: She can see her, flickering out in the hallway. Looking in with one bright dead eye. *She's still hunting.*

Bridget sits up quickly.

Mark pulls off his undershirt and glances back at her over his bare shoulder, on his way to the other side of the room. In that one look, Bridget can see all she needs to know. That he's angry. That what she said to him has had its time to sink in, and what he remembers isn't that she apologized or told him she loved him, but that she was unloving, unyielding, unfair—and that she had the gall to be surprised that he notices the simplest, stupidest things about Julie. That she caught him off guard and attacked. He's exhausted, he's had a terrible, long day at work, and whatever wounded or ashamed part of him she might have stepped on this afternoon has decided to rise like a gravestone and make its coldest stand. This is married life, Bridget supposes. You start the day intending to be a good person, a good partner, but there are usually significant detours before bedtime.

He reaches into his back pocket, pulls out his wallet, and takes a thick sheaf of twenties out. He tosses it onto the foot of the bed, where her feet are tucked under the covers. He steps out of his pants, and his belt jingles to the floor. In his boxers, he makes for the door, to take a shower and change before he heads back to the office.

"I don't make *little comments,*" he says, and it would be ridiculous if he weren't so angry. And if he hadn't just left a spiteful little pile of money at the foot of their bed.

Bridget hears the bathroom door close out in the hallway and knows there will be no more sleep for her that night. Soon Mark will go back to the office. Soon she will be alone again with the ghost.

CHAPTER EIGHT

Rebecca could hardly stay in bed for the entire harvest season, however much Frau and the Doctor and perhaps even John might have wished it. Whether or not she could walk without feeling like her insides were falling out, there was simply too much to do.

And besides, by October Dusana had made a few remarks too many about how tired-out Frau was ("she not a young woman, after all"), how exhausted John and the men were, how no little boy so healthy should be spending so much time indoors, even at his tender age, how, really, her color seemed to be coming back. How every other homestead in the county but theirs was full to the rafters with people helping to pull in the grain, neighbors and relations and even children, all sitting down to the table at dinner with clean hands but otherwise bodily coated in sweat and sweet smells from the fields, oh, the prodigious amount of baking and cooking it took to keep that many friends in full stomachs during the busy weeks. "To me, that is a harvest season, although I know you and Mr. Hirschfelder do things different. Ah, but me, what fun!"

"There's plenty I can do sitting down," Rebecca snapped at her father one afternoon during a follow-up call, and that was the end of her time in bed. *Never would he argue with her,* as Frau had often said of her parents. Rebecca was beginning to realize just how much the Doctor and John had in common in that regard.

After emerging from the hot bedroom upstairs and rejoining the world where her work was welcome, Rebecca carried her little boy around the farmhouse and the yard in a cotton sling between her shoulder and her hip, and when he couldn't be there, he was in a crib with wheels that John built for him. Frau went back home to her room at the Doctor's house.

Those final days of autumn, every man and woman on the place worked from darkness to darkness to get the farm through the late season, John and the men wagoning the harvest to the grain elevator and the railhead in town, all the while simultaneously plowing for the winter crops, and Dusana and Rebecca gathering and preserving the late vegetables from the garden plot while undertaking the strenuous annual effort of ridding the house of a summer's worth of dust.

It would be far from true to say that the work invigorated her—in fact Rebecca found herself dreamily focused on sleep, thinking about it throughout the day, weighing pieces of sleep in her mind, tasting it like a broth, imagining with longing the sweet, swift decline into sleep, like a fall off a ladder. Matty woke twice every night to nurse, once at midnight or so and once at four, maddeningly close to Rebecca's usual waking time at five A.M. Between feeding sessions she slept so hard that she often awoke disoriented, unsure where she lived, who she was, or why she was alone with an infant.

But at least now she knew the difference between a dreaming life and a waking life: Whatever else one could say about it, a farm in late harvest left no one feeling listless and purposeless and about to be consumed by her own bedsheets. While getting back to work on the farm with John and the hired help didn't energize her, it did strengthen her. Because it was more obvious to her than ever what she was truly working for—she thought she would have needed to be a stupid woman indeed not to see it, when she carried it with her day in and day out and it woke her up in the night. The point of all this effort was not to outpace John's mother or hide from her own mistakes but to help build a life for herself, for her boy, for her family. The point wasn't whether she was good at it. The point was doing it, with every bit of will she possessed.

Rebecca and Dusana struggled at first with caring for the baby after Frau went back home; the farm's demands were an unyielding machine that didn't—couldn't—stop its ratcheting gears for a hungry infant. Matty was an insistent squaller when he wanted to feed, and despite Dusana's repeated, embarrassed, and finally short-tempered tutorials, Rebecca had a difficult time learning how to nurse the baby while he was in his sling. "But that what the sling is for!" Dusana exclaimed in exasperation, her imperfect English breaking apart. "It's no reason for carry him all day if you sit down to feed him!" Of course, Dusana was right—it would have been the better way. But Matty was as little and floppy as a hot water bottle, and Rebecca couldn't balance him correctly. He would lose the breast and be inconsolable, and the milk springing forth would ruin her dress. More laundry. It seemed unfair. The nursing hurt less by now, but she was still a novice, and she finally acknowledged that she simply couldn't feed the baby while standing up—Dusana's older sisters and their superior mothering abilities notwithstanding.

But she made of it a wiry little math problem to solve, and she made good use of the time whenever she found herself dropping into a chair, or even cross-legged on the floor, with Matthew in her lap, whether in the cellar or outside the linen closet or on the porch or in the kitchen garden. She learned to arrange the baby in the sling across her lap so that she could keep her hands free, and she sewed larger pockets into her aprons and kept her spectacles and some mending work there. She spent many a pleasant half hour that way, sitting in the warm, sun-baked grass under a denuded peach tree with a happy baby at her breast and her sewing kit spread out around her, her fingers working at something, her eyeglasses on her nose, her back aching as it almost always did. If she talked to Matty while he nursed, she found that she could keep him awake long enough to nurse each breast to empty. So she would mutter stories to him like the ones Frau used to tell her as a girl, only the hapless heroine was herself and not Florencia. John found her in such a state one afternoon, midstory.

"Once upon a time your mama was trying to pluck a chicken. Nobody had told her how to do it, and she didn't want to ask." (All this, so far, was true.) "She was looking forward to a nice hot chicken for supper. So she pulled and pulled and plucked and plucked, but it seemed to her that no sooner did she get a feather pulled than another one grew in its place. She began to think she must be doing it wrong. She said to the chicken, 'How do I pluck you, silly old thing?' Wasn't that a funny thing to do, to ask the chicken? But your mama is a funny one. And do you know what? The chicken said, um . . ." Rebecca paused here to bite off the loose end of a thread with her teeth.

"The chicken said, 'Ask the fox.'"

John, ducking underneath the branches of the peach tree behind them, was almost laughing. Rebecca could hear it in his throat, and the sound of it made her long to trace the length of that throat with her mouth. She turned her head to look up at her husband, aware that she wasn't exactly at her prettiest, with her spectacles slipping crookedly down her sweaty nose and her hair falling out of her coronet braids, unwashed and lank looking. But she found that he was looking at her with warmth nonetheless, and it fortified her heart.

John came around the peach tree to kneel in front of them and admire his little boy, who came off the breast to stare at his father with interest. "Hello, little fellow." With soft, sure fingers, as if he did it every day, John pulled Rebecca's chemise over her damp breast, and then he stroked Matthew's thick wheat-brown hair. "And how are you this afternoon, Mrs. Hirschfelder?" he asked quietly.

Everything in her was shivering as if she hadn't been sitting in eighty-degree heat all afternoon. His touch had awakened every nerve. "Thirsty," Rebecca managed. "I've been out here too long and it's hot."

"I'll get you a drink," he offered in a soft voice. He kept his eyes trained on Matthew, deliberately it seemed to her. The boy made no secret of his excitement at his father's voice and presence, so close by.

"It's all right, don't bother. I'll go in," Rebecca said immediately, then regretted rejecting his offer. She knew it was a fault of hers that had become an ingrained habit—pushing off Dusana's offers of help, and Frau's, and her father's, and of course John himself, his entire being. Her solitary ways hadn't done much for her happiness thus far, and nothing reminded her of how lonesome she could make herself so much as her little sweet companion, her dear constant audience. "Don't go," she added in a gentler way. "He loves it when you hold him." She transferred the bundle of boy into John's arms and stretched her back and waggled her sore fingers while John stood with Matthew and raised him.

"So how does it end?" John asked, still looking at Matthew, who kicked his legs mightily in the sunshine over his father's head.

"Excuse me?" Rebecca felt a bottoming-out sensation. *I think it's bound to end the way it began, my dearest. With me saying something you can't forgive.*

"What does the chicken say?" And he grinned down at her, his handsome face looking relaxed and joyful. The flash of the old John was almost too much for her to bear. Rebecca looked aside hastily into the browning grass.

"The chicken—the chicken says . . . 'I'll make you a deal. You can pluck me and eat me for supper if, and only if, I can have a kiss.' And being a funny woman, Matty, your mama thought, 'Well, it can't be *so* bad, to kiss a chicken.'" John released a husky laugh. Rebecca lay back in the grass and squinted up at the two of them outlined against the bright afternoon. "So Mama said, 'All right, chicken. That seems a fair exchange.' And she bent toward the chicken to give it a kiss, and only then did she realize how she'd been fooled."

Rebecca stopped. This story, the ending of which she'd heard from Frau many times before when Florencia had played the starring role, suddenly seemed like the wrong one to tell. She was seized with a moment of doubt that was like looking into a mirror and seeing a face she didn't expect to see.

"Go on," John said, almost smiling.

"Well . . . a chicken—a chicken has no lips."

John laughed heartily.

"So she couldn't kiss the chicken, and the crafty chicken came back to life and regrew all its feathers and hopped back out into the yard, and Mama was despondent and sat down at the kitchen table to wonder what on earth they'd eat for supper, because all the men were due in from the fields soon. But then she smelled a delicious scent in the air, and she looked up, and the oven was glowing merrily, and she went to the oven and opened it up, and there inside was a fat, juicy roast chicken, all brown and glistening in the pan, and ready for their supper."

John pulled Matthew into his chest and sat down beside her in the grass, looking at her fondly. "Is that one of Frau's stories?"

"It is," Rebecca admitted with a slight smile. "I'd better ask her for a fresh lot, I suppose. I'm running out of Frau-and-Florencia stories Matty hasn't heard before."

They let a moment's silence elapse while Rebecca put a blade of grass into Matthew's fist and let him examine it. "Do you ever miss living at home with Frau and your father, Rebecca?" John asked absently. He seemed to have withdrawn behind some invisible barrier again.

He could not have foreseen how the question would outrage her, else he would never have asked it, but Rebecca's heart was suddenly ablaze in her chest. After the past few months, after what it had cost her, after what she had put into getting back into the rhythm of the work around the place, for him to ask her whether she wanted to go back to that old, indolent life, sitting on chairs and reading newspapers and waiting for something to happen—it was as if he simply wasn't looking at her, as if he didn't know her heart at all. "This is my home now," Rebecca replied hotly. "I work just as hard on this place as you do. It's *my* home. And don't you forget it."

John nodded stiffly. He bent over to kiss his little boy in the grass, and then got up and strode down the line of trees toward the barn.

A good German farmer was a man who planned for and overcame the everyday catastrophes of farm life, of which there were as many as there were days in the week: broken wagon wheels or tools, recalcitrant or wounded animals, not enough rain, too much rain, early frosts, too much heat, yields that were low or, what was often just as bad, too high to bring in without hiring extra help. The farms in German Texas had an old reputation for being run by good farmers. Ever since the German folk had first begun arriving in the hill country, many years before the Civil War, their farms were known to be the neatest, the best equipped, the best run; besides their competence in the field it was often declared that German farmhouses, too, had the brightest gardens, the sweetest water, the cleanest sheets. German farmers were said to have a gift for high yields. It was not unheard of, in their county, to see melons planted neatly among the cornrows, as equidistant between the corn stalks as if the farmer had planted them with a yardstick. No one here in the German country grew just corn, or just wheat, or just cotton, the way farmers farther east toward Galveston were doing. For that matter, no one raised just hogs, or just sheep. Here where the Hirschfelders lived, their way was to plant more crops, and more kinds of crops, on smaller parcels of land that were then relentlessly tended, usually with the inexpensive help of other, more newly arrived Germans. From New Orleans and from Galveston, Germans had kept coming and coming, learning by working for other Germans what farming could be done here on the verdant, rumpled edge of the western desert, before setting out for the new settlements their people had made to the east and to the north. John's own parents had arrived in the seventies. They had worked together at a farm close to New Braunfels for several years before buying their own land and moving farther inland, in the same direction as the others who had arrived around the same time they did, as if Texas were a hungry ocean that demanded more and more little ships.

An accident severe enough to delay the business of the farm was a source of frustration and embarrassment for a good farmer's family. Yet the day came on the Hirschfelders' place when the exhaustion and grind of the season, along with the heavy burdens that John carried mostly on his own, resulted in their inevitable catastrophe.

One warm early November day after dinnertime, while Matthew was napping in his crib in the shady cool of the front parlor, Dusana and Rebecca were in the kitchen finishing what they thought might be the final batch of pickled green beans—the fall crop had turned out even better than the spring beans, sweet and tender and straight, and Rebecca was feeling a little sorry to be packing the last of them in jars. She had been smelling smoke for some time without consciously deciding that it was a different kind of smoke than the one her modern, grouchy kitchen stove tended to put off when they used twists of hay for tinder as they sometimes did—they always had more hay than the animals would eat, since most of the livestock disdained the barn unless the winter took a turn toward unusual cold, preferring to stay out to pasture.

She looked up at Dusana drawing water from the reservoir on the stove and realized that the girl's eyes were slightly red, and that the sting in her own mouth wasn't of vinegar but of smoke, and the light filtering through the kitchen had a golden-gray cast. Feeling

Rebecca's eyes on her, Dusana glanced toward the table, and something in Rebecca's expression made her hands slow, still, stop.

Pushing up from the table, Rebecca said to Dusana in a low voice, "Go to the baby. Go. Go now." Dusana started and dropped the metal cup she held, still staring at Rebecca, whose face seemed, even to herself, strange and frozen, as if she'd looked at Medusa.

"What—" Dusana whispered. Then they heard the first screams from the yard.

"Go now!" Rebecca ordered, rising and finding herself on the other side of the kitchen doorway before she even felt herself move, as if she'd transported herself five feet just by leaning in her chair. She scanned the green-gold perimeter lines of the fields for the men and saw John and the Heinrich brothers running for the barn. And curling around the side of the barn like a gloved, suggestive finger, a pale-gray plume of smoke, white and hot.

Fire. The barn. Rebecca raced across the kitchen garden and past the pump toward the outbuildings. No way of knowing how much of the barn would be destroyed, how many of their tools, how much of their seed, their milking implements. She thanked God from her heart that most of the animals were out in the pasture, although she knew there was a clique of old, fat sheep that sometimes liked to make a nest for themselves in the shady area just inside the barn door. The screams continued, but she knew now they were not human. And no sheep could make a sound like that, piercingly high, loud enough to set her eardrums buzzing. She ran.

Barn fires weren't exactly unusual in that hot, dry country, of course. No one kept any quantity of hay in a wooden barn in summer. Some of the more prosperous farmers erected stone barns as soon as they could afford the materials and the time. One Comal County family had been forced to watch a fire in their barn spread across their fields and yard and eventually set their house ablaze. They had moved to San Antonio, where the wife had family that could take some of their children in. They'd had nothing to put in the wagon, nothing to take away from the stage where their lives, the work of their hands, had come to ruin. Everything they owned had been eaten alive.

Rebecca rounded the corner of the barn, coming onto the wagon path that led from the barnyard back to the farmhouse drive and from there out to the farm-to-market road. There in the wagon path she skidded to a halt and promptly dropped to her hands and knees, so flooded with gratitude or horror or some hellish combination of the two that her legs momentarily failed her.

Pledge, the dray mare, an animal whose leaden, dappled coat usually put Rebecca in mind of a winter field in bleakest January, typically spent her days harnessed to the spring wagon the men used to drive into town and to move light tools and equipment from the sheds to the barn or the fields. Pledge had spent a long, sweaty youth tied to a series of cultivators, gang plows, and threshers, and had earned a little ease in her middle age; her left forehoof was also prone to splits and infection, although she was otherwise a strong old girl, not in the least dainty, if a bit on the haughty side for a workhorse. Rebecca didn't know their farm horses as well as she knew the cows—the horses were usually out in the fields with the men. But Pledge she knew by name because by now she was more or less a fixture around the barnyard and because she would, if she felt like it, respond to her name if it were called from not too far beyond the ridge that separated the barnyard from the acreage. From where Rebecca worked in the house or the garden, she had often heard this horse's name called with humor, with mock longing, with affection.

The wagon Pledge was harnessed to was in flames. With the heat and the lick of the fire at her back the horse was in a panic, charging and bucking through the barnyard, tearing her head side to side, panting, eyes rolling. Her hindquarters had been badly singed, and her tail was smoldering. Smoke and the smell of blood and the horse's fear roiled through the air. The animal had somehow ripped a gash open across her breast—a pitchfork and broken backhoe lay strewn across the hard dirt, along with the smashed pieces of the barn animals' wooden barrel trough, surrounded by an irregular pattern of darkened dust, where the water inside the barrel had disappeared into the earth.

Rebecca forced herself to her feet as the men appeared atop the ridge and Pledge ran for the fence, trailing a racketing terror of flames and anguish. John and the Heinrichs didn't pause until they reached the barnyard, but they were forced to back away as Pledge reared up and threw herself against the gate that led to the empty cow pen. Impossible to think of catching her reins, impossible to think of getting close enough to unhitch the harness.

"John!" Rebecca shouted. She felt tears streaming down her face and sensed by the hitch of her breath that she was either sobbing or choking on the smoke, although she felt curiously clear and pure, as if the terror of the horse made all other emotions impossible to feel for oneself. She advanced toward her husband, who caught her shoulders in his strong grip.

"Rebecca. I have to get her past the fence. If she runs into the fields she'll trail fire into the—" He released her and shouted to Paul Heinrich, the younger of the two brothers, "Get the horse blankets from the barn! All of them!" To Rebecca he said grimly, "We need the blankets wet—we can try throwing them over the wagon to smother the fire, or over Pledge's head to calm her long enough to set her free."

"God help her—and the trough is destroyed, the only water's at the pump!" Rebecca grabbed John's hand and wrung it in her own. "If we can contain her in the cow pen, may she yet knock the wagon loose?"

"If she can, if she's strong enough." John paused. "Can you help me?"

"How? How?"

"We don't have time to get the water from the pump—we have to take the blankets there and soak them, then get them back across the yard—help Paul, direct him."

"Where will you be?"

"I have to try to drive her past the fence. And I have to try to unhitch her somehow."

"Oh God, be careful, John. Please. Please."

His face was terrible in that moment. She saw it all, all across his eyes and his mouth as if the truth were literally written there: An understanding of how he wanted to feel toward her had intruded on his determination to feel nothing for her, and it had only gouged the gulf between them deeper. "I will."

The younger Heinrich emerged from the smoke-filled barn, staggering under a heavy armload of horse blankets, and Rebecca raced up the slope toward the house to prime the pump. She was working the pump handle so hard her arm felt as if it would fly off when Paul caught up to her and dumped the load of blankets upon the dirt at her feet. She heard the chickens in their yard nearby beginning to raise a clamor about the smoke-filled air and the commotion, and she glanced quickly back at the inscrutable windows of her house, and then back to the pump, where mercifully the water had begun to flow. Paul, she saw with some surprise, was weeping, standing still and wringing his hands. With the stout toe of her laced leather boot Rebecca kicked one of the horse blankets beneath the stream of water from the pump. She glared at the wretched farm boy.

"My God, what is the matter with you?" she said. "We must be quick and sharp and smart now, not falling to pieces! We could still save the mare!"

Paul was scarcely older than Dusana. He was a strong, broad, handsome boy, with some habits that Rebecca knew John frowned on: cigarettes, some drinking, some familiarity with the shopgirls in town. "I should have shot her in the head when we came back from town, better than lead her to this state," he wept.

John and Martin and Paul had been down to the depot and the grain elevator that morning, Rebecca recalled. They'd taken Pledge and her wagon and returned just before dinner.

"What are you talking about?" she demanded.

"I had a smoke in the barnyard, ma'am, before I went out to the fields after dinner."

"You mean you think your cigarette started this?" Rebecca wiped her eyes with her sleeve impatiently.

"There were some straw and some husks in the wagon, ma'am—I were supposed to sweep it out and I didn't, and I had my cigarette and tossed it aside as I went out, because they were calling for me and they couldn't wait, and I forgot all about Pledge. I forgot." Paul's eyes streamed. The air in the yard was gray, as if a layer of fog had settled over them. Rebecca thought with dismay of the stink that would pervade the house, the hours of washing of drapes and cushions and bedclothes that faced her. And of Pledge, poor Pledge, who must have stood in the barnyard, attached to a smoldering wooden firetrap, for some time before the pain started, before realizing the danger she was in.

"Take this down— *Warten Sie,* can you manage more? Then take these," she snapped, pointing at the sodden heap at her feet and working the pump handle with a rage that clarified her thoughts and hardened her heart. The cries of the poor horse provoked a harsh sob from Rebecca's own throat as she watched the Heinrich boy dragging the soaked horse blankets through the dust down the slope. She finished dousing the last of them and followed behind Paul as quickly as she could manage, with the corners of two blankets clenched in each fist, pulling with all her might against the weight of the water and the flannel and the dirt that quickly caked on the underside of her burden.

When she returned around the corner of the barn onto the wagon path, she saw immediately that John and Martin had managed to chase Pledge into the cow pen, but the horse's suffering, which had seemed only minutes earlier as if it could hardly have been worse, was amplified unbearably within the fenced-in space. Pledge galloped from one end of the enclosure to the other, screaming and thrashing, bleeding from fresh wounds on her neck and her right foreleg, now rearing up and smashing one powerful hoof on a fence post, now dashing her own head against the gate in her frenzy. The wagon was charred and smoldering, the wheels turning and lurching like medieval torture devices, and chunks large and small of still-fiery wood littered the dirt. John knelt inside the cow pen, breathing hard, recovering from his last attempt to corner the horse, his expression resolute and pained. Martin and Paul were straining to heap the wet horse blankets over the top rail of the cow pen fence. As Rebecca approached, Martin climbed swiftly over the fence and joined John inside, but both men had to scatter as the horse made another mad charge in their direction.

Paul turned and, seeing the mistress of the house dragging two horse blankets that weighed almost as much as she did, moved to help her, shouting, "John and Martin are going to corner her! John said for you to go get the gun!" This last was yelled into her face as he reached her side. Rebecca stared.

"Surely not—not yet? Can't we save her?"

Paul shot her a grim look.

But I can't leave him here, she almost said, but the boy had turned already, taking the horse flannels from her as he did so and, with a holler of effort, throwing them atop the other blankets piled along the cow pen fence, which bowed noticeably under the weight. John had already seized one and Martin followed suit.

Now the horse's strength had begun to flag, or perhaps she understood that within her fiery prison help was finally at hand, and Pledge staggered. She took a labored step toward the center of the cow pen, and Rebecca watched as one of the horse's knees buckled and gave. The proud animal sank, whinnying weakly like a foal, and the blackened and blazing oven behind her reared up, tipping forward on its front axle. There came a tremendous crack as the axle split.

"Now!" John bellowed, and the men charged forward, looking almost like a ragged trio of bullfighters, hauling the soaked horse blankets between them. John threw his blanket over Pledge's head and neck and held her fast, although she fought to regain her feet when Paul slapped a wet flannel over her burned hindquarters. Meanwhile Martin worked to smother the fire in the wagon, staggering back and forth between the fence and the center of the cow pen.

Instead of running for the house, Rebecca climbed the fence. Pledge suddenly threw her head back and screamed again, although there was less terror than pain in the sound. John clung to the horse's neck and pulled her to him with all his strength, shouting to her, "Pledge! Calm, girl! Be still! Still, girl!"

Still her mighty body surged forward, toward Rebecca, almost as if the animal sensed her there and wanted to warn her, to expel her, or indeed perhaps to urge her to come closer. Caught by a corner of the wagon as it lurched behind the horse's weight, Martin fell to his hands and knees and knocked Paul down as he went. How John managed to keep from being kicked was a miracle and mystery to his wife.

"Steady, Pledge! Steady!" John said firmly.

Rebecca dropped to the ground inside the fence and pulled a sodden flannel over into the dirt, hauling it toward Martin, who was on his feet again and didn't spare her a glance. The smoke was everywhere, thick and stinking and dry. The smell of charred horseflesh and the iron tang of blood curdled in her nostrils. She saw with some admiration that the plan had worked—that while John restrained the horse, the Heinrichs had mostly succeeded in smothering the fire. Martin and Paul smacked fearsomely with the blankets, driving down the flames. Rebecca squinted through the haze at the remains of the horse's harness. One of the long wooden shafts that followed the horse's flanks all the way back to the wagon had broken off at the coupling, but the leather traces underneath had remained in one piece, unburnable and unbreakable. The check lines that ran along Pledge's back could not be seen, buried as they were beneath the damp horse blankets on her rear quarters. Rebecca didn't like to think that they might have burned into the horse's flesh, but she supposed it was possible and likely.

Pledge was breathing heavily. John said, in a voice that was low but commanding, "Martin, come and take her. I'm going to cut her loose." Martin obeyed immediately, stepping around Rebecca and wrapping his arms tenderly around the horse's neck. Her fight was gone. At Martin's touch she stretched her neck forward along the ground and groaned. Martin, kneeling beside her, groaned in sympathy.

"Poor girl. Poor old girl," he murmured. "*Ach*, you poor sweet girl."

At this Rebecca could not help but feel her heart lurch as if a powerful hand had pressed it. She wiped her sleeve across her eyes, and when she saw again, John was watching her across the ruined horse's back. The horse, the wagon, the harness itself—all these things cost money, and money was dear to them, would always be. A stupid accident like this one, preventable and painful, was like a deep bite, through skin and tissue all the way to bone, that might never really heal properly. They had hard times ahead—that much they'd already known—but the real sorrow was that for some reason they'd both long forgotten, they couldn't face anything down together. Because they weren't together. They could have been.

His knife was out. She met his gaze steadily.

"Go on," she said. "Go ahead."

John pulled on his gloves and knelt behind the horse, and set to work.

CHAPTER NINE

The adults are all drunk, and the kids are all wild. It's a hot Friday night, and occasional tribes of teenagers skitter past the little park in clusters, glancing nervily at the party inside the gates, the women and the men all taking turns holding beers and small children and plastic cups of wine spritzer. It's as bad an idea as it usually is. Which is not to say that everyone present, young and old, isn't enjoying themselves immensely.

For Bridget it is an opportunity to show off her friend Martha, who has come with her good-looking husband and her well-dressed kids and is truly, tonight, a force to be reckoned with. Every sideways smile she flashes is a powerful signal, something like the elusive smirks that Michael Jordan used to wield on the basketball court at the height of his powers to convince refs, opponents, and teammates alike that they were *on the inside,* within the charmed circle of some understanding with him—and *on the inside* with him and his mysterious, God-given gifts was indisputably the better place to be. Being at the Friday night neighborhood party with Martha at her side feels to Bridget like being escorted through the zoo by the lion.

Martha herself isn't especially pretty, although her children are the kind of kids you see in clothing catalogs, bathed in golden sunshine and walking through wheat fields. Martha has thick, off-blond, curly hair cut into a somewhat hit-or-miss shape, and her nose and forehead are both slightly too long. Her legs are thick and pale. She and Bridget are the two rare women at the gathering who aren't in near-perfect physical condition. Most of the mothers in Bridget's neighborhood got back to their pre-baby weight within months—months!—although she knows each one of them worked at it with a self-discipline that she herself seems to lack, declining pastries and eating quinoa and getting up early to run in a ponytailed pack in the predawn hours before their children awoke and their husbands left for work.

The husbands, meanwhile, have clustered in a group near the grill. They don't know each other especially well—certainly they see less of each other than their wives do—and their banter, while easy, tends to be lightweight and uncollected and difficult to grasp, like the loose strings descending from a roomful of balloons. They've fallen into playing their game, the same game every Friday night, where each guy in turn has to quote a line from a children's book, since bedtime stories are the most obvious thing they have in common. The rules are simple: You get five seconds to come up with something, you can't repeat a line or even a book that someone else has already quoted, and a point value is immediately assigned by everyone else playing the game, which is based on the quotation's obscurity, inanity, or, most often, its previously unrevealed vulgarity.

"'With some on top, and some beneath, they brush and brush and brush their teeth.'"

"Twenty." Laughter.

"Okay, twenty. That *is* pretty filthy."

"'If you are the wind and blow me, I'll go flying on a flying trapeze.'"

"Wait, is that how it actually goes?"

"No. It's not. Five."

"Someone uses that one every week. Zero."

"Damn. It's like *that*."

"It is. You gotta start reading more books to your kid."

"Meanwhile Dave has had, like, a half hour . . ."

"No, I got one. 'Madeline woke up four hours later, in a room with flowers.'"

"Fifteen!"

Martha and Bridget drift away at this point, having refreshed their drinks from the seltzer bottles and the discreet cartons of white wine in the cooler near the grill, and Martha murmurs to Bridget, "They totally want to be overheard. They totally want extra man-credit."

"For coming up with that game?"

"For knowing those lines. They're showing off."

"You're probably right," Bridget acknowledges. This game is one of her least favorite features of the Friday night cookouts.

Mark hasn't joined the rest of the fathers. Bridget can see him over in the playground, pushing Julie in the baby swings, with his closest guy friend from around the block, Asha's husband, Dev, who is pushing his son, Jashun, in the swing next to Julie's. Dev and Mark both manage development teams at competing mobile gaming companies, although Dev's company is the larger of the two. They usually find each other at these gatherings and peel off to talk shop, helplessly, angrily, almost involuntarily, as if they are powerless to keep their jobs from following them everywhere, like starving stray dogs they once showed a moment's kindness to.

She and Mark have hardly spoken to each other all night. They are moving glacially through one of their marriage's ice ages. If this one is anything like the others, they'll work out all right in the end, but for now there's a lot of satisfying jaw-jutting and silence to deploy. Eventually either Bridget or Mark will get bored of it, or something will happen to force them to speak and work together, like the weekly grocery shop or a call from one of their parents.

Or they could be on the edge of permanently breaking up. All it takes, Bridget thinks, is one of them saying something really unforgivable. Sometimes she thinks he's really about to do it, say something from which there's no going back. And sometimes she imagines she'll be the one to let it out, the thing, the black evil thing that lives inside their perfectly unextraordinary love.

"It's funny the things you can get used to," Bridget hears herself say.

"Which one is Sandra? Which one is Gennie?" Martha asks. She knows the supporting players in Bridget's life much better than Bridget knows Martha's—Bridget thinks she might know Martha's nanny's name, and she can just remember Martha's paralegal's name, and if she squints into the tight-packed filing cabinets of her mind, she can almost manufacture the name of Martha's boss, a senior partner at her firm, one of the names on the letterhead. Of Martha's working-mother friends Bridget knows very little. It could be that they don't exist.

Martha has confessed on more than one occasion to feeling envy at the casual sociability of Bridget's neighborhood, dense as it is with children. Martha's envy is, she would be the first to admit, why she is here with Bridget tonight, and it is a relief for them both to discover that, despite Martha's envy, she is also unable to smother a certain amount of contempt for the entire scene, lovely and summery and relaxed as it really, truly is. There's something excellent about Martha's contempt, and Bridget finds herself briefly, triumphantly sharing in it, even at her own expense.

It actually feels good to share a little bit of bitchiness with a friend—it feels normalizing, somehow. It makes a nice change from being the object of the contempt of a ghost, anyway. Since the catastrophic outing yesterday, Bridget has avoided being home. She spent the day with Julie shuttling between the pool, the playground, and the stores, and at midday, while Julie napped in her car seat, Bridget drove up and down long swaths of the interstate and tried to think what to do, or tried not to think what to do.

The ghost had ignored *Pat the Bunny,* of course. No real surprise there, she'd been forced to admit. *So what is she looking for? Haven't I already given up everything I'm supposed to?*

"Sandra. Hm. Well, our paths wouldn't have crossed yet because we're working on getting drunk," Bridget explains faintly. "She has opinions about parents who drink when their kids are around. She doesn't really approve of these parties, to be honest, which is something she'll tell us right out, if we give her a chance."

"Oooh, goody." Martha lights up. "Let's find her. But I also want to meet the *pretty* one—Gennie, where's Gennie?"

She can't wait. She can't wait to hate them. Bridget can't help but laugh aloud. *God, me neither. I'm not what they are. Even though I am, and I'm also what they're not. Wait, how does that go again?* Bridget scans the party in search of her friend Gennie, to whom she hasn't quite gotten around to apologizing. She meant to—she really did mean to call Gennie to explain her rudeness and weirdness and to arrange to return the beautiful sweater, no doubt over Gennie's own protests. Gennie is her ally, the person on earth who is most consistently nice to her. There's nothing special about her niceness to Bridget, of course; it's just part of how Gennie carries herself in the world. But when you get down to it, what's the point in even apologizing to a person like Gennie? She's just going to insist there's nothing to apologize for. Bridget could keep Gennie's three-hundred-dollar sweater forever, without mentioning it once, and Gennie would probably act exactly the same toward her, as if the sweater had never existed. *That's what happens when you're always, always, always the bigger person. Your sweaters get stolen.*

All the same, Bridget isn't proud of her lapse in manners. It feels strange to be here, at one of these parties, without having so much as texted with Gennie beforehand. Yet here she is, enjoying the spectacle of Martha's condescension at the party Gennie plans for her and her friends every week. Martha's every droll aside ups the ante on the sweet perfection of the night, the neighborhood, the neighbors, their children, what everybody's wearing and drinking and how they're holding their liquor. She's already made two John Cheever jokes. If you could call them jokes.

"Even the fireflies look like they're CGI," she remarks now.

The night splashes a sweet, mown-grass breeze in their faces, and light cotton skirts across the park all lift as one. Bridget is still scanning the horizon line of the party for Gennie when she takes in the fact that her husband seems to have removed Julie from the swings and disappeared from the inky, tree-shrouded dark pooling around the swing set, where Jashun and Dev are being joined by

Asha, elegant and lovely in a sundress, and carrying two plastic cups of beer.

Martha herds her, in the way that only mothers of small children can, toward her husband, Graham. And with a sinking heart, Bridget sees that Graham is talking to Sandra.

"Graham! Where are our infernal hellbeasts?" Martha asks merrily as they approach.

"They're off eating squirrels. We never gave them dinner. You didn't bring me a drink?" Graham shows them a hurt, surprised expression. He wears expensive, stylish glasses and has been shaving his head since the turn of the century. He always looks effortlessly great, for a tall bald man, although Martha confides to Bridget that Graham is relentlessly particular about his products.

"Oh God, I *suck*. I'm sorry. The cooler's right there, though. Don't you think the kids can grab something on their own? There's so much food—go make them a hot dog."

For the moment they're all ignoring Sandra, all except Bridget, who cannot help but notice the arched eyebrow that Sandra has manufactured for Martha's benefit.

"Hot dogs are a choking hazard," Sandra informs them, just as Bridget knew that she would. For a moment Bridget feels sorry for her. The inevitable moment has arrived. Martha won't be able to help herself. Sandra is so prickly, so easily offended. She's like a wall of elevator buttons, and Martha's going to make sure she stops at every floor.

Martha, undeterred, introduces herself with a cowgirl grin. "I'm a friend of Bridget's from her lawyerin' days."

"I hear those were great," Sandra says remotely.

"Are you fucking kidding me?" Martha laughs.

Sandra goes on, "If you don't want to give your children hot dogs, there's lots of kid-friendly food here. I'll be happy to make a plate. Where are they?" Sandra smiles, pauses. "Do you know?"

Martha's eyes narrow. "You *must* be Sandra." She turns to Bridget. "Do I get the stuffed pony?"

"You do," Bridget replies.

Sandra looks to Bridget. But it's too late to explain; the show has already begun.

"I am *so drunk*!" Martha announces, throwing an arm around Graham's shoulders. "There is *no way* I'm going to be able to find my children now. *If they're even still alive.* You're going to have to go look for them, honey. But get me another drink first. Wait, first, give me a big sloppy kiss. In fact, let's make out."

Graham obliges with a slightly openmouthed peck. "Sandra was pre-law in college, too," he offers blandly, eyes scanning the party over their heads for his children. The beautiful warmth of the violet night drifts among them like a magical cloak, sequined with the fireflies that have begun to dart. Children are chasing them, shrieking. A dog someone has brought—one of the good kinds, a long, loping wolflike beast—has joined the hunt, although he is already panting desperately. "Someone needs to give that dog a drink of water," Graham observes.

"How can you be worried about someone's dog at a time like this? Our children must be *starving*!" Martha smiles wickedly. "I don't know how we forgot to give them dinner. We must be the *world's worst parents*."

Sandra opens her mouth but then shuts it.

"It's because it's a Friday," Martha explains to Sandra. "I'm so blown out after work every day, I can hardly think straight. And at the end of the week I'm just a *zombie*. And then when I get home I just want them *off* me, you know? Like I *should* be so happy to see my kids but I just need a fucking *second* to myself!" Martha is shaking her head widely. She concludes, "You know what that's like, you're an attorney, too."

"No, I'm not," Sandra says in a small, satisfied voice.

"Oh. Sorry. Graham said you were pre-law. I guess you just . . . what, dropped out?" There's a large blink here.

"I finished college," Sandra says. "I'm not a dropout."

"Of course you're not," Martha says soothingly. "I just meant . . . you dropped out of, you know, the world. The *working* world," she amends.

"You are unbelievable," Sandra says, eyes wide. She takes a step backward.

"Wow, that took even less time than I thought it would!" Martha crows. Graham, who has been doing an excellent impersonation of someone with a train to catch, excuses himself and moves away into the violet green. Bridget watches him go, envious.

"I have the best, most important job in the world," Sandra says crisply. "I am a mother."

"Oh-em-*gee,* we work for the same people!" Martha exclaims, and cracks herself up. Bridget tugs on her hand.

"Let's go find Gennie," Bridget murmurs. She tugs again. Martha's fingers are warm and plump. Martha makes some elaborate verbal gestures about the end of the conversation, but Sandra is already striding across the grass. Graham has disappeared.

"I can't believe she let me have the last word!" Martha cries.

"It's too easy, Martha. It's like that game the guys play. Just let her go," Bridget says distractedly. She is still looking for Mark and Julie. Did he leave? Did Julie have some kind of meltdown? Are they on their way home to the ghost right now? *And what would happen, anyway, if it was just them, just the two of them, alone in the house with her?* The thought produces a sensation that's equal parts terror, curiosity, and vindictiveness. *I'd love to see just five seconds of how he'd deal with it if he could see her. I really would.*

"You're right. You're smarter than me and the rest of these gals put together. Which is why it *kills* me that this is your world now. That woman"—Martha points directly at Sandra's well-toned back in its retreating tank top, shouting—"is a fraud and a fool!"

"Okay, okay."

"Don't dismiss me, missy. Knowing what we know about longevity rates, divorce rates, unemployment rates, the state of health care, the expensiveness of getting old, the disappearing social safety net, the fact that we're all going to be supporting our parents *and* our kids in twenty years, the likelihood that at age ninety we'll all still be alive, increasingly sick, with homes that have run out of equity and children who can't afford to care for us, and only the money we earned and invested twenty and thirty years ago to support us—if a woman doesn't *actually* shit gold bricks *directly* into her IRA, she's got *no business leaving the workforce just because she has children.* Study after study shows that women don't reenter the workforce at the same pay scale where they left it, study after study shows that—"

"I know. You hate them. I know." Again, Bridget can't help but appreciate Martha's baldness, her forceful heart, although her own thoughts, her heart, are elsewhere, far away—sometimes it feels as if she's far beneath the earth, looking up at everyone she used to look in the face. "I know, I know, I know."

And now Bridget finally sees Mark, on the perimeter of the gathering, near the hydrangeas that mark the border of the green central square. He is talking to a beautiful woman holding a child: Gennie. And Gennie is actually holding not Miles but Julie. The three of them are serious, not laughing, but still, it's like seeing him kissing someone else.

What could they possibly be talking about?

Her. Of course. They're talking about her. Gennie is concerned. Mark is bemused. Julie looks worried, as if she's trying to follow the conversation but can't quite. As Bridget watches, she sees her daughter's mouth shape the word "Mama," and she sees Julie strain away from Gennie's arms, not toward Mark but rather as if she wants to be set free to waddle in the grass. Which does look delicious and cool and green and fine right now, as Bridget stares down at it in an attempt to regain her composure, blinking back the strange series of emotions that seem to have overtaken her. *This isn't panic, this isn't jealousy, this isn't humiliation, this isn't love. This, this, what is this?* She wonders where Miles and Charlie are. She scarcely knows Charlie, Gennie's husband. She knows that he works like a dog and makes piles of money and takes Gennie and Miles on three insanely great vacations every year with an au pair for Miles: Paris, Anguilla, Greece.

She thinks of Gennie's question. *Is he cheating on you, Bridge?*

How would you know, Gen?

She looks back up, across the park, to where her husband and her friend stand with her daughter.

"Oh, she must be the pretty one," Martha chooses that moment to say, following Bridget's gaze. "Hey, are you all right, hon?"

But Bridget is now striding across the grass toward them, her eyes trained on Julie like a searchlight.

* * *

Perhaps she is crazy after all.

Her father, even before he disappeared into the desert, had been a little bit *not all there.* On the rare occasions when Bridget still wonders whether the ghost is actually real, she speculates about whether her father's strangeness has finally begun to manifest in her. *Here it is at last, the bad case of the crazies you were born to inherit sooner or later, and here is what it causes to happen: arguments, accidents, insomnia, neglect, divorce. Sound familiar?*

There's something about having a ghost in the house that truly is familiar to Bridget. In some ways it reminds her of nothing so much as her father. Like the ghost, her father left traces of himself around the house even when he was nowhere to be seen: the trailing scent of a joint, a cabal of empty bottles, a run of bad checks. Like the ghost, her father had a way of standing still and appearing to retreat into himself; he'd open the refrigerator and stand looking into it forever, or he'd swing open a window and lean perilously far out, seeming to search the parking lot below their apartment for a visitor. He took up jobs and left them, took Bridget and Carrie-Ann to the playground and wandered off. It hadn't taken Kathleen long to understand that whatever charisma she'd loved in him was bound up in his vagueness and his dangerousness, but that making him leave—really leave, and for good—would in the end be harder than enduring either. It was all the more ironic that the accident that had killed Carrie-Ann was in no way her father's fault—if it *had* been his doing, it was the kind of thing that might have seemed inevitable to a cruel observer. The accident was not his fault, but it meant the decisive conclusion of her father's attempt to live like a normal person, with a family and a wife and a job and a roof. All of that ended, to the extent that it had even begun. Her father slipped away into what really seemed like a hovering, insubstantial world, one that, like a harmless planet, drifted occasionally into a neighboring orbit, throwing Kathleen and Bridget's tides into brief disarray before moving off again on its inelegant route.

Given what her father had been like, Bridget supposes it's little wonder that she's preprogrammed to believe the worst about her own husband whenever he gives her the opportunity. But then again, Mark could give her fewer opportunities, right? He could be a lot less shady and remote. Mark is *not all there,* either. Mark has some ghostlike qualities of his own, oh, certainly—for instance, where is he, half the time? Who is this disembodied voice she keeps having these frustrating conversations with? Like the ghost, he comes in and out of view without any perceivable pattern, leaving mostly an impression of bitterness and things left undone. Even the product of his work, the work that keeps him from appearing fully real to her anymore, is insubstantial—it's technology, but it might as well be magic for how real it seems to be in the world. What does he do all day long? Where is he?

Bridget marches up to them, the three of them, and Julie lights up. Mark notices and follows Julie's smile to Bridget's face, which she knows is not exactly set in a welcoming, loving expression. Mark moves a step closer to Gennie in order to help her with Julie, who is now squirming like a seahorse, entwined against another body with no knowledge of how she got there. Bridget knows it is her imagination, but he also seems to move toward Gennie as if to protect her. There's something in Bridget's face, perhaps, that he's not familiar with.

Mark is too handsome, too funny, too nice. Like Gennie, he can be indiscriminate in his gifts, without exactly realizing it. Without exactly realizing that after what *she's* given up, given away, everything that's *him*—the loose-limbed stance, the warm skin and straight, intelligent gaze, the extravagantly furred forearms with the texture she loves—all of that needs to belong to her, and only to her.

Gennie meets her eyes, but barely—it's exactly as if Bridget is the wife she's heard Mark talk about. Martha is trailing her. Bridget ignores them all and simply plucks Julie out of Gennie's arms. Partly because Bridget is still holding her drink and partly because she doesn't so much as acknowledge Gennie, the transition comes off a little wobbly. Julie's leg swings out and just misses clocking Gennie in the face.

Mark says to Bridget, "Be careful."

You be careful.

"I'm Martha," "I'm Gennie," and the two of them shake hands. Bridget isn't sure what she'd been expecting—maybe a thunderbolt—but Martha seems content to behave herself now, having had her fun with Sandra.

"Gennie and I were just wondering where you two got off to." Mark steps into the middle of the rough circle they've formed in the grass, bringing himself closer to all of them but particularly, as it happens, close to Gennie, who does not shrink away. In one of his large hands he is holding Julie's sandals, the sweet, chubby little sandals that he brought home from work one day in April, having ordered them online based on a coworker's recommendation, and they *are* great sandals, sturdy and pretty and waterproof, so he's not completely *not all there,* is he. "Jujubee is super tired, Bridge. Do you want to take her home?"

"Do *I* want to take her home?" Bridget echoes, flustered. "But Martha and Graham are still here!"

"Fine, I'll take her."

"Wait, you actually meant for *me* to take her while you stayed?"

"God! No, I meant we could both go," Mark says defensively, which is how she knows she was right. He works all week, she does not; ergo, he deserves to have fun more than she does.

Gennie puts her hand on Mark's arm, and Bridget has to restrain herself, physically restrain herself, from giving the smaller woman a shove. "It's okay, I can take Julie home and sit with her for a while—you guys stay out and have fun. Miles and Charlie are home tonight because Miles has a cold. So I was going to go home early anyway. I feel like a bad mama being out when he's sick."

"What a lovely person," Martha remarks, without, it seems to Bridget, much of a motivation to do so.

"Where's Julie's stroller?" Gennie persists. "I can take her home and put her to bed. You guys stay out. Your friend's here, Bridget. You guys have a good time. I wish I could stay, too."

For an inflated moment Bridget feels herself staring at Gennie in disbelief—it really feels as if she has time to read all the way through her, her pretty, funny friend, the only other mother she hangs out with regularly who has a sense of humor, and who seems to do everything right without taking anything too seriously, who always knows what to say and how to give comfort. Despite all the kindnesses Gennie has showed her, despite the essential goodness and uniqueness of this person she's staring at, Bridget suddenly *hates* her—she can't help herself. How else can a person, a flawed normal person, possibly hope to feel with Gennie around?

It's Mark who finally says, "Gennie, thanks so much for the offer. But we couldn't make you do that. We're going to hang out for a little while longer and then we'll take Julie home."

"Well, I'm digging in," Martha announces grandly, with a yawn. "I'm digging into this damn party for the long haul. I'm going to be here until midnight. Midnight still exists, right? I haven't seen it in a while, but I hear it's still out there."

Gennie laughs. She's never heard anything so funny. Good old Gennie. Even Martha can't help but be gratified.

Mark says ruefully, "Yes, Martha, midnight is definitely still happening. Every night."

"You would know." Gennie nods, all exquisite sympathy.

"You know, when I had my kids, I just stopped *being available* for the late-night bullshit. I just *delegated*," Martha says to Mark, eyebrow cocked high. "And it was hard, but you know what? The sun continues to rise and set, the shit still gets done, and I get to have dinner with my kids." She pauses for effect. "Every damn day. The little filthy hellbeasts. So lucky, lucky me." Gennie is laughing helplessly. "All I'm saying is, I want a job at PlusSign so I can eat dinner at my desk again like a civilized human being. Better yet, why don't you give *Bridget and Julie* both jobs at PlusSign and you can all have dinner and whatever the hell else there together. It's one of those offices with, like, a fro-yo machine, right? Babies love yogurt." Gennie is wiping tears of laughter from her eyes, the only one of them besides Martha who finds this remotely funny.

"That's a great idea," Mark says with a slight smile. "There are a hell of a lot of diapers to change around that place, that's for sure."

"That would be my job? Changing diapers?" Bridget demands.

"It was a joke, Bridget. I guess I could change the diapers if you would do my job for me," Mark says, holding his hands up in a mock-surrendering gesture.

"I guess that's a joke, too, right? You think you could have done *my* job? The one I left right when I was about to be making more money than you?" Bridget snaps. Mark doesn't have a reply to this. He just looks at her.

"I take it back, I don't want a job at PlusSign, I want a job at Bridget's old firm," Martha deadpans. Gennie snorts.

"Because I could never get it back, right?" Bridget turns on her. *Yes, maybe I am a little crazy after all.*

"Well, no." Martha looks at her calmly. "You probably couldn't. I wish you nothing but good things and good luck and all the rest of it, but after a year or so you probably couldn't."

Bridget feels gut-punched, and this sensation, on top of feeling as completely out of control as she almost always feels these days, is enough to make her want to sit down in the grass. So she does, with Julie in her lap.

"Are you all right, honey?" Gennie asks immediately. She is the first to kneel down, the first to touch her shoulder. "Do you feel sick? I'm probably giving everybody at this party Miles's cold. I'm the Typhoid Mary of Texas."

"I think she's just sick of standing," Martha says neutrally. "So am I, for God's sake. I've been on my feet at this party forever—where are the damn benches? Isn't this a park?" She plops down heavily in the grass next to Bridget and leans back on her elbows, surveying the violet hour of the cookout party with an appraising air. The children and the ice are beginning to melt down, the adults are beginning to shift on their feet, the dog has drifted away into the night, and the human figures collected beneath the young trees overhead are now draped in shadow, all half-glimpsed, half-disappeared, half-real. More than one adult has a sleeping or squalling child in his arms, or in a stroller that's being rocked absently back and forth, back and forth across the short grass.

"I just think we're all ready to go home," Mark says, already moving away. "I'll go get the stroller. Martha, do you and Graham and the kids want to come over? We've got beer. I think. Right, Bridge? We've got beer?" This is all called over his shoulder.

But Bridget is looking at the little girl sprawled comfortably in her lap. Julie has been busy working with the braid that Bridget has worn her hair in today, a side braid that she did quickly and tightly over one shoulder this morning while her hair was still wet, rushing to get them out of the house. Julie plays with her own hair when she's tired and has been known to reach up to twirl Bridget's hair sometimes, too, while nursing or working on a sippy cup or just trying to keep her eyes open.

It's past nine o'clock by now, and Bridget sees that Julie is painfully tired. Her small pale face is still and expressionless, and her sea-bright eyes are ringed with dark purple. Her mouth is slightly open, and Bridget can smell her sweet milky breath, tinged with a vinegary hint of ketchup, her favorite vegetable. Julie is focused on the tip of Bridget's braid, squishing it between her fingertips, using it as a paintbrush on Bridget's collarbone, smoothing it down against Bridget's shoulder. Bridget kisses the corner of Julie's hot, dry mouth. "Like a horsey's tail, right?" she whispers.

Julie glances up at her briefly. "No," she breathes. Her expression does not change.

"Hey, Bridge, I'm sorry about that. I didn't mean to be a jerk," Martha says without looking at her.

Gennie sits in the grass across from Bridget, who has momentarily forgotten that Gennie is still there. "I'm sure Bridget can do whatever she wants to—she's so smart," Gennie says faithfully.

"Anything except get back into law with any hopes of being a partner after taking time off," Martha agrees, deadpan.

"I bet Bridget could convince them," Gennie insists. "She's analytical, she's ambitious, she cares about making things right. And anyway we're not living in the nineteen fifties—women have power now."

The compliment feels so nice it's almost painful. Martha looks at Gennie and then Bridget with some real amusement, but declines to pursue the subject. Bridget would like to think that this is out of deference to her own feelings, but she suspects it's just because Martha is feeling mellowed out and bored. She would have felt the same way once—most lawyers love a good argument and loathe a pointless one.

Martha had once told Bridget (probably right before Julie was born, that would have been like her) that her three months of maternity leave with Harriet were the hardest thing she'd ever done, harder than the bar exam, harder than her parents' divorce, harder harder harder. She had hated being away from work *that* much—it was one of Martha's irrationally passionate things, whereas Bridget had liked her job well enough but it never even occurred to her to resent three months away, even if half of them were unpaid. Martha liked to joke about how she would never survive in "one of those godforsaken *real* first-world countries like Scandinavia where maternity leave is more like a year." The way she told the story had made Bridget laugh, almost against her will, as was often the case with Martha: "Once upon a time, a queen with bad hair and a good job decided to have a baby. This queen wasn't lucky enough to live anywhere near her parents and didn't have a support network of any kind other than her other childless friends and her husband, the king, but they decided to have a baby anyway because they were stupid horndogs and thought it would be fun to spend a few months trying really, really, really hard to have a baby—on the couch, in the kitchen, in the car, all over the place. And of course because they knew children were amazing and made life meaningful and all the rest of it. So. After all this the queen gets pregnant and everybody at her job starts treating her different. Like, *immediately*. Cases are reassigned; the single women start shooting her dirty looks—which the queen recognizes perfectly well, having shot a few nasty looks of her own at other women at the firm who got pregnant, because everybody knows that an attorney with a baby means extra work for everybody else, and believe it or not the queen used to like to go out and get drunk after work. The queen's coworkers throw her a shower and give her a bunch of expensive shit, and then she has the baby princess and they throw her out of the office and now she's On Maternity Leave, which for the queen means sitting in her castle, stapled to a chair, trying to learn to breast-feed, not showering, unable to walk right, not sleeping, freaking out about how this little princess is going to survive being her daughter. For three months. There was a ferocious fucking heat wave that summer, and every time the queen thought about leaving the house with the little princess she got freaked out about infant heatstroke. Anyway, two months of this go by—the queen has like two visitors this whole time and no help because the queen and king's parents are useless balls of wax—and finally the queen goes to the king, 'Lo, this maternity leave shit is bullshit. I want to get back to work ruling the country forthwith.' And the king, who is no idiot, and a nice guy besides, says, 'Girl, I hear you, because lo, they would never ask a *guy* to be happy sitting around the house for three months nursing a cute baby but not doing much else.' And for that the king got his first postnatal fuck, and then a month later the queen went back to work and the princess was cared for by a really kick-ass nanny she'd spent the last month of her maternity leave finding and they all lived happily ever after. The end."

Now Graham finds them, with the children in tow. The little girl, Harriet, has a face smeared with ketchup, dirt, and the remains of a Popsicle. The little boy, also named Graham but referred to by his parents and their friends as G2 or G-Dos or sometimes just Dos, has his legs and arms looped around the tall tree trunk of his father, and his face buried in Graham's long brown neck. Harriet runs up to Martha and launches herself bodily at her mother, knocking them both backward into the grass, screaming.

"Overtired Theater presents *Harriet,*" Graham says.

"I'm concussed! I'm concussed!" Harriet yells. In Bridget's lap, Julie stares at Harriet, interested despite herself.

"Time to say good night," Martha groans from beneath her daughter, who is all arms and golden hair and sundress straps. "Oh God, you hellbeast." She wraps her arms around Harriet tightly and somehow swings herself up onto her knees. "Did you have fun? Were you a good girl? What's all over your face?"

Gennie looks on wistfully. "I sometimes wish I had a girl," she says.

"Have one. They're great. Have this one!" Martha says, slinging Harriet over her shoulders and lunging at Gennie. Harriet screams "*No no no!*" with delight.

"I don't think Charlie wants another one," Gennie says. She shrugs. "Whatever. We'll see."

"You're young," Martha observes, with Harriet squirming around, trying to get onto her shoulders again. "How old are you?"

"Twenty-eight." Gennie blushes.

"Infant!" Martha accuses. "Babies having babies!" Gennie smiles at this; she has already fallen for Martha's odd charm, that inclusive insultingness that Martha wields, when she wants to—when she feels like letting you inside by reminding you that there's such a thing as being outside.

"Let's get a move on, ladies," Graham says. "Harriet, stop mauling your mother." He holds his hand out to Martha and pulls her up. Harriet wails. "No more horseplay. Let's go." But Harriet is not done, and Martha ruefully rubs Bridget's head and then Gennie's by way of farewell.

"I got her worked up. I'll pay for it all the way home," she says over Harriet's increasing volume. "Good night, y'all. Thank you for having me." Martha looks suddenly friendly, as if she really means it.

"Oh, sure. Sure. Thank you for coming." Gennie stands up and glances awkwardly down at Bridget, clearly not wanting to be left alone with her. For her many talents, Gennie is neither a great actress nor a good liar. "Bridge, should I send Mark back here for you guys? I'm headed home. I'm beat. I think maybe I'm a little sick myself."

"Sure," Bridget says indistinctly. She feels a little like weeping. Her friendships have sustained a breakage. Haven't they? But maybe she's just being oversensitive. It might all be nothing. Gennie might call Bridget up on Wednesday to arrange to bring the kids to the coffee shop as usual before yoga class. But then she might not. Bridget has been waiting for Mark to say simple, unforgivable black things, but in fact she herself seems to have released them, and now they're swimming in the air between her and Gennie and Martha, darting little fish with poison in their veins.

Graham says his good nights to Julie and to Bridget and to Gennie, and he and Martha and their kids lope off across the park, G2 now picking up the thread of his sister's complaint and raising a cry about having to leave. Gennie watches them go, then looks down again at Bridget and Julie. Bridget senses her friend is looking for an excuse to get away from her, but she doesn't want to part on such a sorry, strained note.

Bridget manages a weak smile. "I think Julie would fall asleep right here if we told her a story."

Gennie's beautiful face is suddenly alight with pleasure. She kneels next to them and puts her hand on Julie's back and rubs gently. "Okay. You start."

As if they've done it a thousand times, as if they are sorceresses in an enchanted wood whispering ancient inherited incantations, Bridget and Gennie take turns whispering down onto the top of Julie's sweet, soft head while Bridget rocks her. The fireflies swim around them, and the grass is cool and dark.

"Once upon a time there was a little fish named Julie," Bridget begins.

"This little fish lived in a dear little fishpond in a lovely garden."

"But she wanted to see the ocean and meet the dolphins and the seahorses."

Gennie is briefly silent. "Er, one day she woke up and said, um, 'I'm going to see where that pipe leads that puts all the water into the fishpond.'"

Bridget smiles into Julie's hair. "Julie the fish swam into the pipe, and she swam, swam, swam with all her might against the current, and finally she broke free. When she reached the other side, she saw she was in a beautiful sparkling river that led through a forest all the way to the ocean."

"And the river was full of other little fish just like her, named Miles and Ruby and Jashun and Honor and Madison and Aidan."

"All the little fish felt brave because they had each other, and they swam to the ocean together."

"The ocean was a little scary at first. It was so big! One of the fish said, 'I think maybe we better swim back home. I think I hear my mama fish calling me.'" Here Gennie did a very passable timid-fish voice.

"But then Julie the fish said, 'Let's explore! I want to meet a real seahorse and a real dolphin.' And so she and the other little fish swam to a beautiful coral reef . . ."

"And then who should swim by but a school of dolphins! They said, 'Hello, little fish! Would you like to go for a ride? Hang on tight!' And the little fish rode with the dolphins all around the wide-open ocean. Then the dolphins brought the little fish back to the coral reef and said, 'Time for you little fish to head home to your mamas. Thanks for visiting us. Good-bye.'"

Bridget whispers stubbornly, "But the Julie fish decided to stay in the ocean rather than go back to her little fishpond, so she gave all the other little fish a hug and then curled up to sleep in the coral reef. And from then on her life was full of adventures and beauty. The end."

Gennie blinks, then smiles uncertainly at Bridget. She leans down to kiss Julie's head. Gennie smells delicious, like a field in blossom. Although in the moment that she is bending near, Bridget is almost certain that she can smell Mark's soap on her friend as well.

"Good night, hon," Gennie says quietly. "Have a good weekend." Without another word she vanishes into the park.

Bridget nestles Julie into the curve of her lap and waits while the night unravels around them. Throughout the park, groups of people are breaking apart, spinning off into the streets with strollers and coolers. Locusts shrill and laughter bounces off the blacktop. Streetlights and park lights are on, and the moon is a round dumb show.

She doesn't want to think about Gennie and Mark but finds that it's impossible not to. They could be together right now, kissing secretly somewhere among the hydrangeas. Helplessly she finds she can recall a hundred moments when *she* was that person in Mark's arms, when they'd stolen kisses from each other as if they didn't already belong to each other. They'd played out some bold sexual challenges when they were first together, like they wanted to test each other. On their early dates and nights out, they'd done now-unimaginable things to each other in the posh, darkened lobbies of smart downtown hotels, in restaurant parking lots, in little tacky wine bars. The rules were simple enough: Whatever the one proposed, no matter how outrageous, the other one had to accept the dare, no questions. She'd even surprised him at his office, exactly once, and that is the memory that comes to her now: The two of them in a tree-shaded picnic-and-smoking area between the rear door and parking lot of his office building a few jobs before he'd started at PlusSign, her back against the wall of the building, her skirt shifted up, her thigh on Mark's shoulder, and the vibration of his mouth shocking her all the way through her body as he groaned at the first taste of her. His thumb sliding into her and her knees buckling.

That could be him and Gennie, right now. She sickens herself, deliberately, seeing if she can make herself imagine it. If it could be Gennie, here in the park somewhere, surrounded by rustling leaves in the secret dark, cupped in Mark's palm, her hair wild and pretty around her flushed face.

You don't really believe it of him, do you? You can't really mean this craziness? Stop it, *for God's sake.*

"Are you sleepy, baby?" Bridget asks Julie. Julie doesn't respond. Bridget pulls her little girl up onto her shoulder, and they rest their heads against each other. "My bee. My Jujubee," Bridget whispers.

That is how Mark finds them some minutes later. He reaches down and puts his hand across Bridget's head and Julie's. "Come on, dear ladies," he says gently. Bridget sees that they are the last to leave. Even the fireflies seem to be gone. *Where were you all this time?* she wants to ask, but does not.

Mark has loaded Julie's stroller with all the things Bridget packed to bring to the cookout, Julie's diaper bag and their cooler and a mesh bag with long handles that she uses for picnics. It's all a mess, everything rumpled and half tumbling out, but it's all there. So Bridget carries Julie on her shoulder and the three of them venture out into the street, walking down the block toward where the sidewalk picks up again, across the intersection from the park. They are quiet, and the night holds only the sounds of their sandals flicking and of the crickets and locusts and far-off teenagers crying to each other, even though Bridget can clearly sense the inevitable prickling of questions and statements and challenges between herself and Mark, whole schools of those poisonous, darting little nightfish. They're going to have a fight tonight. They won't be able to help themselves. And maybe that will be the end of it. Maybe the ghost will have what she wants, then.

"I was talking to Dev tonight for a while. I . . . I might be laid off next week," Mark says suddenly. "In fact I'm pretty sure it's happening. I didn't want to tell you earlier. But I'm pretty sure it's happening."

Bridget looks at him in astonishment over Julie's small round back.

At that moment a car materializes from around the corner where the park meets the turnoff to the neighborhood's southernmost exit road, and it's coming way too fast. Teenagers. Music is everywhere all of a sudden. There's a swerve and a shout. Bridget screams and holds out one hand as if to stop the car with it, her other arm tight around Julie's back, but now the baby's legs are dangling and she begins to slip from Bridget's arms. Mark lunges in some direction—she can't tell where or why. The headlights are wild.

Then there's a shriek of laughter from a young girl in the car, and the headlights yank away, leaving Bridget and Julie standing in the purple dark again. She scoops her arm back under Julie's rump and catches her before she slumps any further. The car's wheels ride up onto the grass and then whump back down harmlessly onto the blacktop beyond them. "Shit!" Bridget hears a boy say, maybe the driver, maybe not, and the car swings off again down the street and curls around the next corner with its music and bass and shouting inside, but leaking out behind it in echoes all over the street as well, like the liquid leavings of a cracked radiator.

"Fucking kids!" Mark spits. He's all the way at the curb, visibly shaken, his hands in fists and his shoulders bunched up tensely beneath his shirt.

Bridget looks at him coldly. "Did you just jump out of the way over there?"

"What?"

"Did you just jump out of the way and leave us here in the street?"

He stares at her blankly. "Bridget, I jumped *toward* the car. I just missed punching that fucking driver in the face."

Bridget stares back, keeps her face still.

The problem with being married, of course, is that you always know when the other one is telling the truth, but also when they are lying.

Julie flops one cheek on Bridget's shoulder and starts crying weakly, exhausted. Bridget pats Julie on the back and resumes walking in the direction of their house.

"Bridget? You're kidding me, right? You really think I'd save my own skin before yours and Julie's?" Mark is still standing on the curb where she left him.

Bridget doesn't answer, and then she hears him behind her, his flip-flops scuffing to catch up. She feels his hand on her un-Julied shoulder.

"Bridget. Stop. Look at me. You've got to be kidding me with this."

"Let's just go home. Let's just get home. I can't have this conversation without air-conditioning," Bridget says wearily. In her head she's rehearsing a future-of-the-next-few-minutes in which the ghost meets them at the door to their house and rises up before her husband, vengeful and horrifying, and scares him Scrooge straight.

"There's no *conversation* to have! You're judging me for something I didn't even do—you didn't even *see* me!"

"What I can or cannot see, and what you can or cannot see, is a very big deal. A very big deal," Bridget allows, and she nuzzles her head against Julie's in the vain hope that it will make her cry less, or at least more quietly, but of course it doesn't, and they're followed down the street by the echoes of Julie's crying and their own quiet, stony fortifications. The quiet of the suburbs is rarely true quiet, especially at night.

"Bridget, I don't even want to dignify this bullshit with a defense.

But I jumped toward the car to make them turn—I guess I thought something crazy like I could make them dodge us, I don't know—I was just acting on instinct. But my instinct was to *protect* you. You really aren't paying attention if you don't believe that."

Bridget's eyes are prickling, and she kisses her baby's hot shoulder.

"Fine. Don't talk to me. Don't believe me. Don't answer me. But we do need to talk at some point about what the hell we're going to do when I lose my job next week."

"How do you know you're going to lose your job," Bridget demands in a sullen, thick voice. She knows how she sounds—she won't react to anything but the problem of how he's going to continue to support them—but right now she doesn't care.

Mark is briefly silent as they turn onto their street. Then he says, "Brian and Mike let me know tonight that they've got to cut from both the marketing and development teams. They said they just wanted a clean cut, one cell. They said it was hard but they picked my group. And they decided to go all the way up."

"Did they say why?" Bridget is still avoiding looking at anything but the street passing beneath her feet, and Julie's little bare feet, swinging and bouncing against her thighs.

"Budget. What else. They don't want to go after another round of investor money until after they get this release out. And the shittiest thing is they're not even *letting* me tell the guys they're going to be let go. Not until after the release date. *That's* how they do things, those two."

"Why your team, though?"

"Oh, I don't know," Mark says, almost moans, his voice enlarging as if he wants to yawn even though he's anything but bored by the question. Her heart aches for him for a moment. "I guess I just don't put in the hours that the other team leads do. Those guys live there. They really live there. I can't do that right now."

"I don't know," she mumbles. "It looks to me like you live there."

"You'd be surprised at how much is happening during the hours when you're asleep," Mark says bitterly. He's pulling his house keys from his pocket, and they're turning up the walk. "I don't know why I even bother coming home at night. You're both asleep and I miss you anyway. But there's a lot happening in the office during the overnight hours, believe it or not. I haven't been there enough, but I haven't been here enough, either.

"You know what, though, I cannot *wait* to get out of there. Seeing how they're burning up my team, *after* they get as much out of them as they possibly fucking can. It's the last fucking straw. It's all been a waste," he concludes. His voice is tight and hollow. Bridget blinks, her eyes burning.

"I'm so sorry, Mark," she says. "You work really hard. It's not fair."

"Fair isn't what life is about," Mark responds. "Not for anybody." He opens the door to their house, and the air-conditioning inside swims out to touch their faces and bathe their sticky bodies. He leans across the threshold to turn on the light in the foyer and then holds the door open for Bridget and Julie to pass through ahead of him.

But Bridget cannot move. She can't enter the house.

Her way is blocked by the ghost, waiting in the doorway just as she had imagined a few minutes ago that it might, although its gaze is fixed not on Mark but on Bridget. The stench of wet earth is overpowering, carried toward them much more forcefully than the gentle press of the cooled air inside the house, and Bridget's throat lurches.

"Oh God," she hears herself say.

Its mouth hangs open hungrily, a black maw. Bridget sees to her horror that the ghost no longer really resembles a woman—in fact, whatever was human in its formless shape-shifting is actually disappearing within an indistinct mass of white limbs and black gulfs, its eyes, its mouth, the hollows of its cheeks and throat. But the woman is still there, inside the mass of flickering movement, thin and hungry, a melting ghost inside of a ghost. *What will happen when she is gone inside of it?* Bridget's heart is hammering. *What will happen to us when she's swallowed up? What will it come for next?*

Is this what was happening to her while I refused to see?

"Oh God, I'm so sorry!" she cries out.

The form, or possibly the woman inside of it, lurches toward her but cannot cross the threshold. It is penned inside the house, and she is trapped outside of it. To go back home she needs to—to what? A membrane she cannot bring herself to violate hangs just inside the door.

"Bridge, it's okay," Mark says. He is looking back at her, leaning halfway into the house, his arm holding the door open. He has one foot in the house and one foot on the front step. Around his body, all over his outstretched arm and his shoulder, against his cheek, against his chest, the whiteness and blackness flicker and curl together, vicious like smoke. "Let's talk about it inside."

Then Mark's expression changes. He has seen not the ghost but Bridget, her obvious terror. And also Julie, who has turned in Bridget's arms and is staring at the ghost, her glassy, exhausted eyes blank and wide, her little mouth open and exhaling. Bridget can feel herself beginning to gasp for air, can hear her breath coming harshly. *There she is, she's inside of it, she's allowing herself to be* eaten, *she's allowing herself to be consumed by it, what is it, what is it, why didn't I see before that she's* inside *of it, inside of it and fighting her way out toward us—Jesus, God, look at the way Julie's looking at it, she can see it, too—*

"Bridge?" Mark reaches for her. His warm arm is around her shoulders, embracing her and moving her.

"Don't pull me in, oh God, don't move us!" Bridget screams, but it's too late. He has gently, gently, so gently pulled them right into the whiteness and the blackness, so close to it that the smell of the grave is closing over Bridget's face, shutting out the air, and she thinks for a second that she might pass out from the stench and the cold, but she remembers Julie in her arms and yanks desperately out of the way, stumbling over the doorjamb, falling against Mark's body and then down onto the floor, where her head and Julie's little head both smack smartly against the wood. Julie is screaming now, and Bridget scrabbles to cup Julie's head with her hand, curling up around her girl on the floor, trying to protect her from what she knows will now come, having tasted them both and needing to bite deeper.

"Bridget! Jesus!" Mark drops to his knees and leans over them. "What happened? Is Julie all right?" He is between them and the ghost, his face large and scared over Bridget's, his hands between her body and Julie's, looking for blood, feeling for broken bones.

And behind him, over his head, it comes: The ghost of the woman is now a flickering shadow trapped like a moth inside of some white, staticky haze that seems to be eating her, dissolving her—and it is this haze, this seething and searching and shapeless and hating thing, that is coming for them with its black mouth open.

"*Can't you see it? Why can't you see it?*" Bridget cries. She tastes blood in her mouth. She can't say the word "ghost," she can't say something so crazy and terrifying, she can't make it real by giving it a name—but how much longer can she be alone with it? How much longer can she live in the same house with a thing that she can't name or speak of to anybody, not even her husband, not even the little girl who sees it as plainly as she does?

Mark, helpless and frightened, shakes his head down at Bridget. "What are you talking about? What are you looking at?" Shaken, uncertain, he looks back over his shoulder, then back down at Bridget. "I see nothing. I see nothing."

Julie is still screaming and screaming.

CHAPTER TEN

The magician's first exhibition took place on a bleak December night during Christmas week. It was a good time for an entertainment to come through town, with the harvest shipped and the country families gathering for the holiday. Magic had passed the height of its popularity in the large cities and in Europe, but here, on the telegram- and railroad-laced waistline of what was left of the frontier, the two-week engagement of the magician Herr Robert Krause, young and handsome, brought in most of the families in the county. He was said to be from Munich, and he spoke with a heavy accent during his performances. On the street he was said to have hardly any accent at all.

It was by coincidence that the magician's stay in town coincided with the Hirschfelders'. They had settled at Dr. Mueller's house for a holiday visit, leaving the little there was to be done with the livestock and the farmhouse in the care of the Heinrich boys and Dusana. The real occasion of their visit, besides celebrating Christmas with their only relatives, was to borrow money from the Doctor. John's misery and mortification had not been able to wait: He had taken the old man by the elbow and into his confidence the very first night of their visit. Rebecca understood without being told that the Doctor had agreed to the loan. Indeed, judging by the old man's forced yuletide jollity, he was almost as mortified as John.

At first Rebecca felt shy about asking John the terms. But the more she thought about that, the more her own shyness irritated her. It was her property, too, was it not? She ran the farm, too, did she not? She supposed it would have been irregular and embarrassing for both John and the Doctor if she'd insisted on joining their conversation—or if she'd so much as been in the room while a loan was discussed. But plenty of things about their life were irregular and embarrassing, beginning with the fact that Frau had arranged for John to have his own bedroom, separate from where she and Matthew slept. She wanted to know. She deserved to know about the money.

One night as they were all preparing for bed, she cornered her husband in his upstairs bedroom, crowded with thin-looking, austere furniture that Rebecca couldn't remember seeing in the house before. "What did Papa say about the loan, John? You haven't told me."

John studied her carefully before answering. "He agreed. I thought you could tell."

"But is that all? How much did we borrow? On what terms do we pay him back? What did he say to you?"

John's expression registered a mixture of amusement and pain. "Well, first of all, he said he was prepared to give us this house. I told him that wouldn't be necessary. Then he said he'd give us any amount we wished."

Rebecca shook her head. "He isn't that rich."

"No. But I think he meant it. He would put himself and Frau Nussbaum out in the street if it would help us. If it would help us, I believe the two of them would be prepared to come out to live with us on the farm."

"That would be hard for his practice," she observed.

"Certainly it would."

"So then."

"We left it with him writing me a check. Which I have deposited."

Rebecca waited.

"We'll pay him back, Beck. I promise," John said softly, meeting her gaze with a sure, determined nod. Now it was her turn to feel embarrassed. She realized that to John, it must seem that she was accusing him of taking advantage of her father, of not doing enough to provide for his family, when really she was just curious to know how much money he'd given them and how they'd invest it, how they'd pay it back. *How much trouble are we in, exactly? Why can't you tell me?* She opened her mouth to try to explain, to ask, and then Matthew began to cry, and she had to excuse herself, and had never found a moment to speak to him about it again. And after a few days it began to feel too late to reopen the subject, and she decided she'd ask him later. And then she never did.

It was luxurious and wild to be back in her girlhood home in town, where the smell of animals was absent and the library was full and nothing was required of her but to watch her boy and to help Frau in the kitchen, where she comported herself mostly without disgrace. But being here was maddening, too—knowing, now, how little she'd been prepared for. John, meanwhile, was all restless energy. He spent hours wandering around the place, finding odd projects, like a hinge that needed rehanging or a bolt that could be tighter. Her heart ached for John's humiliation, and her father's, too. She counted the days until they could return home.

In the end, the awkwardness around the house drove them to attend several of Herr Krause's magic shows, the five of them, Rebecca, John, Matthew, Frau, and even the Doctor wrapping up in blankets after supper for the quick, lantern-lit ride through chill, starry blackness to the schoolhouse. Rebecca sat with little Matthew on her lap in the third row of the auditorium of the brick schoolhouse where she and John used to sit in assembly as children. Afterward, the family shivered excitedly back through the streets to the warmth of the Doctor's fireside. John and Dr. Mueller drank thick wine in the parlor while Rebecca and Frau put the little boy to bed.

Rebecca invented lavish bedtime stories about magicians and magic shows she pretended to have seen. Listening to his mother in the minutes before sleep, Matthew would turn brooding and thoughtful in the depthless way of children who have learned to be serious in their efforts to try to understand the world. (Rebecca liked to imagine his baby thoughts at these moments, whispering, "Such a grave young man we are," and kissing his soft forehead over and over again.) Meanwhile, Frau sat nearby, that comforting old presence, sewing by a dim lamp and voicing infrequent, guttural signals of approval.

Both Frau and Matthew had a favorite among Rebecca's stories: the tale of the robber. Frau liked the tale because it clearly borrowed from her own inventions, and Matthew liked it because of the little twist his mother gave to the end. It went this way: "Once upon a time there was a famous robber who stole from all the best houses in Germany without ever getting caught. The robber came from a long line of robbers and had inherited from a distant robber relation a magical sack that could hold anything—as much as could be put into it and much more besides. The sack could hold the contents of an entire noble house, and many nights it did. Well, success made the robber bold, and one night the robber decided to steal from the great dark house of the great dark magician who lived on the great dark hill. So the robber took the magical sack and, late one night under a new moon, crept into the magician's house. The robber was afraid in the magician's house; it was shadowy and cold. But the robber found marvelous things: a time machine, a ring that granted wishes, a potion that allowed you to speak to animals and understand them, and, most precious of all, a small mirror, little enough to fit in my hand, that showed images of your loved ones' faces and told you all their thoughts. After putting everything that could be carried off into the sack, the robber was hungry and tired and decided to try the magician's kitchen.

"To the robber's great surprise, though, the magician was sitting in the kitchen, at a table spread with cheese and cakes and sausages, with a single candle to light his handsome face. 'Welcome to my house, master thief,' said the magician. 'Please, sit down with me and eat.' The robber was startled, but the food looked so delicious that it was impossible to refuse. When the robber sat in a chair to take a delicious bite, the magician caused the robber's chair to grow arms and hug the robber tightly, too tightly to move." Here Rebecca squeezed Matthew tight, to demonstrate. "The magician said, 'I see you have taken my magical things and put them into your sack, master thief. But I will make you a deal. Give back what you've stolen, and I'll take only what's mine.' The robber said, 'I'll keep what's in my sack, magician.' The magician laughed and said, 'Think twice, robber. The police are coming.' And the robber sighed. 'All right then, magician. Have it your way.' Then the magician caused a great, sweet-smelling wind to blow through the kitchen—" Rebecca blew softly on the little boy's face. "The wind caused the robber's hood to fly off her head. For the master thief was a pretty young woman, with hair black as night that flowed like water." And here, at the moment the little boy had been waiting for, Rebecca would brush Matthew's face and arms gently with her hair, and he would smile mightily and kick his small legs and grasp at it. "The magician held out his hand to her and said, 'My dear, everything I have is yours, for I have loved you since I first saw you in my mirror, the very one you've stolen. Let me take what is mine, your heart and your hand.' And the magician and the robber maid were married and did good magic together the rest of their days. The end."

Herr Krause began each of his performances in the same way. Wearing a dark suit and tie and a magician's straight-sided hat, he strode to center stage, removed his hat while bowing deeply, and wished them good evening in English and in German. He would then attempt to put his hat on his head, whereupon a dove would fly out, or colorful streamers of ribbon, or one night an actual rabbit. This simple, silly opening gesture was enough to endear him to the audience and in particular to the children. His face would betray just a flicker of amusement at the apparent disaster, and then Herr Krause would become stern. Then the magic would begin in earnest. His next trick was typically something a bit frightening, and most nights it involved fire. He walked through it, swallowed it, put his hand through it.

The final performance was one that Rebecca and John attended alone. It had been advertised as inappropriate for children, so the Hirschfelders left Matthew with Frau for the evening. Dr. Mueller had intended to come, had bought the ticket, but at the last moment was compelled to stay at home. He wasn't well. He had chest pains, was often weak and green and short of breath. Rebecca didn't like to leave him, but the Doctor insisted.

"The rumor is that tonight's performance will be special. I want you to tell me about it when you return home. I will wait up for you with a cigar."

"Not a cigar," Rebecca protested. "Not when you're breathing like this."

Dr. Mueller wheezed for her benefit and grinned, the little old gremlin. "Never let's pretend that we tell each other what to do, daughter."

Rebecca and John had had few occasions since their marriage to ride out together into the dark alone in a wagon as they did that night, wheeling through the town toward the schoolhouse. They were quiet for most of the drive, each of them wading in their own thoughts.

"The last time we rode together like this might have been the night we were married," Rebecca remarked eventually. She had been worrying about her father, recalling him in his stronger days as a younger man, which had led to thoughts of John, and of how often she and John had done this, just this very thing, when they themselves were younger. The wagon routes from her father's house. They'd all led to the same place in the end. She was surprising herself with something like sorrow. Had there been love between them on those old rides? She thought now that perhaps there had, sitting between them on the buckboard like a little bundle, wrapped up and disguised as something insignificant, and she had been too inexperienced, too angry, too confused, to acknowledge it. Shutting her eyes tight against the cold night air that rushed toward them, Rebecca thought of the hour again, the hour of her life that her mother had bartered so that the two of them could be together, and wished fiercely for the chance her mother had been given. *What wouldn't I give,* she thinks, *for us to love and be loved by each other. What wouldn't I pay to make my little family whole, real, unburdened.*

"That might be so," John allowed.

"Do you think Matthew will keep Frau up tonight?" Rebecca asked as they pulled onto the starlit schoolhouse road.

"I expect she gave him extra milk," John said.

"She wants to spoil him," Rebecca agreed.

"It's good to let her."

"But not too much. A farm boy can't grow up in luxury, expecting women to dote on him," Rebecca said lightly, before she realized how she sounded.

John's face, always so capable of concealing what he felt it was better not to express, changed very little as he said, "I suppose you're right, Beck."

Their wagon joined the others outside the schoolhouse, where the chill night air plumed with the breath of horses and harnesses chimed like bells. Boot soles of women and men they'd known most of their lives were heard to crunch and slide against the hard-packed earth on their way to clop up the schoolhouse steps. The air smelled of stove fires and cold leather. Some of the men, clustered together to smoke before heading in to rejoin their wives, were laughing a bit louder than was strictly necessary, as if to prove they weren't afraid of anything they were likely to see or hear inside.

The rumors about the magician's final show had been dark ones. The handbills had declared that Herr Krause possessed the power to read minds, predict the future, and foresee death, and that his final performance would be devoted to the exhibitions of those blacker, more mystical talents; therefore, no one under the age of fifteen would be permitted to attend. It was said that this was the pattern of his engagements from town to town: a few shows of straightforward magic, of the sleight-of-hand, cabinet-of-wonders, knife-throwing variety, and one final performance that revealed such grim mysteries that afterward, presumably, no one in the town would want to see the magician again and he'd be welcome to depart. It was said that his performances had ruined families and driven men to desperation. How exactly these wreckages had been accomplished was less clear. To Rebecca it all sounded delicious.

The Hirschfelders skirted the crowds huddled in the cold on the schoolhouse steps and made their way into the close, smoky, gaslit interior of the building, weaving their way through the throngs to the ticket taker and thence to their seats. Men came to say hello to John, and women nodded their braided heads to Rebecca. While John made small talk over the seat backs, she looked around at their neighbors, at the curls of smoke hanging in the air overhead, and at the lantern stage lights and the heavy curtain that had been contrived for the magician's performances. What a strange place to find oneself is a theater, or a room made into a theater, she found herself thinking. Lines and lines of people, their heads and shoulders, a whole bobbing sea of consciousness, are all laid out in neat rows like supper on a table. A monster's dream. Rebecca could positively swear that she wished no harm to a single person in the room, and yet she imagined a dragon laying waste to the entire assemblage with the swing of a thorny tail or a single breath of fire. It was easy enough to imagine, in fact, that they had all gathered here for precisely that purpose.

The appointed hour arrived, and the lights dimmed in warning, and the good country people said their good-byes to each other and found their seats in a great clamor. The old hinges on the bottoms of the auditorium chairs sang and yawned like an orchestra tuning in the moments before the opening note.

The magician appeared from behind the curtain and bowed deeply to their applause. He removed his hat, and they all held their breath. Nothing came out. Herr Robert Krause treated them all to a wry smile and put the hat back on his head.

"I'd like to tell you some stories," he announced, adding, "There's no reason to be afraid." He turned then, and the curtains parted on a cue. "As I tell my stories, you may, if you choose to look, see the truth of them revealed in the mirror behind me." They could all now see emerging from the gloom the frame of a tall, wide, oval glass—just the sort of thing, Rebecca thought, delighted, that Snow White's stepmother would consult for wicked ideas. The audience shifted, dimly seeing themselves in their rows.

"You will see by my demonstrations that the mirror is an ordinary mirror."

He walked closer to it so that they could all see his reflection in the glass, and themselves behind him, nodding in the glimmering gray.

"It is as solid as I am myself," Herr Krause said. He put his hand out and touched it, then made a fist and knocked on it. They all heard the sound. He removed a cloth from his coat pocket and efficiently polished the evidence of his hand away from the glass.

"It is, in short, a plain mirror. If one of you ladies would like it for your dressing room, I'll sell it to your husband," he added, again as if he were ejaculating a few last thoughts he hadn't intended to vocalize, and again they all laughed in surprise.

He turned back to them and pointed to an old woman seated at the end of the front row. "Beautiful *Fräulein*"—and there was some charmed laughter here—"will you come up to the stage by yonder stair and inspect my mirror? I will meet you and guide you to it," he blurted, in what seemed to be an unpremeditated flash of gallantry, as she began to start up with some difficulty from her chair. He fairly dashed across the stage and down the five steps that descended to the first row, and the audience clapped. The two of them made a dear sight, the young blond man in his straight black clothes with his arm extended supporting the older woman, bonneted and yellow faced. She smiled handsomely and he smiled back at her and they ascended the steps and the cheering grew louder.

"Who is that?"

"Mrs. Brandt, the dear thing. Her daughter teaches at the school."

"Oh, yes, the pretty teacher—"

He led Mrs. Brandt to the mirror and invited her to touch it, which bravely she did. Her hands, in the old-fashioned fingerless lace gloves women who'd lived through the war sometimes still wore, flattened against the glass as if it were a windowpane, then withdrew, leaving the impressions of her fingers.

"*Ach,* let me clean that off for you," she said, reaching instantly for her handkerchief, and the audience roared with laughter as she set to work on the glass with it. Herr Krause bowed again, and gently put his hand over hers.

"Allow me, *gnädige Frau.* If you would touch the frame, there? Is it solid?"

Mrs. Brandt laughed and ran her hand around the wooden frame of the mirror, nodding as she did so.

"And if you would, please, walk behind it?"

"Are you sure?" Mrs. Brandt said, surprised, and the audience laughed and clapped for her again. Herr Krause allowed a smile himself.

"Oh, yes, please. If you would do me the kindness."

She was seen to disappear briefly behind the tall mirror, and while she was gone, if the room did draw itself up into a plate-just-dropped silence, then what of it? What did it mean but that the magician's performance had already begun? Mrs. Brandt emerged on the other side and gazed at Herr Krause. "It is only a mirror," she said distinctly.

"*Danke, verehrte Dame.*" He bowed to her and with a wave of his arm invited the audience to applaud her intrepid explorations again. "Will you remain here with me while I tell the first of my stories?"

"I will," she said.

"Good sirs, will you bring a chair for Mrs. Gerda Brandt?" Herr Krause called offstage. While the audience, no less than Mrs. Brandt herself, absorbed the information that he in fact *knew* her, knew her name, two of the young boys from the high school who had been trained in lifting and lowering the curtain and obeying the magician's calls for remarkable articles bustled a high-backed dining room chair out onto the stage and left it in the position to which the magician directed them.

He saw Mrs. Brandt settled into the chair and said to her, "Are you ready?"

She looked at him as if to ask, *What has it to do with me?* "All right," she said, and they all laughed again.

Herr Krause nodded to her, then to the audience. "I shall turn toward the mirror, then, and begin. Whatever you should see, and whatever you should hear, you should not repeat outside this room."

Herr Krause smiled at his audience. "We are all friends here," he added.

"If I may ask also for your silence. These stories are very old, and it is difficult for them to hear. Now then."

Rebecca wondered briefly if he'd meant to say that the stories were difficult *to* hear, but then understood that the magician wanted them to believe that the stories were in fact listening to *them,* somewhere on the other side of the mirror, and waiting to be drawn into the world of the living through the medium of the magician. She shivered with some excitement and thought how much Frau would have loved to see this. How Aunt Adeline would have relished being the old woman on the stage! But then the young man turned his back on them, allowing the full force of his features to be reflected in the mirror that held all of their faces, too, and the lights behind him dropped to almost nothing, and he began to speak.

He said to the mirror:

"Once there was a poor woman who loved children and wished for a child of her own. She and her husband prayed and prayed for a child to be born to them, but for many years their prayers went unanswered.

"This woman who loved children was also well loved by the children in the town, and they followed her everywhere while she sang to them and told them stories and taught them games. The people in her town were poor and worked hard, and they often had little to feed their children, but this woman fed them with her love, and the children always went home happy and rosy-cheeked as if they'd eaten cake and milk all day long, and they went to bed with their heads so full of songs and games that they didn't hear their bellies groan with hunger."

In the glass could be perceived another dim shift, as if everyone in the theater had just turned in their seats at once.

"One day while the woman was in the fields with seven of the children from the town, a band of murderous thieves found them. Before the woman could call for help, catastrophe was upon them. One of the children was trampled to death under the men's horses, one of the children ran in fright into the river and drowned there, and two other children, a brother and a sister, were snatched up by the robbers and never heard from again. The woman gathered up the three remaining children and hid them under a haystack and, seeing there was no more room for her there, crawled under a haystack nearby to hide. But the men saw the children moving in the hay and stabbed into the haystack with pitchforks until the children were all dead. The woman hid until she heard the robbers ride away, and then she crept out, weeping, and locked herself in her house. No one in the town knew what had happened, and even the woman's kind husband could not convince her to tell him why she cried and cried and couldn't stop. The parents of the dead children looked everywhere for them, but the children, even the ones under the haystack, were never found, and winter came suddenly that year and covered the town with snow and ice."

The surface of the mirror shifted as if smoke had blown across it, and a pale face was seen to emerge: a woman's face, smeary with tears, not beautiful but not ugly, either. Mrs. Brandt glanced at her and then stared fiercely at the floor, looking very much as if she would like to return to her seat in the front row next to her husband. A few people in the audience were heard to gasp, but as the sounds of alarm and amazement rose in the auditorium, the face in the mirror was seen to fade slightly.

"Please," the magician said, and for the first time he sounded out of breath and tired. "Please, I must ask for your silence."

They quieted. The face in the mirror began to shine with a terrible whiteness.

"The children's bodies slept under snow and ice, and during the winter that the woman wept and wept in her house, she and her husband found that, unknown to them both, just before her great sorrow descended, their dearest wish had been granted, and by spring they would have a child of their own. As the snow melted the woman's womb grew, but to her husband's dismay the woman's soul was melting away with the snow. She could not stop thinking of the dear babies she had allowed to die."

In the mirror, as the magician spoke, the woman's face could be seen to change. An expression of anguish came over her, and she seemed to turn partly away, then force herself to look back. She wasn't pretty enough to be an actress, Rebecca thought.

"Her husband couldn't understand why she, with her dearest wish finally granted, would not be happy. She only melted further away. Even when the child was finally born, healthy and bloodred and snow-white, the woman was tormented with great unhappiness. Finally the husband took the child away to raise in the kitchen while the mother remained locked in her room, crying and crying, unable to stop, even with her happiness right outside the door."

A second face appeared in the mirror, and to no one's great surprise, it appeared to be a child, infinitely beautiful and sad, neither boy nor girl. Mrs. Brandt shifted uneasily in her seat.

"Time passed, and the child grew, and the woman stayed in her room and wept. Times were hard, and they were often hungry. The child was a good girl with a generous heart who saw how unhappy her parents were, and tried always to be obedient and helpful. With her mother locked in her room and her father working hard, she was constantly alone.

"But *not* alone. Because the ghosts of the seven dead children came to the house of the woman they'd loved so well, who'd always fed them with her good heart. They were hungry and cold from their first winter under the snow and always would be. Even though the child gave them her blankets, her bread, and even her clothes, the ghosts were always cold and hungry, and always wanted more."

Murmurs of horror and alarm were heard throughout the theater. The faces of the woman and the child in the mirror had been joined by the spectral faces of sad, hungry ghost children: eyes huge and dark, mouths open and pleading. The face of the young magician, solid and handsome in the mirror with the ghosts, remained stern, and old Mrs. Brandt on the stage refused to acknowledge them by so much as a glance.

"The day finally arrived when the little girl had nothing else to give to the hungry, scared ghosts. There was no bread left in the house, and no wood for a fire, and the little girl's clothes were ragged and thin. The father worked hard, but times were bad, and many families were hungry and making do with little.

"The ghosts said to the little girl, 'Please, please feed us and let us come by the fire. We're so cold and hungry and tired.'

"The little girl said sadly, 'I don't have a fire, and we have nothing to eat.'

"The ghosts said, 'Then you must let us eat your insides hollow and warm ourselves inside your skin.'"

In the mirror, the little faces became monstrous, prompting some cries of dismay.

"The little girl was afraid, but the ghosts were so pitiful that she was afraid to say no. What could she do? She said, 'It might be better for my parents if I let you eat me, because then my mother would be happy and my father would have one less mouth to feed. You may eat me, but let me kiss my mother good-bye first.'

"The ghosts said, 'Please, please hurry. We are so hungry, and so cold.'

"The little girl rose sadly from her chair and went to her mother's bedroom door. The key hung on a peg, and she unlocked the door and went inside.

"There she found her mother sitting in her chair by the window, crying and crying, unable to stop. Her mother's hair had grown very long, and her face was pale as the moon for being washed so constantly with tears. The little girl thought her mother's hair looked as if it might warm her, so she went toward her mother and nestled into her long thick hair.

"The mother looked down at her and said, 'Daughter, why are you here? Leave me alone.'

"The little girl said, 'I'm here to kiss you good-bye.'

"The mother said, 'Where are you going?'

"The little girl said, 'I don't know. Somewhere far away, where the ghost children live.' Then she cried, thinking that where she was going, she would be a ghost child, too, and always hungry and cold.

"The mother said, 'What do you mean?'

"Then the little girl explained about the ghost children who lived in the house with them, who could never be made warm and whose bellies could never be filled. She told her mother that she was going to let herself be eaten by the ghost children because she couldn't bear their hungry cries.

"The mother was horrified and wrapped her little girl tightly up in her hair. 'You won't be eaten, not while I live.'

"The little girl had left the bedroom door open, and the seven ghost children had crept into the room with them. They were hungry for the sight of the woman they had loved so well when they were alive, and hungry to eat her little girl, too."

The little ghost children in the mirror reached out their hands, opening their mouths like hungry birds, their eyes dark and shining. It was a terrible sight. Rebecca shivered and slipped her hand into John's.

And now the magician turned and looked at Mrs. Brandt, still in her chair, refusing to glance at him or the mirror. He said something to her in a low voice.

The older woman shook her head sharply—*no, not that*—and responded, loud enough for the auditorium to hear, "They save each other."

The magician nodded, then briskly concluded:

"When the ghost children saw the little girl wrapped up warm in her mother's long hair, they began to melt. They melted away like snow and became the woman's tears. Finally the woman's tears dried on her cheeks, and as her tears dried, the little ghost children were no more."

The faces in the mirror disappeared, and the lights rose again. The audience shifted creakily in their chairs and then burst into heated applause. The magician stood for a moment, shoulders slumped as if projecting the figures in the mirror had exhausted him. Then he turned and thanked the audience with a brief, professional bow. He strode to Mrs. Brandt's chair and helped her to her feet, then, inexplicably, invited the audience with a broad sweep of his arm to applaud her, as if she'd somehow had a hand in projecting the figures onto the glass or supplying the tale, and in fact Mrs. Brandt did look a bit strange and moonlike as she stood, stone-faced, accepting their applause.

Herr Krause told three more tales that evening, each time inviting an audience member to come up on the stage first to inspect the mirror and then to sit onstage in the chair, revealing each time that he knew exactly who they were. The stories were all made from the same pastiche of Grimm fairy tale and German *Volk* talk that he must have known would particularly appeal to them. One story was bawdy and funny and violent and involved a miller's wife who fed her husband his rivals in a series of stews. The final story was about a princess who pulled her entire country underwater, as if pulling it under a blanket with her, house by house, rather than marry her father, the king. And each time, before concluding the tale and the mirror's ghastly show, the magician consulted the person sitting in the chair onstage, as if he didn't know without asking how his story would end. There never seemed to be any apparent connection between the stories Herr Krause told and the people who sat onstage during the telling—these were people well-known to other people in the audience, and there were no dramatic revelations or trembling fingers pointed that night. But as the magician spoke, eerie images flashed and grew, waxed and waned on the mirror, and the people seated on the stage were not the only ones who were perceived to grow silent and unhappy.

After the last story was told and the images had faded away, the magician caused the mirror to be rolled back behind the curtain and offered for his final act to predict the circumstances of a single volunteer's death.

"No one?"

No one stood up or came forward. The audience laughed uneasily as the silence unspooled.

Rebecca, feeling reckless, rose to her feet. John looked up at her, and she smiled down at him, as if nothing she did could really harm him, which sometimes she thought was in fact the case.

"Oh, but you, my dear"—Robert Krause squinted at her from far away, through the haze of the stage lights—"you won't ever die."

Rebecca laughed. "But surely—"

"Ladies and gentlemen, I thank you, but I've reached the extent of my powers when a beautiful young woman asks me to imagine the end of her life." Robert Krause smiled and bowed, sweeping off his hat, and the audience applauded expectantly, but then he strode off the stage in long-legged lopes and they were given to understand that he meant it, and that the show had truly concluded.

The night, therefore, ended on a strange, deflated note. John and Rebecca found themselves forcefully congratulated on the way out of the theater.

"Well, the immortal beauty! You've caught quite the wife, John!"

"What will you do with the rest of your eternal life, Rebecca?"

"If you don't plan to die, make sure you've got a lot of money."

"Brave of you to call his bluff, Mrs. Hirschfelder."

John and Rebecca were all laughter and easiness with their neighbors, but it seemed to her that they were afraid to meet each other's eye. They accepted an invitation from Betsy Hart to come to her house for punch and cake, along with a good number of their old friends from school, where Betsy's sister pounded away on the piano and a group of the men sang "Das Glühwürmchen" and "In the Good Old Summertime," and the piano-playing sister was serenaded with "I Can't Tell You Why I Love You, but I Do." It was a merry night, and the hour was late when the party broke up.

Rebecca was conscious that she looked to be in higher spirits than she perhaps felt as she and John made their way back through the chilly streets to her father's house. She was thinking that if she hadn't stood up in the theater and reminded Betsy and her town friends that she existed, she and John probably would have just driven home in silence.

John, for his part, had retreated back to the dark-lidded place in which he dwelled when he was with her. She'd seen the other John, her old John, at Betsy's, in conversation with the people they used to know, and she'd had to acknowledge anew what everyone else seemed to understand already: He was handsome; he was good-natured. He was often friendly. He was well-mannered and gentlemanly. He could be funny. But he lived behind a wall.

Out in the cold, her breath creating vapors, Rebecca said to him, "Did you enjoy the party?"

"I enjoyed it more than the show," John returned, with a charged glance at her. *Here it comes,* she thought. *Well, I gave him the opening after all. Even if I was feeling tenderly toward him just now, it's clear enough he's been angry at me all night.* "What could you possibly have meant by it, Beck? Why did you stand up? What on earth could you possibly have wanted to know from him?" He caught himself short and shook his head quickly, staring straight ahead at the road.

"Oh, I don't know. I don't have an idea. I'm sorry if I embarrassed you." Rebecca shrugged. "I was curious. I suppose I did want to call his bluff, as Mr. Bieder said."

"You were charmed. You were snake-charmed."

Rebecca stared at John, astonished and amused. "You're jealous."

John turned on her a brief glare, then looked away.

"Herr Krause is a handsome devil, everyone says so," she teased. John stared ahead at the horse's cold-bitten ears. "He fell in love with me upon the instant and couldn't bear to think of me in peril," she put the back of her gloved hand on her forehead in pantomime.

John grasped her hand a bit roughly and pulled it away from her face. "Don't," he warned.

"You're a funny one," Rebecca said, letting her hand rest in his but looking a challenge into his eyes. "As if you had any real reason to fear," she finally muttered. "You must know you haven't any rivals. You never have."

John turned away to frown at the horse's ears. "I don't know what you're talking about."

Rebecca sighed, watching his profile against the passing darkened houses. "No, I don't suppose you do," she said. "I don't know why I feel such impatience tonight." She shook her head. "I can't say. But I'll show you. I *will* show you," she added, with something of the magician's abruptness, and she lunged across the wagon's seat with her husband's hand in hers and took his chin in her other gloved hand. The reins jerked with a metallic chime. Rebecca brought her mouth to John's and curled her arm around his neck. *I'll feed you, I'll warm you,* she thought crazily. *What's gotten into me?*

She felt his arm encircling her waist, and suddenly the layers of woolly clothing that she wore felt as restricting and cold as a tightly wrapped shroud. She was bursting outward from within, the heat of her self—her real self—spreading and reaching out toward the surface, penetrating her own skin from within, hot inside and cold without, warming the surface from below.

They were in the middle of the street, exposed together alone. John released any pretense of driving the wagon and pulled Rebecca's body into his. She felt her knee lifting, felt his hand pulling her, and then she pushed herself off the wagon seat and straddled his lap, holding his face in her hands and driving her tongue down into the heat of John's mouth. He made a sound then, a sound that she remembered from their first kiss, and it broke her heart afresh even as she felt a delirious triumph rising from her chest. She answered with a moan against his lips and felt his body stiffen.

She pulled her mouth away with a laugh, feeling dizzy and untamed. "We're out in the middle of the road, John."

"I don't care. Kiss me again."

"We'll be arrested," she said, dipping her head to brush her lips against his. "Thrown into separate cells."

"Frau Nussbaum will post our bail," John murmured, and she cracked a decidedly snort-like laugh. His body surged up against hers. "Don't let go of me," he said. She tightened her legs around him, and he pulled close about their bodies the lap blanket she'd disarrayed in her mad lunge. In the protected embrace of the blanket, in the dark, his cold hand slid under her skirt and up her woolen stockings to where her legs parted, and her cold hand reached down between his legs, rudely forcing his pants open. She heard herself beginning to pant with hunger and eagerness, and felt herself, too, drawing from behind John's wall some burdened, hungry thing that she'd been allowing to starve.

"You," she managed, his mouth hot on her throat. "You. You must know. You must know by now."

Meanwhile, the horse continued slowly down the street without either of their guidance, moving methodically toward home, a warm barn, a little sleep.

When they arrived at the Doctor's house sometime later, Rebecca's mouth swollen and John's thin face flushed with exertion, they found all the downstairs lamps lit, blazing into the street at nearly one in the morning. It was their first sign that something was terribly wrong.

Neither of them leaped to react, although the sight of the glaring house was a bad omen at this hour. Rebecca looked a question at John, who shook his head, eyes dark, and swiftly steered the horse down the lane toward the shed behind the house. He paused at the post that marked the corner of the Doctor's yard, though, and without a word between them Rebecca jumped down.

In an instant, despite the sweetness of the cold night, they were separate again. Perhaps they'd grown too accustomed to the old, hard habit of answering challenges alone and in their own distinct ways, she with decisive, swift movements and he with the quiet relentlessness of a stone. If she had known in that moment what would happen in the weeks to come, she might have taken John's hand and insisted that he come with her, that the horse could wait—that, indeed, it might be better to leave the horse harnessed and ready in case they had to go for help. She might have waited for John instead of dashing off into the house alone. She might have remembered, in that moment of stomach-freezing fear, that they belonged to each other, that they had married each other in part to help each other through just such moments as these, and she might have tried to reinforce the tenuous thread that bound them to each other. If she had known that in the weeks to come that spider-skein thread would seem to snap entirely, leaving the two of them floating aloft and tetherless in a terrifying blank space, she might have done something differently. But she didn't because they weren't together in that way, not even yet. They'd never found a way to be.

Rebecca felt herself moving with effort up the walk, pulling herself against the weight of her own fear as if she were dragging heavy, wet horse blankets again.

She opened the door from the front steps and discovered Matthew sitting unsteadily on the parlor rug near the stove, eyes red with recent crying and purple shadowed with baby exhaustion. He was holding something in his plump, dear little hands, frowning at it, busy in thought in that way small children can be. It took her some moments to recognize the object he grappled with, its tubes flopping horribly across his lap.

Rebecca closed the door behind her, and the little boy looked up from his study of the sticky, mysterious tubes of her father's stethoscope. At the sight of his mother, Matthew's face curled into a smile that was also half a cry. Under the heavy glass-globed lights of the parlor, Rebecca, still in her coat and gloves and hat, scooped up her little boy and held him, looking around her in real fear for the remainder of the disaster, wherever it might be.

Just as Matthew was setting out to protest the situation, the scratchiness of her coat, and the stethoscope abandoned like so much forbidden fruit on the warm rug near the stove, Rebecca heard the back door open and the heavy step of her husband on the kitchen floorboards. "Rebecca?" he called.

He met her in the downstairs hallway, which formed a dim tunnel between the brightly lit kitchen and parlor. John was openly dismayed at seeing Matthew in his mother's arms at this hour of the night, rather than asleep and safe in his cot.

"Where is everyone?" John asked, and Rebecca felt a cold stone against her breast. "They must be upstairs," John looked up. "Hello up there. Dr. Mueller? Miss Nussbaum?"

There came a sound from above, a thud like something falling from a shelf. Rebecca and John looked at each other, startled and afraid.

"Stay here," John murmured. "Until I know it's safe." Then John made for the stairs with his long-legged gait. Rebecca stood with Matthew in her arms, both of them watching as John disappeared into the dimness of the upper hallway.

A fearsome quiet followed. Rebecca felt as if a hook in her rib cage were tugging her toward the staircase. She had to know what was up there, but she was suddenly afraid to let her little boy see whatever might be waiting. She forced herself to blink her burning eyes and look away. Matthew leaned his little head against her shoulder. His warm, round cheeks were a soft, kissable plumpness that curved down past his tiny chin, making of his face a darling round pear, creamy white and sweet. Matthew didn't look like her—he had John's dark eyes and his lighter hair—and as he lifted his head again to turn his serious, tired baby smile on her, Rebecca's heart tightened with love so crushing she thought she might die of it. *I would do anything for you, but I can't stay here with you,* she thought at him fiercely. *Forgive me.* She moved into the parlor and set the boy down in his former nest on the rug near the stethoscope.

"Stay here and play quietly, my own sweet love," she said, kissing his head and his cheeks and his little dry mouth. He looked at her expectantly. So small. Was he too close to the stove? There was no time to lose. She would return to him. She breathed him in and then stood and made for the stairs, backing toward them while smiling insincerely at the little boy on the rug, afraid of the quiet up there, so afraid of it, but still impelled toward it by something she knew but couldn't name.

Matthew's small face crumpled at the sight of her retreat. He began to wail in earnest as she reached for the banister and began to climb.

"Sssh, sweet love," Rebecca whispered. "Sssh, sssh." But he only sobbed the louder. Rebecca looked over her shoulder at her baby, grown purple faced with the rage of incomprehensible loss. "All right, all right." She dashed back to the parlor and put the stethoscope back in Matthew's hands. He flung it away, reaching for her instead. "No, no, little love. You can't come with me," she whispered, unhooking his fingers from her skirt, scarcely able to think. *What is happening up there? Why is it so quiet? Why hasn't John come down?* She stood hastily, and Matthew fell over with a graceless flop and began to scream into the rug. She righted him as softly as she could and then turned and ran for the staircase.

She didn't make it far. His screams escalated. "You're going to hurt yourself," she cried down to him. "Be still! Be still and wait for Mama!" Rebecca looked up into the darkness awaiting her at the top of the stairs and tried to still her heart. *God help me,* she prayed forcefully, staring at the black upstairs hallway and searching for the strength of heart to climb up into it. *He's only a baby. I can't bring him into that.*

She heard the baby fall over again, and his screams intensified. Fearing that he really had hurt himself, she hurried back down the stairs and craned from the landing to look into the parlor. Matthew was on his side, perhaps too close to the stove after all, fists clenching and unclenching, eyes shut tight, screaming.

"Matthew, hush! Stop that now! Your mama is going to be right upstairs!"

Matthew's eyes opened at the sound of her voice, and he reached for her, his tiny fingers spread open like a forced flower, his sobs hoarse and pleading.

It was too much for her. "You poor thing." As fast as she could move, she went to him, scooped him up, pressed him against her shoulder, none too gently. There was no time to lose. Something was happening up there. She had to get to John. Her shoes made the staircase shudder. "We'll go together. We'll go together. Be brave, little one."

She raced toward the dark at the top of the stairs, where all the light seemed to have been sucked out of the world by some tremendous leave-taking force, like a wind that sweeps a door closed. But three-quarters of the way up, midstep, she felt herself overreach, her body overbalancing, as if the next stair had sunk, suddenly and without warning, three feet into the bottom story. As if the whole staircase belonged to a different house, one built just a bit lower and to the left of her father's house, the house where she knew herself to be. Clutching her baby boy to her side, she felt herself hanging perilously close to a fall.

Dream, this must be a dream, I must have fallen asleep in the wagon on the way home, afterward, and I'm tucked up against him under the blanket and dreaming this, dreaming this entire disaster.

But as much as she wished it, she knew it wasn't true. She was falling, with her baby in her arms, on stairs she'd traversed a thousand times.

In the half seconds that felt like days during which her body overcorrected and searched for a reality that was no longer there, she saw the house as if through a film of smoke or bright linen gauze, the sort her father used for bandages, but the house was utterly changed. Here it was bright, it was hot. Here the top of the stairs led to a hallway with three doors on one side—not the eight doors, four on either side, that she'd raced in and out of as a girl. As hideous and sickening as the sensation of falling was, and even as the unfamiliarity of the place in which she found herself doubled and redoubled the terror of what was happening, she felt more impelled than ever to get to the top of the stairs. Something she wanted was up there. Something she wanted very badly. She had to get to it. She had to get to it—no matter what it cost, she knew she was willing to pay.

She urged herself forward, hurling her body and angling her shoulder—the opposite shoulder from the one that cradled Matty—toward where she knew the staircase ought to be, ought to be. Although here in this dream house it was as if she were throwing herself over the banister. And for a stomach-dropping moment she thought she'd done just that.

The staircase spun back into place before her. *I'm going to hit—*

Her shoulder and the side of her head thudded against the edge of the wood. Matty screamed on and on. She cradled his small head, pushed up onto her knees with her sore free arm, gathered her heavy skirt out of the way, and lunged again for the top of the stairs.

Her father's door was the first on the left. As her fingers closed over the knob, it turned. John was there. She launched herself into him bodily, and he took her in.

"He's gone, Beck."

Still holding Matthew, she pushed past John into the room, as peremptorily and instinctively as she'd run into his arms. There was a light past him on the bedside table, illuminating a room in which nothing seemed possible—surely this was a play, a stage? Not her home. Frau was on the floor. "Oh God!" It burst from her throat in a sob.

John managed to gather the boy away from her. Rebecca, still not seeing, or unwilling to see, what was in her father's bed, knelt at Frau's side. She was warm, but breathing shallowly.

"She's unconscious. She fainted, Beck; she's still alive."

"What—" Rebecca, with her hand on Frau's cheek and her little boy screaming and screaming behind her, and her husband pushed away like so much unwanted food, finally looked at what was in her father's bed.

It emerged that on the night of the Doctor's death, poor Adeline had passed some nightmarish hours. Dr. Mueller had gone up to bed not long after John and Rebecca left for the schoolhouse, and sometime later, at around the hour that popular songs were being sung at Betsy Hart's house in town, a repeated sound, like a choking cry, had stirred Adeline Nussbaum from her bed and brought her to the bedroom door of her old friend and protector, her one remaining cousin from the old days in Duisdorf, before their small, rudderless family had scattered to pieces all across the cities and America and left each other to make their own ways as best they could. Adeline had lived in America long enough to see that not all the Germans here came from luck and large families. Some came here lonely and died here lonelier still.

The sounds had continued behind her cousin's door, and so eventually, after calling softly through the wood to him, she'd pushed the door open and found the old man strangling on his own blood, purple in the face, eyes bulging, unable to speak or breathe but not yet dead, horribly not yet dead. As she stood in the doorway, the Doctor, that sturdy and inscrutable man who had always seemed invincible in his way, vomited blood onto his chest.

Her shriek of horror awoke the baby, who tumbled from his cot in Rebecca's room across the hall with a ragged thump that jolted Frau's heart, and that was followed by screaming of such an intense pitch that she was convinced the little lad had broken his arm. From that moment she was consumed by the effort and the helplessness of trying to find a way to aid them both at once, by herself. She ran to the Doctor, who didn't seem to recognize her, his whole body thrown into the effort of fighting something that seemed to have exploded within itself. So then she ran to the boy, who seemed mercifully unharmed, although she could hardly pause long enough to examine him. She hastened downstairs in the dark with the still-screaming boy, where she found herself alone and in a terrible conflict. Could she leave the boy to get help? She couldn't bring the baby with her into the cold, and she didn't have time to dress him. Did she even have time to run to the neighbors for help? In a fever of indecision she lit all the lamps she quickly could, hoping somehow that the brightness of the house might alarm the neighbors. She left the boy in the parlor with the only toys that came to hand: the topmost items in the Doctor's old medicine bag, which customarily sat on a table in the hall by the door.

From there Adeline pulled herself as quickly as she was able back up the stairs, carrying the Doctor's bag with her. In narrating the evening's events to Rebecca and John later, she tried, she did try, to explain what happened in the Doctor's room over the course of the unending hour before the Hirschfelders arrived at home, but was largely unable. Her English seemed to fail her. No one who lived nearby had noticed the lights blazing from the house or heard the boy's screams, or if they had, they hadn't made it their business to come. She said merely, "After some time, the little boy, he stop crying downstairs. But I could not leave him alone, your father, in his *Leiden*."

The Doctor had only just finally died when Rebecca saw him, and the blood on his bedclothes was still bright and fresh.

CHAPTER ELEVEN

Bridget manages, somehow, to scramble partway up from the floor, with Julie half in her arms and half in Mark's. Crabbing backward, away from the ghost in the door, Bridget whangs her head, for the second time in seconds, on the stair banister post. Tears start in her eyes, and she realizes that in falling she has also bitten the inside of her cheek hard enough to draw blood—it feels like there's actually a little loose flap of skin in there, and the pain is both needle sharp and throbbing. There is no air in the house, no air in the universe, and her lungs are white pain. Standing, running, getting away, is impossible. Her arms are shaking so hard she can hardly keep herself propped up.

The ghost has turned effortfully in the doorway and is staring down at them with hunger in its eyes. Inside the shape-shifting open-mouthed whiteness Bridget can still just see the blackened figure of a woman, melting and struggling. And now it moves, taking a shuffle step that throws it off-balance, and it brushes against the doorframe with a revolting thud like a hand flapping against the inside lid of a coffin.

Mark, of course, cannot hear it. He has struggled along on the ground with Bridget, keeping low to prevent Julie from falling out of their arms, and with a grunt he lands on his ass on the polished wooden floorboards. He pulls Julie away from Bridget to his own chest, smooching and rocking the girl and looking at Bridget with betrayed astonishment in his eyes.

"What the hell, Bridget?" he demands. "Are you drunk? How much did you drink?"

As Bridget watches in nauseated terror, the ghost reaches out its flickering, grotesque arm and closes the front door to the house behind it. *Now we are all here. Now you are mine.*

"We have to move. We have to get Julie away from here," Bridget whispers.

"I'm getting her into bed," Mark snaps, exasperated, and rises to his feet with the sobbing little girl in his arms. Like it's nothing. He steps over Bridget at the foot of the stairs and ascends quickly, making funny *nom-nom-nom* noises into the crook of Julie's neck that cause her to insert one giggle, exactly one giggle, into the line of sobs she is producing. Bridget hears the upstairs bathroom door close, hears Mark's comforting voice talking to their girl, hears the bathtub faucet come alive with a hiss that runs through the walls.

Meanwhile neither she nor the ghost has moved.

"What do you want?" Bridget manages through numb lips.

Around its blackened center the ghost actually enlarges—spreads itself wide like a hellish preying bird. The world grows momentarily dark and bone-chillingly cold. *I want it all. Everything you love is mine.*

"Please don't," Bridget begs. "Please, please just leave them alone. Take me, take just me."

The ghost's head dips low, as if bending to a trough. Then its jaw lowers like a mantis, and its black and earth-stinking mouth opens wide enough that Bridget can see directly into the chasm. There the dark-eyed woman inside is trapped and reaching. *Join her, then. Go on. Climb inside. You knew all along you were going to be swallowed alive.*

There's a happy squeal and a splash upstairs.

Bridget's mind stutters to Julie. *I would do anything for you, but I can't go in there. Forgive me.*

"I have something for you," Bridget extemporizes. "I have something you want. I promise." *It's slow it's slow it's slow, I can lure it away from them, I can lure it into the dark, and then I can escape and get us all out of here.*

It flickers and then preens again, growing and stretching, a mindless wall of cold and anger that dissolves all the air around it into nothingness. *Everything you love is mine. You know yourself that you already gave it all away.*

"Follow me. Follow me. I'll show you," Bridget pants.

Keeping her eyes on the ghost, her breath a thin and painful whistling in her throat, Bridget gropes behind her for balance and begins slowly to pull herself up. The airless world spins, and for a heart-stopping second she's sure she's going to black out. The ghost tilts its maw toward her, as if to scoop her in, and Bridget almost loses her determination not to scream. She scrambles backward into the dark, moving faster now.

She is halfway into the darkened living room before the ghost makes its move, throwing its weight forward to drape halfway over the banister post, flopping horribly, half impaling itself. Then it swings its weight forward and begins its struggle after Bridget.

She needs to outflank it again. She tries to think how she can trap the ghost somehow, corner it and then get away with her family. But whether because of her terror or because of her struggle to breathe, her mind can't focus. She staggers, lurching from one support to the next, gripping the arm of a chair and then reaching for the corner of the low bookshelf by the entrance to the dining room, pulling herself to the entryway and holding herself up by clinging to the wall. The smell and the airless void of the grave pursue her. *This can't be happening. This dead thing can't be chasing me through my own house.*

It doesn't want my baby's story. It doesn't want my deepest grief. It doesn't want my house, or my marriage, or my daughter.

I already gave it all of those things. I already dissolved myself into the white.

It's just ready to finish the job.

And then something like a cloud descends over her eyes, over her mouth, like the view from an airplane window when the craft is overtaken by a cloud. But this cloud isn't water vapor suspended in air. This cloud is made of knives.

It has me it has me—

The pain is excruciating. Bridget's mouth opens in a shriek, and now it's in her mouth, the whiteness seeking a way down her throat, seeking a way into her heart, a way to gut her from within.

She falls to her knees, out of the white—she can no longer stand, but also it feels as if some force has come from behind her and given her a push. *It was her.* The woman—the one struggling in blackness inside of that hateful cloud.

Bridget gasps for air and begins to crawl again, digging her fingernails into the dining room rug to pull herself along. She makes her way to the corner of the kitchen entryway and pulls herself to her feet, looking back into the darkness behind her for the ghost.

What is silhouetted against the faint light coming from the entryway brings tears of horror and pity to her eyes.

She is tall, the dead woman, but painfully thin. She is more solid than Bridget has ever seen her because with one arm she is trying to pull herself out of the white. The other arm looks broken, somehow useless, bent at a wrenching angle. But she is trying to pull the white off, pull it up and over her head like a dress (*or like a nightgown*) that was found, too late, to be made of something dangerous, something that would eat her alive. (*I know that feeling, I know it. I've been the ghost in my house, that whiteness is mine, too—or—or I made it—dear God, I made it, I chose it.*) As Bridget watches, the woman's thin frame doubles over and shudders. She pushes up from her knees and forces herself to stand. Her hands clutch at the edges of something around her that Bridget cannot see—she is nothing but a shade, with the entry light behind her as she struggles for her freedom in the darkened doorway. It is clear that the woman is in terrible pain, that she is fighting for her life with what might be the last, the utmost that she has.

Bridget can no more watch a person struggle through that kind of pain than she can let someone hurt her baby girl. Before she knows herself what she is doing, she is moving back toward it. Back toward the shape-shifting, the flesh-dissolving, the hungry and hateful *it,* because the *she* (*she could be me, she could be me—I am what you are*) cannot hold out much longer. She's across the room, but Bridget feels as if she reaches her merely by summoning the will to move, as if she has folded the space in the room like the corner of a tablecloth and erased the few feet between them.

"I can reach—let me help—" She puts her arms out to the woman, into the space where she seems to be, although even as she approaches she's not sure what her hands will encounter there, what her arms might enclose. She lunges in, reaches through, and for a half moment she thinks their fingers touch, and it's not painful, it's not like the press of hot knives through her skin—but it is cold, and wet, and hard where this woman is, and she has become that place, and it's a place she does not want to be.

In the dark, her eyes change. In the dark, in the second before Bridget realizes neither of them is strong enough, not yet. They haven't beaten it, not yet.

It slips over the woman's face like a caul and changes her into a horror. The eyes suddenly black and bottomless and huge, the mouth like a grave tipping her in (*YOU'RE MINE, TOO, MINE MINE MINE*). Bridget screams and yanks herself backward, but her hand (*it's got my hand, dear God, I can't take it*) is agonizingly held in its clutch.

"MARK!" She screams his name. But what could he do, even if he were here? This is the ghost that she chose. She's the only one who can see it or fight it or free herself from it. There is pain here, unimaginable, but it's pain she made, inherited, stepped into, was born into. It's almost familiar. It's almost like birth.

Let me go, please—I'm sorry, I can't get through, I'm not strong enough—

She's no longer sure which thoughts are her own and which are the thoughts of the woman—or the raw, frequency-annihilating broadcasts of the staticky, flickering white ghost. She's connected to both; she's inside of them as surely as they are inside of her. She's not sure who lets go of whom, who was pulling or clasping, but somehow she's released. For now. But the ghost is still a hungry mouth, it still wants her—and as she falls backward, it lunges again.

Bridget lands on her back and rolls. There is a thud behind her—something hitting the floor. She staggers to her feet and runs into the darkened kitchen, where for a moment, in a panic of fresh pain and bewildered instinct, she thinks the impossible (*I could just leave, I could just run out the door into the night, a madwoman, get into the car and leave this horror show*) and then she stops. She forces herself to think.

Mark might be safe, it's true—he might not even be living in the same layer of reality that admits such things as the ghost, or the woman inside it. He might not even have heard her screams; the struggle of the last few moments simply took place in a house he doesn't inhabit.

But there is another person in the house who can see the ghost. Who could always see it, who would go on seeing it, even if Bridget somehow found it in herself to leave her behind. There's another person here that the ghost might accept, a compromise, if its first choice became unavailable. A girl, clever and special, worth everything.

It won't stop. It can't.

What does it want? Everything, everything. And it knows just where to find it.

A shuffling sound has arrived at the kitchen doorway. Something hisses like static in her ear, the piercing sound of an empty frequency. The air thins out; the smell of damp earth and wet mud overtakes her.

Bridget is shaking. Her legs won't move. She feels literally rooted in fear. She tries to force herself to put one foot in front of the other. She cannot do it.

But it's slow, it's slow, I can get there before it—

A thud. A dead step. Then a draft of air wafting over her shoulder, like a dreadful mockery of a summer breeze, cold like the grave and moving the loose hairs that have escaped her braid. Like a breath on her neck.

You're all mine now.

Her paralysis shatters, and she is running for the stairs.

CHAPTER TWELVE

In the weeks that turned into months after Dr. Mueller's funeral, Rebecca, numbed as she was by the sadness and the lonely hideousness of the end of her father's life, found herself wrapped up tight in an isolation from which she could not see an easy way to extricate herself. For her, of course, it was not an unfamiliar sensation.

For the Doctor had left his house to her—to his beloved daughter, "Rebecca Mueller." And John, insulted but not wanting to reveal it, had seemed to align immediately with the notion that his mourning wife should remain in her childhood house in town, along with Frau and Matthew.

John went back out to the farm without them, coming into town for weekend visits, as if the family had decided to prolong their terrible holiday visit long, long past the date of its exhausted and joyless expiry. At first the separation seemed temporary, or at any rate they all assumed it to be so. But it was not long before an air of fatigued permanence and failure attached itself to the split household.

To Rebecca it seemed as if she had put on seven-league boots and stepped not forward but backward in time, to the days when she was a young and indolent beauty, except the small man in whose thrall she was held was not the Doctor but her little boy, for whose sake this arrangement purportedly made the most sense: He must be with her, after all, and she, oh, she must not be asked for anything, not now. And it was true that she was tired all the time, terribly tired.

Sometimes she stood at the foot of the stairs and looked up, just being quiet. Sometimes she found herself standing there without remembering when she'd moved into that spot, or why, and she'd think, *Oh, what was it, what was I doing here?* Thinking she should make some excuse to go up the stairs and look for something—just to see. Just to see if it might happen again: if she might suddenly drop into another house, onto another stair. At these moments she sometimes found herself thinking, *Who is waiting in that place for me? What was I trying to get to, up there?* And then the questions themselves would seem as unlikely as her own behavior, and she would force herself to move away and try to find something useful to do.

Perplexing as it was, Rebecca sensed that her father's house was a box she herself had stepped into, closing the lid over her own head. The listlessness of the place crept into her bones. She was as unaccustomed to inactivity now as she had been unprepared for the endless work that had awaited her when she'd moved out to the farmhouse after her marriage, and to her amazement she found herself as exhausted by drifting around her father's house as she'd been last year working through her first winter on the farm. Now, here, without the purpose that the farm gave her or the heightened awareness that she and John produced in each other's company, everything she thought she was simply dissolved. All the self-doubt and the loneliness and the self-loathing she'd come to associate with her own many mistakes—

everything she'd done wrong in her marriage, on the farm, even as a mother to Matthew—became a shroud in which she felt herself being embalmed, day by endless day. She lacked the power to fight her way out. It was a frightening sensation, this helplessness, and yet she supposed it ought to have felt familiar, perhaps even welcome: Wasn't this how the fortunate among women lived, or dreamed of living? Comfortably in place, tending their dear babies and their dear homes and their dearly beloveds? Shouldn't she feel *more* real and not less? But something was missing, something she wanted badly, and without it she felt she might become so insubstantial as to fly apart into pieces.

As the winter ended and the spring reared up, John was at the house in town less and less.

Frau was not herself, either. The Doctor's death and the way she'd lost him—the long night that had rendered her as helpless as a girl in a dark, pitching boat leaving her homeland, never to return—stayed with her. She let the few remaining servants do whatever they would, whenever they would do it, while she sank into her chair by the kitchen window for long hours. She even allowed her garden to go to weeds.

"My father's will was out of date," Rebecca suggested out loud one afternoon, sitting with Frau in the kitchen. They avoided the parlor when they could help it. Her father's chair and pipe stand still stood there.

"*Ja,* no doubt it was," Frau replied, without conviction.

"Perhaps he meant us to keep this house as a Sunday house." In the old times in their town, as in other hill-country towns where Germans had settled, farm families had kept little dwellings that were known as Sunday houses, two-room cottages with sleeping lofts for the children. Entire families would trundle into town on the farm-to-market road on Friday evening with wagonloads destined for the Saturday market, crowding into their Sunday houses and remaining until after church and Sunday dinner, then towing themselves back out to the farms for the week's work. The houses themselves were half squalid and half charming, as was the custom itself, which had been mostly abandoned, although some of the little houses remained. Rebecca knew even as she made the suggestion that the notion of her father's roomy, well-built house as a Sunday house, even for a successful farmer, was a preposterous one. But she couldn't quite believe it of her father, that he had meant to maroon her here like Rapunzel or brick her up like the tell-tale heart.

"I ought to sell this place," Rebecca said, feeling at the same time a wave of crashing exhaustion at the very thought. "You should come out to live on the farm with me and John," she went on. But with their debts, the house in town was now more valuable than the farm. They'd be foolish to sell it—even John had said so. The question was what exactly they should do with it, and that question, lacking any better answer, was to be met in this way: she, alone with her boy and her old relative, drifting through the rooms every day, either looking for something to do or doing nothing at all, playing with the boy or looking out the window or reading the Doctor's newspapers.

"*Ja*," Frau said, and then said no more, and Rebecca dropped the subject and went upstairs to take a nap with Matthew.

March arrived, powerless to stir them from their torpor despite the near-violent greening of the countryside beyond their windows. Rebecca longed to clap eyes on their old friendly fields.

She knew she was needed on the farm—she could be useful there, when John and the Heinrichs and Dusana were working themselves half to death with the first planting. John warned them that there would be several weeks during which he wouldn't be able to come to town. He was in a fever of planning when Rebecca had last seen him, scarcely able to talk for the thundering pressure the corn and oats were producing in his imaginings. This year had to be a good one for the farm, and too much depended on beginning the season the right way, right now. "Dusana will cook for us and keep things up a little. As much as she can. We'll be out in the field so much we'll scarcely see the inside of the house," he said distractedly, climbing into the wagon for the return trip.

Rebecca held Matthew in her arms, both of them blinking up at John from below. She thought with a surge of intense homesickness of the yellow-green yard around her house, the kitchen garden she ought to have started planting in February, the smells of growing things reaching out to them wherever they stood, inside or out, in the barn or the orchard, like the good strong handshake of the earth. Even standing in her father's yard outside the horse shed, she was assailed by powerful smells: Frau's old garden, looking fresh even in neglect, the shivering bushes and grasses that crowded up against the house, even the pungent oat and manure smell of the horse shed itself. "I want to come home," she said to John suddenly. "Please take us with you."

John looked down at them, troubled. Matthew reached up to his father, and John released the reins and took his boy with a grunt of happy effort. "Strong fellow," he said, smiling into Matthew's dazzled face.

"John. I can't think here. I want to come back out to the farm and do something useful with my time instead of sitting around the parlor, growing roots." Rebecca put a boot up on the wagon's side step and pulled herself up, balanced there on one foot, holding to the side of the wagon board and leaning close to her husband, who sat stiffly with his boy on his lap, avoiding, it seemed to her, both the question of her return and the pressure of her body. "Please. Answer me. Why won't you take us with you?"

"Beck," he said quietly, "I think it's better this way."

She swallowed a gulp of the muddy, green-scented air of the yard for strength. John was so close to her she was practically pressing her breasts against his arm as she stood balanced on the wagon step. She saw him so clearly then, as if the spring air were a lens. Sadness and resolve had hardened him into a whetting stone that made his body—pressed against hers but even now beginning to pull away—into a knife-edge sharp enough to cut her heart.

"How can it be better?" she whispered miserably.

John shook his head. "We have a chance now to stop making each other unhappy. I'm sorry that it had to happen this way, but now that it has—"

"You mean my father's death is looking to you like a good opportunity to get away from me?" she flashed out.

"I don't see it that way, no," John said, his careful, neutral tone signaling his characteristic retreat from conflict. "We're both orphans now, and I'm nothing but sorry about that," he added softly. Then he said nothing else for a maddening pause, and Rebecca realized that was all he intended to say on the subject. Her exasperation pounced.

"You won't *fight* with me! Don't you think we'd be better off if you'd just *fight* with me, just one time? We could have it all out between us!"

Matthew, seeing his parents in disagreement over his head and hearing his mother's sharp tone, immediately turned on his peacemaker's charms, smiling and unleashing a squeal, giving his father a hearty pat on the chest and struggling to stand up in his lap.

"He's just like you. He won't brook an argument," Rebecca observed.

John wrangled Matthew in his arms until the boy discovered and fell to examining the leather strap his father held loosely in one hand. "I won't fight with you, Rebecca. It's not respectful to you. My parents taught me that a man who fights with a woman is worse than the lowest dog," John said slowly. "I just want to give you both a good life. The best I can anyway."

"That's foolish," Rebecca snapped. "How are you supposed to understand me if you won't fight with me?"

John looked at her with some real amusement then. His eyes were fond and tired. "How indeed."

Rebecca felt her cheeks grow hot. She looked at the ground below the wagon, the compressed little grasses and the pale-yellow earth of the lane. She struggled for a moment, then said, "I know I'm—not always good to others. To you. But try. Try, please, to understand me. If you can't, nobody will. I want to come home, and I want to get back to work. I want to be part of your life. I want us to be together and make something, mean something. Don't leave me here."

Having delivered her final plea, Rebecca forced herself to look up again. John's dark eyes were on his son, and a small smile was on his lips as Matthew bounced in his lap on springy, rubbery legs.

"You aren't listening," Rebecca said.

"I am, Beck. I am." He made a face at Matthew, who chortled with joy.

"Well then, if you are listening, and you still take the absurd position that we should be apart when you know I want the opposite, then in fact you are *arguing* with me, and as you said, only a lowly dog would do that," she pointed out reasonably.

John spared her a wry glance then.

"Think about it. Please. Take us back." Rebecca leaned in and kissed his cheek, then stepped back onto the ground and squinted up at the two of them, shining down from above her like a sun. "I'm not so terrible, am I?"

"You are the love of my life," John said simply. He handed Matthew down to her, and she took him and kissed his sweet, soft temple. "You both are. Good-bye."

"Good-bye, then."

A few lonely weeks later, Frau and Rebecca were in the kitchen, sewing and reading while Matthew played on the floor, when the bell hung on the scrolled iron hook outside the house's front door rang once, tentatively, then again with strength. The women looked at each other mutely, then rose and went into the parlor, Rebecca carrying the boy.

They rarely had visitors. Rebecca, with Matthew on her hip, opened the door to the house and saw an unknown figure bathed in gold spring sunshine. She stepped back and the darkened figure resolved into a man, and then a man she thought she half remembered, and then his hat was off and he was bowing deeply and saying with a trace of an accent, "Mrs. Hirschfelder, I may assume?"

Rebecca peered into the man's handsome, shadowed face. "Herr Krause? Is that you, sir?"

Robert Krause smiled thinly. "Indeed, and thank you for remembering me, Mrs. Hirschfelder."

"How could I forget? You promised me eternal life." Rebecca laughed. "Please, come in. May I introduce my aunt, Miss Nussbaum."

Again the deep bow. "But I am afraid I have come to visit you during a time of sorrow."

Rebecca smoothed her hands down the skirt of her mourning dress and said, "My father, Dr. Mueller, passed away this winter. My son, Matthew, is our bright consolation. Will you sit?"

"I will fetch some coffee," Frau offered. "It would be my pleasure, sir."

"You are from near Bonn, madam?" the magician asked abruptly.

"I am," Frau said, a flush of pleasure in her face. "Duisdorf, in the western country outside of Bonn."

"I knew within a moment," Herr Krause said warmly. "I am from Bonn myself."

"Then my pleasure is doubled," Frau replied. "Excuse me, I will return in a moment."

"I thought you had left our town in January for your next engagement," Rebecca said, seating herself opposite the magician with Matthew in her lap.

"I had. I returned," the magician said, fixing her with such an odd stare that she felt herself obliged to sit up straighter. His look wasn't amorous—far from it. He seemed almost irritated by her.

"I hope you traveled well," she said politely, not sure how else to broach his hostility.

"I confess I did not," Robert Krause answered. "I found I had unfinished business here. I see now that I am not likely to gain any satisfaction of it despite the effort I made in returning." He paused, then blurted, "Tell me, Mrs. Hirschfelder, you are not of— Your parents, they are not both German, are they?"

"My late father was born in Duisdorf, like my aunt Adeline with whom you are acquainted," Rebecca answered calmly. "My mother's people were from Italy."

"Ah." Herr Krause nodded with a great upward jerk of his cleft chin. "That explains it. Your darkness, you know. You stand out. When I saw you in the theater, I thought, this woman cannot be from Germans."

"You did seem rather swift to make up your mind about me," Rebecca said, with some haughtiness she couldn't restrain. He really was hostile, she thought. She kissed Matthew's creamy cheek, then set him on the floor near her feet on the rug with some of his scattered toys.

"I did, I am afraid. I apologize if I seem rude," Herr Krause said. He jerked to his feet and strode across the room to Matthew, then knelt beside the boy before Rebecca could make a motion to protect him. The magician gazed into the boy's face; then suddenly in his hand was a toy wooden turtle, brightly painted.

Altogether it was the most astonishing thing Rebecca had ever seen—at such close range, Krause did seem to have magical powers—and she laughed and clapped her hands before she could stop herself. The young man relinquished the toy to the little boy, who promptly put it into his mouth. "*Danke sehr!*" she exclaimed, delighted.

The magician settled back into a seated position on the rug and looked up at her in a way that was now familiar and friendly. But his cheeks, she saw, were as scarlet as if he'd ridden through a rainstorm. *Is he ill?* she wondered. She fought an impulse to pluck away the turtle in Matthew's mouth, as if it were poisoned. "I'm more comfortable down here with the little creatures, if you don't mind, madam," Herr Krause said.

"Not at all." At that moment Adeline returned with a tray of quick breads and fragrant coffee, and if she was surprised to find a young man who was not Rebecca's husband seated on the floor at her feet like a conquered swain, the woman gave no sign of it. She merely poured the man a cup.

"Black, *bitte,*" he said.

"*Sehr gut,*" Frau replied, and handed him the cup without a twitch.

"Miss Nussbaum attended your performances, of course. My entire family saw them. Matthew included."

"You did me more credit than I deserved. My performances here were flawed by a multitude of mistakes," the young man said. "I reentered town this morning expecting to be met with flaming pitchforks at the train station."

Rebecca wondered at his casual reference to pitchforks—the story of the murdered ghost children had returned to her many times in her disquieted winter hours. She had theorized, too, about its application to poor Mrs. Brandt. A woman like Mrs. Brandt, who had been young when the country was at war, might have witnessed atrocities, but something as horrible as seeing children stabbed to death with pitchforks seemed beyond the pale even for those grim times. She had turned over the possibilities like playing cards but never produced a satisfying explanation. "Your effects seemed so well done," she protested. "You had us all believing you could read our minds."

"A woman is invited up to the stage, and everyone in the theater begins to whisper her name—it's not a difficult thing, if you have a sharp ear, to surprise her and everyone else by having overheard it." Robert Krause tapped Matthew's little ear gently and produced a penny between his fingers. "A mirror may function as a screen. A box may have secret compartments, themselves with mechanical surprises. The truth is, Mrs. Hirschfelder, the tricks of my trade are so well-known that to make a living, a man like myself must seek out those rare pockets of humanity that haven't already divined that magicians are far from divine."

"Oh, no one accused you of that, I hope." Rebecca smiled.

"I haven't seen your like before," Frau put in. "You are a gifted young man, Herr Krause. You should not sell yourself short."

"No one has accused me of doing that, either." Herr Krause nodded. There was a brief pause, followed by a tumble of words: "But I did feel that I needed to return here, Mrs. Hirschfelder, to find you and to—if I could—rectify my error."

"But not to apologize for dooming me to a long and lonely life here on earth?" she teased.

"Ah, is it so lonely?" He looked at her with sharp eyes. If the question had been posed by a young man similarly seated at her feet even two years ago, that young man's purpose might have been romantic. But she sensed that something else entirely was afoot here and began to feel uneasy.

"No. I have my little boy, as you see. And my good friend—" She nodded to Frau across the room. "My husband also, who has a successful farm not far from here." She was surprised at how naturally the lie came to her.

"But a long and solitary existence, that's what you perceived me to mean," Robert Krause pursued, his eyes narrowed and stark. When she didn't respond, he said bluntly, "That was what I saw for you, madam. If you will forgive me. What I saw was that you will not remain in the earth when you are buried. You will not remain quietly interred."

After a shocked pause, during which everything in the room seemed to wheel around and come to a stop in front of the young man looking at her with such intensity, Rebecca regained herself enough to retort, "You just said you weren't a divine medium. You admitted you had nothing but a few well-worn tricks." She shrugged. "I didn't take you seriously, whatever you saw."

Krause, however, hardly seemed to hear her. He went on, with some of the relentlessness that they had paid good money to watch on the stage, while Rebecca stared at him in growing consternation over her little boy's fair head. "I thought I might have made a miscalculation, you see. It's rare to see a ghost on earth before she walks, and I thought I'd made a fool of myself—I *did,* I did indeed make a fool of myself that night, rushing off the stage without pausing to bow! I was— How do you say it? I was rattled. Do you know how it works? You have heard how this trick is done?"

Rebecca shook her head, lips dry.

"I will tell you. It is simple. You observe what everyone else in the theater expects for that person, and you calculate the difference between how that person expects to die and how others expect him to die. The difference is the sum! The sum of the years the person has left, multiplied by the way those years will end! Another magician taught me the trick of it in Chicago, years ago. Really it is simple once a few times you have done it."

His words were coming fast now indeed, his accent thickening in his excitement. "One never—almost never—calculates a difference of nothing. Of zero. Do you see? Everybody else thinks you are already dead! But what is plain in you, my dear Mrs. Hirschfelder, is that you don't know it yet!"

He nodded briskly, professionally, and Rebecca saw with a profound sinking of heart that the golden-haired young man was mad.

"No. You don't, and you never will accept that you will die. *And,*" he added significantly, his face turning cold and rude, "you won't sacrifice a second of your life for anyone else, neither! Ha! What do you say to that, *Fräulein*?"

"Get out of here," Frau thundered, suddenly rising to her feet like a mountain with a storm gathering over its head. "Get out of here, you terrible man. What you know about death and about this woman would fit in my hand, here." She thrust her cupped hand toward him. "Imposter."

Rebecca stood hastily as well, tears of pity in her eyes. "It's all right, Frau. I think Herr Krause is tired. He may be saying things he doesn't mean. I'm sure he didn't come here intending to offend me."

Sitting on the floor beside her son, the insane magician stared up at her with a narrowed focus; then his brow cleared abruptly and he scrambled to his feet, looking lost. She extended her hand to Robert Krause, and he clasped it in his. His hands were slick with sweat, cold and hot at once. *The poor man,* she thought. *Such a waste.*

"I apologize, Mrs. Hirschfelder. I do apologize. But this may save you yet."

He leaned toward her over her little boy's head, uninvited, and kissed her gently at the corner of her eye, then in the center of her soft, dry mouth. He was so shockingly hot, perhaps with fever, that she felt his body radiate warmth at hers like a coal. Then in the stunned silence that followed his transgression, the magician Robert Krause turned on his heel and left the house.

Rebecca got to the parlor window in time to observe him leaning heavily against the ash tree in the front yard, as if overtaken, and then he stumbled to the street and made his way out of their lives.

In the brooding, quiet hours after Matthew had been put to bed, Adeline and Rebecca had been in the habit of sitting in neighboring chairs by the kitchen stove in silent companionship, like a pair of old spinster sisters. With the weather beginning to take a pleasant turn, Rebecca and Frau now sat outside on the small back porch in the evenings, wrapped in shawls against the crisp oncoming spring, and they found themselves on the back porch that evening, both of them unhappy and preoccupied.

On the porch in the dark with Frau in the cool spring night, breathing the fresh scent of the growing things around them and longing for the home she had abandoned and for the love she had wasted, Rebecca said softly, "What do you think he meant, the poor man?"

Frau grunted.

"Don't you think it was strange? What he said—that I would be a ghost? And that I would never sacrifice anything for anyone? Didn't it remind you of— And the kiss? Aren't you thinking of my mother?" Rebecca pulled her wrap around herself. She'd been feeling chills all afternoon. "I am. I'm thinking of that story you always told me," she said accusingly. "If I had never heard that story, I would just think Herr Krause was a sad wandering madman with a few clever tricks."

She looked at Frau. "It's as if he *knew* that story about my mother. But he couldn't have, could he? And if he did, he knew it wrongly."

Frau cleared her throat with a great, defensive harrumph. "He *certainly* knows it wrongly, if he knows it at all. Men *always* observe women's lives to be *sacrifice,*" she said brusquely. "It is a word I dislike."

Rebecca looked over at her old friend with some surprise. "That's quite a declaration, Frau," she said with a little laugh. "What on earth do you mean?"

Frau sniffed. "We women have lives that are not easy, never easy. But they are not for *sacrifice.* That makes it seem like a thing that is weakly done, a surrender. I believe in more like *Tausch.* Exchange. Whatever a woman does, she must get something for it, if it is done with will and with purpose. Your mother say to me once, 'A woman cannot have happiness without purpose, or purpose with no happiness.'"

Rebecca chewed on this for a moment out of deference to Frau, who she knew had faced deprivations of the sourest and loneliest sort, and who she believed had lived without much love, purpose, or happiness in her long years, other than what little she and her mother and Matthew had given her. She then said slowly, "I don't think it's that simple."

"Simple. What she did was simple?" Frau demanded, pointing to her. "Would *you* have done it? Give up an hour of your life, and your Matthew's? And for what would you make this exchange? To save his life, or yours? To save your marriage? To save your family?"

Rebecca stared at Frau, startled. And then the older woman's indignation began to seem like an insult.

"What are you suggesting, that our lunatic fire-breathing magician was right?" Rebecca retorted, mocking. *But he did take my kiss. He did take my tear.* "Or that because *you* made up a story about it, my mother really bartered the last hour of her life to save mine?" She had never spoken harshly to her Frau before. Her chest hurt; it felt like she was stomping boot-shod on her own heart. But Frau had never before flung in her face what was so obviously, openly wrong between John and herself. Neither Frau nor the Doctor had ever once commented on how cool Rebecca and John were with each other, how they seemed to speak to each other and to everyone else with bitterness, how they'd lost touch with friends and grown remote toward their loved ones, how even their little boy seemed afraid to misbehave, afraid to be anything but good, good, good, reluctant to prompt any more love to fall out of his universe than was already so clearly missing. Frau, of all people, wasn't supposed to have eyes to see or ears to hear. What could this old woman know about the thorn in Rebecca's heart? "I don't believe that simply telling a story makes it real, Frau. And I certainly don't believe I am to be an unquiet, graveless, lonely soul, who never gave anything to anybody . . ." But here her archness failed her, and she found that she couldn't go on.

Frau burrowed into her shawl and shivered. "I have no opinion."

Late and starry and dark. Only a quarter-moon lights the road. It is difficult to see, but she thinks the animal may have traveled this route a few times. The horse seems to be able to pick her way through the darkness as if picking berries with her dainty hooves. Only the wind courses through the grasses and the distant live oaks. She is out here on the country lane alone, the lantern is insufficient, and the farm feels farther distant than it ever has before. Still she knows she must get there.

It is now several hours since she began to feel peculiar, dizzy, uncertain. The world clouds over, then clears, clouds over, then clears. Like a white sheet flung across a bed and yanked away, or like a nightgown floating over her head and coming to rest around her ankles before being pulled up again.

She feels as if she is dissolving.

She is trying to understand what is happening to her. Perhaps the magician has cursed her and she is dying. Or the magician's stolen kiss was laced with a slow-acting poison that is only now taking effect. Or perhaps she is mad with the magician's madness, because she, too, is seeing things, as if she is projecting them on a mirror from which she cannot turn away. She keeps closing her eyes and willing the visions to leave her be, but there they are, right in front of her on the road she travels: A cold house in a burning place, filled with magical objects, unimaginable luxuries. A woman curled up around a little girl, filled with fear, and with love, love, oh, desperate love. The beloved face of a mother suspended on a rope swing, wheeling far overhead, moonlike and as far out of reach as the moon. A window overlooking a dark street like a river, a pool of shockingly blue water, other houses, too close, with ugly eyes glaring in like a giant's face at the panes. A staircase she must climb and climb and then descend and descend, tirelessly, even though the scissor of every step is like a blade slashing through her limbs. A beautiful little girl, clever and special like her own Matthew, worth everything.

She is gasping for breath, the night air thin and cruel. Perhaps simply by making his prediction about her, the magician also made it come true. She won't reach home in time, but she also won't die. She'll always be on this road.

She feels as she felt standing at the foot of the staircase: There is something she wants badly just ahead of her, if only she can get there.

She opens her eyes and looks up at the stars and realizes that she has slumped backward in the cart's seat and she must sit up again. It is hard, so hard. But she does it, and she is relieved to see that the horse is still moving ahead, good old girl, dear old girl. Whose horse it is, she scarcely knows. She came out of Gruber's livery stable down the street, and Rebecca hasn't given her a name yet. Mercy, Prudence, Patience, Courage, Fortitude.

What is inside me? What am I looking for? The visions descend from the sky overhead like a screen swinging into place, and begin to flicker and fade on the road ahead of her, just past the horse's ears. The good thing about closing her eyes is that the images cannot follow her here into the dark. The bad thing about closing her eyes is that it becomes difficult to breathe.

When she can no longer stand it, she opens her eyes again, and the stars and the road and the horse and the window and the house and the mother and the girl are all still there, seething and growing and shrinking on the other side of some unthinkable membrane.

John. Be there waiting for me. Be there, love.

She thinks of what will happen to them if she doesn't make it home, if she's trapped on this road. She thinks about John, his beautiful face and his sad, hard eyes, and she sees his face become a little boy's face, her Matthew's. These thoughts are intolerable.

The hour is unimaginably late. At some point that evening Frau went up to bed, but Rebecca stayed out on the back porch alone, thinking and then not thinking. The wind picked up, lifting leaves and grasses across the darkened yard and flying up the steps to where she sat draped in her shawl. And there on the back porch, something overcame her. Something: her own soul, a tribe of witches, her mother's spirit. Something. It lifted her. She went into the house, moving toward the stairs, and, climbing them, felt herself dropping through them again and into this horrible place, not here, not there, knowing neither. Pulling with all her might, she finally gained the house's upper story and hovered like a mist over her darling boy asleep in his cot, cheeks flushed scarlet, breathing too rapidly. She knew it then, didn't she? *He's ill, he's dying, but I can still save him.* She called for Frau, called and called from Matthew's bedside, and the old woman never came. *My boy is ill, we're dying, but I can do what my mother did. I can give up an hour of my life and an hour of my darling's, and in that way we can save each other.* But some thing, some crucial part of the exchange, was still absent: She was still missing something, looking for something. Something she loved and needed.

And then she was out in the night, at the stable, taking a neighbor's light horse cart for the journey home, with these images flashing before her eyes.

She has been on this road a long time.

Something has overcome her—her self, that hot and hungry thing, latent in her but growing all along—and caused everything inside her to rise to the surface and evaporate. That must be it. She has finally turned her insides out. And the fear and loneliness and doubt in which she has encased herself are causing her to dissolve. Her self, her real self, that thing she felt rising to the surface from within its cold container that night in the wagon with John, the night her father died and the magician's calculations failed: It is here, now, outside in the world, but it is disintegrating inside of an acidic mist, a sheet of white, a cloud. She knows well this kind of evil whiteness that envelops and imprisons: the nightgown, the smoke, the snow. The bedsheets.

She is trapped inside, looking out. Watching these scenes.

Can she touch them?

She can try.

The night is black.

She wants to be home. She wants to see her fields again and see John's dear, good face.

She left her little boy behind.

She is a monster.

But not forever, she wouldn't leave him forever.

Just for an hour. An hour of his life, sleeping and unaware, and an hour of hers, out here alone on the road. The hours are given freely in exchange for their release from the tower and her release from the white, and in exchange for their return home, to each other, to safety together. What mother wouldn't exchange an hour of her life for her child? What child, if he understood what it meant, wouldn't exchange an hour of his life to save his mother?

Make the barter that I made. I am what you are.

She's ready to do it now.

In exchange for love, I give this hour. In exchange for happiness, for purpose, for worth, I give this hour. It's that easy—it's such a small thing, to give and to take. On the road in front of her she can see the burning house in its tiny matchbox of a field, and the terrified mother curled around her little girl, and she wants to tell her: *It's not so hard as you think. Make the barter that I made, and you can both be free.*

The farm is over the next rise, she's sure of it, and in the farmhouse she will find her happiness, her purpose, and her power. It's not just John, although he's part of it, and it's not just the work and the farm and the things she learned how to do there, but that's all part of it, too. It's not only Matthew, either, although he is always there with her, a part of herself that she's always known and yet has a whole lovely lifetime to learn. Joy rises in her throat, and she urges the horse onward, hurrying toward the woman in the road.

Don't you know who you are? Don't you know by now what you can do?

You are the only one who can give so monstrously. You are the only one.

The horse missteps in the dark, and her foreleg is suddenly off the road. She is a light animal, and the cart is not heavy, but there is a bank by the roadside here, protecting a ditch through which a shallow springtime creek runs. The angle is not steep, but it is enough to render the horse off-balance, unable to correct her stride, and the front wheel of the cart follows the animal off the road and catches her on her back hoof. All at once the cart is on its side, and then the horse is beneath it, bucking with her heavy hooves against the muddy earth until she is upright again. The cart rears up with her weight and then crashes back down again, still attached to the horse and still on its side, dragging behind her on a broken harness. The horse takes a few lurching steps, and the cart's rear wheel catches on a rock emerging from the creek's gravelly bank. The horse pulls mightily, making a frustrated sound of effort, and the cart's cheap wheel breaks off. Up onto the road the animal pulls herself, the wrecked cart trailing. With a triumphant little shake of her head the horse continues on her way, slowly, dragging the ruined cart on its side and favoring her back left leg.

There is a woman by the side of the road.

She is still moving.

She followed the little cart's cartwheel into the ditch and shattered her right shoulder on the rocky outcrop that just a minute later would catch the cart on its way back out of the ditch. Striking her head on the ground at the creek's edge and then tumbling into the water, the woman saw the cart following her flight into the creek, and then the cart's weight landed on her body and rolled, breaking two ribs. She was aware of a forceful, splashing lunge, a whicker of air overhead, and then the horse's flailing hoof struck her skull.

This woman is able, after some time, to fight her way out from the creek water to lie on her side, and then on her back, lying in her blood- and mud-soaked black dress in the grass on the edge of the road, smelling the wet earth all around her and gasping up at the stars.

And then, because she's strong, and because if she's gone this far she might as well go on, she might wait here, and in an hour, after the sound of the broken, riderless cart clattering past the farmhouse over the next rise awakens the farmhouse's occupant, she might be discovered and, after a long night of anguish and uncertainty, ultimately saved by the doctor who replaced old Dr. Mueller. She might in time recover and build a successful farm with her husband. Because of her, Matthew might survive the night, too, and grow up to distinguish himself at school and marry a smart girl of a good family. He'll be too young for the Great War and too old for the one that follows it. He'll be one of the lucky ones. And after enough time passes she might not think of the barter she made—like the meaningless, random accident that followed, it simply won't seem to have taken place. She could almost have imagined the white flickering images, the road, and the magician's cursed kiss. She might still go on to have a happy life, with few regrets. She might die an old woman, loved and accomplished.

She might survive this. Or she might barter her hour and still die, just as her own mother did.

But she still wants to tell the woman ahead of her on the road something—*I have something for you. Something important.* Even here by the side of the road, she feels so alive with power that her body seems to be singing with it: She's outside of the white now, and she knows what she passed through it to do. She wants to tell this woman, wants to tell her—what? To do exactly as she herself has done. Risk the safety of an hour for what it might yield in exchange: power. *You are the only one who can do this.* The power to define the meaning and shape of your own life, and not have it shaped for you by an acid shroud of fear, self-doubt, misperception, powerlessness. *You* are *what you are looking for.* The power to walk right through that white, shapeless barrier of fear and self-loathing and render it meaningless, a bedsheet flapping on a clothesline in the breeze.

Even now, even here poised on the crumbling edge of this road, she is filled with compassion for the woman ahead of her—the other one, the one she'd been racing toward through the white of her fear and the black of the night. If only she can be brave enough to make the same barter. *Let me show you. Let me help you. My mother did it, and now I will do it, and you must do it, too. An hour, it is such a small thing, and it could save all of us. All of us.*

She can taste blood in her mouth. Every breath brings with it a shocking pain, and then an awareness that the pain is fading. She's sorry to feel it leaving her, but she feels ready to reach out for whatever might be coming next.

CHAPTER THIRTEEN

She makes it to the top of the stairs, chest heaving—there's some air up here, now that she's put some distance between herself and the thing downstairs. But her legs are still shaking so badly that somehow on the last riser she trips and falls to the floor. The ghost is coming. She keeps her eyes on the rectangle of air above the stairway. She knows what she will see there, soon, very soon. Behind her, on the other side of the yellow-outlined rectangle that is the bathroom door, Julie is gamely splashing with her father, her rarely glimpsed great love. And in front of her, just over the horizon line where the upstairs hallway meets the staircase, something is coming for her, something so hungry and insistent that even though it can move only by shambling, shuffling grasps at the air, it won't stop until it reaches her again.

Without pausing, Bridget pulls herself down the runner carpet of the darkened hallway, reaching into her skirt pocket for her phone. *Time to call in reinforcements. If she were here, I really think she could see it.* Bridget taps her mother's name on her phone and forces herself to wait, inching backward down the hall on her elbows, listening for sounds on the stairs.

"Bridget? Hey, how are you, how's my baby?"

"Mama. We have to come stay with you for a while. Please." Speaking is almost impossible. She can't get enough breath in. *It's closer now.* "Can we stay with you? Can you come and get us? Tonight?"

Kathleen's voice is suddenly octaves deeper. "What happened, honeygirl?"

"Nothing. We just— We need to get out of this house, Mama, tonight. Okay?" Bridget can hear the panic rising in her voice and struggles to get enough air in to talk, to get the words out. "Or we'll come to you. We'll drive there. We're on our way. We're on our way," she repeats, to reassure herself more than anything.

"Listen to me, honey," Kathleen Goodspeed intones sternly. "Okay? You and Mark have a good thing. A good thing. It's worth something, what you have, and I know it's hard, but if any woman ever balanced it all, her self and her marriage and her work and her babies, it was through love, hard work and hard love. What I'm saying, and I want you to listen to me, is that you have it in you to make this work, but you're the only one who can do it."

Bridget closes her eyes. "Mama, I have to tell you something."

"Go ahead, honeygirl."

I am crazy. After this, there's no going back. Bridget gulps for air and can smell nothing but the grave coming after her, up the stairs in her own dear house. *After this I don't know what.* "There is a ghost in my house. It's a woman. Or—there's a woman inside it, but I—I think it ate her. It ate her. And it wants something from me. I don't know what it is. I can't tell Mark. He can't see her. But Julie can." She is panting. The ghost is below her on the stairs, scrabbling and thumping. "I tried, I—I gave her my favorite picture of you and me and Carrie, I gave her Julie's favorite book. She wants something else and I don't know what it is. She wants it now. The ghost is right here, Mom. She's *right here.*"

Silence on the other end of the line, but scraping, shuffling, a revolting flopping sound from the stairs. And then it is there, its head, rising up before her, its mouth, its black and starving mouth, and its eyes full of hate. *Found you. I'm so hungry. Let me.*

Bridget's mother says, "Help her, honey."

A shattered white arm slaps against the hallway floor. Bridget screams and drops the phone.

Warm yellow light sweeps over her as Mark and Julie emerge from the bathroom. "Bridget? What— Who are you talking to?"

Julie begins screaming again.

"Oh God—Mark, get her into her room—" Panic and terror shoot a sudden strength through her limbs like voltage, and Bridget scrabbles to her feet and grabs her husband and her little girl bodily, throwing her arms around the two of them and pulling them with a cry of effort into Julie's dark little room, then slamming the door. In the blackness her fingers fumble for the lock. *Not that it will work—against that—what is she now, where is she now? What do we do? How do we get out? Does it even matter, now that I'm crazy? I'm officially crazy. Even my mother would say so, and she would know, wouldn't she? Jesus, Jesus Christ.*

"Okay. I'm getting Julie into her pajamas. And you can nurse her down. And then we are going to have a goddamn *conversation,* Bridget." Mark's tone is that of a man who has reached the end of the proverbial rope.

"Just—get her changed—and then we have to hurry—we'll run down the stairs as fast as we can and get in the car right now and go to my mom's." Bridget has found the lock, she's found the light switch, and as she swipes the light on in the room and flattens her back against the door, determined to protect them even if she is insane, even if it is impossible, she turns to face her husband and her daughter.

Who stare back at her, both of them as hurt and scared and confused and sorry as she has ever seen either of them. They have never looked more alike. If it weren't so heart-wrenching, and if she weren't so terrified, she would laugh, she really would.

"What?" Mark grates out. His eyes are bright. "Bridget, are you—are you trying to say you're leaving me? Is that what this craziness is all about?"

Julie lets out a sobbing wail and begins to squirm out of her ducky towel. Mark wheels about suddenly, not waiting for Bridget's answer, and brings his little girl to the changing table, where he lays her down and begins diapering her with stiff, unpracticed movements.

"Because if you are, Bridge, I can tell you, it's one of the shittiest things you've ever done. Not just because of the timing, although, my God, like, you would *think* after what I just told you, you could at least wait until the morning. Or until we got Julie down so we could actually *talk* about—"

Here Bridget interrupts him with a muffled shriek. "Mark!" The ghost is in the hallway, thudding against the door—*I can hear it thumping out there I can* feel *it God help us*—

"Well? What? For Christ's sake *what*?" Mark bursts out, picking Julie up and looking at Bridget over the girl's head.

She is not so insensible with fear that she doesn't feel her heart lurch at the expression in her husband's eyes as they meet hers. Because he is her friend, her one real ally—not Gennie, not Martha, but Mark. *He* is the one she chose, and she chose him knowing him well: He is smart and good-hearted and true. He works hard; he tries hard.

He doesn't always know what to do, and if he's the type of man who often makes that into a problem for her to solve, then at least it means he values her instincts and her abilities. Even if he doesn't always understand her, he loves her; she sees clearly enough that he does love her. She's hurting him terribly without meaning to.

She can't bear to stand across the room from Mark with him looking at her like that.

Bridget releases her panicky grip on the doorknob. If it means the ghost can enter the room, so be it. Let them face it together.

The door shakes in its jamb. Bridget flinches. Her daughter's mouth is slightly open, and her eyes are dark with anxiety. *I'm going to keep us safe,* Bridget thinks at her, but her heart is screaming, *She can hear it out there, she can hear everything it's doing, God help us.*

She extends her arms to Mark and Julie and seems to cross the few feet from the door to the changing table just by leaning closer to them. "I'm sorry. I know you must think I'm crazy," she says to Mark. "Please, please, please believe me, I'm not, I'm not."

Now Mark has Bridget in his arms, has them both in his arms. He kisses her mouth, and she feels his shudder as he pulls her shoulders close, holding both Julie and Bridget against him. Julie is cupped in the crook of his elbow, wedged between the two of them and holding her little self still. "Don't scare me like this," he mutters into Bridget's neck. "Don't leave me. Bridget. I'm begging you. I know I've been out of it. I know I've been gone a lot. Things are going to change. I want them to. You and Julie—I want things to be different for us."

Bridget hears the ghost in the hallway thudding against the wall, the door. Something is knocked over and drops to the runner carpet with a rumbling roll—the little bird vase? Bridget closes her burning eyes and concentrates on the bodies, the bodies: her little warm girl, who always smells of honey and pee and soap, and Mark, lean and hot and urgent. *I love these let no harm come to these let me protect these let not a single part of these come to grief God help me help me be strong enough.*

Mark is saying, "I'm sorry. I'm sorry I haven't been paying attention. Gennie was telling me tonight that she's worried about us—not that it's her business. But I'm trying, I'm really trying. This news about my job is—hard. I'm scared I can't keep it all together by myself. It's making me sick—it actually feels like something's eating my guts. I don't know how we're going to live. The house—"

"You don't have to do this all yourself. I'm here. I can help. I can go back to work," Bridget says. Her burning eyes are closed; her throat is full. "We should be facing this together."

"If you want to, fine. It's always been your choice. You know I'm fine with whatever you want to do," Mark replies instantly, his voice ardent and thick. "Just don't give up on us."

From the hallway the sounds cease.

Then there's a scraping, a sly scraping, like bones trailing along the floor.

She doesn't want to ask it, but she does. It's the only thing that might still separate them, the only thing she doesn't yet know about him, for sure.

Bridget says, still in his arms, still holding on to him and their daughter with her eyes closed up tight, "You're having an affair with Gennie, aren't you."

There is a numb pause and then Mark steps back. She forces herself to open her eyes, and right there and then she can see the truth. She's wrong. He's done nothing.

But for the moment Mark is so amazed he can't answer. Her

heart breaks a little bit—she's sorry, of course she is—and then she gently takes Julie under her hot little armpits and lifts her away.

"Please just get the car," Bridget says quietly. "We have to leave tonight. We can't stay here."

His face changes. He is furious. "I don't even *like* her," he bites out.

"I know. Never mind. Forget I said it." One-handed, Bridget opens Julie's drawer and begins to pull out clothes, pajamas, tiny little shirts, tiny little leggings. Now the house is filled with silence, so thick and terrible it's like a snow that has fallen hard enough to fill up every room and smother every thought, movement, heartbeat. Bridget can see tears, her own, dropping onto the little cotton flowers and turtles and gingham checks that make up the pile of Julie's clothes in front of her on the dresser top. Julie puts her arms around her mother's neck and burrows in, glossing her own cheeks with her mother's tears.

"I have *never* liked her," Mark says distinctly. "*You* are the one who's, like, *fixated* on Gennie. I know what she is for you—and I know you know it, too. It's like you needed to make her into this *thing* just to remind you to feel bad about yourself for some reason. But I don't give a shit about her. You know that."

"I know." Bridget shakes her head. A hot salty drop flies from her nose. "Forget it. Forget I said anything. But we need to leave. Please, please believe me, Mark, we have to leave tonight. All of us."

She can't hear anything in the hallway, but that doesn't mean nothing's there.

When she can bring herself to look at her husband, she sees that he has pulled a veil over his feelings for the moment and is gazing at the floor, eyes shuttered.

"I don't understand what you want to do, Bridget," he says at last. "I don't understand what's happening to us."

She gulps in a strengthening breath and pulls her little girl's body close to hers. The air all around them smells of the ground in spring, pungent and reeking and yet full of insects, living things, everything struggling and green.

"I have to *give* something," Bridget says, her throat aching. "I don't know why, I don't understand it, but I know I have to give something up in order for us to be—safe. Saved. But I think—I think it wants something from *all* of us. Me, you. Even Julie." She strokes Julie's back and feels the girl's fingers clutching in her hair. *But how can I ask it of her, how how how?* "Oh God, this is so hard," Bridget gasps and feels her knees buckle. *My baby, my baby.* She sits down heavily on the pretty braided rug, pulling her girl into her lap, and she can hold herself steady for a second but then the sobs come and she is racked and racked. Julie gazes at her in astonishment and alarm. She puts her lips to Bridget's trembling ones and makes the "mmmm-ma" sound that is her notion of a kiss. She does it again and again. Her baby.

Mark comes over to them. He kneels down and puts his arm around Bridget's shoulder, and his head against Julie's soft little head. He is quiet for a minute, and the three of them just hang on to each other, their family, the three of them, their own little boat.

Then he says, "I'll drive us to your mom's if you really want to go. Let's just get out of here, like you want, and we'll figure it all out tomorrow." Bridget sobs with relief, with gladness. "I'll go get the car."

He rises, goes to the door, and opens it, and then she hears his footfalls descending the stairs.

And then nothing else.

As if he's stepped into snow.

The two of them are alone, Bridget and Julie, in the girl's room.

Julie is so tired. Bridget can feel it in her little body, in the stillness and the warmth of her velvety limbs. She gathers her girl up against her and waits for what she knows is coming next.

She has known for some time now that the ghost wants something, something dear and unnameable, and it comes to her now, as clear as a pang of remorse, as charged as an afternoon sunray, who can tell her what that is. The woman inside the whiteness. She's the only one who knows. Bridget will have to face her. Ask her. Help her, maybe.

"Not much longer now, Jujubee," Bridget whispers. Her eyes are hot with tears. "I'm right here. Not much longer now. It'll be over soon."

She folds herself around her girl, drinking in her sweetness. Julie rests her head against her mother's shoulder, and Bridget brushes her lips across the little girl's mouth. *Not much longer now. Be brave, little bee. We have to be brave together. Because she's here.*

The door opens wider, as if pushed by the breath of a dragon.

The scent of the ghost enters the room before she does, and by now it is so familiar, so understood, that it seems borne by a current of powerful, deep associations, just the way certain smells carry back figments of Bridget's childhood to her whenever she experiences them. The high, bitter fragrance of gas stations, for instance, will always remind her of her father, of sitting in the backseat of an old car, waiting for him to come back, longing for him and dreading him at once, the beloved and frightening ghost of her own baby girlhood. The ripe, cakelike smell of the makeup aisle at the drugstore is the smell of her mother's purse, the home of all the world's great mysteries and delights when she was a girl. And whenever Bridget pours her daughter a cup of apple juice, she is three again herself, in a warm and comfortable room, sitting drowsily on a sofa, watching leaf shadows play with each other on the ceiling like kittens with a ball of yarn, and it is early evening and she is at Mrs. Washington's apartment, waiting for her mother to come pick her up, it has been a long day and she is little and she loves Mrs. Washington, she loves her juice, she loves being comfortable and small and safe, and she loves her mother with an intensity and a force that seems to make the leaves take the shape of her mother's face on the ceiling, round and loving and beloved overhead, like the moon, the moon in the bunny's room, the moon winking in the window.

The ghost is here now. Like the moon it is white, like the moon it is cold, like the moon it is crossed by shades of darkness. And like the moon, it pulls.

It is pulling itself through the doorway.

Bridget's pulse is a thick, heavy thudding in her throat. Julie rolls forward in Bridget's lap, tucking her knees up and making herself a ball. They face the door together and watch the ghost come in. *My brave girl. God help me, please help me keep her safe.*

First the arm, then the head, which seems hideously larger, almost square, like a block swiveling atop a frail body. The white static of its form seethes, grows, shrinks, approaching and retreating like a tide. As Bridget watches, trying to breathe, the ghost's limbs slice into the room, jerking and stuttering. The dead thing brings itself forward with great effort and great hunger. And inside the white, Bridget and Julie can clearly see the blackness, and the woman being endlessly eaten and eaten and eaten alive.

The thing turns its gaze on Bridget and Julie, and its maw drops open, ravenous. Bridget bites back a scream and clutches at Julie, who buries her head against her mother's chest, staring and silent.

"Don't be afraid, baby. It's going to be over soon. Don't be afraid, Jujubee," Bridget gasps, staring at the hungry, long face that flickers and waits. *I'll find a way to keep you safe. I've got to. I've got to.*

She is looking into the thing's black mouth. Bridget forces herself to look, although her heart is hammering and all of her physical instincts are pleading with her, begging her to get up and run, run, run.

The ghost of a woman is in there. *Inside, inside of it, I'm so sorry, so sorry, how did this happen to you?* Bridget is sure of it—she can see her more clearly now than ever before. She's so close, and yet, as Bridget watches, she seems to be melting away, or perhaps consumed, as if the whiteness all around her is the whiteness of a smoldering coal. She is in terrible pain.

Bridget pulls Julie tighter into her chest and leans forward into her knees, putting one hand on the floor in front of her. Julie clings to her neck, her fingers a fist in Bridget's hair.

Staring into the white hungry static with its stink of the grave, Bridget sees that the woman inside is not what she'd thought. Either something has changed in the ghost, or Bridget never really saw this woman for what she was. But she is beautiful. Her hair is black; her eyes are piercing and intelligent and gray. She is wearing a black dress, not a white one. Her lips are full but pale, and the skin of her throat above the high black collar of her dress is also a nacreous white, except where it has been darkened by the blood flowing from her mouth and over her chin in a dreadful caul. Her hair is in disarrayed braids.

Part of her skull is horribly misshapen.

The ghost within the whiteness has one arm wrapped around her own side protectively, and with the other hand she is reaching out to Bridget and Julie.

What happened to you, what can help you? Bridget's lips are dry with terror, and her throat is choked with pity.

She is suddenly aware that as she leans toward it, the white stinking hateful fire is also leaning toward her and Julie: *Yes. Yes. Let me. I'll eat you, too, you stupid woman. I'll eat you all.*

It lunges at them, releasing a ghastly sigh like the air escaping a tomb. Bridget screams and scrabbles backward to her feet, holding to Julie with one arm. Julie's legs dangle hazardously close to the open mouth, but her arms are painfully tight around her mother's neck and Bridget manages to yank them both upward, backward, away. She staggers under Julie's weight in the direction of the window.

"Mama," Julie says pleadingly, and her small high voice reminds Bridget that they have to get out of this. She has to find a way. She can't be backed into a corner and out the window. They are alone with this thing, she and her daughter, and she has to see them through to the other side.

Bridget hisses at the thing. "I won't be swallowed! Shut your mouth!"

It cocks its head, for all the world a disgusting parody of a human. *Surely you've always known this would happen.*

It advances.

Bridget clutches Julie and calls out to the woman again through the fearsome seething that surrounds her. "*What do I do? Please, please, what can I do?*"

The dead woman's arm is extended, and her hand is outstretched. But not to ask for something, not to beg for help. Incredibly, in her agony she seems to be reaching out to offer something, an invisible thing, the only thing that can save them, small and insignificant but worth everything, and cupped in her outstretched hand.

You. You are the only one. The only one who can give so much.

Don't you know by now what you are? Don't you know what you can do?

As if she is reading it on a page in the ghost's outstretched hand, Bridget sees the answer unspooling like the hours she's lost and looked for, the hours she hoped to gain but kept watching helplessly evaporate, the hours she would give her life to retrieve and make meaningful, the hours she'll never get to live again. That is all that it wants, all that it requires. An hour of her life. An hour of Julie's. To save the ghost, to save Bridget's marriage, to save them all. She's holding it in her hand. All Bridget has to do is walk toward her and take it—and give her what she needs in return.

The woman beckons to them. *Come to me.*

The whiteness rears back to attack, its limbs eager and curled inward like a spider's. The blank, numbing reality of it strikes Bridget as she watches it prepare: This is really happening, there is a poisonous and hateful presence in her daughter's room, and it will consume her and her little girl and leave Mark with nothing. Unless she can find the courage to move, to act. To give and to take—the thing that means so little and yet means everything.

Bridget looks at the little girl in her arms, panicked and heartsick. *How can I ask it of you, my own love?*

Julie gazes back at her, in just the way she always looks at her mother. The way that the lucky and loved children of this world all look at their mothers, reflecting back the promise that brought them into the world to begin with: *You are the beginning of everything in my world, and I would do anything for you.*

"I have to go through it," Bridget tells Julie in a whisper. "We have to go through it together. Don't be afraid. I'm right here. I won't ever really leave you." She kisses Julie's cheek, again and again. "We're giving a little something away, but we'll get so much more back if we can just be brave together. You'll see. We'll be okay. We'll be okay." Her heart is pounding. She is terrified, so terrified. She closes her eyes. She takes a step forward, and the smell of the room, the grave and the stink of death, shifts like a lock clicking into place and becomes the smell of a wet dirt road, earth after a rain, green and struggle and reward.

I give it freely, this hour. In exchange for love, I give this hour. In exchange for strength, for meaning. Your heart makes me brave enough.

"It's okay, Julie. It's going to be okay," Bridget murmurs. She doesn't dare open her eyes, but she senses herself on the cusp of something larger than herself, and she can feel hands reaching for her, strong hands that can set her free.

It doesn't hurt. I thought it would hurt.

She feels the warmth of a hand on her face, on her cheek, on her lips. It is Julie's small hand, placed there as if to comfort her. But it's actually to bring her back to life.

EPILOGUE

The warm November afternoon has given itself over to a golden evening. Something is burning in one of the valleys—he can see the smoke rising over the trees as he drives. Leaves, probably, or an autumn brushfire. He takes in the scent and urges the minutes to move slower and the wheels to move faster.

He's hungry, thinking of dinner. He's restless because the drive is so familiar. And he's tired, thinking about all the things he still has to do that evening and tomorrow. As he drives, his thoughts take the indistinct shapes of a thousand things, big and small, orderly and disordered, practical and unwise. It's the movement of the trees and the landscape all around him that makes his thoughts scatter and fly like this, he thinks. As hard as he tries to bring his attention back where it belongs, his consciousness wants to wander away to the side of the road. He has a hangnail on his left index finger, and it's been throbbing all afternoon because he never found the time or the right tool to cut it. He didn't eat enough at lunch today and he feels a little light-headed, although a hot cup of coffee might set him straight. And the right rear wheel is making that whirring noise again; he'll need to look at it soon, try to figure out what the problem is, but to be honest he likes mechanical problems, he always has, so he's not entirely sorry that the wheel is speaking to him now. It sounds like a voice in his head, spinning out the same phrase over and over. *You miss her, you miss her, you miss her,* it says. And also, *Here I come, here I come, here I come.*

The little creek skirting the road has receded into the earth now, but he knows that during the spring it will resurface, during those months when the whole world smells like the beginning of the earth must have smelled: pungent, promising, wet, and black. He drives this road infrequently then.

Back at the house he knows what he'll find—or at least, he loves to imagine it. He urges the wheels toward it with a great swelling of anticipation in his chest: the gold fields, the busy yard, the good straight house, and in them the familiar heads young and old bent over familiar chores. But for all its familiarity, and for how much it is loved, it's not a peaceful place, and it never has been. With a child growing up in the house, you can expect something wild and inconsistent every day. Even when you think you've finally understood them. You never know what you'll come across, rounding a corner or coming up the stairs.

Sometimes, even now, coming up the stairs in his own house, he expects to see something waiting for him at the top, just waiting and looking for him. Something he recognizes and honors from the deepest mirror in his heart, something he longs for, loves still.

Here I come, here I come, here I come.

Mark yawns with a bone-cracking stretch of the jaw and tries to keep his eyes on the road and not the golden, outrageously gorgeous hills tempting his attention just past the car windows. He's got eight minutes by the dashboard clock. He should make it in time.

Their days are driven by clocks. Sometimes he feels the urge to step outside of the little machine they've made, just stop the relentlessly moving gears and try something easier, but he knows better than to believe that *easier* necessarily exists. Bridget likes to tell him her ideas for magical, amazing tools for a better world—she comes up with them by the hour, it seems like. She says mothers and geeks have that in common: the creative compulsion to *make it better.* Clocks that let you swap wasted hours for better ones, mirrors that reconfigure the symbols in your dreams so you can see their meanings more clearly, books where you can write down things you want to come true—but only within the next two days. Sort of like enchanted objects from fairy tales but addressing the particulate vexations of modern life. He's always thought it was funny that he was in the business of game development when she had the better imagination. Once, when he asked her if he could use an idea of hers in a game they were developing back when he was at PlusSign—was it the eye camera? or the thought clock?—she'd made a face, screwing her pretty mouth over to one side, saying, "What would you want to do with *that*? Sure, take it. Although, wait. Is it going to be, like, a weapon thing or a status thing? You should earn it. It shouldn't be just sitting in a . . . a yeoman's abandoned cloak at ye old mill town tavern, you know."

Mark glances at the phone on the passenger seat of the car, its unblinking face reflecting the car ceiling and the dim dashboard lights.

I have an idea for a new one, Bridge. I want a text message service that reminds you to stop compulsively looking for text messages. It would be activated by elevations in certain . . . hormones. I wouldn't even have to look at the phone—it would detect that I was about *to look and supply the reminder preemptively.*

Either that, or a teleport that will get me to day care pickup on time regardless of when I leave the goddamn garage.

"Almost there," Mark says aloud, and turns on the car radio to try to keep himself alert. Still his mind wanders, picking up familiar objects and putting them down. Work, mostly. But also: his girl, his home, his wife.

He doesn't like to indulge in it too much, but he loves thinking about his girls. He saves up thoughts of them like Halloween candy and dips into his store when he's feeling bored or off-center.

His wife is the one thought that usually brings him back to something like a center. She is the engine that turns the wheels in a lot of ways. She got them out. After those dark days when PlusSign pushed him out and there was no work for either of them and they lost the house. When he was at his lowest. Bridget kept them looking, moving. She was the boat and the water and the oars and the sails, the boards and the hammers and the nails.

It makes him turn ever so slightly inside out to think about those times, but those times are stuck in his candy store of Bridget thoughts, too. Hard times but good times, in their way. That was when they were finding each other again, a process that he can admit is still *in process,* but it's happening. He needs it to happen. That brightness between them coming back, flame point by flame point in a hard glass window. She's happier now, even when she's tired, which is often, or always. He tries not to think that he wasn't good enough, that he somehow failed to carry them all on his own and he let his girls down. Or that he was somehow responsible for Bridget's unhappiest times, that he had penned her up inside of a bright idea. Bridget, for her part, never fails to reject that notion, to lop off its head whenever it pokes up out of the ground like a deranged gopher. "You and I are supposed to do this together. It's better for us to do this together. We need to have each other's backs," she usually says. Sometimes she just says, "Shut the fuck up, honey. Really."

Tonight it's Bridget's turn to leave the office later and get home in time for the bath, and it's his turn to pick up Julie and get her dinner. So. Dinner. What should it be? Fishies and peas. She loves those. Like Lola in that book about the tomatoes. Easy. Food groups. Think food groups.

As he turns the corner into the parking lot, he feels his heart quicken, and a goofy swat of joy smacks him across the face. It's always the same.

He parks the car and lets himself run, really run (okay, trot) to the door. Inside the golden-yellow main room the day's artworks are tacked up to dry, cubbies hold water bottles and jackets and small shoes like dinner rolls, and a sweet cluster of little heads is visible in the center of the room, all the kids on the rug listening to a story from Miss Henry, who catches his eye in the doorway and says, "Julie, your daddy's here."

Her dear, shining face. Her glorious, spazzy grin. Her curls and creamy cheeks. Her bright rascal eyes. Here she comes. Mark drops to a knee and holds his arms out for her, and she begins her toddle across the room. *I can't wait, I can't wait, I can never wait to hold you.*

As Julie makes her unsteady way toward him, Mark smiles a thank-you to Miss Henry, who, as she nods and turns back to her storybook, reveals a strange, elongated figure behind her, dark and light at once, like a smudge of charcoal across a sheet of paper or like the trail a warm, swiped hand leaves across a frosted windowpane. The figure flickers like a flame and then grows stronger, straight, sure, impossibly tall—*is that a woman? who is that?*—but then Julie falls into his arms with her scent of honey and playground dust, and he isn't sure he saw anything at all.

ACKNOWLEDGMENTS

The author wishes to acknowledge her debt to, and admiration for, the late scholar Terry G. Jordan-Bychkov of the University of Texas at Austin, whose many works on German Texas (especially his book *German Seed in Texas Soil*) inspired and informed portions of this story. Thanks are also due to Eleanor Arnold and the Indiana Committee for the Humanities for their wonderful oral history project *Memories of Hoosier Homemakers*, and to the late midwestern nature writer Rachel Peden, whose beautiful, funny, deeply human writing about farm life is a treasure worth seeking out.

Thanks also to Betsy Lerner, Denise Roy, Andrew Roth, Amy Shearn, Sarah Gerkensmeyer, Melanie Lefkowitz, and Amanda Touchton for their encouragement and to Ryan Plumley, Marie Muschalek, Stephen and Ursula Baniak, Demetri Detsaridis, Fawn Horvath, and Matthew Daddona for their timely help.

ABOUT THE AUTHOR

Siobhan Adcock received her MFA from Cornell University, and her fiction has appeared in numerous literary magazines. She has worked as a writer and editor for *Epicurious, iVillage,* and *The Knot,* among other digital publishers. She lives with her family in Brooklyn, New York.

A 150-YEAR PUBLISHING TRADITION

In 1864, E. P. Dutton & Co. bought the famous Old Corner Bookstore and its publishing division from Ticknor and Fields and began their storied publishing career. Mr. Edward Payson Dutton and his partner, Mr. Lemuel Ide, had started the company in Boston, Massachusetts, as a bookseller in 1852. Dutton expanded to New York City, and in 1869 opened both a bookstore and publishing house at 713 Broadway. In 2014, Dutton celebrates 150 years of publishing excellence. We have redesigned our longtime logotype to reflect the simple design of those earliest published books. For more information on the history of Dutton and its books and authors, please visit www.penguin.com/dutton.